RHAPSODY IN RED

DONN TAYLOR

RHAPSODY IN RED

Moody Publishers
CHICAGO

Overton University (formerly Overton Grace College), its faculty, and its students exist only in fiction, but they share many denominational colleges' conflicts of academic standards vs. commercialism, education vs. indoctrination, and Christian heritage vs. secularism. The town of Overton City and the geography of the novel are also fictional.

Editor: Michele Straubel
Interior Design: LeftCoast Design
Cover Design:Kirk DouPonce, DogEared Design (www.DogEaredDesign.com)

Library of Congress Cataloging-in-Publication Data

Taylor, Donn.
Rhapsody in red / Donn Taylor.
p. cm.
ISBN: 978-0-8024-5116-3
1. College teachers—Fiction. I. Title.

PS3620.A943R53 2008
813'.6—dc22

2008019260

We hope you enjoy this book from Moody Publishers. Our goal is to provide high-quality, thought-provoking books and products that connect truth to your real needs and challenges. For more information on other books and products written and produced from a biblical perspective, go to www.moodypublishers.com or write to:

Moody Publishers
820 N. LaSalle Boulevard
Chicago, IL 60610

1 3 5 7 9 10 8 6 4 2

Printed in the United States of America

For Karen and Katherine, *Warren* and *Walter*
in gratitude
for the delight they have given Mildred and me
these many years.

ACKNOWLEDGMENTS

Preston Barclay's class in Theories of the American Revolution is based on a graduate seminar taught by Professor Philip White at the University of Texas.

Piano techniques described in the novel are those taught to me years ago by the late Jemmie Vardeman, formerly of Cincinnati Conservatory of Music.

The novel's brief quotations from Plato's *The Republic* are taken from the now-classic translation by Benjamin Jowett.

My special thanks to the National Association of Scholars and the Council for Christian Colleges and Universities for allowing me to make brief mention of them in the novel—but more so for their excellent work toward improving the substance of higher education. Thanks also to David Lehman for guiding me to the council.

I wish to thank Guida Jackson for frequent encouragements and Wanda Dionne for astute and helpful chapter-by-chapter suggestions. Thanks also to Zac Doyle and James Husum for sharing their expertise on computer networks.

Special thanks to my agent, Terry Burns, for leading me to Moody Publishers, and to Moody's Andy McGuire and Michele Straubel, both of whom greatly improved the novel with their editorial skills.

Most of all, I am deeply indebted to Mildred Taylor, my wife, for encouragement, understanding, and fruitful suggestions throughout the writing—but even more for her sound literary judgment, on which I rely when mine falters.

Why else was the pause prolonged but that singing might issue thence?
Why rushed the discords in, but that harmony should be prized?
—Robert Browning

Wake up, and strengthen the things that remain, which were about to die;
for I have not found your deeds completed in the sight of My God.
—Revelation 3:2

CHAPTER 1

That Wednesday two weeks before Thanksgiving was a bad day to find a corpse on campus. It was already bad when Professor Mara Thorn came to ask my help.

She did not know, but she found me battling the incessant music in my head and grieving for past Wednesdays when Faith was alive. That had become my Wednesday ritual: close the door of my office in the history department at five o'clock, return to my desk, and linger alone in memories of my wife while darkness brought in the chill of Midwestern evening. I would put off as long as I could my return to the home where Faith and I had raised our daughter, for that house with its silent piano now formed the center of the world's vast emptiness.

That afternoon, the orchestra in my head was augmenting my grief with Samuel Barber's *Adagio for Strings* when someone knocked at my door. The office was dark, but through the door's frosted glass I saw a shadowy form against the dim lights of the hallway.

"Come in," I called.

The door opened and the dark form paused on the threshold.

"Professor Barclay?" The voice was feminine, hesitant.

"I'm Preston Barclay," I said. "The light switch is beside the door to your right."

The shadow's arm moved. Light flooded the office and revealed Professor Mara Thorn. I had never spoken with her, but I remembered her introduction last August at the year's first faculty meeting. She was perhaps thirty-five years old, slender, with a pleasing face and shoulder-length blonde hair. She wore no makeup, and her blue eyes held the faculty in a gaze that some described as earnest and others as defiant. I held with the latter view. It's said that eyes are the windows of the soul, but hers were the embrasures of a fortress.

Her expertise was comparative religions. And that raised the question why a nominally Christian institution like Overton University—the school we knew before The Crisis as Overton Grace College—would hire a Wiccan in its department of religious studies. Most faculty assumed she was part of the new administration's diversity program.

"Come in," I said again. My internal musicians shifted suddenly from the solemn *Adagio* into a series of hideous discords. Harmonious or dissonant, though, that music is all I have left now of Faith. It's not just a tune here and there, but constant, uncontrollable torrents of music inside my head. The clinical term is "musical hallucinations." Psychiatrists and neurologists don't know what causes them, but they say these hallucinations duplicate the ordinary function of listening to music—except that the hallucinated "sounds" don't come from outside, but are generated internally through a weird malfunction of the brain. The experts have their theories, but I live with the reality. This internal music makes my life like living in a movie that some insane editor has mismatched with the music score from another.

Professor Thorn began to close the door. "I've come to ask your help."

CHAPTER ONE

"Leave the door open," I said. "Come have a chair." I gestured toward a hardwood straight chair to the left of my desk.

She removed her winter jacket and hung it on the rack next to my overcoat. She wore a long-sleeved violet blouse, and her blue jeans showed none of the currently fashionable fading or fraying. Still hesitant, she kept her eyes on me as she settled into the chair. To ease her mind, I circled the right side of my desk and took a chair opposite her. I hoped my coat and tie wouldn't make her self-conscious about her jeans.

The open door and the width of the room between us were minimum precautions in these days when a careless word can get a male faculty member accused of sexual harassment. Music may bounce around in my head, but I don't have any loose screws.

Professor Thorn let the silence linger, broken only by a few clicks from the computer under my desk as it ran one of those automatic programs I've never understood. I thought she might have changed her mind, but then she spoke in a rush.

"Professor Barclay, I've come to you because everyone on campus respects you."

I adjusted my trifocals and tried not to look self-conscious. "A lot of people would disagree with that."

"They also say you're not afraid to take an unpopular stand."

. . . but that was in another country; / And besides, the wench is dead.

The quotation flitted across my mind, but I must have spoken aloud because she answered: "I've read Christopher Marlowe, too. Though that line may have been added later by Thomas Heywood."

Score one for her unexpected erudition.

She moistened her lips and turned that blue-steel gaze on me. "Do you know Laila Sloan?"

"I've talked with her a few times in groups over lunch."

I knew more than I was telling. Six years ago our administration added a nursing program to the school's offerings. Too many of its students failed the required chemistry course, so the nursing faculty and administration tried to drop it from the curriculum. It made no sense to me to graduate nurses ignorant of chemistry, and I led a faculty movement that defeated the curriculum change. So the administration took the course away from the chemistry department and brought in Laila Sloan from a high school across the state, inserting her in the nursing department to teach it. Suddenly, all the nursing students passed chemistry. That made the administration happy.

Except with me.

That's why I denied being courageous. We work on annual contracts here, with no provision for tenure. Teaching history is all the life I have left to me now, and I'd make a lousy used-car salesman. So ever since then I've been quiet as a church mouse with laryngitis.

"I have a problem with Laila." Professor Thorn looked down at the floor. "She has been friendly with me, more so than the rest of the faculty has." Her eyes lifted and speared me again with that blue gaze. "But lately she hasn't kept her hands to herself."

"She's an . . . outgoing person," I said. "Maybe she doesn't mean any harm."

Laila was a large woman of about forty, strong and robust. Rumor said she'd been cautioned about "inappropriate touching" of female students, but apparently no one had accused her of an overt advance. And her value to the nursing department ensured that the administration would overlook quite a lot of questionable behavior on her part. They apparently see no contradiction between their laxity in her case

and their Draconian approach toward even the appearance of impropriety among less-favored faculty.

Score one for institutional hypocrisy.

I confess I didn't want to get involved. For all I knew, this Wiccan professor might have invited the situation and then changed her mind.

Professor Thorn's lips tightened. "Laila still makes me uncomfortable."

"Then tell her positively to keep hands off," I said. "The campus gossip mill says you're into weight training and karate. You ought to be able to make it stick."

Her chin rose a fraction of an inch. "I've told her twice, and I've told her why." Professor Thorn looked like she didn't know whether to curse or cry. "In my teens I made a bad marriage to an older man. It took me three years to work up nerve enough to break out of it. By then I was sick of being touched in ways I didn't like. I swore I'd never let it happen again."

She glared at me as if daring me to come across the room and touch her. I noticed for the first time that she held a cell phone in her hand. This seemed like a good time to study one sleeve of my coat. The cuff had frayed, showing a pinhead-sized patch of white thread. A few strokes with a Sharpie would hide it, and I wouldn't have to buy a new suit.

"This afternoon," Professor Thorn continued, "Laila asked me to drive her to the post office to mail a package. I did, and we went through the same problem again. I told her again, and she threatened to complain about me to the administration. I'm new on faculty, and I can't afford complaints. I need this job."

"What does this have to do with me?" I asked.

I made a mistake then. I have a habit of walking back and forth

while I'm thinking. A professor's folly, Faith used to call it. When I stood, Professor Thorn tensed and flicked the cell phone open. Her fingers lingered over its buttons while her gaze searched mine.

What was she going to do? Dial 9-1-1? I sat back down and made a show of adjusting my necktie. "I'm sorry if I startled you. Pacing is a bad habit."

"It's . . . it's all right." She flushed slightly and closed the phone. "Will you go with me to talk to her? I can't go to the administration, and the women faculty members haven't exactly made me welcome."

I didn't want to go because it would mean a nasty scene with Laila Sloan. For obvious reasons, I'd always been persona non grata to her. Still, Professor Thorn's position as a new faculty member was precarious, and she did need a disinterested witness. I admit my conscience was bugging me because I had doubted her. She didn't act like the kind of person who would invite an advance. Indeed, she seemed the pathological opposite.

"All right," I said. "Will we find her at home or on campus?"

"At her office." Professor Thorn's tension eased a bit. "I dropped her there about an hour ago. She said she had papers to grade."

We stood, and I waited while she retrieved her coat. I didn't help her into it because that might involve touching. When she had it on and moved out into the hall, I sauntered over and collected my overcoat and hat.

Outside, trees and hedges bent before a gusty November wind off the plains. The beige globes on campus light posts sent nervous shadows skittering along the concrete walkways. Without warning, my mental music shifted from a Chopin nocturne into the frenetic finale of Beethoven's *Appassionata*.

We crossed the campus circle to what used to be called the chem-

istry building until the new administration renamed it the Center for the Natural Sciences. (Everything now is either a Center or a Service.) Without speaking, we climbed to the second floor, where the scent of floor wax surrendered to pungent odors from a chemistry lab down the hall. Professor Thorn stopped at the closed door of the only lighted office. We could see nothing through its frosted glass window. No one answered our knock.

We knocked again and received no answer.

Professor Thorn called, "Laila?"

Still no answer.

I called, "Professor Sloan?" She was an instructor, not a professor, but in the present situation I would not quibble over niceties of protocol.

Again no answer. I twisted the knob and eased the door open a crack. "Professor Sloan?"

Only silence. Even the music in my head shut down. I opened the door and stepped inside, with Professor Thorn close behind. I looked to my left and saw nothing. Then Professor Thorn gasped. Her gloved hands fastened on my arm like those of a giant blacksmith trying to crush an anvil. She buried her head on my shoulder.

Quite a performance for a woman who didn't want to be touched.

Then I saw her reason.

Laila Sloan lay on her side on the floor near the right wall. On a table above her, a desktop computer clicked a few times, then fell silent. Her head had received several hard blows—apparently not long ago, for her temple still oozed blood that darkened the floor nearby. A large bruise disfigured her neck below the ear. But the lividity of her face suggested death by strangulation. And a silk scarf lay open-ended beneath her neck.

I shook off Professor Thorn's grip and pushed her back into the hallway.

"It's time to use that cell phone," I said.

Weeping, she gave it to me. Somewhere in the building a window banged open, and a blast of cold swept through the hall. With it came a premonition of some unseen force taking control of my life, boxing me in, making me remember things long forgotten.

I dialed 9-1-1 and made the report, then stood in the doorway, brooding and staring down at the battered remains of Laila Sloan.

Incongruously, the musicians in my head launched into the piccolo obbligato to a John Philip Sousa march.

CHAPTER 2

While Professor Thorn and I stood silently in the hallway, the shrill twitter of my internal piccolo felt like rinsing out my ear with ice water. Except it was my brain that was frozen by what we had found.

Professor Thorn stopped crying and stood staring out into nowhere. I probably shared the vacant staring, and I confess my thoughts were not on Laila's death. I was wishing Professor Thorn had chosen someone else as her witness, and I wondered how soon I could get back to my comfortable rut of teaching history.

I should have known that wasn't going to happen.

Acrid fumes from the chem lab irritated our noses, and the open window, wherever it was, kept banging every few minutes. Occasional gusts of cold wind purified the air momentarily, and then the chemical stench would return.

"Shouldn't we call someone else?" Professor Thorn threw a worried glance at the cell phone in my hand. "I mean . . . someone at the college . . . the president or dean?"

"Not just yet," I said. I made no move to return her phone.

She looked doubtful but said nothing. The window banged a few more times, and we weathered a few more blasts of wind. Then, faintly, I heard police sirens.

"Now," I said, and dialed the home telephone of the college dean, who is known since The Great Renaming as the vice president for academic affairs.

Among faculty it is said cynically, though not very originally, that his affairs would necessarily be academic. His actual name is Dean Billig. He was promoted to dean while we were still Overton Grace College, and thus he became Dean Dean Billig. The faculty immediately shortened the name, not entirely affectionately, to Dean-Dean.

Years before my time, Dean-Dean came to Overton with a master's degree in psychology and gradually worked his way up to department chair. His lack of a Ph.D. posed no accreditation problem because the psychology department was folded into the division of social sciences. The division head was my boss, the well-credentialed chair of the history department.

However, Dean-Dean later earned his Ph.D. via correspondence without ever leaving our campus. That solved his personal accreditation problem but created another. He still grows self-conscious around faculty who earned degrees in residence at major universities, going eye-to-eye with tenured professionals in cutthroat oral examinations.

But that is ancient history.

Dean-Dean's high-pitched voice answered the third ring.

"This is Preston Barclay," I said. "We have a problem. Professor Thorn and I are at the college—"

"University," he corrected.

". . . in the science center," I continued. "We've found Laila Sloan dead in her office."

There was a silence, after which Dean-Dean several times invoked the Deity to himself sotto voce. A faint rustle came through the line as if the phone were trembling against his ear.

"Are . . . are you sure she's dead?" he asked.

"I'm sorry. There's no doubt." I resisted the temptation to use the phrase *dead as a frozen mackerel*. Although accurate, it seemed a bit insensitive.

"Do you . . . can you tell how she died?" Dean-Dean had his breath back now and took a tentative step toward controlling the situation. The sirens grew louder, and I wondered if he could hear them through the phone.

How she died? I told him in words he couldn't misunderstand. "It looks like somebody slugged her and then choked her."

Dean-Dean invoked the Deity again, reflexively rather than conscientiously. "Don't call the police," he said. "I'll be right there. Whatever you do, don't call the police."

"I won't," I said.

"Good boy." He slammed down the receiver.

I guess that answered my question about whether he could hear the sirens.

I handed the phone back to Professor Thorn.

"What did you tell him you wouldn't do?" she asked.

"Call the police," I said.

The loose window banged again.

She frowned. "You've already called them. Why didn't you tell him?"

I grinned. "You'll see." I was feeling less and less like a history professor.

She again looked doubtful but said nothing.

Sirens came closer and the chemical odor grew stronger.

Concern showed on Professor Thorn's face. "Will we have to tell the police why we came here? It's so embarrassing. . . ."

I gave her a straight look. "We have to tell them exactly what happened. If we lie or hold anything back, they'll dig it out and confront us with it. Our interviews won't be pleasant, but we haven't done anything wrong."

It had not yet occurred to me to question her story.

Sirens whined outside, then stopped, leaving an eerie silence. Even my internal music rested, bringing a welcome interlude of relief. Running footsteps sounded on the stairs, and two uniformed policemen burst into the hallway.

I pointed to the open office door. The lead policeman took two careful steps through the doorway. One look was enough. He came back outside and used his hand radio to call for backup. His partner sealed off the office with yellow tape.

Dimly heard mutterings from outside the building indicated that a crowd had formed. Mostly students, I supposed. There must have been more police restraining them, for none entered the building.

The lead policeman inside was a well-groomed man of about thirty. He turned to me now, his manner tentative. "I don't know if you remember me, Dr. Barclay, but I was in your Western Civ course eight years ago."

"You're Ron Spencer, and you wrote a research paper on 'Anti-Semitism in Elizabethan England.' " I tried not to sound like a professor. "Those sergeant's stripes look good on you."

He glanced at his sleeve with a self-conscious grin. "Yeah. But I'm still embarrassed about that paper."

"Don't be," I said. "With one exception, it was a fine paper." He showed too much deference, so I added, "You have to forget you were

a student here. Forget we're faculty. Treat us like you would anyone else at a crime scene."

"Right," he said, suddenly all business. He pointed his partner toward Professor Thorn and led me a few steps up the hall. I told him, briefly, how we happened to find the body.

It's a good thing I was brief, for I'd no sooner finished than people started arriving. I'd thought the building was deserted because we saw no lighted windows as we approached. But it turned out several people were in rooms on the opposite side.

First to arrive was Bob Harkins, a tall chemistry professor with curly blond hair and a pink-cheeked complexion that made him look as young as a student. When cornered, he would confess to thirty-eight years. But he usually avoided being cornered. Dressed in a black lab apron and shirt sleeves, he came out of a lab at the far end of the hall.

"What's going on, Press?" His voice revealed nothing beyond normal curiosity.

Before I could answer, Sergeant Spencer intercepted him and took him aside. They were about the same size and looked about the same age, though Spencer could not be a day over thirty. Bob gestured freely during the questioning, his face the picture of injured innocence.

Next to arrive was the college's lone philosophy professor, Gifford Jessel, another tall, late-thirties-to-early-forties type. His head was adorned with a garland of short-cropped, raven-black hair around a doorknob-bald pate. He stepped out of the stairwell, apparently having descended from his office on the third floor. In point of fact, his office *was* the third floor. Assigning him an office carved out of what had once been the building's attic presumably reflected the low priority our administration placed on his subject. But Giff accepted the assignment with a grin and quipped that it was the best place to teach Attic Philosophy.

Now he looked from Professor Thorn to me and asked, "What's the problem?"

I gave it to him straight. "Laila Sloan is dead."

His mouth dropped open, but before he could say anything, the second cop interrupted and separated him from the rest of us.

A high-pitched voice sounded angrily above the mutter outside, and presently a breathless Dean-Dean trotted out of the stairwell. His head jerked around in quick, birdlike motions as he took in our group. Then he moved directly to the office door and lifted the tape as if to step through.

Both policemen converged on him, and Sergeant Spencer warned, "Sir, you mustn't go in there."

"I have to see what's going on. I'm in charge of the university in President Cantwell's absence." Dean-Dean drew himself up to his full five feet eight inches, which was not too impressive since he stood among two policemen and two professors, all of whom stood about six feet three. Matter of fact, he wouldn't have been too impressive beside my five foot ten.

Whatever Dean-Dean was wearing when I phoned, he now wore the super-dark blue suit that's supposed to make him look authoritative. He means well for the college, but he seems to think he can make the ship go faster by running along the deck. Most of us don't mind that until he wants us to run beside him.

With a policeman at each elbow gently ushering him away from the yellow tape, he looked at me accusingly. "I told you not to call the police."

"I followed your instruction to the letter, sir," I said. I tried to look innocent.

Dean-Dean's gaze flip-flopped from one of my eyes to the other

like a moth trying to choose between two lightbulbs. I don't know what he expected to find there, but he spoke in an accusatory tone. "Well, *someone* must have called them."

"That sounds like a safe bet," I said, now trying to look stupid, which does not require great effort on my part. My internal orchestra suddenly detonated like a bomb into a lively scherzo with a bassoon cavorting in the lead. Something about Dean-Dean always evokes that bassoon.

Professor Thorn, who'd been standing just out of Dean-Dean's line of vision, caught my eye with a barely visible nod. I'd told her she'd see why I didn't tell Dean-Dean I'd already called the cops, and now she let me know she understood. That was an improvement from the skittishness she'd shown in my office.

While that exchange was going on, another person arrived. This was Luther Pappas, a thick-shouldered, barrel-chested, swarthy man with a handlebar mustache and bristly black hair. Pappas was the janitor, though the administration's Great Renaming gave him the title of custodial associate. He said nothing, but looked from one face to another until Sergeant Spencer took him aside for questioning.

Dean-Dean seemed to notice Professor Thorn for the first time. "My dear, I'm sorry you had to witness all this. It's not the usual way we welcome new faculty." His face put on its best imitation of an overly attentive undertaker.

"This is terrible, terrible," he said to no one in particular. "Things have gone so well for us since The Crisis. . . . This is terrible . . . a terrible thing for the university . . ."

"It's kind of hard on Laila, too," I said.

Dean-Dean glared at me and turned away toward Sergeant Spencer.

Professor Thorn murmured, "I see why you're the campus recluse."

"More like the campus leper," I said. Someday, maybe, I'll learn to control my tongue.

Or my mind, which now noted that Professor Thorn's eyes had widened when Dean-Dean mentioned The Crisis. I thought all faculty knew our school's recent history. But maybe she hadn't been briefed.

Dean-Dean confronted Sergeant Spencer. "What are you going to do now?"

"Nothing." The sergeant's eyes twinkled. As a former student, he seemed to enjoy telling the dean what to do. "We're all going to stay right where we are till Homicide gets here."

As we waited, a feeling crept into me that something unpleasant out of my past was about to rise up and smack me in the face.

We stood around without saying anything while the tension grew and our already-glum mood subsided to grim. Someone must have thought to close the banging window, for the cold gusts had ceased and that chemical stench permeated the hallway without opposition. The various professors exchanged occasional glances or shrugs, Dean-Dean tapped an impatient foot, and both policemen watched us with expressions that would make Snow White feel guilty.

My cerebral orchestra abandoned the scherzo in favor of a Chopin-like waltz played on strings rather than piano. Under its influence my tension receded like an ebbing tide. I pushed aside my forebodings and told myself the campus would quickly return to normal.

The crowd's murmuring outside had stilled, but now came the siren of another approaching police car. Its shrilling dwindled into silence. A car door slammed and curt orders sounded.

"Homicide," Sergeant Spencer explained.

As if on cue, Overton City's captain of homicide entered.

He was the one man in the world I'd hoped never to see again.

CHAPTER 3

I had hoped never to see Clyde Staggart again, yet after twenty-three years he'd turned up as captain of homicide in Overton City. I'd heard he'd arrived in town recently to take the homicide job, but I'd found it easy to avoid running into him. Who could know I'd become a prime witness in a homicide investigation?

Staggart was five years my senior, which would make him about fifty-five. But time had made few changes in him. About six feet tall, he had the thick neck and rounded shoulders of a football lineman who'd spent extra time in the weight room. He looked like a dumb ex-jock until you saw his eyes. Jet-black and deep-set, they reminded me of a starved rat about to charge out of a dark hole at a sleeping baby.

As he passed through the hall, his gaze flicked to mine for a moment. His lips twisted into a sarcastic smile, but he said nothing and moved directly to Sergeant Spencer. Three more plainclothes detectives, one carrying a camera, came close behind him, along with a small, sloppily dressed man I took to be the medical examiner. The one with the camera had a face remarkably like that of a basset hound, though not quite as pretty.

Staggart lifted the tape and entered Laila's office, returning a few moments later to beckon the medical examiner forward. I lost track of the action then, for the detectives broke up our group of bystanders. The dogfaced one beckoned me into a classroom. Without speaking, he pointed me into one of the ancient student chairs, the bare hardwood kind with an arm for a right-handed notetaker and a flat seat that made no concession to the varied shapes of students' bottoms.

Without a word, Dogface returned to the hall. Maybe he thought if he left me alone long enough I would ferment.

I didn't, but my mind slid back to dwell on Wednesdays past. At this hour, Faith and I used to attend prayer meeting at Saint Mark's Grace Church. During the hymns and prayers, we would hold hands and feel close to each other and close to God in a way I haven't felt these three years since the cancer took her away. I don't go to prayer meeting anymore.

Forcibly, I brought my mind back to the present. Some lazy instructor had left a complicated equation on the blackboard without adding a "do-not-erase" caveat. Most of the campus has upgraded to dry-erase whiteboards, but this was one of the antique original chalkboards we still use in the older campus buildings. I walked up and changed the arabic number 2 on one side of the equation to 5. I wondered if the instructor would notice that it no longer balanced.

I was just returning to my chair when Staggart loomed in the doorway. "It's been a long time, Press," he said. He nodded toward the blackboard. "I see you're still playing cutesy."

"I'm allergic to people who leave loose ends for other people to tie up."

Staggart motioned me into a student chair and hovered over me. "What kind of trouble have you gotten yourself into now?"

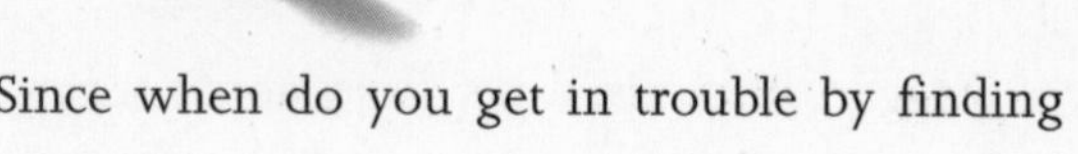

I grinned at him. "Since when do you get in trouble by finding someone dead and reporting it?"

"That depends on the circumstances."

He stood with hands on hips. Dogface slipped through the door with a notepad in his hand and eased into a seat behind me.

"All right, Press," Staggart said, "tell me about those circumstances."

"I'll be happy to," I said, "if you'll back up a couple of steps."

It occurred to me that I was acting less and less like a professor. I seemed to have regressed a couple of decades into a self I hadn't visited in years. But that self hadn't had a head full of mad musicians. The madmen now played a German *oom-pah-pah* waltz with a tuba so loud that the *ooms* overshadowed the *pah-pahs*. The internal music is a constant distraction, but at least I'm in famous company. Beethoven and Schumann both had musical hallucinations. Schumann even wrote them down, and it's said he thought he was taking dictation from Schubert's ghost.

Staggart exhaled in impatience, startling me out of my thoughts. He didn't like it, but he backed off onto the classroom's raised dais and sat on the corner of the instructor's desk. That put him looking down at me, which I suppose was the main thing he wanted.

I summarized Professor Thorn's coming to my office with a problem and our finding Laila Sloan dead.

His skeptical gaze never left my face. "So you were alone in your office for a couple of hours before the Thorn woman arrived?" His lips twisted again into that sarcastic half-grin. "And why would she bring that problem to you? I'd think she'd go to another female or to the college administration."

"*University* administration," I corrected. For heaven's sake, I was beginning to sound like Dean-Dean. "You'll have to ask her about her reasons. All I know is that she did come to me."

"And you believed her story about sexual harassment?" His voice grew derisive.

"It wasn't up to me to believe it or not. She seemed sincere, and I could see she was worried. If she'd been lying, that would have come out when we met with Professor Sloan."

I'd promoted the deceased again, but that didn't seem to matter now.

Staggart sneered. "What would you have done then?"

I grinned at him again. "I'd have taken them to the dean. He gets paid for refereeing faculty catfights. I just teach history."

"Get out of here, Press." Staggart jerked his thumb toward the door. "And keep your nose clean."

"I always keep it clean," I said. "I thought you'd remember."

Professor Thorn stood waiting in the hall. Her lips were drawn tight, her body tense. I didn't envy her—a new faculty member, apparently without friends, and now forever associated with this incident.

"I need to depressurize," I said, "and you look like you could use some of the same. There's a former faculty member I need to catch up on all of this. He's in an assisted-living facility across town. You'd enjoy meeting him."

She waited so long to answer that I thought she'd refuse. Truth to tell, I was wishing she would. Then she said, "All right. Frankly, I don't want to be alone right now."

"Good," I said, not meaning it. "We can catch a bite to eat on the way."

"I don't feel like eating," she said. Her words were straightforward enough, but her tone said, "I don't want to be seen with you in public." Her eyes became the embrasures of a fortress again, and I could almost hear her hoisting the drawbridge.

"We'll use my car," she added. "It's parked near your office."

"No use wasting your gas," I said. "We can park your car at my house and take mine."

Her chin raised a fraction of an inch, as it had once before in my office. "I can spare the gas. We'll take my car."

I should have known she wouldn't want her car parked in front of my house at night.

Walking back to her car, we briefed each other on our interrogations. Our stories matched, but my suspicious mind kept reexamining hers. Her account of her drive to the post office with Laila Sloan could surely be verified. But she said she'd spent the hour before she came to my office pacing her own office and wondering what to do. So, if I was right in thinking Laila was killed shortly before we found her, Professor Thorn had no alibi. Her iron grip and karate experience suggested she might have strength enough to commit the crime. She could have killed Laila and then come to me with a credible cover story. With Laila dead, she wouldn't have to worry about getting caught in a lie.

My historian's instinct warned me that was the simplest explanation of Laila's murder. Caution said I'd better be careful around Professor Thorn. I couldn't teach much history if I got conked on the head and strangled.

Her car turned out to be an experienced Ford Taurus at least fifteen years old. Its doors rattled, its engine ran loud, and the heater didn't work. I had visions of frostbitten feet.

We clattered down the steep hill from the university and across the flat, mile-wide plain of the Overton River valley, through the city proper, and up the hills on the other side.

As we drove, I spoke of the man we would visit. "Lincoln Sheldon was the history department chair who hired me back in the eighties.

He lost the use of his legs to a stroke a couple of years ago and had to move into assisted living. But he likes to keep up with what's going on at the college."

"*University*," she corrected. "I'll be glad to meet him."

In the dayroom of the assisted-living center, elderly people looked up from board games as we passed. We found Dr. Sheldon in his room, sitting in his wheelchair and reading. No board games for him. The sight of his broad mouth and brow, together with his iron-gray hair, always made me think of the cliché "an old lion." Certainly, his manner was leonine.

"Hello, Press." His deep voice echoed as he laid the book aside. His gaze moved to Professor Thorn. "Who is this young charmer?"

Professor Thorn surprised me by not bristling.

I introduced her as a specialist in comparative religions but didn't mention that she was a Wiccan. He said something conventional about being glad to meet new faculty. Before we got too conventional, though, I asked how he was getting along.

"Bored to death except when I find a good book," he said, raising the one he'd been reading so I could see the title. It was David McCullough's *1776*.

"That's a good one," I said.

"It reminds us how close we came to remaining a British colony." He made a face. "And these people want me to play board games. I'd be bored, all right."

Professor Thorn smiled. "Maybe you should offer the residents refresher classes in history." Her defensiveness with me disappeared completely in Dr. Sheldon's presence.

His face lighted up. "That's an idea." He'd always loved to teach with that great voice of his.

CHAPTER THREE

"We've brought bad news," I said. "Somebody killed Laila Sloan on campus this afternoon."

His face fell. "She didn't deserve that. Nobody does." Then his historian's curiosity took over. "Give me the details."

I told him what we knew, glossing over Professor Thorn's problem with Laila as "personal differences." His eyebrow flicked up at the euphemism, but he didn't question it. When I finished, he looked from one of us to the other and stroked his chin while he digested the information.

"This won't be the end of it," he said. "Both of you must be extra careful."

"We shouldn't be in any danger," Professor Thorn said. "Neither one of us had much of a connection with Laila."

She glanced at me for confirmation. I nodded.

Dr. Sheldon leaned forward and pointed his finger. "But you may have knowledge that's dangerous to the murderer. You won't know if you do until you know who killed her and why." He tapped the finger on his knee. "And the police will be on you like sand on the Sahara. According to what you told me, neither of you has an alibi for the hour or so before you found the body."

"I think you're too pessimistic," I said. I hoped I was right.

Professor Thorn took the conversation in another direction. "Since you've taught here a long time, maybe you can tell me about this thing called 'The Crisis.' What was it, and why do people talk about it like it was an earthquake about to come back for an encore?"

Dr. Sheldon blinked. "They hired you without telling you that? They ought to be horsewhipped."

He continued in full lecture mode. "Before The Crisis, Overton Grace College was an underendowed but respectable liberal arts institution with about eight hundred students. When enrollment suddenly

fell below seven hundred, it caused a panic and a change of presidents. The new one brought in a high-paid consultant to lead us into the promised land." Dr. Sheldon waved his hands like a magician. "Voilà! Instantly, we became a university with new and relevant programs designed to attract students in droves. Satellite campuses sprang up like mushrooms wherever money could be found, and some of them faded just as quickly. We invested in a high-profile athletic program to increase our public visibility. And somewhere in the rush, 'Grace' fell out of the college's name and the crosses disappeared from the campus entryways because the consultant said those things were scaring students away."

Dr. Sheldon's scowl left no doubt as to his opinion. "Secularization, renaming everything, and offering juicy new courses with catchy titles seems to have solved the enrollment problem. But I hear the new administration has a conniption fit every time a student gets unhappy."

"Thank you for telling me," Professor Thorn said, and turned to me. "I think I'm depressurized enough now."

I stood and moved to the door. She followed.

"Comparative religions, eh?" Dr. Sheldon said with a satirical wink. "Come back and tell me about pagan religions that have wild Bacchanalian rites." Suddenly serious, he looked from one of us to the other and said, "Take care of yourselves. There's a murderer loose out there somewhere."

In the hallway I said, "I apologize for some of his remarks."

"It's all right," she said, visibly tense again now that we were alone. "Shall I drop you by your place?"

I glanced at my watch and grimaced. "Yes. There's another visit I usually pay while I'm here, but it's getting late."

"Someone I should know?"

"Not really. It's Gifford Jessel's mother over on the full-care side of

the nursing home. She doesn't know much anymore. Half the time she thinks I'm her son. But she always enjoys being visited."

Professor Thorn made no reply. By then we'd arrived at her car, so we climbed in and renewed the process of freezing my feet. We said nothing during most of the drive back across town. My internal music played something wistful on a marimba, and my mood grew pensive along with it.

"Sad and strange," I mused aloud. "Dr. Sheldon is dying from the feet upward, and Mrs. Jessel is doing it the other way around. I wonder which way we'll go when it comes our turn."

"If we last that long." Professor Thorn's hands gripped the wheel. "Dr. Sheldon didn't seem optimistic about us."

Her comment replaced my pensiveness with apprehension. An unknown killer was at large on campus or at least in town. And I wondered how deep a grudge Clyde Staggart still held. He'd directed his questioning more toward personal harassment than toward solving the crime. And I still held nagging doubts about Professor Thorn. She seemed innocent enough, but she'd had both opportunity and motive for the murder. There had to be a reason for her defensiveness.

"I appreciate Dr. Sheldon's concern about us," I said, "but I don't agree with him. The university administration will go bananas for a while, and we'll have a two-day frenzy on campus. Then things will sink back to normal as if this had never happened."

And I won't have to deal with this unpredictable woman.

I should have known when I said it.

I was wrong on both counts.

CHAPTER 4

But I was right about the frenzy. On Thursday morning, an army of grief counselors descended on the campus like the plague of gnats on Egypt. One met me at the door of my office with word that Dean-Dean had personally assigned her to me. I got rid of her by explaining that I'd had enough practice grieving so I could do it efficiently without assistance.

I'd arrived that day determined to make routine prevail in spite of all obstacles. At times it looked like I was succeeding, but then my house of cards would get scattered by something I couldn't control. Nor could I shake that feeling of unseen forces driving me toward places where I didn't want to go.

When I got rid of the grief counselor and opened my office, my computer was missing.

I called Dean-Dean and reported the theft. "They left the printer, cables, and keyboard," I said, "but the computer itself is gone."

"It wasn't stolen," Dean-Dean explained in his high-pitched voice. "Captain Staggart asked for the computers of all the suspects, and I told him to take what he needed."

"Why am I a suspect? All I did was find the body."

Dean-Dean grew impatient. "They took the computers of everyone who was in the building when the crime was committed. They searched the offices, too, with my permission. They're getting a warrant to examine your home computer."

"I don't own a computer," I said. There was no use reminding him I wasn't in the science center when the crime was committed.

"No computer? When are you going to join the twenty-first century?" His voice squeaked, as it always does when he gets excited, and he skipped illogically to a new subject. "The president rushed back last night and has called a campus-wide meeting at eleven this morning. Be sure and make the announcement to your class in case anyone missed the e-mail. We'll have a faculty meeting immediately afterward."

He hung up before I could respond. He was definitely running along the ship's deck again. That was okay by me, but I got paid for teaching history—*just* teaching history. At least, I kept telling myself that. I glanced at the notes for my nine o'clock Western Civilization class while my personal musicians played a nice string quartet.

Then the phone rang. It was my daughter, Cindy, calling from the state university where she was a junior. She'd read about Laila Sloan in the morning paper—*Good for her! She's reading the papers!*—and she was concerned because I found the body.

"Do you want me to come home, Daddy?"

My soul melted, as it always does at her voice. It sounds so much like Faith's, yet Cindy's has its own special sweetness.

"No, honey," I said. "It's not that bad. I didn't know her well."

She sighed. "I *do* have a big exam in psych on Monday. . . ."

I found myself smiling. "Then you'd better get psyched up for it."

She laughed and said she loved me.

She would have rung off, but I asked, "How's the car doing?"

Cindy drives Faith's seven-year-old Camry. My finances being what they are, we have to keep it running until she graduates. Meanwhile, I make do with my old stick-shift Honda Civic from the mid-eighties. For us, good maintenance is a must.

"The car is fine, Daddy." Cindy's voice held that special tone children reserve for over-attentive parents. "It doesn't need an oil change for another thousand miles. I have to go now. Bye."

Well, at least she knew when the next oil change was due.

I made it to class with a minute to spare and opened with Dean-Dean's announcement, naming him with due respect as "Dean Billig." Then my mind clicked into place, and teaching brought me alive again. History is a marvelous tapestry woven from facts and aspirations and accomplishments, all intermingled with the tragedies of mistaken motives and forgotten truths. Introducing new generations to that grandeur is all I care about anymore. By the end of class I'd almost forgotten I was a murder suspect.

The president's convocation was held in the old auditorium, a place I usually avoid. Its familiar smells and the feel of hardwood benches bring bittersweet memories of my world that used to be. I particularly remember Faith's last recital, the week before she began chemotherapy. She feared it would be her last, and she put every ounce of her being into it. After a varied program of Beethoven, Chopin, Liszt, Mussorgsky, and Prokofiev, she closed with Dohnanyi's C-major Rhapsody, subtly inviting us to smile at the playful staccato passages but moving us deep, deep beyond words with the sweep of its impassioned melody.

Since then, I only visit the auditorium when I can't avoid it.

Today's convocation was so typical that I could almost believe routine would prevail. We opened with a nonsectarian prayer in which no

specific deity was named. After all, we wouldn't want to offend any Taoists or ancestor worshipers who might have wandered in.

Routine again prevailed as our president spoke. I have to say that President J. Cleveland Cantwell is an impressive person. He's about forty-five years old, tall and thin, with a long, serious face like John Carradine in the old movies.

He came to us soon after The Crisis, chosen by the trustees to lead us out of financial bondage. At the time, he'd been working on a doctorate in elementary education at the state university. The uncompleted degree posed no problem, for our denomination's sister institution in the next state awarded him an honorary doctorate, and he returned the favor by granting one to that institution's un-degreed president the following year.

In sonorous rhetoric, President Cantwell regretted the Terrible Tragedy that had Fallen Among Us. But with police on the job, he said, Our Beloved Campus would remain as safe as ever. Because The Administration was providing The Best Professional Grief Counseling, these Clouds of Tragedy would soon pass, and Life in These Hallowed Halls would return to normal.

I wondered what he would have thought if he'd heard his speech as I did, counterpointed by my internal piccolo.

The convocation had only one unusual feature: no one mentioned a next of kin for Laila Sloan.

After students were dismissed, faculty were asked to remain. President Cantwell again regretted This Terrible Tragedy and exhorted us to Persevere, Go For The Gold, Run The Good Race, and continue The Pursuit of Excellence. After he left, Dean-Dean called the faculty to order, and the education department chair presented his department's new mission statement for faculty approval. If it passed, certification of

students for public-school teaching would require their signed pledge to promote social justice, work to stop global warming, and combat institutional racism, sexism, homophobia, and a number of other social ills.

This was a typical Dean-Dean operation: to slip through a major policy change while the faculty's minds were numb with something else. Fortunately, we mustered enough votes to postpone consideration so that everyone could study the proposal. Thus thwarted, Dean-Dean pronounced the meeting adjourned *sine die* until Tuesday at eleven.

Dean-Dean has a problem with Latin. An intrepid member of the language faculty once explained to him that *sine die* (without day) means *indefinitely*, and that naming a specific time to reconvene created an oxymoron. Dean-Dean reportedly replied that the distinction didn't matter because most of the faculty couldn't understand Latin either.

As I said, these things were so normal I could almost believe routine would prevail. The key word was *almost*, for I had the nagging sense that something else bad was about to happen.

Still, it was normal for the faculty to leave the meeting with directly opposed opinions. One member praised President Cantwell for an excellent speech, while another complained that there were three clichés the president failed to use. As for me, I was grateful I'd been able to keep quiet. I don't know what happened with Professor Thorn. I'd seen her earlier on the opposite side of the auditorium, a bit blinky-eyed but otherwise no worse for yesterday's excitement. I did not see her leave, so I didn't know how she received the convocation.

After catching a grilled cheese sandwich in the campus grill, I returned to my office and found Sergeant Spencer waiting. This looked like the bad thing I'd expected to happen.

CHAPTER FOUR

Spencer greeted me with the same grin I remembered from his student days. "Professor Barclay, I thought you might want to know how the investigation is going."

"I'm always interested," I said, inviting him in, "but don't tell me anything you shouldn't. The dean says I'm a suspect."

Spencer took the chair at the left of my desk, and I took the one on the right.

"We worked all night on the crime scene," he said. "The search of the victim's office gave negative results, unless something shows up in the fingerprints."

I was glad I hadn't touched anything except the doorknob.

He rubbed his chin and continued. "I guess you know we took the computers from everyone who might have been involved."

"When do we get them back?" I asked. I keep everything on hard copy, too, but I don't like people fiddling with my things.

"I don't know." A sheepish expression appeared on his face. "We searched your offices, too, you know."

"I heard," I said. "Thanks for not tearing up the place."

He frowned. "The main people Captain Staggart is looking at are the ones in the science center building yesterday—you and Professors Thorn, Harkins, and Jessel. And Pappas, the janitor. He says he was downstairs."

I thought for a moment. "Actually, the murderer could be anyone on campus. For that matter, anyone off campus could walk on, kill Laila Sloan, and walk right off again."

Spencer nodded. "Staggart knows that. Today he's trying to narrow the possibilities."

My skepticism set in. "That's a big job. Eight hundred students and fifty-odd faculty. And he still can't be sure about walk-ons."

"The critical time is the hour before you found the body. Several meetings were being held then, and the chief has given Staggart plenty of manpower to see who was where. He can eliminate a lot of possibilities."

As we talked, Spencer kept fidgeting and looking at the door.

I decided to find out why. "Look, you've told me more than you probably should have. What did you really come to tell me?"

Spencer looked at the door again, and his hands clenched into fists. My stomach muscles tightened, though my internal string quartet was playing a lullaby.

"Staggart doesn't like you at all," he said. "I think he'll pin the murder on you if he can."

CHAPTER 5

Sergeant Spencer's visit left me more determined than ever not to be distracted from my normal life. That included avoiding the kind of interruption Professor Thorn had brought. So I concentrated on reviewing my notes for my afternoon class.

The phone rang. Another irritant. It was Dean-Dean, saying President Cantwell wanted to see me and Professor Thorn. He told me to bring her when she finished her afternoon class.

"Doesn't her office have a phone?" I asked.

"She doesn't answer it." He made that sound like a criminal offense. "You'll have to give her the message."

He could have sent a secretary or a student worker. Then I wouldn't have to dismiss my class early to connect with Professor Thorn. But there's no use arguing when Dean-Dean has made up his mind.

Attendance was off a bit in my class, which was to be expected since the swarm of grief counselors gave a ready-made excuse to anyone who wanted to cut. I was teaching my specialty, Renaissance History of Ideas, and the subject for the day was virtue. Most educated people of that time, all over Europe, took that subject seriously and

spent a lot of time discussing and cultivating the virtues.

The assigned text was Baldassare Castiglione's *The Book of the Courtier* and its idea of perfecting oneself like a work of art. Students raised on today's "whatever" philosophy find that an alien concept. Some received it like I was a guest lecturer from the University of Pluto, but most perked up and listened. They were on the edge of their seats when I described the Platonic "ladder of love" and the courtier's progress by willpower from the sensual love of his youth to completely cerebral love at the moment of his passing into the next world.

By the time I finished, I'd forgotten my premonition and forgotten I was a murder suspect. My adrenaline was flowing like water through the floodgates at Grand Coulee. It's moments like these that I live for. Musically, my emotions sought expression in something like the glorious *Festmarch* from *Tannhäuser* in full, triumphant brass. But my uncooperative hallucination played "Arkansas Traveler."

We can't have everything, I suppose.

I arrived outside Professor Thorn's comparative religion class in time to hear her closing discussion. I confess I was leery of her Wiccan theology, but what I heard made me think we might find some common ground after all.

A student named Arthur Medford was arguing that there was no such thing as objective truth: every person had his own truth, and it wasn't the same as anyone else's. Professor Thorn explained the difference between truth and individual perspectives, and then I heard the scratch of chalk on the blackboard. (She taught in one of the older classrooms, too.)

Her voice came again. "Now, Arthur. Read what I've written on the board."

His voice: " 'Truth does not exist.' "

Hers: "Is that statement true or false?"

A ripple of slow laughter spread around the room, followed by Arthur's voice, subdued with wonder. "Oh, I get it. It's like . . . that statement has to be false in order to be true, and it can't be both true and false at the same time."

Professor Thorn, approving: "Thank you for helping us settle that question. And that's as good a time as any to dismiss. I'll see you next Tuesday."

Her class straggled out with that dazed look students get when they've actually learned something. Professor Thorn came close behind, still fiery-eyed from the encounter.

"Don't they ever question that pop-culture nonsense?" she said to no one in particular.

"The dean called," I said. "The president wants to talk with us now."

"What about?" The blue eyes burned me again.

"'Ours not to reason why,'" I misquoted. "He didn't tell me what it was about."

She gave me another hard look. "'*Theirs* not to reason why,' you mean. I hope it's not *ours*."

Score another point for her. First she knew Marlowe, now she knew Tennyson. I'd have to watch my step around her.

But I didn't. I made a bad mistake. As I might have done with anyone else, I touched her elbow to move us in the right direction. I'd forgotten her aversion to being touched.

Her arm jerked away as if she'd touched a hot frying pan, and she gave me a look that should have turned me into stone.

"Don't color outside the lines," she said.

All I could say was, "Yes, ma'am."

I should have left well enough alone. Outside, Professor Thorn walked steadily into the November wind, looking straight ahead. That and her fixed expression should have told me to keep quiet. But, stupid me, I tried to patch things up. Truth to tell, my adrenaline was still flowing from my class. So I complained about having to cut my lecture short.

"I had to leave out the best part about the courtier in love," I said. "Although Castiglione values cerebral love above physical love, he justifies kissing on grounds that the kiss is a mingling of souls. . . ."

She gave me another gorgonizing look. "It's more like a mingling of bacteria and viruses."

"You have to remember," I said, still hoping to get out of the doghouse, "the germ theory of disease wasn't invented until the mid-to-late nineteenth century, and viruses weren't discovered until almost the twentieth. Those things weren't known when Castiglione was writing."

"That's why they had plagues."

For once, I was glad to arrive at the president's office.

We were greeted there by Mrs. Dunwiddie, whose official title is Administrative Assistant to the President and the Vice President for Academic Affairs. She appears to be a harmless person fighting a losing battle to remain middle-aged, but it's still best to watch what you say around her. She ushered us into the president's office and made her exit, shutting the door behind her.

President Cantwell sat behind his desk, while Dean-Dean occupied a comfortable chair beside it. Professor Thorn and I were relegated to small hardwood chairs facing them.

Dean-Dean spoke first. "I've been informed that both of you dismissed your grief counselors. Whether you make use of them, of course, is entirely your own decision. . . ."

He made it sound like it wasn't.

Then President Cantwell took over. "It was Most Unfortunate," he said in full rhetorical mode, "Most Unfortunate that I was away on Business when This Terrible Thing occurred."

"How was the fishing?" I asked.

The president spends most of his time away from the campus chasing money for the university, which is what university presidents are supposed to do. President Cantwell does a good job of it. But it's also well-known that much of his time in absence is taken up with his true passion, fishing. He never goes anywhere without his rods and tackle box.

He barked his reply. "I was meeting with an Important Person about a Donation for the new Fine Arts Building. I expect him to give at least a Million Dollars."

I didn't ask on which lake the meeting took place.

"Professor Sloan's death is a Terrible Thing for the university," he continued. "Just when we've Passed Through The Crisis and begun to Grow As An Institution, this Horrible Event threatens to Blacken Our Good Name. I am Greatly Concerned that it may hinder our Institutional Progress."

Professor Thorn moved restlessly beside me. She evidently didn't know where this was going, but I was afraid I did.

President Cantwell droned on. "It is important that each of us Put Our Shoulders To The Wheel and minimize this kind of Unfavorable Publicity."

When he paused for emphasis, I tried to visualize one person simultaneously putting both shoulders to the wheel without beheading himself. It seemed politic not to inquire how he thought this could be done.

"Each of our faculty members have a Sacred Charge," he said with questionable grammar, "to take Great Care of our actions. The reputation of our Fine Institution must not be Further Sullied."

Professor Thorn was less experienced than I in situations of this kind, and ventured a question. "What specifically have we done to bring any kind of discredit on the university?"

I could have told her that was like Oliver Twist asking for more. President Cantwell and Dean-Dean bristled.

The latter answered. "You must not take this as any kind of accusation, Professor Thorn. We only want everyone whom the police have named as suspects to realize their responsibility to minimize adverse publicity."

"We are on the Monthly Budget of More than One Hundred Churches," President Cantwell orated. "You can imagine how they would react if we become known as a Habitat for Violent Crime."

I could imagine how they would react if the administration followed the consultant's recommendation to establish coed dorms, but I thought it best not to raise that issue.

Instead, I asked, "Who are the suspects? There must be a thousand possibilities."

Surprisingly, Dean-Dean actually answered. "Captain Staggart has narrowed the field somewhat. The athletic teams were practicing, and the coaches know who was present. The same applies to many student activities. Most of the faculty have witnesses as to where they were, and most of the faculty wives and female faculty attended a tea honoring Mrs. Cantwell."

I heard Professor Thorn breathe heavily beside me, and guessed she hadn't been invited. She later told me she hadn't. My mental warning flags flew up to full mast as I wondered how Dean-Dean knew so much

about confidential police business and why he would bother telling us.

"Some stories must still be checked," Dean-Dean continued, "but Captain Staggart's prime list includes Bob Harkins, the custodian Luther Pappas, Gifford Jessel, Brenda Kirsch, and, of course, you two."

"Why Professor Kirsch?" I asked. "She wasn't in the science center at all."

Brenda Kirsch was a physical education instructor who'd once coached women's basketball but now only taught courses. Her specialty was a workout of her own invention called "Hop-Bop"—calisthenics performed while loudspeakers blared rock music at top volume.

"Uh . . ." For once, Dean-Dean looked embarrassed. "The ladies who put the tea together had the unfortunate impression that Professor Kirsch would be teaching a class. She was not invited and says she was alone in her office. She was also the person who recommended that we hire Professor Sloan."

"In summary," President Cantwell concluded, "neither of you is Under Any Cloud with us. But we wanted you to understand the Full Implications of further Unfavorable Publicity."

"I understand perfectly," I said. Professor Thorn nodded.

President Cantwell stood. Dean-Dean ushered us out and closed the door behind us. In the outer office, Mrs. Dunwiddie showed us her special secretarial smile, which meant exactly nothing except that she was a secretary . . . uh . . . *administrative assistant*.

Professor Thorn gave me a quizzical glance. "What . . . ?"

"Outside," I said, cutting my eyes toward Mrs. Dunwiddie.

As soon as we cleared the steps of the executive center, she stopped and put her hands on her hips. "Now tell me what's going on."

"Welcome to the college faculty," I said. "What this means is that the administration is frustrated out of its wits by events it can't control.

So it responds by transferring that frustration onto people it can control. Interesting psychological phenomenon, isn't it?"

Her face still reflected incomprehension. "They can't possibly blame us for what happened."

"They actually don't," I said, "and if we walk a straight line for the rest of the year and all of this blows over, we'll get our contracts renewed."

She exhaled disgustedly, clenched her teeth, and stalked off without further comment.

I turned and headed back to my office. Gusts of cold wind sprinkled my face with grit, and my brain-based orchestra held forth with a cute pizzicato piece by Benjamin Britten.

With pressure from the administration within the university and from Clyde Staggart without, it looked like my efforts to lead a normal life were doomed to failure. And that weird, invisible something I'd felt closing in on me before loomed nearer than ever.

CHAPTER 6

Friday had a heavenly beginning. Then it U-turned into a day straight from the pit.

It began with a dream of my waking up with Faith the way we used to. In the dream I woke to early morning sunlight and Faith's face close above mine. Unbound, her light brown hair cascaded about her shoulders and glistened in the sunlight. She gazed into my face, and her smile confirmed her delight in simply being with me. It was a delight I never understood despite the fact that her presence brought me sheer enchantment. I always felt guilty because I could never deserve love from such a delightful person.

In the dream she sang to me softly and intimately, as she had in life, putting her own words to that sad song from the sixties, "What Now My Love." I think she knew all songs as far back as they'd been having music. And they all pleased her, for her life consisted of music and me. To be held coequal with music seemed to me the ultimate honor.

As I said, she made up her own words. She'd always begin, "Hello, my love . . . I'm glad to see you . . ." But after that she'd invent words fitting for that particular day in our life.

I'll never know what words she would have sung for that Friday, for the jangling telephone woke me into the emptiness of reality. No sunlight streamed through the windows. All that came in was the dim gray of a November dawn.

I rolled over and uncradled the phone on the bedside table. Professor Thorn's voice conveyed something close to panic.

"Professor Barclay, I have to talk to you. Now. Something . . . something has come up."

I suppressed the impulse to suggest she swallow it again and be more careful what she ate. All I actually said was, "What has come up?" Silently, I awarded myself a medal for discretion.

"I can't tell you on the phone. Can I see you in your office?"

"All right. I'll be there at eight thirty." It was easier to give in than argue, and my nine o'clock class would make a handy excuse for ending the discussion.

Friday was a blue-suit day this week, and I took time to ink in the frayed cuff with a Sharpie. I might be too cheap to buy another suit, but I didn't want to look slovenly.

I reached the office first. Its familiar smells of floor wax and furniture polish were soothing, though, surprisingly, I missed the random clicks of my absent computer.

Professor Thorn steamed in with panic on her face and took the left-hand chair before I could ask her to. I took the right-hand chair, as I had before.

"I need your help," she said, her hands clasping and reclasping in her lap. "Captain Staggart thinks I killed Laila Sloan."

"Then you don't need me. You need a lawyer."

Her jaw clamped and her blue eyes burned right through me. "I can't afford a lawyer. I'm still paying off debts from graduate school."

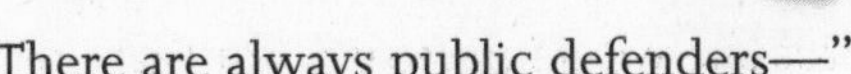

"There are always public defenders—"

She scorched me again with that blue gaze. "You can't get a public defender till you're indicted. You know that as well as I do."

"What does Staggart have on you?" I had no intention of getting involved. But if Staggart was after her, maybe he wasn't after me. After all, she'd had opportunity to commit the crime. I had only her word on what she'd done Wednesday before she came to my office.

She looked at the floor. "He found an e-mail on Laila's home computer. It demanded that she break off her relationship with an unnamed third party and come back to me. And it said there would be unpleasant consequences if she didn't."

"Did you write it?"

She flushed. "No. But it appears to have come from my university e-mail account."

"Who do you think wrote it? And why?"

"I don't know. Maybe Laila. She has . . . *had* . . . a way of entangling people. But I don't know why she would imply that kind of relationship with me."

I adjusted my trifocals and thought a minute while Professor Thorn's lack of an alibi screamed in my head. Maybe she was more involved with Laila Sloan than she'd admitted. My arm still had bruises where she'd gripped it—through my overcoat, no less. The only good part of her story was that I wasn't named in that e-mail. There was no reason I should be, of course, but I still felt relief that this was one campus mess I wasn't a part of.

"I don't see how I can help," I said at length. "I'm neither a lawyer nor a detective."

"I visited Dr. Sheldon again last night," she said, her voice now calm. "He told me a lot of things about you."

"He overrates me," I said. "I just teach history."

"Not according to Dr. Sheldon." Her blue gaze made me feel like a bug pinned to a display board. I wondered what label she'd hang on me.

"You began graduate school at the state university," she said, "but you got disgusted because some professors used their classes for political indoctrination. So when it came time to write your dissertation, you quit and joined the Army."

She had it almost right. Actually, I'd earned a commission through ROTC as an undergraduate. The Army had approved my request for active duty.

"Dr. Sheldon acted skittish about what kind of military work you did, so I assume it was classified. But apparently the Army didn't meet your standards either, so you resigned your commission and went back to graduate school."

"I didn't resign. My category—my term of service—expired and I didn't renew it."

"You put together a supervising committee of older, nonpoliticized professors and wrote your dissertation on something in the Renaissance that was hard to get political about."

"It was then. It isn't now. Some people say everything is political."

"You had trouble finding a job at a first-line university because of your military service."

"We don't know why I lost out. Other people may have been better qualified." I felt more and more like that bug.

"Dr. Sheldon says your selection committee here deadlocked because of the military angle, but as department chair he hired you anyway."

"I was grateful to get a job. Any job."

She sighed. "I had the same kind of trouble getting a job. That's why I need so desperately to keep this one." She cleared her throat and went on. "He says you were a crusader from day one. You went after the national blame-America-first crowd with that essay, 'A Critique of Cold War Revisionism,' exposing basic errors in the revisionists' methods. That was before the Cold War ended. When the Soviet archives were opened, they proved you right on every point."

I shrugged. "'. . . but that was in another country; / And besides, the wench—'"

Her eyes flashed blue fire. "Don't you *dare* quote Marlowe to me again. That wench is *not* dead. She's only asleep, and you need to jolt her awake. You've led two faculty movements here. The first voted down the administration's move to throw out the traditional core of required courses and make almost every course elective. The second was the move to drop chemistry from the nursing curriculum."

"You're wrong about that wench. She's completely and finally dead, with a wooden stake driven through her heart."

"Doctor Sheldon says you became persona non grata with the administration. Between that and the shock of your wife's death, you've let yourself degenerate into a recluse and a cynic."

"Guilty on both counts. I like it that way."

Her hands tightened into fists. She seemed close to tears. "You *need* to come out of your shell and do something constructive. And I need help before I lose my job and get put in jail."

As if being pinned to a board wasn't bad enough, now she was twisting the pin. But I let her down as gently as I could. "I'm sorry, Professor Thorn. As I said, I'm neither a lawyer nor a detective. I don't have the qualifications to help you, much less the authority."

"All right, then." She stood. If her blue gaze had scorched me

before, it now became an acetylene torch. Her chin raised that telltale fraction of an inch. "I've done everything else by myself. I'll just have to do this, too."

She showed commendable determination, yet a single tear trickled down her right cheek.

After she'd gone, I sat for several minutes, half-stunned by the sheer force of her, while my internal music grumbled away with something too obscure to identify. She had a lot of things right, but there was one factor she'd failed to mention. On the two faculty votes I'd carried, I'd moved for secret ballots and Dr. Sheldon had seconded. With that shield of anonymity, faculty members could vote their conscience without fear of retribution, so Dr. Sheldon and I were the only ones with our necks bared to the guillotine. As I fell into disfavor with the administration, my faculty friends withdrew from me. I think they still respect me. But they do it silently and from a distance.

I'm still angry about that. So now I just teach history.

My emotional downer lasted only until my nine o'clock class, Theories of the American Revolution. That's a senior seminar studying how successive generations have interpreted the same historical facts in different ways according to the circumstances of their own times. It always inspires me, and by the end of the period I was not only walking on clouds—I was walking on air above them.

But not for long. Captain Clyde Staggart met me at my office door with his dogfaced detective in tow. Staggart was grinning and holding something behind his back. I'd heard that police procedures in Overton City were . . . uh . . . somewhat informal, but until now I'd had no occasion to gather empirical data on the subject. It looked like Staggart was about to fill that gap in my experience.

I didn't invite them in but they came anyway, taking the two chairs

Professor Thorn and I had occupied earlier. I sat behind my desk, that being the most available signal that they'd invaded my territory.

When they were well-settled and waiting, I said, "Come in."

Staggart laughed, the muscles of his bull neck bulging. "You always were a sarcastic one." His hand still hid something on the side away from me.

I asked, "To what do I owe the honor of your visit?" As long as we were being sarcastic, we might as well be trite.

Staggart held up the thing he'd been hiding. It was a small book with a light blue cover. "What do I have in my hand?"

I tented my fingers on the desk and said, "It appears to be a book. What's the catch?"

His grin broadened. "Its title is *The Elizabethan Love Sonnet*, and it's by somebody named J. W. Lever."

My skin began to crawl but I held his gaze. "So?"

He opened the book to show the inside of the front cover. "It has your name written in it in what I think is your handwriting."

I could recognize the book from where I sat. But to be sure, I got up and moved to where it should have been in my bookshelves. In its place there was an empty space. I pointed and said, "It should be right here. Where did you find it?"

"In Laila Sloan's office, this morning. Why did you give her a book of love sonnets?"

"It's not a book of love sonnets. It's a book *about* love sonnets. I didn't give it to her."

"So you say. Then how did it get there?"

I shrugged. "I have no idea. And I don't know how long it's been missing. I haven't looked at that book for years."

His grin changed to a frown. “And just what might a history teacher be doing with a poetry book in his office?”

I sat down again behind my desk. “My specialty is history of ideas. That book explains that the sonnet forms themselves have meaning even before they’re filled out with words. It also says that one form illustrates sixteenth-century methods of thought and another one was better suited to the intellectual revolution of the seventeenth century.”

Staggart grimaced. “What kind of gobbledegook is that?”

It was my turn to grin. “Take my course and I’ll teach you.”

“All right, Big Brain.” His mocking grin returned. “How do you explain what we found on Professor Sloan’s computer?”

He took a folded sheet of paper from the book and held it close enough for me to read it through the middle lens of my trifocals. My skin had crawled before, but now a hot brick settled in my stomach.

The paper contained a printed-out e-mail:

> Laila, my sweet, I can never get enough of you. Yes, I’ll keep this a secret, but when can we get together again?
>
> Fondly,
>
> Press

The sending address was my university e-mail account. Anger blazed up in me until my temples throbbed. My words gritted out between clenched teeth. “I didn’t write that.”

His grin became a leer. “Press, boy, you’re blushing.”

I ground out more words. “I didn’t write it. If I ever do start writing love notes, I won’t use a computer. When did you say you found the book?”

“This morning when we searched Sloan’s office again.”

"How did you miss it when you searched Wednesday night? A book is a pretty obvious thing, even to a cop."

Staggart glowered at me. "The point is that we found it. That door has been locked and the office marked 'off limits' with yellow tape. Nothing was tampered with."

I met his gaze. "The fact remains that I didn't write the note. There's never been anything between Laila Sloan and me."

His leer broadened. "The note sounds like there wasn't anything at all between you. Literally. Do you want to talk now or later?"

My jaw ached from gritting my teeth. "There's nothing to talk about."

Staggart hurled his bulk out of the chair and leaned across my desk, the veins in his temples pulsing. "You'll talk, Press, boy. You'll tell me all about it at a place and time of my choosing."

He whirled with surprising speed for a man that big and made his exit, with Dogface trailing behind.

I sat for a long time trying to cool down, my fingers drumming occasionally on my desk. That bogus note apparently made me the unnamed third party of Professor Thorn's note. Instead of my being pleasantly outside the mess she'd described, this note dumped me right back into the middle of it. Beyond that, this Friday had brought me two disastrous meetings thus far, and it wasn't yet noon.

There was a whole afternoon left for things to go wrong.

CHAPTER 7

My spinning thoughts went nowhere.

At noon I caught a grilled cheese sandwich and coffee in the campus grill. That hot brick seemed to have established residence in my stomach, but I needed to eat something before my afternoon class.

I wanted to be alone, but the only open seat was at a table of faculty. Bob Harkins and Gifford Jessel—my fellow suspects—were there along with two members of the English faculty, one male and one female. Harkins waved his hamburger as an invitation for me to join them, and Jessel welcomed me with a nod and a grin. None of us said anything about the murder.

The female, a composition specialist, showed us a student paper with one sentence circled in red: "The problem is not young people, it is our effluent society."

"He meant to say 'affluent,' " she explained, in case we didn't know the difference.

"I don't know," Bob Harkins said. His eyes had a mischievous twinkle that made him look as young as a student. " 'Effluent' is sewage.

Maybe he meant it as social criticism."

The composition teacher's mouth hung open. "I never thought of that."

The male beside her said, "I thought you were complaining about the comma splice."

The female teacher objected, and they argued over the relative merits of "content" and "mechanical correctness." You might say it was a typical faculty lunch.

My Western Civ class went well—good student interest, good questions—and by the end of it that hot brick had absented itself from my stomach. But not for long. A student met me at the door and said I was wanted in the dean's office. Like right now.

When I got there, though, Dean-Dean was in conference behind a closed door. Mrs. Dunwiddie avoided eye contact, which was not a good sign. Presently, the door opened and two faculty members emerged. Close behind came Dean-Dean, who motioned me in.

One half of his office is the archetype of disorder. His desk sits there, with a computer monitor perched on one corner and the miscellaneous scatter of a month's papers covering the rest of it. Behind the desk is his swivel chair, and behind that stands a table with more scattered papers and a telephone.

The other half of his office is an archetype of order. Above several hardwood chairs, the walls display framed photographs of fields and streams. Dean-Dean's precisely labeled key rack graces the wall by the entry door.

"Come in and close the door, Professor Barclay." Dean-Dean's head jerked about in the usual birdlike motions. "I must have had twenty people through here today, with seven more to come."

Dean-Dean likes to let everyone know he's busy.

He took a seat behind his desk. That, his use of my formal title, and the closed office door were storm signals for his authoritarian mode.

My internal music swung into an awkward bassoon solo. No surprise there. I've wondered if I didn't make a subconscious sound association of *bassoon* with *buffoon*. Maybe a psychiatrist could figure that out, but I'm not about to ask.

Buffoon or not, though, faculty have to take Dean-Dean seriously. He may not be very bright, but neither is a rattlesnake.

"Captain Staggart talked with me this morning," he said, looking down at his desk. "He says he's found evidence of a . . . uh . . . *personal relationship* between you and Professor Sloan."

I don't mind his running along the ship's deck to make the ship go faster, but this was different. On this run he seemed to carry a harpoon pointed at me. I thought it best to file a nonconcurrence.

"There has never been anything personal between me and Laila Sloan." I said it as bluntly as I could, deliberately omitting her title. I wasn't going to promote her again, even posthumously. "I've spoken to her a few times on campus. That's all."

"Captain Staggart says he found a love note."

"I have never sent her a note of any kind."

"The personal lives of our faculty greatly affect public opinion of our university." Dean-Dean glanced at me and looked away again. "If evidence from this investigation leaks out, it could make trouble for us. We can't afford to get a reputation for . . . for *untoward conduct*. We're on the monthly budget of more than one hundred churches."

By now my temper was up. I knew it was a vain effort, because Dean-Dean always believes the first person he talks to, and it's next to impossible to change his mind. But I tried anyway.

"If you were worried about what the churches think, you shouldn't have taken the crosses off the entries to the campus. You shouldn't have hired a Wiccan on the religion faculty. And if you carry through with the coed dorms idea, you'll stir up more untoward conduct than either one of us can imagine."

Dean-Dean flushed. "Those are matters for presidential decision. President Cantwell's consultant recommended the coed dorms, and he said that flaunting the crosses would alienate students who might otherwise enroll. He said we need to create an environment of inclusiveness."

"Then President Cantwell should fire the consultant. You know the biblical text: 'Ye cannot serve God and mammon.'"

"The president has made his decision about the crosses, and our enrollment is up. He thinks the coed dorms will make us even more attractive."

I wanted to ask, "Attractive to whom?" But I'd pushed as far as I could, so I took us back to the original subject. "Nevertheless, there's never been anything between Laila Sloan and me."

Dean-Dean leaned forward. "Then how do you explain that e-mail? And how did that book get into her office?"

I shrugged. "Staggart is the detective. Ask him."

"There is one other thing." Dean-Dean clasped his hands on the desk in front of him. "Years ago, you gave us false information on your application for employment. Your military service: Captain Staggart says you were in Special Forces, but your application said it was Infantry."

I laughed. It was a forced laugh, but it seemed appropriate. "The application was correct. My basic branch was Infantry. Special Ops was an additional qualification. I also completed a course in chemical warfare and fired expert with the rifle, but I didn't list them, either. They weren't pertinent."

Dean-Dean drummed his fingers, his usual ploy when he's

stumped. "Your application still raises questions. And Captain Staggart says you were active in that . . . that *nastiness* in Nicaragua in the eighties. He also said you had some kind of trouble in the Army. If all that had been known, you'd never have been hired here."

"The Army trouble wasn't my trouble." I didn't want to get into that, and I certainly didn't want to rehash a dead issue in Latin American politics. That got settled in 1990 when the Nicaraguans voted out the Communists.

"What I'm telling you," Dean-Dean said, his hands again clasped on his desk, "is that you're skating on thin ice as far as this administration is concerned."

The telephone rang. Without so much as a "Pardon me," he swiveled his chair around to answer it.

"Mind if I stretch?" I said to his back.

"Go ahead," he muttered. He picked up the phone and launched into a heated conversation about something or other, his free hand gesturing for emphasis.

I stood and stretched, my mind whirling again from the impact of the three disastrous interviews that day. Staggart might, as Sergeant Spencer said, want to pin the murder on me. But the printed e-mail he'd shown me proved nothing, even though it appeared to confirm the one involving Professor Thorn. Staggart hadn't arrested me, so his purpose still had to be harassment rather than anything concrete.

On the other hand, he'd told Dean-Dean things about the investigation that he shouldn't have, and his skewed version of my Army service was clearly intended to poison the dean's mind. Staggart's minimum objective, then, was to get me fired. That didn't surprise me.

But if Staggart hadn't planted those notes, someone else had. The only person with reason to do that was the murderer. The notes prob-

ably meant the murderer was someone on campus, someone actively working for nothing good. And while Staggart concentrated on Professor Thorn and me, he might not be looking for the real killer. So someone else would have to.

Like it or not, that someone would have to be me.

A weight of responsibility I hadn't felt in years descended on my shoulders like a leaden overcoat. I felt as Julius Caesar must have felt just before he crossed the Rubicon in rebellion against the Roman Senate. But unlike Caesar, I'd already been forced out into the river. My only choices now were to drown in place or swim to the other side.

I decided to swim.

Dean-Dean still had his back to me while he argued on the phone. I sidled over to his neatly labeled key rack, lifted the university passkey, and slipped it into my pocket. If I was going to be fired, it might as well be for cause rather than false rumors.

I was seated again when Dean-Dean finished his call and turned back around.

"Is that all?" I asked before he could refocus on me.

He looked a bit disoriented, which is not unusual for him. "I . . . ah . . . well, I suppose it is."

I stood up, said "Thank you," and left before he could get himself back together. He hadn't stated a definite conclusion, ordered me to do anything, or issued an "or else" ultimatum. I made it through the door before he could do any of those. Two more faculty crowded in as soon as I left. With that kind of traffic, he'd never know who stole his key.

Outside the executive center I stopped and took a deep breath. It might be the last calm breath I got for a long time. Dark clouds hung low overhead and the chill November wind stung my eyes.

The wrong side of the Rubicon was not a comfortable place.

CHAPTER 8

I sat a long time in my office thinking things through while my private orchestra ground away at something eighteenth-century that I didn't recognize. Decision and darkness arrived together, a congruity I hoped was not prophetic. I phoned Professor Thorn at her apartment and hoped Staggart hadn't bugged my phone. I also hoped I wasn't doing too much hoping lately.

"About your visit this morning," I said to her, "circumstances have changed. I'd like to get together and compare notes."

"What made the change?" I couldn't blame her for sounding doubtful. I'd been pretty blunt.

"Not on the phone," I said. "I'd rather explain in person."

She said nothing while she thought it over. I could hear her breathing, quick and short, the way a person breathes when he's deciding whether to hold his temper or let it fly.

"I'm not about to come to your office or home at this time of night," she said, "and you certainly can't come here."

"Neutral ground, then," I said. "How about Dolt's?"

Her tone grew ironic. "That might be appropriate."

So it was agreed.

Dolt's Café is a student hangout below the hill from the college but well short of downtown. The owner's name is actually Dalt, so he put up a neon sign with *Dalts* written in script. That's right: no apostrophe. On public signs, the apostrophe to signal possessive case has become an endangered species. Dalt's was no exception.

Soon after he put up the sign, college kids used duct tape to convert the *a* to an *o* so that it read *Dolts*. Mr. Dalt liked the joke and left it that way. Students claim it refers to the owner, but he says it refers to his clientele. Judging by the noise level inside, both opinions may be correct.

Professor Thorn was there ahead of me, wearing an expression that said she'd marked me tardy. She'd taken a table for two against a wall where everyone in the place could see us. The café was packed, and the speaker system blasted out a beat so loud and fast you could hardly hear the vocalist caterwauling behind it. With that racket going on, no one could overhear us.

We had better insurance than that. At the nearest table sat four students, two boys and two girls. Each was totally immersed in a cellphone conversation, shouting to be heard above the background noise. I wondered why they'd bothered to come together. At any rate, they were too self-absorbed to eavesdrop.

The café smelled of beer and burnt hamburger, but we each ordered coffee and a sandwich. Professor Thorn made a point of having separate checks. I briefed her on my interviews with Staggart and Dean-Dean while we waited. Her expression subsided from skeptical to neutral as I explained. She relaxed a bit when I told her my conclusion: "That love note with my name on it puts a different light on the threatening note with your name."

"I should think so," she said, still noncommittal.

"It looks like someone wants to implicate both of us," I said. "I propose we form a partnership to find out who. But there's one thing I have to ask you first. Just what *was* your relationship with Laila Sloan?"

Her jaw clamped tight and her eyes became blue fire. "Nothing like you're implying."

The server delivered our orders and commanded us to enjoy them. I had a ham and cheese and she had a Reuben with sauerkraut hanging out the sides. She dawdled with it for a minute, perhaps deciding how much to tell.

I used the interval to attack my sandwich and test the coffee, which compared unfavorably to Tabasco sauce mixed with rubbing alcohol.

After a thoughtful bite of Reuben, Professor Thorn turned her blue gaze on me again. "I haven't been well-received on this campus. As a female Wiccan in a Christian department full of married males, I've been as welcome as the groom's ex-mistress at his wedding reception."

"How about the single women on faculty?"

"I didn't toe the party line, and that was that. I had lunch once or twice with Brenda Kirsch. She was nice enough, but we had nothing in common. Then, last month, Laila Sloan started dropping by my office for chats. We could at least find something to talk about, so we had dinner together a couple of times. She invited me to her house to watch a DVD, but by then she was getting too free with her hands, so I said no."

The heavy beat from the speakers pounded my ears while I digested that information. It still wasn't quite enough. So I said, "But you were on good enough terms that she asked you for a ride to the post office."

"Yes. I'd told her definitely to keep her hands to herself, that I wasn't demonstrative in that way. She seemed to accept it. She said her car was

in the shop and she needed to mail a package. I thought she meant the post office just down the hill from the campus, but she'd had trouble with one of the clerks there. So we used another one."

"Which one?" Overton City has a main post office in the city center plus two branches, east and west. The west branch was in the valley close below the campus.

She paused, looking puzzled. "The one on the east edge of town," she said. "Now that you mention it, I wonder why she didn't use the main office. It's so much closer."

"But she did mail the package . . . ?"

"She mailed three. I didn't question that at the time, either." She looked more puzzled than ever.

We were getting off the subject, so I asked, "And that was the extent of the . . . uh . . . friendship between you and Laila?"

She gave me that gorgonizing look again, but she only said "Yes."

We sat there awhile with the music battering our brains. My internal orchestra counterpointed mildly with Schubert's *Trout* Quintet. Then Mara said, "You mentioned a partnership to find out who planted those notes. What did you have in mind?"

I pushed the remains of my sandwich aside. "It's possible Staggart dreamed up that bogus love note to get revenge on me. But even so, I can't see why he'd write a threatening note to implicate you. The only other person those notes would help, as far as I can see, is the murderer."

She showed a sardonic smile. "So you've finally decided I didn't do it?" I must have looked either surprised or guilty, for she added, "You know I had opportunity and a possible motive. What changed your mind?"

I decided to come clean. "I never had a firm suspicion, but I did harbor some doubts. You might have clobbered Laila in a fit of temper, but I couldn't see you choking her afterward. You might have written a note to make police think someone was throwing suspicion on you, but it wouldn't have been a threat. And you wouldn't have written a second note to implicate me in a way that would throw even more suspicion on you. When Staggart showed me that second note, he put you in the clear with me."

She pushed her own plate aside. "There's something I have to know before we form a partnership. Why does Staggart hate you?"

I looked away for a moment, making up my mind. "It's complicated," I said, "and there's too much noise in here. I'll tell you sometime when our eardrums aren't splitting."

She arched her eyebrows. "Promise?"

"Promise. It happened in the Army back in the eighties."

"And he still holds a grudge?"

"Apparently. I haven't thought much about him for twenty years or more, though I'd heard he'd arrived in town. It looks like he's done all right for himself: captain of homicide in a fair-sized city. But we've managed not to cross paths until now."

"That's because you haven't gone around murdering people." Her foot bumped mine under the table. "Oh," she said. "Sorry."

"Don't color outside the lines," I said. As soon as I said it, I wished I hadn't.

But she laughed. "I guess turnabout is fair play." Then her face grew serious. "That doesn't change the rules."

I raised my right hand as if taking an oath. "I won't even bring my colors."

She skewered me with another glance. "Just what does this partnership involve?"

"We investigate the murder and every person who's been identified

as a suspect. Some of it I can't do alone. I should warn you that I have no qualifications as a detective, and we may have to cut some corners. That may land us in trouble with the administration and with the law. It could also be dangerous. We're dealing with a murderer."

That's when my pastor, Urim Tammons, stopped by the table. He is a portly man a bit past sixty, thoroughly knowledgeable and comfortable with himself and his calling, always sympathetic but never overbearing.

"Hello, Press," he said. "I heard you had some excitement the other night." He was too kind to say that if I'd gone to prayer meeting, someone else would have found the body.

"It was harder on Professor Sloan than it was on me." I'll be John Brown's butler if I hadn't promoted her again. So I switched to introductions. "Professor Thorn, this is Pastor Urim Tammons from Saint Mark's Grace Church. Pastor, this is Professor Mara Thorn from the department of religious studies. She and I found the body together."

"Glad to meet you," the pastor said to her. "Not the best experience for someone new in town. . . ." He let the thought hang in the air.

"I managed to get through it," she said, suddenly all sweetness and light. "But I'm sorry it had to happen to her."

Score another couple of points for her. In less than a second she'd switched from serious discussion to make a gracious response to the pastor. And she hadn't let herself be haunted by the trauma of finding a dead body.

"We all are sorry it happened," Pastor Tammons said. He looked from one of us to the other and said, "Let me know if I can help in any way."

We thanked him and he left. It was so like him to offer himself without pushing. He'd checked on me every month or so since Faith's

death, and I'd explained that I wasn't bitter against God. Just spiritually numb. Everything about Saint Mark's Grace Church reminded me of Faith and drove grief deeper into my heart. He'd told me, and I'd conceded, that someday I'd have to get through it and come back. But after three years I still wasn't ready. His stopping by was a gentle reminder that he and the church were still there.

He'd said one other thing, too: "God isn't through with you yet, Press. If He were, He'd have taken you along with Faith." Theoretically, I knew he was right, but since her death I hadn't felt any development.

While I mulled those memories, Professor Thorn sat there without saying anything, her jaw tight and her blue gaze focused on the bridge of my nose. The beat of amplified music battered our eardrums, counterpointed by the random clatter of dishes and the muddle of shouted cell-phone conversations.

Gradually, she relaxed like a stiff apron siphoning up water.

"All right," she said. "We'll be partners. How do we begin?"

I came back from memory land. "We start with Laila. Why would someone want to kill her? Meet me at the corner behind her house at six thirty tomorrow morning. Wear a dark warm-up suit and running shoes."

Her eyebrows lifted again. "We're going to search her house? What about the police?"

"They have one car staked out in front. That's why we're approaching from the rear."

"What about fingerprints?"

"No problem," I said, trying to look confident. "I've taken care of that. And one other thing: If we're going to work together, I don't want to keep saying 'Professor Thorn.' Is there something I can call you that you wouldn't find offensive?"

"Call me Mara," she said.

"That sounds like something Naomi said in the book of Ruth."

"I know." She showed a secretive smile. "That's why I chose it."

I wasn't about to follow up on that. "My given name is Preston," I said. "They call me Press."

"All right, Press," she said. She picked up her check and stood. "Six thirty, then. I'd rather you didn't see me out."

I waited five minutes, pondering all the while about the enigma that was Mara Thorn. Then I paid my check and left. The cold wind outside struck me between the eyes, but it wasn't as cold as the polar ice in my heart.

Tomorrow morning I would begin my career as a burglar.

CHAPTER 9

Laila Sloan had lived in an old-fashioned frame house four blocks from my own. Its backyard was enclosed by a wooden privacy fence, with a gate opening into a mid-block alley used for garbage collection. Yellow crime-scene tape surrounded the entire property, and we'd be in deep trouble if I got caught violating it. I wouldn't have risked it except that trees and bushes restricted the neighbors' view. The pre-dawn darkness would cover our entry, but we'd need luck for our exit.

At six thirty Saturday morning, my private orchestra worked busily at something in sixteenth-century counterpoint. Professor Thorn—Mara—arrived at the corner behind Laila's house exactly on time. She wore a dark blue running suit with dark gloves, and she'd added a black toboggan to hide her blonde hair. My dark hair needed no cover, and my running suit was black. It dated from the eighties, and I'd dug it out several years ago to jog with Cindy until she left for the university. For two years since then it had hung with other garments in a mothproof bag, and it smelled of mothballs. But I guessed it was good enough for burglary.

Burglary was a lousy occupation for a couple of professors, but, I told myself, we'd been forced into it. My premonition seemed to be proving true.

"Put the gloves in your pocket," I told Mara, "and put these on." I handed her a pair of latex surgical gloves. Faith had used them for dishwashing because she had a water eczema that split the skin on her fingertips. As a pianist, she couldn't afford wounded fingers. Regular rubber gloves didn't agree with her, either, so she switched to surgical gloves. I'd never bothered to get rid of them after she died.

We opened the back gate in the alley and slid between strands of yellow tape into Laila's backyard. The grass there hadn't been mowed for a couple of months before the November cold killed it. But it presented no obstacle, having apparently been trampled down by several herds of policemen.

I peeked around the house to make sure the cop was still in his car out front, then stationed Mara as a lookout while I worked on the back door. I still had trouble thinking of her by her first name, but maybe I'd get used to it. The door brought the first surprise of the day. I turned the knob and it opened. My penlight showed fresh tool marks on the doorjamb.

Another burglar had been there before us.

Mara joined me, and I warned her about the other intruder.

"So what do we do?" she whispered.

"We hope he's gone. If he hasn't, we'll do whatever we have to. But we can't waste this chance. Heaven knows when we can get in here again."

She gave a quick nod, and we slipped through the door. It opened into the kitchen. In the half-light of approaching dawn, I could recognize the stove, refrigerator, and an island, but I couldn't see any details.

Because our fellow burglar might still be in the house, we stood for several minutes in silence, listening. We heard nothing, not even a creaking board, so I finally decided no one was there. Still, the possibility put our nerves on edge.

Mara whispered, "All right, Sherlock, what do we do now?"

"We wait for full daylight," I whispered back, "and I can't be Sherlock because you're too feisty for Dr. Watson."

She cocked her head to one side. "I always thought he was too much of a doormat. What are we looking for?"

"I don't know exactly," I admitted. "Anything that might suggest why Laila Sloan was murdered. Use your imagination."

Her eloquent expression showed her opinion of that guidance.

As the light improved, we saw that the kitchen was organized by someone who'd made a fetish of neatness and intended to spend quality time there. The stove and refrigerator were late models, and an impressive array of cutlery hung on racks above a wooden-top worktable. On a small table at one side stood a collection of recent cookbooks—all gourmet. Maybe that's why Laila was a bit overweight.

On one side, the kitchen opened into a utility room containing a washer, dryer, and built-in shelf of the kind used for folding clothes. The only anomaly was a commercial-sized roll of brown wrapping paper on one end of the shelf.

The other side of the kitchen opened into a large living room, the nearest corner of which held a small dining table with four chairs. But it was the rest of the room that held us in momentary shock. In one corner stood a huge flat-screen television. Speakers were mounted overhead in each corner of the room. A small table beside the TV held a slick-looking DVD player/recorder and a top-of-the-line stereo with an iPod in the dock. A nearby set of shelves contained a hundred or more DVDs and CDs.

"Wow!" Mara gazed at the profusion of equipment. "There's no doubt what she thought was important."

The sheer number of electronic gadgets raised questions in my mind, but I said nothing.

We checked the titles on the DVD/CD shelves. All of the movies were hits from the last fifteen years. The music disks also looked recent, though I renewed my qualification as a dinosaur by not recognizing most of the musicians' names. When it comes to popular culture, I can't even remember if the magic dragon was named Puff or Snap.

A car stopped outside and a car door slammed. My pulse pounded a drumroll in my head. I had to check on the car, but it took all my self-discipline to stand back from the windows where I couldn't be seen from outside.

The occasion was the changing of the guard, and the new arrival was another cop. The old one stayed while the new one made a check of the premises. We retreated to the kitchen while he mounted the porch and made sure the front door was locked. I pressed the button on the back door to activate the spring lock. I hoped he wouldn't find the jimmy marks on the doorjamb.

When the new cop left the porch and circled toward the back, we eased up toward the front. The house seemed suddenly colder. We listened closely for the cop to fiddle with the back door, but heard nothing. Presently his voice sounded from the front. I should have known he'd stay outside the yellow tape. I'd been anxious for nothing.

We peeped out the window and saw the old guard drive away. The new one got in his car and launched into a take-out breakfast with coffee. I envied him the breakfast and the security of his position. History professors don't make good burglars.

Mara kept lookout while I searched the study. That was easy, for it

held only a writing desk, one straight chair, and a small throw rug. Beneath the desk, exposed ends of computer cables suggested that the police had taken Laila's computer.

The neatness of Laila's kitchen did not extend to the desk. It contained mostly bills thrown haphazardly into drawers. Some were marked paid, others not. I looked for checkbooks and bank statements, but the police must have taken those.

I relieved Mara on lookout duty while she searched the master bedroom. The cop outside had finished his breakfast and busied himself with sitting and looking bored. In the silent house, my private musicians changed to something dreamy with a lot of strings—a nocturne by Borodin, I think.

"You need to see this." Mara's subdued voice registered surprise. "I wouldn't have believed it."

I followed her into the bedroom. A queen-sized bed lay unmade, half-covered by the folds of a heavy, quilted comforter. One feather pillow bore the imprint of a head while the other contained none. Outer and inner garments lay scattered across floor, bed, and dresser as if Laila had dropped everything wherever she happened to take it off. The quantity of clothing indicated at least three days since the last pickup. The bedroom's contrast with the impeccable kitchen could not have been greater.

"You haven't seen anything yet." Mara gestured toward a walk-in closet. "Look here."

On one side hung the everyday garments Laila wore on campus. They weren't slovenly, but they'd obviously come off the rack in discount stores. In contrast, the opposite rack sported the latest fashions of a quality not found in Overton City. Few of these were daytime apparel. Most were evening wear—cocktail dresses for after five, evening gowns

for later on. Our faculty had never seen her in any of those.

So where did she wear them? Around the house for her own pleasure? Or did she head out of town on weekends?

Similarly, the floor beneath that rack held a proliferation of shoes—not enough to rival Imelda Marcos, but more than six ordinary faculty members could use.

"What do you make of it?" I asked.

Gazing in wonder, Mara ticked off her observations on her fingers. "A house of her own, HDTV with wireless surround sound, and a wardrobe that would have made Jacqueline Kennedy proud. How could she afford all that on a teacher's salary?"

"The short answer is that she couldn't," I said. "But a lot of our people have outside money—extra jobs or family sources. The question is where hers came from."

Mara nodded and beckoned me into the bathroom.

It looked like a high school athletic team had showered and left without cleaning up. Used towels hung from the shower curtain rod, and some had been flung on the floor. A washcloth lay half-wadded and half-draped on the edge of the tub.

"I suppose we ought to look under these," Mara said. Before I had time to answer, she began picking up towels. She put them back as they were, so I saw no reason to stop her. She lifted the washcloth and gasped.

Hidden beneath it lay a key, the kind of key used to open safe-deposit boxes. It bore the arabic numeral 34, but no mark to identify the bank it came from.

"Leave it there and put the washcloth somewhere else," I said. "We have to leave that one to the police."

She frowned, but complied. "I want to see the study," she said.

I led her there, forgetting for the moment that we needed to keep an eye on the police guard.

She stopped at the door and surveyed the room, then asked, "What's that by the rug?"

A tiny bit of white contrasted with the dark area rug and hardwood floor. I couldn't see how I'd missed it. She turned back one corner of the rug, revealing two scraps of off-white stationery. She picked them up and showed them to me. Each bore fragments of words written with blue ink in bold script. One scrap said "y husband." The other said "ter leave h."

She tried to fit the pieces together like a jigsaw puzzle, but they did not fit. The words were not contiguous, nor could we tell which came before the other. We lifted all corners of the rug but found no other scraps of paper.

Another car approached outside. Again we heard a car door slam, followed by a voice that sounded like Staggart's. My heart banged around in my chest, and that hot brick found its way back into my stomach. Mara held up the scraps of paper, silently asking for instruction.

"Drop them on the floor in plain sight," I whispered. "Let's get out of here."

She complied, and we hurried to the back door. Footsteps sounded on the front porch, and a key turned in the lock. We had no time to see if the coast was clear; we simply left the house as quickly as possible. I left the back door unlocked, as we'd found it, and deliberately left the back gate open. I didn't know what the burglar before us had done inside the house, so the police needed to know someone had been there.

"What now?" Mara asked as we cleared the alley.

"We go jogging," I said. "Follow me. But first take off those surgi-

cal gloves. They're not standard equipment for runners."

We both pocketed the gloves, and I led her by a circuitous route to my house. My aging Honda Civic stood in the driveway, and we stopped beside it to catch our breath.

"Where are we?" she asked between gasps.

"That's my house," I said, also breathing heavily.

She gave me a hard look. "I'm not going in there."

"Neither am I," I said.

She looked doubtful. "Then what's next on the schedule?"

"First we get in this car and find some breakfast. After that we commit another burglary."

I hoped I sounded more confident than I felt. Our first burglary had come within a hairsbreadth of disaster. Our next might not be so fortunate.

CHAPTER 10

Mara balked at the idea of breakfast. "We were seen together last night," she said. "If we have breakfast together, people will draw the wrong conclusion."

"We can't do two burglaries on an empty stomach," I said, "but we won't be seen. We'll do takeout from a donut shop."

That quieted her objections, but she watched me with suspicious eyes as we climbed into my car. She did not fasten her seat belt until I fastened mine. I respected her reticence but thought she carried it a bit too far. My Honda has a stick shift, and it would take an acrobatic contortionist to reach across that apparatus to impose on a passenger.

We got our takeout at a drive-through: coffee for both of us, three glazed donuts for me, three chocolate-covered for her.

"There's something I want you to see," I said as we pulled out of the drive-through.

She looked doubtful but said nothing.

I drove us eastward across the Overton River valley and up the line of hills on the other side. The river, by the way, isn't much more than a respectable creek. It straggles northward through Overton City before

turning to flow into the Missouri somewhere up in Nebraska or Iowa. Strange geography. Thirty miles to our west, another river flows south into the Arkansas.

On the eastern range of hills, I circled into a public park and stopped facing the best view of the valley. When I cut the ignition, Mara released her seat belt and sat with her back to the door, watching me warily.

"The view is that way," I said, pointing toward the front windshield. "We can enjoy it while we eat." I took care not to release my seat belt while I dealt out the breakfast.

She threw a glance in the direction I'd pointed and looked back at me. Then the suspicion on her face changed to surprise, and she turned back to devour the view.

It was worth devouring. The Overton River isn't much, but its valley is magnificent—flat and a mile wide with dramatic two-hundred-foot ranges of steep hills on either side. On the brink of the hill facing us, the windows of Overton University's red-brick buildings reflected the morning sun.

Mara gazed in silence for several minutes, entranced. My personal musicians furnished appropriate music: sustained strings behind a cello melody.

Finally, Mara turned back to me, her face full of wonder. "It's beautiful," she whispered. "I've never been up here before."

"Good burglars earn the right to enjoy beautiful views," I said. "We can savor it while we eat."

We did exactly that, wasting no time with words. I finished first, having made a head start while she gazed.

When she took the last bite of her chocolate donut, I decided to share a confidence. "There's something I've wished for," I said, pointing

back across the valley. "That open spot to the left of the university buildings is where they'll build the new fine-arts center, three stories high. The original architect's drawing capped it by a steeple with a cross on top. It would have been the most dominant feature on the whole ridgeline, announcing to the entire valley what Overton Grace College was about."

"You said 'would have been.'" Her expression was grave. "What happened?"

"You've heard about The Crisis and the paid consultant. He convinced the administration our denominational heritage would turn students away. So no new crosses will be built, and the old ones came off the entries to the campus."

"And they hired a Wiccan to teach comparative religions," she mused.

"We could have been, literally, the biblical 'city set on a hill,'" I said. "That isn't going to happen, but it's still nice to dream about."

"I'm outside of that tradition now," she said, her words coming deliberately, "but I can understand your disappointment."

My historian's curiosity got the better of me then. "I don't understand your tradition," I said. "Can you give me the short course?"

I guess I expected a personal testimony, but what I got was a classroom lecture. The early sunlight struck blue sparks from her eyes, but neither that nor the chocolate smudge beside her mouth made her any less the lecturing professor.

"Wicca is a modern reconstruction of an ancient earth religion," she said. "It concerns itself with living fully in this life, right now. Wiccans regard the earth as divine, and they try to live in harmony with it. Divinity divides into god and goddess, and Wiccans worship one or both."

CHAPTER TEN

She paused, so I asked, "Do you belong to a coven?"

Her eyes narrowed. "No. I'm a solitary. I do my own thing."

"What about ethics?" I asked.

Her gaze held mine, but her eyes again became a fortress. "The ethical guidelines of Wicca are the Wiccan Rede—'An it harm none, do as ye will'—and the Threefold Law, that whatever you do in the world comes back to you three times. Do something bad, and three bad things come back to you."

"That sounds nice," I said, "but where do the *harm* and the *bad* come from? What's the source of badness?"

She looked away. "Let's get back to business. If we're going to work together, I need to know something about the people we're investigating. I don't really know anyone on campus."

If I wanted her willing participation, I had to take time to share information. "The only suspects we know of are the ones Dean-Dean named on Thursday: Bob Harkins in chemistry, Gifford Jessel in philosophy, Brenda Kirsch in physical ed, and Luther Pappas, the janitor."

"Let's start with Jessel," she said. "You said his mother lives in the nursing home."

It occurred to me that I didn't know much about my fellow faculty members, but I told what I did know. "Jessel holds a Ph.D. from the state university. He's been here eight or nine years. Soon after he came, his mother had to go into the nursing home. He visits her several times a week. He's around forty years old, a bachelor. I've never heard of any romantic interest. He's not popular with the administration because he's hardheaded about academic standards, but students keep taking his classes because he challenges them. He hangs pretty much to himself. That's about all I know."

"It's a good start. Bob Harkins?"

"A different story. Married, late thirties, looks young for his age. Ph.D. in chemistry from a prestigious school in the East. Solid worker with students on research, fine record getting them into jobs or graduate study. He had a promising research project a few years ago, one he thought would make him rich. He says it got stolen, he doesn't know how, and someone back East patented it. He's been pretty glum since then. Bob stays out of campus politics. He's a good family man with two daughters about junior high age. He spends his spare time at home, so far as I know. If you saw his family, you'd think the fifties had made a comeback."

"Another straight arrow." She sounded disappointed. "Brenda Kirsch?"

"I know less about her. Master's degree in physical education from somewhere out of state. She's been here ten or eleven years. Began as instructor and coach of women's athletic teams, worked her way up to director of women's athletics with the rank of associate professor. She doesn't coach now, just teaches and conducts exercise classes."

Mara arched her eyebrows. "You haven't given any personal information about her."

"I don't know much. She's in her late thirties, I guess. Not married. My wife, Faith, and I saw her occasionally in restaurants in town. Always with a man, but never the same one."

"What kind of men?"

"I never noticed." I thought a moment. "Well, I remember Faith saying they were all big men and looked like athletes. I didn't pay much attention. I've never heard any talk about her."

Mara took a deep breath. "All right. How about the janitor?"

"He's been here nine or ten years. We speak in passing. I know nothing about him."

She looked out across the valley again. "And you know nothing to connect Laila with any of these?"

"Nothing."

She made a face. "So all we have is three respectable professors and one complete blank. Not one motive among them, unless Laila stole Professor Harkins's research project."

"That's why we're starting with her: to find a connection to that or anything else. And don't forget those scraps of paper . . . the fragments *ter leave h* and *y husband*. They must mean something."

We dumped our trash in a litter barrel and headed back to the campus.

Mara stared out the window, then turned and said, "We found a lot of things in Laila's house that she couldn't afford, but did you notice that she didn't have the one thing you'd expect to find?"

"What's that?" We crossed the river and climbed the campus hill.

"Books." She paused. "The only books she had were cookbooks. Most teachers I know have more books than picnics have ants."

"What do you make of it?" I'd noticed the same thing, but wanted her interpretation.

"It means her interests lay elsewhere. Let's hope that 'elsewhere' will tell us why someone killed her." She let that sink in, then showed a wry smile. "Where's our next burglary?"

"Laila's office. We're still trying to find connections."

She looked at me in alarm. "There's only one way in or out of her office. What happens if we're caught?"

I showed a grin that belied the near-panic in my heart. "We exchange our business suits for the latest fashion in jailhouse coveralls."

CHAPTER 11

The second burglary didn't happen. At least, not the way we'd planned.

"The science center ought to be deserted on Saturday morning," I said as we parked in front of it. Few cars and no people were in sight.

On the campus circle, the grass had turned gray and the elm trees stood bare in the November chill. Snows would fall soon, and the bleakness of winter would prevail. Even now the sunlight showed a cold, silvery cast, and the wind's sharp edge cut at ears and noses.

My companion threw me a doubtful glance. "How do we go about this?"

"You stay in the car and beep if anyone enters the building," I said. "That should give me time to find a safe area."

Her lips tightened. "Does that mean I don't search her office?"

"Not this time. Maybe tomorrow."

Her frown let me know she didn't like the setup, but she accepted it. When I got out, she maneuvered herself across the stick shift into the driver's seat and rested her hand on the horn button. I walked boldly into the building, my hand clutching Dean-Dean's passkey in my pocket. Although I still wore running shoes, my footsteps on the stairway echoed in the empty building. I reached the second floor and turned toward Laila's office.

That's when my plans went awry. Luther Pappas, the janitor, was pushing a wide wax mop along the floor near Laila's office. The perpetual scowl on his middle-aged brow testified to a hard life. The heated building required no coat, and Pappas's bulging biceps and shoulder muscles threatened to split the short-sleeved shirt he wore. At my entry, he looked up with a gaze half-startled, half-resentful.

"What do you do here? No one comes here on Saturday." His heavily accented voice sounded like a growl. I had to remind myself it always sounded that way.

"I hope I haven't interrupted your work." As faculty, I wasn't going to be intimidated by a janitor, even one with the title of custodial associate. But a bit of conciliation wouldn't hurt. "I . . . I keep seeing images of what happened here Wednesday," I said, pointing to the office still adorned with yellow tape. "I thought if I came back and saw things normal, the way they used to be, it might drive the bad memories out of my mind."

"Miz Sloan was not a good woman," he said. The muscles of his hairy forearms flexed and unflexed as he gripped the mop handle. "She made me much trouble."

"How was that?" I feigned idle curiosity.

"Bad temper." His brow drew into a deeper frown. "One afternoon when I go to clean her office, I think no one there, so I unlock the door and open it. She stand behind her desk, wrap some kind of package, jump like I catch her doing something wrong."

His eyes searched my face. "She call me names I never call a dog.

Tell me never come again without knock, or she complain—say she faculty, so they believe her and not me. After that I never clean this floor till she gone."

"What kind of package?" I asked. "How big?"

He studied me again. Then he leaned the mop against the wall and his hands described something a bit more than a foot square and three or four inches deep.

"So you didn't see her after that?"

"Once." His eyes held suspicion. "Why you ask so much question?"

"I don't know." I shrugged and tried to look innocent. "I guess knowing more about her helps get rid of a bad memory."

"Once I walk by here to see if she gone. The door left open. She and that other teacher—Miz Kirsch—stand by the desk, talking. Something between them on the desk, I don't see what. They stop talk and look at me. Miz Sloan put herself between me and thing on the desk. I say 'scuse' and go on."

A car horn beeped outside. I'd forgotten about Mara waiting in the car.

"Thank you," I said to Pappas. "What you've said will help me forget what . . . what I saw here that day." The thought was neither logical nor what I felt, but I hoped he wouldn't notice.

"One thing more." Pappas raised a restraining hand. "You always say 'good morning' to me on campus. Not many do. So I tell you about that policeman, Staggart."

My stomach tensed. Footsteps sounded on the stairs. "What about the policeman?"

"He try to make me say I see you in the building before Miz Sloan killed."

"You know that I wasn't."

The footsteps drew nearer. The car horn beeped again.

Pappas looked down at the floor. "Staggart make trouble. I tell him what he want to hear."

Before I could ask further questions, Bob Harkins emerged from the stairwell. His step reflected the energy of the young, and his face was the face of a man content with the world. When he saw me, his expression changed.

"Returning to the scene of the crime, Press? In any case, you're just the man I want to see. Come in a minute?" His hand gestured toward an office farther down the hall.

Frustrated because he'd kept me from following up with Pappas, I feigned a pleasure I didn't feel. "Of course, Bob. What's on your mind?"

Outside, the car horn beeped again.

Harkins glanced in that direction. "That's Professor Thorn in your car. I parked beside her and we had a nice conversation. She said she wasn't familiar with the car and blew the horn by mistake." He laughed. "I guess she doesn't learn very fast."

His office was arranged much like mine, except he had several photographs of his wife and daughters. We took chairs facing each other beside the desk.

His boyish face grew earnest. "I'm worried about the police investigation. I've never been suspected of anything before. Do you have any idea what's going on?"

"Not much," I said. "Dean-Dean said we're all under suspicion."

He frowned. "I'm probably the number one suspect because I was in that lab down the hall all afternoon. I couldn't see anything from there, of course, and I didn't hear anything out of the ordinary."

"Then keep telling the same story."

"That policeman, Staggart . . ." Worry made Harkins look closer to

his actual age. "He's dug up the background on why they hired Laila Sloan. He thinks the other chemistry professors and I hold a grudge against her because, as he put it, she 'succeeded' where we had 'failed.' He implied that gives us a motive to kill her."

"Given my involvement with the nursing curriculum, I suppose he thinks I have the same motive."

"He implied as much."

I'm not much of an actor, but I put on a huge sigh. "We can hope there's safety in numbers. He can't very well accuse all of us. . . . But look, you did work on the same floor with . . . with the deceased. Did you get to know her?"

Something flickered in his eyes. "We spoke in passing, exchanged remarks about the weather, but we never held a substantive conversation."

I didn't like that flicker. "Sounds like a cold relationship for two faculty with offices so close together."

His jaw tensed. "I kept it as cold as I could. I did resent her being hired, and I certainly resented her lowering the grading standards. We're graduating nurses who don't know enough chemistry to conduct a litmus test."

I forced a grin. "It may not be that bad."

"It's bad enough. Not one of her students has ever taken an advanced chemistry course. They know they aren't prepared."

The conversation was going nowhere, so I put it back on my track. "Do you know what Laila was doing with those packages?"

"What packages?" He seemed bewildered.

I raised my hands, palms up. "People say she mailed a lot of packages. I was curious. How well do you know Pappas?"

"The janitor? Not well. He's a surly fellow, but he cleans what he's supposed to and doesn't fool around with things in the lab. He doesn't complain when someone makes a mess. Do you think he—?"

"I really don't think anything." I repeated the palms-up gesture. "We were talking in the hall, and I gather he didn't like Laila very much."

"He never complained about her to me." Harkins pointed to a pair of photographs on his bookshelf. "Those are new pictures of Amy and Suzie. Their piano teacher was one of Faith's students. Sherry McKeon—used to be Sherry Vogel before she married."

"I remember Sherry," I said. Harkins obviously wanted to change the subject. Out of courtesy, I studied the two photographs. They showed two girls of junior high age, each wearing a white knee-length dress adorned with a pattern of green leaves and yellow flowers. Nature had favored them with the same peaches-and-cream complexions their parents had, and they wore their dark hair in ponytails secured with yellow ribbons. As I'd told Mara, Bob's family looked like something out of the fifties.

"That's a fine-looking pair," I said. "I know you're proud of them."

"You'll be happy knowing Sherry teaches Faith's low-wrist technique." Harkins demonstrated by resting the curved fingers of one hand on the edge of his desk, his wrist held below the level of the desktop. "The girls complained about it at first, but now they hear the different sound it gives them."

"Faith always said it was important." As if on cue, my head echoed with the solemn opening chords of Rachmaninoff's Piano Concerto no. 2, one of Faith's favorites. But I kept the conversation going. "How is Threnody doing?" I glanced at the photograph of Bob's wife, the older image of her daughters even down to the style of dress. She looked exactly like what she was: the polished product of a prestigious Eastern school.

"She's fine." Harkins picked up a pencil and tapped the eraser on his desk, a hint for me to leave. "She stays busy with racquetball, church activities, driving the girls here and there . . ."

"Give her my regards." I stood and headed for the door, the Rachmaninoff still echoing in my brain. "I enjoyed talking to you."

"The same," he said, his head already buried in a book.

Pappas was nowhere in sight as I left. Laila's office door pulled at me like a whirlpool pulls at driftwood, but with an effort I resisted. It would have to wait for a more opportune time.

At the car, Mara greeted me with a set jaw and a visage like a small inferno. "It took you long enough. I've been worried sick."

"You look healthy enough except for your temper," I said. "I got more than I bargained for. Let's go to lunch, and I'll tell you what I learned."

She still occupied the driver's seat. She got out, circled the car, and established herself in the passenger's seat before she replied. "Tell me right now. It's too early for lunch, and I have work to do. This had better be good."

I got in the driver's seat and described my conversations with Pappas and Harkins, omitting the flicker in Harkins's eyes that I'd taken as a warning signal. Her attitude softened as she realized I'd had little choice about my actions.

"Professor Harkins said he'd talked with you before he came up," I said in conclusion. "How did that go?"

She wrinkled her nose. "Embarrassing. He spoke to me, and I had to pretend I'd blown the horn by accident. He recognized your car and asked what you were doing here. I said he'd have to ask you. He laughed and acted like he thought something was going on between you and me. Then he left."

Her temper was back, but at least it wasn't directed at me.

"I'm sorry," I said. "I didn't mean to start any rumors."

She burned me with that glance again. "Do we go on with our investigation, or do we quit?"

"We keep going if you're willing," I said. "I have to go on in any case."

Her eyes narrowed. "I'm still in. What do we do next?"

"Personnel records of all the suspects. At seven o'clock on Sunday morning there shouldn't be anyone around except the security guard. I'd like you to keep him occupied while I look at the files."

Her eyebrows arched. "And how do I 'keep him occupied'?"

I gave her a hard look. "Use your feminine wiles."

Her eyes blazed. "That man is fifty years old if he's a day, and he hasn't had a bath in that long, either—"

"You'll think of something," I said. I admit I was nettled at her thinking fifty years made a person old. "The main idea is that if I get caught, you'll be in the clear. One casualty is enough."

Belligerence left her face, replaced by something like concern. "You know you'll be fired if you get caught."

I showed her a grin. "I don't plan to get caught."

I wished I felt that confident.

CHAPTER 12

The rest of Saturday was the longest and loneliest I'd known for many months. Bob Harkins's idle talk about piano instruction started the memory train out of the station, and I couldn't find a way to get off. My spirits were already low when I dropped Mara at her apartment, and after that they dove "full fathom five." I lay on my bed, stared at the ceiling, and let the memories take over.

Faith, so delightfully pleasant in most things, had been a harridan on low-wrist technique for the piano. She made her new students master it by playing nothing but scales for the first week—fingers arched, wrist below keyboard level, and the full weight of the arm carried on the ends of the fingertips. When they did it correctly, she could tap the underside of the student's forearm and the fingers would not leave the keys. Students could always raise the wrist, she said, when they needed to reach farther back into the keys, but the habit of firm touch would remain.

For the doubters, she would show clips of José Iturbi playing in the old movies. By the end of the second week she'd have the student convinced. Then they'd go on to build repertoire. That technique gave her

and her students a distinctive sound: when they struck a note, it sang.

I've never understood how she came to love anyone as different from her as I was. I came to Overton with a chip on my shoulder from the Army and grad school, on guard with everyone I met. But never with her. That was her special gift, along with one other. She found delight in everything she saw and led everyone nearby to share her delight. She provided the perfect antidote for my saturnine disposition. I never understood what she saw in me, but we found instant companionship and were married the following summer. A little more than a year afterward, Cindy was born.

My thoughts wandered more as I lay on the bed, hoping the ceiling would show me how to assuage the pain. Three years ago Faith had died on that same bed. It was the most heartrending of memories, and yet one I'd consciously revisited again and again.

The telephone on the bedside table rang. I rolled over and answered, then lay back with the phone at my ear. Cindy's voice, so much like Faith's, created its own silken melody.

"How're things going, Daddy? I called to check on you."

You don't want to know, I thought. But I said, "They're fine with me. As you might expect, the campus is in an uproar with a murder on its hands. But the police are working on it."

"I'm glad you're okay." She paused, and I knew she was about to broach the real reason for her call. "Daddy, would you mind too much if I didn't come home for Thanksgiving? My roommate's family invited me to spend the holidays with them."

My heart felt a father's little pinprick that Cindy would prefer someone else's company, but my mind flooded with relief. I didn't know how long this investigation would go on, and I needed more freedom than Cindy's presence would allow.

"This is your roommate, Heather Albright?" On autopilot, my built-in parental caution had to ask.

"Of course, Daddy. She's the only roommate I have." Her tone said parents ask too many questions.

"And there are no men involved?" My caution came off autopilot into conscious control.

"Oh, *Daddy*. Of course not. Eduardo and some other guys are driving with us, but they're staying with their parents and I'm staying with Heather's. We all belong to the same residence life education group. Besides, Eduardo has never tried anything. He's earned my trust."

My caution went on red alert. "Trust doesn't work that way, Cindy. A man has to earn your trust again every day—every minute, actually. Con men set you up by pretending to be good people. Sometimes you don't know the difference till they cross the line."

"Oh, *Daddy*." I could almost see her squirm. "You know I won't do anything like that."

"Of course not, honey. You go ahead and have a good holiday. I just want you to take care of my girl."

"You know I will, Daddy."

She rang off. The house seemed more empty than ever. My internal musicians rollicked through a sprightly rondo, with a fife skipping from note to note like a mockingbird fluttering from limb to limb. But the music could not touch the deeper cloud of depression that descended upon me.

That presented me with a choice. I could lie there and feel sorry for myself, or I could get up and do something, anything, to stop the memory train. Maybe not derail it, but at least park it on a siding for a while.

I picked up the phone and dialed Lincoln Sheldon's number in the assisted-living center. "I'm free this afternoon," I said. "Would you like to run a few errands?"

"Errands?" he said. "Horsefeathers. You're feeling charitable, and you think I need a therapeutic change of environment."

Horsefeathers was a favorite expression of his. He'd once explained it was the name given to shingle-like wood cuttings formerly used for siding on New England houses. He found it amusing when people thought he meant something else.

Before I could answer, he continued. "Well, you're right. I've read books till my eyes are falling out, there's nothing worth watching on the stupid TV, and I'll be hanged higher than Haman if I'll start playing dominoes. Come get me out of this place for a while."

He was waiting out front in his wheelchair when I drove up. I suppose even the November cold gave him a refreshing change. He got into the passenger seat of my Honda without too much trouble, and I managed to fold his chair and wrestle it onto the floor of the backseat.

"Where do you want to go?" I asked as I started the engine.

"Dolt's," he said with a glance that dared me to disagree. "The people there think a lot of noise means something significant is happening. Right now I'm inclined to agree."

When we parked in front of the café, I could tell he was right about the noise. The university football team was playing out of town that Saturday, but the stay-behinds had the place revved up like jet engines in a boiler factory. I hated to think what it would sound like later tonight. The din of iniquity, I suppose.

Inside, Dr. Sheldon wheeled himself up to the same table Mara and I had occupied. We wouldn't have to worry about privacy. At the nearest table, four male students gesticulated and shouted back and forth, but the speaker system's recorded mayhem kept me from catching any words.

". . . tired of reading, and there's nothing worth watching on TV." Dr. Sheldon picked up where he'd left off on the phone.

"You could watch the news channels," I suggested.

"What?" He glowered at me. "And hear gossip read from a teleprompter by some bright-eyed popsy with neon teeth?"

"They don't have neon teeth," I said. "Neon is red unless it's mixed with something else. Fluorescent teeth would be more like it."

"All right, *fluorescent*," he grumbled. "Press, you talk like a nit-picking history professor."

"My mentor taught me the virtue of accuracy." He was my mentor, so he knew exactly what he'd taught.

The server rescued us from that discussion. I settled for a grilled cheese sandwich and Coke. Dr. Sheldon continued his rebellion by ordering a quarter-pound hamburger, french-fried onion rings, and a Heineken beer. So much for his anti-stroke diet.

Dr. Sheldon seemed to have gotten something out of his system, for he didn't pursue our previous conversation. He didn't even flinch when the server commanded us to enjoy our meal. We simply sat there and let the ambience of Dolt's beat on us. If it had beat any harder, I'd have needed an eardrum transplant. I wondered if the college's health insurance would cover that.

Dr. Sheldon assaulted his food like a starved mastiff turned loose in a meat market. I nibbled at mine, timing it so we finished together. With a benevolent smile, he settled back to enjoy his beer at leisure, glancing casually at his surroundings. I matched his style in sipping my Coke.

"What's new with the campus murder?" he asked. "The newspapers don't have much to say."

"According to Dean-Dean, the police have six suspects, including Professor Thorn and me." I named the others.

"And what are you doing about that?"

I could tell he had something up his sleeve, but I didn't know what. "What can I do? It's a matter for the police."

He leaned forward and tapped the table with a forefinger. "That's not what Professor Thorn told me. She visited me earlier today."

I must have reacted visibly, for he laughed and continued. "She felt me out subtly on how far she could trust you, but before she left I'd wormed the full truth out of her. You and she are the prime suspects, and Captain Staggart is the man you had trouble with in the Army. So you and she are turning detective." He showed a satisfied grin. "This is the most interesting thing I've heard since my legs quit on me."

"I surrender," I said. "What do you want to know?"

"Your plan of attack. What you want to find out and how."

I grimaced. "I wish I knew. Find out all I can about the other suspects and hope to get lucky before Staggart hangs something on me."

He squinted, dark eyes sparkling beneath iron-gray hair. "You can find out a lot with computers."

"The police have taken my computer. I don't know when I'll get it back."

He tapped the table again. "When you get it back, you won't dare use it because it'll be bugged. They'll either log your keystrokes or the college network will log what you do. But I have a notebook computer and a broadband connection."

"I'll appreciate any information you develop." That was putting it mildly. He was a tenacious researcher, and it would be great to have the benefit of his wisdom.

He beamed like a kid about to open a birthday present. "I'll see what I can find out about your suspects."

He swallowed the last of his Heineken and I downed the last of my Coke.

"Don't turn around," he said, "but a couple of characters over in the corner have their eyes on us." His own gaze never left mine, and he gestured as if making casual conversation. "They don't look like students or police. Matter of fact, they look kind of tough. Watch your step."

He wheeled back from the table and headed for the door. I picked up the check and followed without looking back. But I did glance at the corner table as I paid the check. Two men sat there. Both had shaggy hair, one black and one dirty blond. The blond one had an overdose of hair gel. The other one's hair flopped around like a wet mop used to swab out coal bins. Both men were big, with well-muscled shoulders showing beneath open-collared shirts.

Dr. Sheldon was right. They were too old for students, and they didn't look like police. But they did look like trouble.

I hoped that, for once, it would be trouble for somebody else.

CHAPTER 13

Sunday morning broke cold and clear, with a sharp north wind off the plains and a steely sun that accented the elm trees' silvery bark. I shaved, showered, and breakfasted on a ham sandwich while my personal musicians played a lively polka. If they were paid union wages, I'd have the richest brain in Christendom.

After breakfast, I risked calling Mara. Our phones might be monitored, but I had to know her part of the plan was on track.

"This is your friendly wake-up call," I said.

"I'm already awake." She put an admirable amount of irritation into her voice. "I have things to do this morning. I'll see you at lunch."

"Okay, then." I tried to sound disappointed.

Our conversation was prearranged, partly due to the possible bugging and partly because we couldn't afford to approach the campus together.

My running suit still reeked of mothballs, but I put it on anyway and made sure its pockets still held my surgical gloves. I climbed to the campus via the walkway Faith and I had used so many times together. But this time I didn't enter the campus circle. After spotting Mara's car

at its far end, I passed behind the buildings and approached the executive center from the rear.

Dean-Dean's passkey opened the rear door, and I walked boldly up a set of creaking wooden stairs to the first level. I wasn't out-of-bounds yet, for I could always say I saw the rear door open and came in to check. Once I'd made sure the building was empty, I entered Mrs. Dunwiddie's office, where the personnel records were kept. If I got caught there, I was out of a job and into jail.

The file cabinets were locked, of course, but I'd seen Mrs. Dunwiddie put the keys in her desk drawer often enough to know where to find them. A moment of panic struck at the thought they might not be there. But they were. With those in hand, I felt my blood pressure sink back toward normal.

The first file cabinet held correspondence, but the second contained the personnel records of faculty and staff alike. I started with Laila's, squinting in the dim light and ignoring the throbbing pulse in my temples, searching for essential facts among the proliferation of trivia.

Laila came from Alfalfa Heights, a small farming community on the sparsely populated western edge of the state. She was indeed the forty years of age I'd guessed. The records held no high school transcript, of course, but the chronology suggested that she'd gone directly from high school to the community college in Insburg, a medium-sized city about a hundred miles east of her home and a couple of hundred west of Overton City. She'd earned a two-year associate's degree at Insburg, then worked four years as a secretary for Insburg Tool and Trucking, Inc.

After that, she'd gone back to school at the state university, graduating two years later with a B.S. degree in home economics. *Home economics!* The words exploded in my head like a thunderclap. With that

major, what was she doing teaching college chemistry?

Had she minored in chemistry? No, the transcript showed minors in secondary education and physical education.

Yet she'd been hired directly from graduation to teach high school chemistry, again in the western fringe of the state. The school was named Bi-County Consolidated, located near a town called Bullerton.

Laila had taught there for eight years before her advent at Overton University. Her file held two glowing recommendations on letterhead stationery, one from Morris Wimberly, M.S., principal of Bi-County Consolidated, and the other from William Murphy, president of Insburg Tool and Trucking, Inc. I thought the second one a bit strange, coming from more than eight years back. I would have expected a more current letter from her department chair at Bi-County Consolidated.

The file held only one other item of interest: a letter signed by President J. Cleveland Cantwell, stating that two nursing students had complained that Laila used her hands in a too-familiar way. The letter warned with characteristic vagueness that any further complaints would be "taken very seriously." Trust President Cantwell to leave his options open.

I made a few quick notes and closed the file. As I returned it to the cabinet, I heard a car engine approach. It stopped outside. A car door slammed and voices sounded, though I couldn't make out the words.

A glance out the window revealed Dean-Dean talking to Sergeant Spencer. Fear surged through me, bringing the familiar pounding of blood in my temples. And my anger blazed, unreasonably—anger at Dean-Dean for coming here at this hour on Sunday when he should have been at home reading his Bible and preparing for Sunday school.

So should you, my conscience shouted at me.

But I didn't have time to argue with my conscience. Spencer pointed

toward the opposite side of the circle, and Dean-Dean pointed toward this building. Then each went in the direction he'd pointed. I heard Dean-Dean fiddling with the building's front door.

It suddenly hit me that I hadn't planned a place to hide, so my eyes frantically searched Mrs. Dunwiddie's office to find one. A closet! I didn't know what was in it, but it would have to do. The passkey opened it. I squeezed in among a profusion of clerical supplies and closed the door behind me. Forcing myself to breathe slowly and silently, I tried my best to look nonexistent. At that moment I would have preferred to *be* nonexistent.

It then occurred to me that I was clutching Mrs. Dunwiddie's file cabinet keys in my hand. And I had closed the file cabinets but not locked them. If Dean-Dean noticed either aberration, my goose was not merely cooked. It was charred to the point of disintegration. But all I could do now was wait.

True to form, my internal orchestra featured a bassoon solo as Dean-Dean approached. A door opened as he entered Mrs. Dunwiddie's office, and I could hear him poking through desk drawers. He must have been pleased with the world, for he whistled as he searched. My internal bassoon neatly modulated into the key of his whistling, and just as neatly modulated again when he wandered off pitch.

He must have found what he was looking for, because the whistling stopped. I sweated. Would he notice the missing keys and the unlocked file cabinets? The office grew deadly silent except for the cavorting of my antic bassoon. I must be the world's worst burglar, I told myself, and waited for the fatal sound of a hand on the closet doorknob.

What would I do if he did find me? The only thing I could think of was to pretend sleepwalking: If he opened the door I could blink my eyes and demand, "What are you doing in my bedroom?" Somehow, I

didn't think that tactic would work, not even with Dean-Dean.

Now I was sweating profusely. My trifocals were sliding down my nose, but in this confined space I didn't have room to adjust them.

I held my breath and continued sweating, but the dreaded hand on the doorknob did not come. Instead, I heard the sound of something light dropped onto a solid surface. The whistling began again, a drawer closed, and footsteps retreated from the office. I didn't move until I heard Dean-Dean's car engine start, rev, and fade in the distance. A glance out the window showed no one near, but across the circle on the steps of the science center, Mara sat chatting with two men. Her hands drew eloquent diagrams in the air, and the men bobbed heads and bodies in response. I had to hand it to her. She provided good cover for my skullduggery.

My heartbeat kept up its drumfire as I turned back to work. Desperately, while every tick of the clock sounded a siren alarm, I reviewed the personnel files of Bob Harkins, Gifford Jessel, Brenda Kirsch, and Luther Pappas. Harkins and Kirsch came from different towns in the western part of the state, while Jessel came from Insburg. One of Jessel's years at Insburg Community College coincided with Laila's stay there, but, with that possible exception, the records showed no logical connection with her. I'd heard Brenda had been married, but the records made no mention of it. Pappas's records did not point to any connection: They listed him as an immigrant from Greece, but told little else about him except that he was married. No children were listed. Employed at the university for ten years, he had previously driven a delivery truck in Overton City.

That wasn't a lot of information for all the risks I was taking.

After another glance out the window, I pulled Mara's file. My conscience protested this invasion of her privacy while she was covering for me, but burglars can't afford much of a conscience. And I have to admit that Mara had by far the most interesting file.

Its most intriguing part was the name change she had hinted at earlier. Her maiden name in her hometown in rural Kentucky had been Alice Thornton. The records did not list a married name or the date of her divorce. They showed that she was thirty-five years old now, so she'd been about twenty when she had her name legally changed to Mara Thorn. Her curriculum vitae showed a four-year enlistment in the Army that I hadn't heard about before. The educational benefits from that helped explain the financing of her undergraduate study, and she'd earned some credits from extension courses while she was in service. Afterward, her college studies spread over seven years, with a few gaps when she apparently had to earn money to continue.

She'd begun at a two-year college, but graduated summa cum laude from a state university. That apparently won her a full scholarship to an eastern seminary, where she earned her doctorate in three years. I didn't take time to read her letters of recommendation. Given her academic record, they had to be good.

I stood in awe of that record. She'd come from Nowheresville and fought her way up to a terminal degree and a position on a university faculty. I could count on one hand the people I've known who had that kind of determination, much less that ability. From what I'd seen of her, though, the only question was how much of her total self she'd stunted while doing it.

But the ticking clock in the executive center continued its siren warning. My time and luck were running out, and I had to get out of there *now*.

As I put the file cabinet keys back in Mrs. Dunwiddie's desk, I saw that Dean-Dean had left two notes on her desk. The one on top

instructed her to tell the "custodial associate" to stop using cleaning supplies that smelled like mothballs. The one beneath it was a memo to all staff and faculty. It complained that three passkeys had been stolen from his office since the beginning of the semester, and that the culprit or culprits would receive severe disciplinary action when apprehended.

When I read that, the familiar hot brick made a sudden reappearance in my stomach. Partly for fear of being caught, of course. But mostly because two other unauthorized people now had passkeys. That explained how the book had escaped from my office so Staggart could find it in Laila's. Similarly, Laila's house had been forcibly entered—no passkey used in that—before Mara and I got there. And who had any reason for those actions except the murderer?

These facts showed we were not dealing with someone who'd killed once in the heat of passion and afterward resumed a normal life. The keys stolen in September expanded the applicable time frame well beyond the four days since Laila's murder. We were dealing, then, with a cunning person whose planned crimes spanned several months. That meant one person on this campus was greatly to be feared.

One person? If the number of stolen keys was any indication, there might be two.

CHAPTER 14

Another glance out the window showed the male members of Mara's threesome departing in different directions. That meant my cover was gone. I hurried out the back door of the executive center and locked it behind me. Then I retraced my route behind buildings and reentered the campus circle via the walkway up from my house. My watch said seven forty-five. I'd been in that office almost an hour.

Mara was waiting on the steps of the science center, her blonde hair a sunny contrast to her dark blue running suit, a slight frown her only symptom of worry.

"About time you got here," she said. "I held them as long as I could."

"Long enough," I said. "How did you do it?"

She gave a sad laugh. "Elmo Koontz is a lonely old man who thinks no one appreciates his work as a security guard. I brought him donuts and coffee, added a few compliments, and he was pleased to sit and talk for a while. It's a shame to take advantage of him like that. How did you make out?"

I ignored her question and asked, "What did Sergeant Spencer want?"

A smile brightened her face. "We talked about his wife and children." Her smile died suddenly, and the light tone with it. "Now, tell me how you made out."

"Only so-so." I still resented her reference to a fifty-year-old as a "lonely old man" but decided not to make an issue of it. Instead, I surveyed the deserted campus. "I'll brief you later. Where did Elmo go?"

"He went to check the liberal arts center. Said he'd already finished this building."

"And Sergeant Spencer?"

"Said he was meeting someone at the gym."

"Good. So let's have a look at Laila's office." I remembered Mara's pique at being left out the day before.

Surprise and apprehension battled for control on her face. "Shouldn't one of us stand lookout?"

"If we hear a car drive up, we'll have time to get out of her office. Any other part of the building is fair territory for faculty."

She needed no further encouragement, but skipped ahead of me up the stairs to the second floor. The hallway stood empty, unadorned except for three strands of yellow tape across Laila's door. I put on my surgical gloves, checked that Mara was wearing hers, and opened the door with my passkey. We threaded our way between strands of tape into the office and closed the door.

"What are we looking for?" she asked.

I shook my head. "I wish I knew. Anything out of the ordinary, I guess. Especially anything that might connect her to anyone else."

We made a quick survey of the office. I looked toward where Laila's body had lain and saw that a dark bloodstain still marred the floor. I

wondered if it could ever be cleaned. Cable ends lay open on the table that had held her computer. The only other furnishings were a desk with a swivel chair behind it and two hardwood straight chairs facing it. Laila apparently talked to students from behind her desk. Most of us come around in front because students respond better in a less formal setting.

My personal orchestra broke into something loud and dissonant—the Shostakovich Symphony no. 5, I think. Nothing distracts you quite like orchestral heavy artillery when what you really need is a quieter heartbeat.

Shelves on two walls of the office stood mostly empty. The third wall held no picture or other decoration, nor did the walls on either side of the door. The only sign of academic activity was a desktop cluttered with papers.

"Let's have a look at the desk," I said. "You go through her papers, and I'll take the drawers."

Irritated even more by Shostakovich's bombardment of French horns and timpani, I opened one drawer and began searching. After a pause, Mara started on the papers.

Neither task took long. The middle desk drawer contained the usual clerical miscellany of scissors, pencils, and paper clips. The others contained only a stack of ungraded true-false exams and two chemistry pamphlets. I riffled the pages of these and found nothing of note.

Disappointed, I turned to Mara. "What did you find?"

She wrinkled her nose. "A bunch of ungraded papers. A few memos from the dean. Unpaid utility bills for her house."

A car approached outside, and we stood frozen in apprehension. My heart jackhammered against my ribs again, counterpointing the mental bedlam of Shostakovich. The car passed and the engine sound faded.

"We need to get out of here," Mara said. "What's left?"

I resurveyed the bare office. "Books. You take the shelf behind the desk. I'll take the other."

Not that there were many books. The three upper shelves in my assignment stood empty, with maybe a dozen on the bottom shelf. Most proved to be high school chemistry texts, supplemented by a few on teaching methods. I checked the blank prefatory pages in each book, then held each up by its spine and riffled the pages. Nothing fell out.

Another zero.

I replaced each book where I found it and turned to Mara, who was reading an oversized book with a sculptured maroon cover. She'd had even fewer books to deal with, for I recognized much of her shelf's contents as Overton University yearbooks. Laila had been here long enough to accumulate six of them.

"I found something interesting," Mara said. "Laila's high school annual. Her senior year."

She kept her place with a finger and held the cover up for me to see. It showed the words "Bi-County Consolidated High School," and was dated the year before Laila entered college.

"Laila is listed as a senior," Mara said, "but this is what's interesting." She flipped the book open to the page marked by her finger, then indicated a photo on the bottom half of the page. It showed a much younger version of Laila seated on the lap of a skinny male teenager, her arms around his neck. Laughing and mugging for the camera, she held her cheek against his. The boy's arms were wrapped close around her, one hand resting on her hip and the other on her thigh. But he wore a startled expression, like an altar boy caught sampling the communion wine. A caption in bold print below the picture asked:

Can Dee Laila make more trouble for her Samson, Bobby H.?

I looked more closely at the boy in the photo. He had light brown curly hair and a peaches-and-cream complexion. Though he was very, very young, there was no mistaking the face of the man we knew as Professor Bob Harkins.

Thunderclaps exploded in my head as I put that fact together with what I already knew. At minimum, Bob had given me a false impression of his acquaintance with Laila, and he'd probably just plain lied about it. The name *Bi-County Consolidated* set off another explosion. *Consolidated* meant that students who came from widely different towns might have been schoolmates.

"You need to look at this page, too." Mara held the book in front of me again. That page, labeled "Sophomore Class," held rows of small, square photos. Her finger pointed to one at the center of the page. Again, there was no mistaking Bob Harkins. Mara's finger shifted to the list of names, which confirmed his identity as "Robert Harkins."

"What do we do now?" Mara asked.

Another car engine approached. This one halted in front of the building and remained there, idling. A door opened downstairs. Footsteps sounded on the stairs and then outside in the hall. We had missed our chance to escape from the office. Now everything depended on the visitor's intentions. The office afforded no places to hide. If the visitor came in, we'd be discovered.

I held my breath and I could see Mara holding hers. The footsteps passed our door and continued. They stopped farther down the hall. A key turned in a lock and a door opened. Four more footsteps, then silence.

Mara tiptoed toward our door, but I stopped her with a gesture.

"Don't," I whispered. "That door didn't close."

We waited, motionless, breathing as quietly as we could. The car engine outside continued idling. Presently, the footsteps started again. A few of them first, then a door closing, then the steady *clomp-clomp* back down the hall. Thankfully, back down the stairs. The building's outside door closed, a car door slammed, and the engine climbed from idle into life. It faded as the car moved around the circle.

"Now," I said. "Put the book back and let's go. We've used up our quota of luck for the day."

"Maybe for the decade," she said.

We wove our way back through the yellow tape into the hall, walked less cautiously down the stairs as we pocketed our surgical gloves, then strode openly onto the campus circle. My tension eased with each step of the journey, but by the time we reached her car, fatigue had flooded through me, permeating each limb as if some alchemist had turned my blood into lead.

Mara's face showed the strain, and her eyes looked the unspoken question, "What next?"

"We separate," I said. "You go in your car and I walk home in the usual way. Then we meet off-campus and compare notes. What's a comfortable place for you?"

She turned up her nose. "Not Dolt's."

I took the plunge. "How about Dr. Sheldon's room?"

"Oh." Consternation played across her face. "Then you know I let the cat out of the bag."

"It's more like you uncaged a tiger. You'd know that if you knew Dr. Sheldon better."

We agreed on two o'clock that afternoon, and she departed in her Ford Taurus. It sounded like it could use a new muffler as well as a new

heater. I sauntered down the walkway to my house, accompanied now by an eighteenth-century minuet.

Dean-Dean's memo about the mothball smell bothered me. I wondered if my running suit had left a lingering fragrance in Laila's office, and if it could be traced to me. So as soon as I got home, I stripped off the running suit and started it through the washing machine. I took a long shower in the hottest water I could stand, growing each minute more conscious of my deep fatigue.

After the shower I set the alarm and flopped on the bed, but my mind kept churning with the paltry sum of routine information we'd produced. The only item of real significance was Laila's high school connection with Bob Harkins. I dreaded confronting Bob with that, as I knew I must. And my mind was riddled with fear. Mara and I had taken extraordinary risks and had been lucky thus far. But our luck couldn't hold forever, and who could tell what further risks we might have to take before we completed our self-imposed mission?

And what chance did we have, really, of solving this murder before the effort cost us our jobs or Staggart managed to pin the murder on one of us? Or both.

At some point in those thoughts I drifted into sleep, my mind echoing with the mocking rasp of blues played Clyde McCoy-style on a *wah-wah* muted trumpet. And I dreamed of swimming endlessly in a hostile sea that had no shore.

CHAPTER 15

Fortunately, one can't drown in a dream. At least, I didn't drown in that one. The alarm clock shook me out onto dry land in my own house. The clock reminded me I had an appointment.

I grabbed a quick ham sandwich and headed out the door. At the rate I was eating ham sandwiches, I'd probably turn into a pig, which would be preferable to what I was beginning to feel like. A donkey, for instance.

I arrived at Dr. Sheldon's quarters on time, but he and Mara were already waiting. They wore expressions like a couple of cats poised outside a mouse hole. Whatever they might have learned, they expected my information to be the main course.

"All right," I said. "I'll go first, but I expect some input from both of you."

Mara showed no expression at all, but Dr. Sheldon ventured a knowing smile.

"Before you do," he said, "let's agree on what we hope to accomplish. You both say Captain Staggart wants to indict you for the murder, and you're both under pressure from the college administration. You

think finding the real murderer will solve both problems. I've offered to supplement your efforts with computer research."

Mara nodded and I said, "That's the size of it."

"May I say before starting," Dr. Sheldon said, "my considered opinion is that all three of us are nuts. My computer work will keep me from dying of boredom, and it should bring no negative consequences. But what you're doing is dangerous. You're dealing with a real murderer, and the closer you get to him—or her—the more likely you are to become the next victims. And the probability of your succeeding can best be expressed in negative numbers. Are you sure you want to continue?"

"Yes." Mara showed him her steely blue gaze.

"I have to continue," I said. "The police won't find the real murderer as long as they're focused on us. And on the job front, I like teaching history. I'd make a lousy salesman."

"You would at that," Sheldon agreed. "So our chances are less than zero, but we continue anyway."

Mara and I nodded, and at that moment my internal musicians launched into something appropriate—from Dvořák's Symphony no. 9 (*From the New World*), his variations on "Three Blind Mice."

That wasn't exactly reassuring.

Nevertheless, I summarized what I'd learned from the personnel records, conveniently omitting the fact that I'd peeked at Mara's.

"So the records show no definite connection between Laila and any of the suspects," I said. "Pappas's record shows only that he's a naturalized citizen. Laila, Bob Harkins, and Brenda Kirsch list hometowns near the western border of the state, but I found no other common factor."

Mara stirred as if she wanted to say something, but I went on with my report. "Laila and Gifford Jessel overlapped one year at Insburg Community College, but that has several thousand students enrolled, mostly commuters. It's possible Giff and Laila never met."

Before Mara could break in, I continued. "I talked Saturday with Pappas and Harkins. Pappas says he and Laila didn't get along. He found her in her office wrapping a package. She called him names and threatened to complain about him. After that, he avoided her as much as he could. Another time, though, he saw her and Brenda in Laila's office with something between them on the desk. He didn't see what it was because Laila stepped in front of it. He made his excuses and left."

"What kind of package did he see?" Mara asked.

"When I asked, he made motions with his hands." I imitated the motions. "Something a little more than a foot square and several inches deep."

Mara nodded. "That would describe two of the three packages she mailed with me. The third was much deeper and maybe a little wider. Shaped more like a cube."

"Pappas is afraid of something," I said. "Laila's threat of a complaint panicked him. And Staggart has something on him, enough to force Pappas to say he saw me in the science center about the time Laila was killed."

Mara gasped, but Dr. Sheldon looked thoughtful and stroked his chin.

"Were you in the chemistry building then?" he asked.

"Science center," I corrected. Maybe Dean-Dean had influenced me more than I'd thought. "No. I was in my office. Unfortunately, nobody saw me there until Mara came by."

Sheldon pursed his lips. "If worst comes to worst, your defense counsel can give Pappas a lie-detector test. If he flunks it or refuses to take it, that should create doubt in the prosecutor's mind. Slow him up a bit."

"For heaven's sake," I protested, "you already have me in the docket."

He showed his leonine smile. "Just thinking analytically, as one of my protégés used to recommend."

You might know I was the guilty protégé. Okay, now he'd evened the score for my correcting him about the color of neon and reminding him of his own demand for accuracy.

"What about Bob Harkins?" Mara asked. "You said he denied anything beyond a speaking acquaintance with Laila, but that photograph showed them wrapped around each other like stripes on a barber pole."

"He did lie about it," I said to Dr. Sheldon, "and we did find the picture in Laila's high school annual. I dread facing Bob about that, but it looks like I'll have to. That brings up something else. The personnel records show nothing about high school work. Potentially, Bi-County Consolidated High School could also connect Brenda Kirsch to Laila. But we didn't find anything about her in the annual. We know she recommended Laila to the administration, but we didn't learn how she knew enough about Laila to do that."

Dr. Sheldon's hands formed loose fists, and he struck their knuckles together. "I didn't find much on Brenda, either. Only a hundred or so items about her coaching days here. Nothing about her earlier years, and nothing to connect her with Laila."

He pursed his lips again. "For that matter, I didn't find anything on Laila before she began teaching at that high school. You'd think she'd leave some kind of record."

"Her first name was Dee," Mara said. "Maybe she didn't go by Laila until later."

"Dee Laila?" Sheldon asked. "Sounds like someone couldn't spell. Or played cute with names." He snapped his fingers. "All right. I'll look

for her again under *Dee*. I found the usual information about Harkins and Jessel, but nothing you haven't told me."

He looked at Mara and said, "Your turn."

She gave him an appreciative smile like she'd never shown me and said, "Not a great deal. The security guard—Elmo Koontz—hasn't seen anyone suspicious near Laila's office at any time this fall. He did see a couple of tough-looking fellows walk across campus yesterday, but that's too late for our purposes."

Sheldon and I exchanged glances but said nothing.

She sighed. "That poor, lonely man certainly likes to talk. He thanked me for sharing donuts with him, and I felt really bad for taking advantage."

"Burglars can't have consciences," I said.

Her glance showed me a bit of blue fire, but nothing like the conflagration she'd shown me earlier.

"Sergeant Spencer likes to talk, too," she said, her face now expressionless. "He said Dean Billig told him he'd fire the no-good who's been stealing passkeys. Except that the dean used a more colorful expression."

Dr. Sheldon snorted. "Dean-Dean has a habit of hip-shooting off the top of his head, which in his case may not be a mixed metaphor."

"I'll take the Fifth Amendment on that," Mara said. "Spencer also said Staggart was beside himself because someone broke into Laila's house. He—Staggart—found new evidence there, but he doesn't know if it's usable because he didn't find it on his first search. He's doubled the police guard."

I thought Spencer had talked too much, but I couldn't complain about it. "Anything else?" I asked.

She gave me her ironic smile, nothing like the approving one she'd shown Dr. Sheldon. "Spencer is happy because Staggart is bringing him in on the investigation. It seems they're short of manpower."

"That's good news," I said. "We'll have someone on their team who isn't prejudiced against us."

Mara's smile changed to a friendly one, the first from her that I could remember. "Prejudiced *for* you, actually," she said. "He told me about that research paper he mentioned just after we found Laila's body."

"What research paper?" Dr. Sheldon asked.

Mara directed her answer to him. "As a student, Sergeant Spencer wrote a paper on 'Anti-Semitism in Elizabethan England' for our distinguished Professor Barclay. Spencer wrote that in 1594 one Dr. Lopez, a Jewish physician, tried to poison Queen Elizabeth I, and the subsequent outpouring of anti-Jewish sentiment resulted in plays like Shakespeare's *The Merchant of Venice* and Christopher Marlowe's *The Jew of Malta*."

Dr. Sheldon waited expectantly.

"Our good professor assigned a grade of A-, but he pointed out that since Marlowe was stabbed to death in 1593, it was unlikely that he wrote *The Jew of Malta* in response to an event that happened in 1594. He further explained that the same applies to the play itself, which was produced on stage as early as 1592."

Dr. Sheldon nodded vigorously.

"This made a great impression on Sergeant Spencer, who says that ever since then he's been careful to get his facts straight before jumping to a conclusion."

Dr. Sheldon beamed. "Press, it's rare for anything we do in the classroom to actually change someone's life. That incident alone means your career is a success."

"I'd like to try for a few more," I said, "but basking in Sergeant

Spencer's praise doesn't help me keep my job. So where do we go from here?"

"There is one factor that may link several of our suspects," Dr. Sheldon said. "Three years ago, someone got up a faculty trip to Las Vegas during spring break. About a third of the faculty went, including Laila and our suspects—except for Pappas, of course."

I'd forgotten about that. At the time I was too tied up with Faith's death to pay much attention. "Did spouses go too?" I asked.

"The only spouse we're concerned with is Threnody Harkins," Sheldon said. "She did go. I remember because one of my student assistants stayed with the children."

"I don't see where it fits," I said, "but I'll keep it in mind when I talk to the three faculty."

"Have you considered the time factor?" Dr. Sheldon asked. "Thanksgiving holidays begin at noon one week from this coming Wednesday. All the suspects will scatter. Our investigation will lose momentum, and we'll have difficulty regaining it."

"So the calendar gives us a deadline," Mara said. "We'd better work fast."

"I'll keep working the computer," Dr. Sheldon said.

Mara turned to me. "What will we do?"

A wave of hopelessness swept over me, but I did my best to ignore it. "Deadline or no, we resume routine school activities tomorrow and try to look as normal as we can. I have three people to interview—Harkins, Jessel, and Brenda Kirsch. With any luck, I should be able to do that within the next few days. Maybe we can work it so you look over their offices while I hold them somewhere else. If you're still game, that is."

Her gaze gave me the full harpoon treatment. "I'm game. I need my job as much as you need yours. And I don't think I'd get along well in prison."

"Now, children," said Dr. Sheldon, "let us not squabble. If we're to be teammates we must work without friction."

Mara nodded again and I said, "Yes, sir."

We left it at that. Mara said she had another stop to make, so we went separate ways. I passed again on visiting Mrs. Jessel because I didn't feel up to coping with her dementia.

I drove home through the gathering darkness, more convinced than ever that mine was a fool's errand, but one in which I had no choice except to persevere.

Appropriately, my mind still echoed Dvořák's variations on "Three Blind Mice."

CHAPTER 16

On Monday morning I climbed the walkway to the campus thirty minutes before my nine o'clock class. For once, I carried my ancient cell phone that usually lies in the glove compartment of my car. A few faculty would kid me about the phone, but Mara and I would need it later today.

The campus seemed trending back toward normal in some ways, but not in others. The toward-normal trend was that the swarm of grief counselors was thinning out. Last week I was tripping over one every three or four steps. Today I might make it to ten.

The not-normal factor was the air of anticipation, intangible but real, that permeates every campus as holidays approach—in this case, the Thanksgiving break that would begin at noon a week from Wednesday. This was also the week research papers were due in all my classes. I learned long ago that a post-Thanksgiving deadline invited mass procrastination and an epidemic of incomplete grades. Having them due this week let me use next week's three class days as an unofficial grace period.

I found my office door open and Earl-George Heggan reinstalling my computer that the police had taken. Earl-George avoids eye contact and doesn't have much to say, which may be why he flopped as an instructor in what used to be called the computer department but is known since the Great Renaming as the division of electronic communication and technology. Because he is President Cantwell's nephew, Earl-George couldn't be fired, so he now administers the campus computer network and fixes the faculty's frequent computer glitches. He always wears farmer's overalls, a denim work shirt, and his hair down over his forehead.

As I came in the door he looked up and muttered, "You're back on the network."

"Is this the same computer the police took?" I asked.

He nodded and grunted something. As if to add its endorsement, the computer clicked several times.

I crawled under the desk and checked the serial number to be sure. It was the same computer.

"Did they put a bug in it?" I asked. "Or a keystroke logger?"

"No bug, no keystroke," Earl-George said. "Someone put memos under your door. Now on your desk." He shuffled out without further comment.

The first memo, from President Cantwell, announced a memorial service for "Professor Laila Sloan" at eleven Tuesday morning. Another posthumous promotion, I guess. A faculty meeting would be held immediately after the service.

The second was Dean-Dean's memo to all faculty:

> Since September three passkeys have been stolen from the Dean's Office, this will not be tolerated. If any person has an unauthorized

key they must return them immediately. Any further thefts will result in disciplinary action.

Dean Billig, Ph.D.
Vice President for Academic Affairs

I looked forward to hearing comments on his grammar over lunch. The computer emitted another succession of clicks—updating itself to network standard, I guess. That started me worrying again about what Staggart and his cohorts might have done to it. A quick check showed that my files were still there. If they later proved to be corrupted, I could correct them from the hard copies I'd kept. The computer age has not weaned me from the habit of keeping paper files.

I worried awhile, then adjusted my trifocals and worried some more. I'm not paranoid, but thinking of the tricks Staggart might have played bothered me. I needed better help than I could get from Earl-George.

Because the office might be bugged, I went outside and used my cell phone to call Richmond Seagrave, an old Army friend now working in St. Louis as a computer expert. He balked at first, but when I mentioned Clyde Staggart he said he'd drive over here before sunset. That should solve the bugging problem, I hoped.

My seminar on Theories of the American Revolution went better than expected. We studied the consensus historians who wrote during the early Cold War period. Strange that the hostile pressures uniting Americans against the Soviet threat should lead historians to emphasize the factors that united American colonists against the British.

But that's part of the majesty of history. I waxed enthusiastic, and my internal musicians celebrated the occasion with a brass fanfare by one of the mid-twentieth-century composers. I forget which one.

My emotional high didn't last long because I headed into the science center for that dreaded interview with Bob Harkins. When I entered his office, he looked up from his desk with an expression that said I wasn't welcome. He did not invite me to sit down, and he stayed seated behind his desk.

I decided the best approach was to throw my skunk on his conference table. "We've been friends for a long time, Bob," I said, "but you didn't level with me about Laila Sloan."

He leaned back and showed a sarcastic smile. "Suppose you tell me how I didn't level."

I adjusted my trifocals. "There's a picture in your high school annual. . . ."

His eyes hardened and his jaw clamped shut. That anger showed a Bob Harkins I'd never seen before. Holding me with his eyes, he got up and came slowly around the desk, his fists clenched tight. For a moment I thought he might attack me, but he moved beyond and closed the office door. Then he motioned me to a chair beside his desk and sat on the edge of one across from it, his fists clenching and unclenching.

"You and I *were* friends for a long time," he said, emphasizing the past tense. "What are you after, Press?"

"The truth, Bob." I thought he still might attack, so I imitated his posture on the edge of the chair. As I said, I haven't always been a professor.

"Why?" Bob's eyes were still hostile, but now they showed the beginnings of tears.

I returned his gaze. "Because someone murdered Laila Sloan. Captain Staggart intends to prove I did, and I don't intend to let him. So I've made it my business to find out all I can about Laila and anyone who

might have killed her. That includes you."

His sarcasm returned. "So you've turned detective and think you're going to catch the murderer."

I showed a quirky smile. "I'm not doing bad so far. I've already caught you in a lie."

His gaze wavered. "What will you do with the information?"

"Nothing unless it's needed to convict the murderer. I'm not interested in personal dirt unless it solves the crime." I showed him the sincere expression that I hope will sell used cars if I get fired.

"And if I don't tell you?" His voice had lost its hard edge.

"Then I tell Staggart about the picture."

"All right." Bob slumped in his chair. "In high school I had a fling with Laila Sloan."

He ran his hands through his hair. I said nothing.

"She was a senior," Bob continued. "I was a sophomore. I felt flattered that she found me attractive. I know now that all she wanted was a boy she could control. She had a way of entangling people."

I'd heard that said about her before, but I couldn't remember where.

Bob leaned back and wrung his hands. "It happened in spring semester. We ran pretty much wild the rest of the year. Then she graduated and moved away. With the reputation I'd earned, no girl could afford to be seen with me. I couldn't get a date during my last two years of high school. That's why I went to college back East, where no one would know me."

"Was that affair the extent of it?"

Bob's eyes flickered. "That was all of it."

"Were you and Laila's group into anything else? Like selling drugs?"

He looked down. "No drugs, nothing else. . . . For heaven's sake,

Press, the relationship itself was all a sixteen-year-old sophomore could handle." His eyes met mine with a haunted look. "In the East I met Threnody, and she taught me what real love is like. I couldn't bear to see her hurt."

"She needn't be if you didn't murder Laila."

"I swear I didn't. I didn't come out of the lab all afternoon. And I didn't see or hear anything, either. That's what I told the police, and it's the absolute truth."

"A faculty group went to Las Vegas during spring break several years ago. You and Laila were among them."

He bristled. "We hardly spoke. Threnody went with the group, you know."

"Did Laila interact with anyone in particular during the trip? Do you remember anything unusual?"

He gave a sardonic laugh. "Laila was always unusual. I can't think of anything. . . . But no, she and Brenda Kirsch—the two single women—paired off and went their own way. I don't know what they did."

A new thought occurred to me. "How about others in the group? Any big losers or winners?"

Bob thought a minute. "None that I know of. Threnody won some, I lost some. We broke about even, overall. People made a lot of casino talk on the flight back, but no one seemed to have won or lost heavily. You don't think . . ."

"I don't have enough facts to think with," I said. "You've told me everything about you and Laila?"

"Yes." His eyes flickered again.

"Do you know anything untoward about Gifford Jessel or Brenda Kirsch? Or the janitor, Luther Pappas?"

He shook his head. "Not a thing. Listen, Press, I'd rather die than see Threnody get hurt."

"She shouldn't get hurt if you're telling the whole truth."

"I swear it," he said.

"Thanks, Bob," I said. I stood up and headed for the door.

"Be careful, Press." Bob's voice came low and thoughtful. "It's dangerous to go poking around with a murderer loose."

"Thanks again," I said.

As I turned the knob, his voice saddened. "It was nice knowing you, Press."

I left him slumped in his chair and staring at the floor through red-rimmed eyes. It was the first time I'd seen him look older than his age.

Saying I felt like a heel is like saying Hitler's treatment of Jews was impolite. But I gritted my teeth and reminded myself that losing friends was better than getting convicted of a murder I didn't commit.

My personal musicians mocked me by cavorting through something that sounded like Liszt—note patterns interesting in themselves but without much meaning beyond.

With an effort, I forced my regret for lost friendships from my mind and headed upstairs to confront Gifford Jessel.

CHAPTER 17

This was my first visit to Gifford Jessel's office. It was located on the third floor just left of the stairwell. Above his door he'd hung a hand-lettered sign that said "Attic Philosophy," his favorite pun and a sly dig at the administration's lack of enthusiasm for his discipline. Giff sat behind his desk, leaning back in his chair with his hands behind his head and gazing at the ceiling. The crown of his bald pate reflected the overhead lights, and the fringe of dark hair around its edges needed combing. Before I could knock, he beckoned me in and pointed to a hardwood chair standing against the right-hand wall.

It was the only other chair in the office. I sat in it and took time to look around. A chest-high worktable occupied the opposite wall. I'd heard Giff preferred to stand up while he graded papers. Shelves crammed with books filled the wall behind Giff's desk.

"Welcome to the eyrie, Press." Giff sat up straight. "You've heard the faculty will vote on the education department's proposed mission statement tomorrow?"

"I hadn't heard," I said, "but I'm voting against it."

He nodded. "I knew you would. I don't know how we'll come out, but there ought to be some interesting speeches. What brings you to the eagle's nest?"

Trust Giff to get down to business. He knew my views on education too well to waste time agreeing with them.

"I came about Laila Sloan," I said, and watched for a reaction.

There was none.

"What about Laila?" he asked presently.

"I'm writing a memorial for her for the college yearbook." That was the most credible lie I could think of.

"*University* yearbook," he corrected with a sarcastic grin. "Why? Are you having a fit of conscience about her?"

"You might say that." I tried to look conscience-stricken. "In a roundabout way I was responsible for her coming here."

"Baloney. All you did was defend the nursing curriculum against dumbing down. None of us knew the administration would make an end run around us. And we certainly didn't know Laila would be the ringer they brought in. Your conscience is hyperactive."

"Still, I'll feel better if I write the memorial." I adjusted my trifocals and blinked a couple of times. "So I'm talking to everyone who might have come in contact with her."

"Hair of the dog that bit you?" Giff showed a sympathetic smile. "I'm no help on that. I hardly knew the woman."

"You worked in the same building," I prompted.

"Different floors." The smile left his face. "We spoke when we passed in the hallway, maybe a few times on campus. That was the extent of it."

The office seemed filled with tension that hadn't been there before, but I tried another prompt. "I thought you might have known her at Insburg Community College."

"I didn't. That place has more students than we do."

The tension grew, and it was obvious I was getting nowhere. I stood up to leave. "Well, there ought to be somebody around here who actually knew her. I'll keep looking."

Giff also stood, his gaze fixed on mine. "How's your Plato, Press? You've read *The Republic?*"

I'd never noticed before that he had gray eyes. He didn't mind using them to show what he thought of me.

I tried not to bristle. One of the worst aspects of academic life is when a specialist in some other field expects you to know as much about it as he does. The instinctive reaction is to say you'd read the work in question a long time ago. But that implies you've forgotten it, which professors aren't supposed to do. Besides, what little I did remember from Plato himself had been contaminated by reams of Renaissance Neoplatonism.

So I didn't bite, but asked, "What did you have in mind?"

"Socrates' definition of justice." Giff went into his lecture mode, his gaze still fixed on mine. "He defined justice in a community as 'citizens . . . doing each his own business.' In another place he put it more bluntly: justice is 'doing one's own business, and not being a busybody.'"

I held his gaze. "I gather you'd like me to practice justice according to Socrates."

"Not just for its own sake." He showed an indulgent smile, but his gray gaze did not waver. "Press, this murder is serious business. The police searched my office, and I imagine they searched yours and several others. I only got my computer back this morning."

"I know," I said. "You and I are both under suspicion."

"Asking about Laila can increase that suspicion. It may be dangerous, too. There's a killer loose around here somewhere. You don't want to stumble onto him."

"I'll leave murder investigation to the police," I said, hoping I could lie convincingly. "Right now I'm going to investigate some lunch."

"Go ahead," he said. "I'll be along after awhile."

The interview left a bitter taste in my mouth as I headed for the campus grill. In contrast with Bob Harkins, Giff was a mature man, poised and confident. I couldn't tell if he was on the level or not.

By arrangement, Mara was waiting on a bench outside the grill. She wore a gray pantsuit and looked very professional. Later, she'd probably let me know, pointedly, how long she'd waited in that chilly wind, but I couldn't help that. I nodded to her in passing and let her see the cell phone in my hand. Hers hung halfway out of her coat pocket. So we were set for our next operation.

I stopped by the campus post office adjacent to the grill and checked my mail. As expected, it was all junk and ended up in the voluminous post office wastebasket. On the bulletin board, some phantom grammarian had posted Dean-Dean's memo with the errors in punctuation and pronoun reference circled in red.

In the grill, I bought coffee and a grilled cheese sandwich—the alternate food group to my recent diet of ham—and found a corner table with a view of the entire room. Mara's targets were the offices of Bob Harkins and Gifford Jessel, but neither man was in the grill.

The male and female English faculty who'd shared my table on Friday came and joined me. The female was laughing about a student-written sentence: "Looking in through the window, the sofa can be seen." In case I couldn't figure it out, she explained that the sofa could not be simultaneously inside the house and outside looking in. The

male argued that the truth of her thesis depended upon one's assumptions about ontology and the possible bifurcation of time. Another typical faculty lunch.

Then Gifford Jessel entered the grill. He carried his order to a table, avoiding mine but trying not to make a point of it. I picked up my cell phone and dialed Mara's number. I let it ring twice, then broke the connection. That signaled her that Giff was eating lunch, so she was safe to use the passkey for a search of his office. She and I were still casting a broad net and hoping something significant—anything—would get caught in it.

The female English teacher raised an eyebrow. "Press, you're notorious for saying you didn't need a cell phone unless you were in jail. I'm glad you've finally joined the twenty-first century."

"Not with that phone he hasn't," said the male, pointing to my six-inch-long monstrosity. "All he can do with that is open an antique shop."

"We have to change with the times," I said. There's nothing like an original statement to liven up a conversation.

"With that phone, you're ten years behind time," the male said.

I tried to look chastened. "That's why I'm a historian instead of a journalist."

The banter went on from there while I dawdled over coffee and watched for Bob Harkins to come in or Gifford Jessel to leave. Bob never showed, but after awhile Giff headed for the door. I hit Redial on my phone and let it ring twice to alert Mara. I hoped she'd remembered to set her phone to vibrate. No use in broadcasting her presence to the whole science center.

Three minutes after Giff left the grill, while the composition specialists argued about coordinate and cumulative adjectives, I excused myself and departed. I hung around outside, looking across the campus

circle once in a while to be sure Mara came out all right.

I saw no sign of her. Giff had made it about three-quarters of the way to the science center. Then Bob Harkins drove up in front of the building, parked, and went inside. Still no Mara. I couldn't warn her about Bob because our prearranged signals assumed he'd eat lunch in the grill, as he always did.

I waited while the cold wind cut a few slices out of my neck and ears. Giff entered the science center. Still no Mara. I was beginning to feel conspicuous, so I walked slowly toward the liberal arts center. I had only five minutes before my one o'clock section of Western Civ.

Then Mara emerged from the science center, accompanied by Brenda Kirsch. What was Brenda doing there? She had her office in the new gymnasium complex on the back side of the campus. We rarely saw her on this side.

I paused at the door of the liberal arts center and looked again. Mara and Brenda were just parting, with Brenda heading toward the gym. Mara looked once in my direction and made a tiny wave with her cell phone. That would have to do until we could talk.

My section of Western Civ went well because students are always interested in the culture of medieval knighthood. They're surprised to learn that, by the twelfth century, knights were expected to sing and write poetry as well as bash heads. Knights were expected to be adept at romance, too, but I don't put much emphasis on that. If I did, it would be all the students remembered. At any rate, we had a good class, and my internal musicians joined in with thundering timpani and blazing trumpets.

All day, though, I felt the tension between pursuing our murder investigation and plodding through academic routine. An air of unreality hung over everything, and I felt a new premonition that something was

about to happen. Something unpleasant.

Or maybe I was just afraid of getting caught.

Richmond Seagrave arrived at my office in late afternoon. He was another six-footer with broad shoulders, copper-colored hair, and brown eyes hard as hazelnuts. Since I'd last seen him, he'd added a copper-colored goatee.

For fear of bugging, I took him outside to talk.

"I don't have to ask how bad Staggart wants you," he said, "but how much evidence does he have?"

"Not enough to arrest me. Not yet." I told him about the coerced false statement from Pappas and the stolen book and bogus love note Staggart had found.

Seagrave nodded. "That's about what I'd expect. Well, let's see if he's played tricks with the computers. I have to get back tonight."

One call on the cell phone set him up to check Mara's office and computer. He came back in about forty minutes.

"No problem with her place," he reported and proceeded to check my phone and office for bugs. This last was not easy, for all offices and classrooms in the older campus buildings—the liberal arts center, science center, and executive center, among others—were given false ceilings when central heating and air-conditioning were installed maybe thirty years ago. The new ceilings were built with Styrofoam ceiling tiles resting on a metal framework. Seagrave had brought a ladder, and he wasn't satisfied until he'd lifted every tile and surveyed the space between it and the old high ceiling above it.

A silent nod from him told me those spaces were clear. Afterward, he spent thirty minutes with my computer while I did a quick first reading of early bird research papers.

"Everything looks okay, " Seagrave reported. "No bugs, no keyloggers,

or anything like that. I added some anti-keylogger software just in case. I installed it on your friend's computer, too." He stroked his goatee and worked his copper eyebrows up and down. "Say, she's quite a dish."

I found his metaphor not only hopelessly archaic but personally offensive.

"I'd never thought of her in terms of tableware," I said.

Seagrave looked like he wanted to pursue the subject further, but I preempted. "I really appreciate your coming, Rich. It's a relief to know everything's okay."

He squinted. "I did find one odd thing on your computer. Have you ever used a wipe program—one that overwrites sensitive documents so they can't be recovered?"

"You're over my head with that," I said. "I have no sensitive documents. When I'm through with something I just hit Delete."

"Delete only breaks up the path to the document," he explained. "It leaves the document itself in place. It can be recovered, even if it's been overwritten several times."

"So everything I've ever deleted on this computer might still be there if somebody wanted to dig it up?"

He nodded. "If it hasn't been overwritten too many times. That's what the wipe programs do: they write over things repeatedly till there's no hope of recovery. You've never used one on this computer?"

"I didn't know things like that existed. And this computer was new when they assigned it to me. So why are you telling me this? What does it mean?"

Seagrave squinted again. "I don't know what it means, Press, but one small section of your hard drive has been wiped so thoroughly that no one will ever know what was on it."

As if to emphasize that fact, the computer clicked three times.

CHAPTER 18

The three blind mice reconvened in Dr. Sheldon's rooms that evening while my musical accompaniment labored through something dissonant and atonal—by Schoenberg, I think.

I described my interviews with Professors Harkins and Jessel, adding that in my judgment they produced no useful information. I repeated their warnings against continuing the investigation, commenting that I didn't know if they intended these as subtle threats or simple descriptions of reality.

From the moment our meeting began, Mara had radiated impatience. She let us know why in a preface to her report. "I'm in more danger of catching pneumonia than I am from our campus murderer."

She directed her ocular acetylene torch at me as she said this, but by now I'd developed an immunity.

"I finished with Jessel as soon as I could," I said. "You could have worn a heavier coat."

"Let me remind you, children, that quarreling is not permitted," said Dr. Sheldon.

Mara's chin lifted and she continued. "I did manage to search Dr.

Jessel's office in spite of my frozen body, though I didn't have time to shake out all the books. No one saw me go up there, and no one interrupted the search."

She looked from Dr. Sheldon to me and then back to him. "Most of what I found was class notes, student papers, and the like. The only thing worth mentioning is that Professor Jessel keeps a pistol in his desk drawer."

Her bombshell had its intended effect. The campus was a designated "weapons-free zone," with a list of prohibited items ranging from firearms and knives down to ordinary box cutters. Rumor had it that Dean-Dean wanted to ban scissors but got overruled by President Cantwell.

"What kind of pistol?" I asked.

Mara met my gaze. "A Colt .32-caliber automatic with a full clip of ammunition."

Dr. Sheldon's face filled with wonder. "Child, where did you learn about such things?"

Mara favored him with a smile. "Country girls from Kentucky know all sorts of things."

They might know squirrel guns and horse pistols, but not cute little hand weapons like a Colt .32. Mara would have learned that in her Army training, for the .32 is a little brother of the old .45 that used to be Army standard. Dr. Sheldon let her explanation pass, and I couldn't mention her Army service without admitting I'd peeked at her personnel record.

"Jessel's keeping the gun there makes a kind of sense," I said. "He knew our offices had been searched. He seemed to think our homes will be searched, too. So if he didn't want the police to find that pistol in his home, the logical place to hide it was a place that had already

been searched." Another thought hit me. "Could that pistol be the blunt instrument that knocked Laila unconscious?"

"Probably not," Mara said. "It had no signs of blood, flesh, or hair on either the barrel or hand grip. I looked."

"Good work!" Dr. Sheldon turned to me, beaming. "This child has real presence of mind, Press. She'll solve this case before you and I even get started."

My respect for Mara was growing. There was a lot more to her than the fearful ingénue she'd seemed when she came to my office.

"The news isn't all good," she said, suddenly grim. "Professor Harkins saw me coming down from the third floor. He came up to the second just when I was coming down to it. He gave me a hard look but didn't say anything."

"You can always say you wanted to check a point of philosophy with Jessel before you covered it in class," I said. I could have kicked myself for assuming Bob would follow his habit of eating lunch in the grill.

Mara gave me a skeptical look. "The murderer won't wait for reasonable explanations."

Dr. Sheldon intervened. "That's taking a rather dark view of an ordinary event, Mara. You seem to assume that Bob Harkins either is the murderer or will tell the murderer about your visit."

"I'd expect him to tell Professor Jessel," she said. "But that's not the worst of it. Brenda Kirsch was on the second floor—near Laila's office, I think. She also saw me come down from the third, and she also drew a hard look from Professor Harkins."

"That at least diverts some of the suspicion from you," Dr. Sheldon said.

"What was Brenda doing on the second floor of the chem build-

ing?" I asked. "She's almost never seen on this side of the campus."

"Science center," Mara corrected. "Brenda was terribly nervous, terribly embarrassed, or something. I scarcely know her, but she greeted me like a long-lost sister. Then she chattered nonstop while we walked downstairs. I couldn't get a word in to ask about anything."

I remembered Pappas seeing Brenda in Laila's office, and Laila stepping between him and something on her desk, the apparent subject of her meeting with Brenda. But I didn't get a chance to mention it.

"Worse yet," Mara said, "we ran into Professor Jessel before we reached the ground floor. That got us another hard look. And the janitor —Pappas—came up from the basement and saw us, too." She sighed. "If you'd been there, Professor Barclay, I'd have been seen by every one of the suspects."

So now she'd distanced me from "Press" to "Professor Barclay." I gathered that meant I was in the doghouse—whether for poor planning or letting her wait in the cold, I couldn't tell. Not that it mattered: a doghouse is a doghouse in any case.

"This is very interesting, children," Dr. Sheldon said, "but I have yet to make my report. As you may imagine, I have been casting a wide net with my little electronic notebook, and I have netted at least one significant fish."

He obviously enjoyed building suspense and making us wait, so I didn't spoil his fun by asking a question. Mara seemed to read him the same way, for she merely looked at him in expectation—whether real or feigned, I couldn't tell.

"I've still had no luck with Brenda Kirsch," he said, "not that I discovered anything we didn't already know about Bob Harkins or Gifford Jessel." He licked his lips and rubbed his palms together. "But I've

learned that Luther Pappas served two years in state prison for assault. He broke someone's jaw in a barroom brawl."

"His personnel record doesn't mention it," I said. "That's probably what Staggart threatened him with that made him say he saw me in the science center before Laila was killed."

Dr. Sheldon grinned. "It also means Staggart won't dare put him under oath where he can be cross-examined."

"We'll hope it doesn't come to that," I said. "But what else do you have up your sleeve? You look like the canary that swallowed the cat."

His grin broadened. "Our dear, sweet, deceased Laila also has a record. In the year she graduated from high school, Dee L. Sloan was convicted of burglary. As a first offender, she got off with two years probation."

Mara appeared stunned. I certainly was. My mind echoed with Bob Harkins's description of his affair with Laila: *It happened in spring semester. We ran pretty much wild the rest of the year.* When I'd asked if the affair was the extent of his involvement, he'd said, *That was all of it.*

But his eyes had flickered, as they had the first time he lied to me.

CHAPTER 19

Tuesday morning began with a bang. It was delivered by a fist to my front door while I shaved. With the first bang, I nicked myself with the razor. Fortunately, I use a safety razor, so the wound was less than life-threatening. The door-pounding continued, but I stanched the bleeding before I answered. Why reward rudeness with courtesy?

My house has a front door of solid hardwood, with an outer storm door of tempered glass. Half shaved and half lathered, I opened the hardwood door. Beyond the storm door stood Capt. Clyde Staggart, accompanied by two uniformed cops and, as usual, by Dogface. I didn't have to guess what they wanted.

"There's a new electronic invention you should learn about," I said, pointing to the appropriate place beside the door. "It's called a doorbell."

Staggart did not take the bait, but held up a sheet of paper. "I have a warrant to search your house. Open up."

I slipped my trifocals on and, through the storm door, read enough of the paper to make sure it was a search warrant. Then I unlatched the

door and stood aside as Staggart and his troops forged past.

"What are you looking for?" I asked. "Maybe I can help."

"Your computer," Staggart yelled back over his shoulder. "Where is it?"

"I don't own a computer," I said.

"You *what?*"

"I said I don't own a computer. The one at the university does everything I need."

Staggart snickered. "Press, boy, wake up and join the twenty-first century."

"You could use a technological update, yourself," I said. "They had doorbells in the last century."

As we bickered, Staggart's men spread out through the house.

There was no way I could keep up with all of them, so I again asked Staggart, "What are you trying to find?"

"Where were you at daybreak Saturday morning?" He gave me a withering glance.

I declined to be withered. "I'm not sure. I was probably still asleep, but in my widowed state I have no witnesses to prove it."

That wasn't a lie. Not quite. Actually, I don't remember my exact location in Laila's house at the precise moment of daybreak. And the word "probably" has saved many a felon from perjuring himself.

Staggart's eyes had been giving my living room the once-over, and now his gaze fixed on the piano. "Oh-h-h-h," he said, his tone mocking. "A Steinway. If you can afford that, you're hardly the impoverished professor."

"My wife's father gave it to her as a graduation present," I said. I could have told him her father gave her the house, too, but he didn't need to know that.

Then he seemed to notice my half-shaved face for the first time,

and he went back to the reason for his search. "Someone broke into Laila Sloan's house. Early Saturday morning, one of the neighbors saw two guys come out of the alley behind it. One of them fits your description. Do you own a black jogging suit?"

I shrugged. "If I do, your storm troopers will find it." Though I feigned indifference, something like an icicle stabbed at my heart. I'd forgotten where I put the jogging suit.

"Have your fun," I said, and turned into the bathroom to finish shaving. My lather had gone dry, so I washed it off and started over. I never had a worse shave, for I remembered that I'd thrown the jogging suit into the washing machine to get rid of the mothball smell. I didn't see how they could miss it.

The icicle kept jabbing my heart and the now-familiar hot brick resumed its residence in my stomach. You'd think the two would neutralize each other, but instead they formed an alliance and tortured me in tandem.

For about forty minutes, the cops searched and I sweated. When they cleared my bedroom closet, I carried my blue suit and accessories into the bathroom and changed. (Tuesday and Thursday were my blue-suit days that week.) A few minutes later I emerged from the bathroom to find Staggart and his men huddled in the front hall.

"We didn't find a jogging suit," one uniformed policeman said, "but we did find this toolbox. It has screwdrivers and chisels in it."

"Give him a receipt and send it to the lab," Staggart said. "The tools may match the marks of the break-in."

My cardiac icicle gave me an extra prod, and my abdominal hot brick did a back flip. I'd carried a screwdriver, chisel, and pliers from that toolbox to jimmy Laila's back door. Thanks to the burglar who got there first, I didn't have to use them. An honest lab test would prove the

tools hadn't been used recently. But could I hope for an honest test?

Staggart left with his usual warning to keep my nose clean, and I followed with my usual response that he should know I always did. I didn't feel confident about that. I'd traveled a long way on the wrong side of the Rubicon, and I couldn't believe Staggart's crew hadn't searched the washing machine.

However, I'm not one to look a gift horse in the eye, or whatever that expression is. So I poked around to see if they'd taken anything besides the tools. They hadn't, but while I was looking I found an old box of mothballs. That gave me an idea, so I put three into a Ziploc bag, used a rolling pin to grind them into powder, double-bagged the result, and slipped it into my coat pocket.

Afterward, I cleaned my trifocals and headed up the hill to my nine o'clock class. It was Western Civ, and that day I made my usual diversion into cultural history to talk about love traditions. I began with the ancient world, where love was at best deep loyalty and producing heirs or, at worst, lust and madness. I mentioned the physicality and promiscuity of the Ovidian tradition. In the twelfth century came the invention of romantic (courtly) love, popularized by Eleanor of Aquitaine and Chrétien de Troyes. And of course there was the purely intellectual love championed by the Renaissance Neoplatonists.

Then in the 1590s, Edmund Spenser struck a compromise between Ovidian physicality and Platonic idealism, added the romance of courtly love, and synthesized it all within the holy sacrament of Christian marriage. I pointed out that Spenser's synthesis reigned as the ideal of Western civilization for more than three centuries until, in the early twentieth century, it broke up under the influence of Freudian psychology and naturalistic philosophy.

For once, I had the students' full attention for the entire period.

That brought me out of class on another emotional high while my internal musicians collaborated on a cute little march by Edwin Franko Goldman, with plenty of brass and *oom-pah*.

I figured that was as good a time as any to talk to Brenda Kirsch so, with Goldman bouncing around in my head, I marched myself beyond the campus circle to her office in the new gymnasium. That wing of the gym featured a hallway with offices on either side. Beyond it, from the basketball court, the *slap-slap-slap* of bouncing balls penetrated faintly.

I didn't know Brenda well, and I hadn't decided how to handle the interview. So I was almost relieved when no one answered my knock at her door. I was about to go back to my own territory when the door to the basketball court opened and Brenda came striding down the hall to her office. I'd never much noticed her before, so I remedied that deficiency as she approached.

She was a tall woman, only an inch shorter than my five foot ten. She wore a warm-up suit of emerald-green velour that emphasized her slender figure and long legs. Her movements combined the strength of an athlete with the grace of a ballerina. She wore a nice perfume that seemed more graceful than muscular.

"Hello, Professor Barclay," she said with a cordial smile. "We don't see you often on this side of the campus."

"I decided to go exploring," I said, hoping my answering smile didn't look as silly as it felt. "Actually, Professor Kirsch, I'd like to talk to you."

"Come in, then." She opened the door and motioned me to a chair —a much newer, more comfortable chair than we had in the liberal arts center or the science center, another indication of the administration's priorities.

Brenda glided around the desk and sat behind it, her elbows resting on it and her chin resting on her clasped hands. She fixed her gaze

on me and asked, "What did you want to talk about?"

As I say, I'd never much noticed her before. She had unusually wide cheeks that tapered down to an almost pointed chin, and these features joined with the widow's peak on her forehead to suggest the shape of a heart. Her dark brown hair, short and fluffy, formed an attractive frame for the face, but her most prominent feature was a pair of narrow, bright black eyes that seemed to glitter when she looked at you.

"I want to talk about Laila Sloan," I said, making a point of adjusting my trifocals and trying to look like a distraught bookworm. "I'm writing a memorial of her for the yearbook, so I'm talking to people who knew her."

Brenda quirked an eyebrow. "So why ask me? I wasn't at all close to her."

I tried to look self-conscious, which in truth was how I felt. "The campus rumor mill says she got her job here because you recommended her. I thought maybe you could help me build a picture of her as a real person."

She smiled like she'd remembered a secret joke. "Right now I have to get back to my gym class, but I'll be happy to talk with you later. Why don't you come by my house for a cup of tea?"

Something about the invitation rang false, but I couldn't very well refuse. "That sounds good," I said.

She stood up. "Three thirty, then."

"Three thirty," I said, and preceded her to the door.

She checked the spring lock, closed the door, and glided away toward the ball court, trailing a faint aura of perfume.

Returning to my office, I decided the invitation was a good thing. While Brenda and I were having tea, Mara could search her office. I would suggest that to Mara after the memorial service.

CHAPTER NINETEEN

A surprise awaited me at my office. That was Penelope Nichols, a tall, angular student who was as awkward as Brenda Kirsch was graceful. Penelope had sharp features, a beaklike nose, and a figure that would lose a beauty contest with the average stork. A senior now, she had not talked with me since her first freshman semester.

She was one of those smart kids who've played through their senior year of high school and try to play through their freshman year in college. Some of them wise up in time to salvage their semester grades, but Penelope Nichols was not one of those.

She'd breezed into college with an attitude that stood out like a crow in a covey of sparrows. She barged into my Western Civ class wearing short shorts on her spindly legs and opened with an outrageous pun: "I'm Penny Nichols, to coin a phrase."

"I can believe the corn," I'd said, "and we'll hope you're just going through the phase."

Those were undoubtedly the worst puns I ever made. They were so hideous that I'm still ashamed of them. But bad or not, they served their purpose. Penny wasn't used to being outpunned, so she quieted down in my class.

But not outside. She put on a show everywhere on campus, especially as one of the bare-midriff cheerleaders Faith used to refer to as the "navel cadets." Finally, in November of that year, Penny decided it was time to play the game of shock-the-professor.

The ostensible reason she visited my office was some inane question about a research paper. But she dressed for the occasion: short shorts again despite a subfreezing day. She matched them with a ridiculously low-necked sleeveless blouse that revealed the tattoo of a serpent's head.

Needless to say, I stayed seated behind my desk, maintained eye

contact, and refrained from adjusting my trifocals while I answered her elementary questions.

As she was leaving, though, she stood facing me and said, "Dr. Barclay, would you like to see the tail of my serpent?"

"No, Penny," I said, "and, frankly, I would have preferred not to see the head."

She looked disappointed and turned toward the door. But my temper was up by then, so I broke one of my cardinal rules and ventured a personal comment.

"Penny," I asked, "do you ever plan to get married?"

She paused in the door and said, "Well . . . uh . . . I suppose I will . . . eventually."

"Good," I said. "Then you ought to save something for your husband that you haven't shown to everyone else."

Her eyes blazed and she left without a word. She never took another of my classes and she avoided me on campus, so I wondered what brought her here today.

Now, as a senior, she remained as sharp-featured and angular as ever, but she'd obviously matured. This time she wore slacks and a high-necked blouse with long sleeves.

"I need some advice, Dr. Barclay," she said.

I motioned her into the office and indicated a chair. But for prudence' sake, I again kept my desk between us.

"I . . . I've been receiving money from Laila Sloan," she said, her eyes searching mine for any sign of disapproval. "For two years now, she's paid me twenty dollars a month to keep a post office box and receive mail for her."

"Nothing wrong with that on the face of it," I said. "What else was involved?"

"I checked the box once a week and gave her any mail that came in—maybe one package a week and one or two letters a month. All I had to do was take them to her."

"These were addressed to you in your name?"

"Yes."

"But you gave them to her without opening them?"

"Yes. I get my own mail at the campus mail office."

"What size were the packages?"

She made motions similar to those Luther Pappas had made, indicating a shape about a foot or two square and several inches deep.

"Do you know what she did with the packages?"

"No. She never told me and I never asked."

"And you don't know what was in them?"

"Not until today." She looked at the floor. "One came in today and . . . and I opened it. It was a notebook computer. That's why I need your advice. I don't know if I should keep it or not."

"That's something the police will have to decide. Penny, Laila Sloan was murdered and no one knows why. Your information may help the police find the killer."

Fear crept into her face. "I don't know if I want to go to the police."

I kept my voice soft. "We don't have a choice, Penny. If you don't go, I'll have to. Withholding pertinent information is pretty serious."

"All right," she said. But she still looked frightened.

I looked up the number for police nonemergency and wrote it on a card.

"You haven't done anything wrong," I said. "Call this number and ask for Sergeant Spencer. Tell him I sent you. He's a former student. He'll treat you right and get your information to the proper people."

"Okay," she said, but her tone sounded doubtful.

I added reinforcement. "I'll be seeing Spencer tomorrow. I'll ask if you contacted him." I made a mental note to call Spencer so as not to make a liar of myself again.

Penny nodded and rose to leave. As she had on that other visit, she paused in the doorway.

"Dr. Barclay," she said, a bit teary-eyed, "I . . . I want to thank you for your advice on my last visit. I did take it to heart." She raised her left hand to show a moderate-sized engagement ring. "I'm glad I did."

I smiled. "I hope you'll be very happy."

"That serpent," she said. "It wasn't a real tattoo. It was just painted on."

"I'm glad of that, too," I said. "I never did like snakes."

She left then, leaving me with a warm glow inside. Penny had matured a lot in four years. Once in a long, long while, a professor is actually able to help a student toward that kind of maturity. It's a good feeling when it happens.

I knew Penny's information would throw light on Laila's package mailings, but I had no time to think about it. I had a memorial service and faculty meeting to attend, and a full afternoon after that.

CHAPTER 20

When I left the liberal arts center for Laila's memorial service, I saw Dean-Dean heading across the campus circle toward the auditorium. As always, my internal bassoon adorned his progress with an awkward tune. I used the opportunity to visit the executive center, where I managed to drop the mothball powder from my sandwich bag into Mrs. Dunwiddie's wastebasket without her noticing. I could not define this as scholarly activity, but at least it would give Dean-Dean something besides me to think about.

The memorial service for Laila was quite solemn. All the faculty were there, though student attendance seemed largely limited to the nursing program. After a musical prelude, Dathan Hormah of the department of religious studies opened with a nonsectarian prayer. It was so nonsectarian that he could have said "may the Force be with you" and accomplished the same result. Then President Cantwell eulogized Laila as a Highly Valued Member of the Overton Community until This Terrible Tragedy came to Rip Her Untimely From Our Midst.

If the English faculty recognized the words he'd cribbed from *Macbeth*, they were too kind to let on.

It struck me then that we'd heard nothing from or about Laila's next of kin. Nor was one listed in her personnel record. So now I had another weird question to answer.

After the service, the students left and Dean-Dean convened the faculty to vote on the education department's proposed mission statement. President Cantwell began his exit up the aisle beside me, but on an impulse I intercepted him.

"Sir," I said, "I think you ought to stay and hear the speeches. This isn't a routine vote for one department. Whatever we do today will affect our entire academic program." It occurred to me that I was beginning to talk like an administrator.

President Cantwell looked surprised, muttered that he'd think about it, and continued up the aisle. Dean-Dean glowered at me, so I sat down and tried to look nonexistent. In my case, that isn't very difficult.

The education department presented, again, its proposed new mission statement. If it passed, department certification for public school teaching would require students' signed commitment to promote social justice, work to stop global warming, and combat institutional racism, sexism, and homophobia as well as a list of other social ills.

The usual faculty catfight ensued. One of the science faculty asked for a precise definition of each ill that had been named. The definitions given in response only muddled the issue further. A sociologist questioned the education faculty's qualifications to practice what was, in effect, social science rather than teacher training. The male English teacher I'd had lunch with said no expertise was needed because any fool would recognize and combat those ills. So if "any fool would combat those ills," one of the coaches asked, why should prospective teachers have to say so in writing? Did that mean the teacher candidates were dumber than fools? Several more faculty expressed shock that anyone

could object to any program to correct social problems.

Gifford Jessel made an eloquent speech quoting Socrates' definition of justice as "citizens . . . doing each his own business" and not trying to do someone else's. We should practice our own disciplines, he said, and not arrogate ourselves as arbiters of society. Naturally, one of the younger faculty denounced Socrates as a Dead White Male and therefore not worth considering. We should be guided, she said, by modern intellects on the Cutting Edge.

That cliché inspired one of the nursing faculty to suggest providing tourniquets for scholars on the Cutting Edge, but Dean-Dean ruled her out of order. He then tried to argue in favor of the education department's motion, but one of the older faculty called him on a point of order: under Robert's Rules, the moderator of a meeting could not speak to the question.

I lost track of the meeting then, for my internal musicians overwhelmed me by launching with full orchestra into the background music from a classic movie. All I remember about the movie itself is that John Wayne and Susan Hayward drowned. Faith didn't care for the story, either, but she loved the music score by Victor Young. What she loved most was the wonderful melody linked to Susan Hayward's doomed romance. It began soft and low, built to a climax of impassioned longing, receded unfulfilled, then climbed again to an even greater height, only to subside once more, still incomplete and yearning.

Faith often played the videotape, but we never watched the movie. We would grade papers or read books, and she would signal me in delight whenever the Susan Hayward theme returned. She loved Victor Young's varied orchestrations of it, particularly in the underwater scenes. So it was no wonder that, taken unaware and plunged suddenly into a flood of poignant memory, I was transported far from the world

of faculty squabbles. I would have stayed in that other world, but the music stopped as suddenly as it began.

". . . bet my laptop no student will sign it," a voice was saying. "It's ridiculous to require anyone to support any political idea, good or bad, before he can be certified to teach. It's like my making students commit to subjective epistemological monism before they can pass my course."

Yes, the speaker was Gifford Jessel. And Bob Harkins, for once, joined in the speeches: "I think I'll make my students certify the superiority of acids over bases."

Brenda Kirsch also broke precedent by calling the question, and one of the coaches moved for a secret ballot. Dean-Dean had ballots ready and named faculty from both sides of the issue to count. The counters withdrew and returned presently to announce that the education department's mission statement had failed by a vote of 26 for, 31 against.

When Dean-Dean called for a motion to adjourn, one of the nurses asked when the faculty would vote on the question of establishing coed dorms.

Dean-Dean drew himself up to his full five feet eight and huffed, "That is a purely administrative decision and not subject to faculty vote." He called again for a motion to adjourn, which was duly made, seconded, and passed unanimously. For once, perhaps exercised by the failure of the education department's motion, he failed to adjourn us *sine die*.

As we left, I saw President Cantwell ease out the back door. Whatever his reason, he had stayed to hear the speeches.

Except for my musical flight on Victor Young's magic carpet, I'd kept an eye on our designated murder suspects during the meeting. Bob

Harkins endured it silently with a worried expression until his one speech. He also made a point of not seeing me. Until she called the question, Brenda Kirsch simply looked out the window. Gifford Jessel, of course, followed the discussion with relish. Yes, I watched Mara, too. She seemed surprised by the vitriol in what should have been a reasonable discussion. I guess she hadn't yet learned about college faculties.

After the meeting, Mara hesitantly agreed to search Brenda's office while Brenda and I had tea—provided, of course, no one was hanging out in that hallway of the gym. There shouldn't be, for team practices would occupy coaches and athletes. Mara's frequent workouts in the gym meant no one would question her being there in warm-up clothes.

I think disappointment was creeping into both of us. All the risks we'd taken had turned up truckloads of dirt, but they had brought us no closer to finding the murderer. Still, with Clyde Staggart breathing down our necks, we had to keep trying.

We agreed to meet later at Dolt's.

I don't know what Mara did for lunch. I grabbed a quick one in the grill, then headed for my afternoon class, one tiny thread of normality in the vast web of insanity that had entangled us. But today even teaching brought no relief.

For reasons I couldn't define, the thought of having tea with Brenda Kirsch filled me with apprehension.

CHAPTER 21

I admit being curious as well as apprehensive when I knocked on the door of Brenda Kirsch's house. I'd known Brenda only as instructor of exercise classes where women hopped around to full-volume rock and rap music. I already wondered at the contradiction between Brenda's trendy image and the austere furnishing of her office. The decor of her house provided another contradiction.

Her living room was rather dark, furnished with an ancient divan, an overstuffed chair, and a number of small tables that looked like antiques. That much was unremarkable. But the surface of every table was covered by intricate lace doilies and filled with displays of delicate ceramics. And I do mean *filled*. Every square inch of horizontal surface was crowded with fragile china plates poised on pedestals. Each plate possessed its own elegant beauty, but they were crammed so tightly together that the total effect was a hodgepodge of undifferentiated crockery.

Several lighted candles gave a heavy odor of musk.

The sitting room where Brenda served tea had a similar decor. Everywhere I looked were displays of paper-thin ceramic, and a china-

filled end table stood so close by my chair that I hardly dared breathe for fear of breaking something. It looked like Martha Stewart gone mad and catapulted a century backward into the Victorian era. I half-expected the ghost of Faulkner's Emily Grierson to materialize with her hand-painted china.

Remembering that Emily poisoned her beau didn't make me feel any better.

Brenda herself, graceful and athletic, sat serenely modern in the midst of the accumulated antiquity. Another musky candle burned on a table at her side. She wore a silken red blouse under an open black jacket, with close-fitting black slacks that called attention to her shapely legs. The blouse's spot of crimson among all the black reminded me of a black widow spider. Brenda's glittering black eyes and her lipstick the color of old blood did not help.

Still, her heart-shaped face showed a welcoming smile.

We sat facing each other, a few feet apart, with a tea caddy on a table at her side. She poured from a vintage pot that President McKinley might have used, and she served me tea in a cup of eggshell china about the size of a thimble.

"Lemon, cream, or sugar?" she asked.

"None, thanks," I said. "I take mine barefoot."

She laughed at my inelegant expression as if she hadn't heard it before. Then she poured herself a cup, leaned back in her chair, and crossed one nicely curved leg over the other.

"Now, Professor Barclay," she said, raising one eyebrow, "what did you want to talk about?"

I took a sip of tea and said, "I want you to tell me all you know about Laila Sloan."

She looked thoughtful. "I really don't know very much. She came from the same part of the state that I did, and I'd heard good reports about her teaching. That's why I recommended her."

"Where did you come from?"

"It's a tiny farm village called Prosperity." She laughed. "It's so prosperous that half of its people have moved elsewhere."

If she was trying to steer me away from Laila, I wasn't having any. "Did you know Laila there?"

She looked at the wall beyond me. "I ran up on her a few times here and there. I never knew her well, but I remember everyone talking about how sweet and considerate she was."

"So sweet she got convicted of burglary," I said.

Brenda changed stories without batting an eye. "I heard she had a wild side, too, and a way of entangling people so they did whatever she wanted."

"That sounds real sweet and considerate," I said. "What was she like in school?"

I'd set a trap with that question—a lead to talk about Bi-County Consolidated High School—but Brenda didn't fall into it. She didn't even pause to think before answering.

"I really don't know. I never had any classes with her."

"What was her reputation around the school?"

Brenda turned one palm up in front of her shoulder. "I don't know that either, Press. Oh . . ." She looked at the floor, then up at me through her eyelashes. "Do you mind if I call you Press? 'Professor Barclay' sounds so formal."

"I don't mind." The room temperature suddenly rose about ten degrees, but I pushed on. "Wasn't there any peer talk about Laila? Most schools are drowning in that kind of gossip."

She shook her head and looked sad. "There wasn't time for it. We

spent hours on buses to and from school, and no one from her age group rode my bus. I'm afraid I'm not much help to you, Press. Would you like more tea?"

"No, thank you. I really ought to be going." I hadn't been able to break through that false facade, so this was another interview going nowhere.

"One more thing." Her black eyes glittered. "The campus rumor mill says you and Professor Thorn think you can solve Laila's murder. That could be dangerous."

So much for my cover story about writing a memorial.

"You shouldn't believe everything you hear," I said. I found an unoccupied square centimeter on the table by my chair and eased my cup and saucer onto it. "I really do have to go."

We stood together. She escorted me to the front door and turned to stand facing me. I wondered what else she was going to say, but she said nothing. She smiled with those lips the color of old blood, put her arms around my neck, and kissed me.

It was not a china-cup kiss. It was more like a mug of black coffee that had fermented on the stove all day and been reheated for the occasion.

Her embrace started down around the ankles and gradually wound its way up to the kiss, inspiring visions of being cuddled by pythons or pumas. I couldn't decide which was more apropos.

After a few minutes she pushed back a step, hands on my chest, and gave me a coy glance.

"I'm glad we're going to be friends, Press."

"Friendship is a wonderful thing," I said.

With commendable concentration, I managed to find my way outside. I sauntered casually down the block and around the corner, acting like nothing unusual had happened and silently cursing my internal musicians, who mocked me with more Clyde McCoy blues on a *wah-wah* muted trumpet.

Once out of Brenda's sight, I used my handkerchief to wipe the lipstick from my mouth. On her it had seemed maroon-and-black, but on my handkerchief it just looked black. My hands bore a faint aroma of Brenda's perfume that I hadn't noticed among all the musk. I half-remembered that she'd made some reference to it as I was leaving. I tried to wipe the smell off my hands with my handkerchief. Then I wadded up the handkerchief and stuffed it as far down in my pocket as it would go.

When you start an investigation, I guess, you never know what will turn up.

Later, in Dolt's, I found Mara waiting at the same table we'd shared before. Her blue warm-up suit emphasized the blue of her eyes and contrasted nicely with her ivory complexion. Under the subdued lighting, every movement of her head put dancing highlights in her blonde hair. But the set of her jaw and her scorched-earth gaze warned me I'd find this interview no easier than the one with Brenda.

"This place isn't as loud as usual," I said. It was still loud enough, for my eardrums already hurt. The other tables were filled with the usual flocks of students who'd come here together so they could yell into their cell phones at people who were somewhere else.

Mara glowered at me and said nothing, so I asked, "How did your search go?"

"All right." She gritted out the words. "And your tea party?"

"I didn't come away with anything we can get our teeth into."

"That's not the complete truth." Her eyes focused on the left corner of my mouth. "You didn't get all of it off."

I wiped my mouth again with the polluted handkerchief. She stared at it in disbelief while I finished the job.

"There," I said. "How's that?"

"Okay on the outside. You missed a spot on your number twelve bicuspid."

"On what?"

"It's a tooth. The first one behind your eyetooth, left side."

"Upper or lower?"

"Upper."

I covered my mouth with my other hand while I used the handkerchief to sanitize the disgraced tooth. When I finished, I asked, "How did you learn the names of teeth?"

"I used to work for a dentist. If you'd shown her that tooth, she'd have wiped the lipstick off with a drill. Down to the nerve."

"Aren't we getting off the subject? I thought we were conducting an investigation."

She looked right through me. "Are we investigating the same thing?"

I returned her hard look. "I'm investigating a murder, and I'm not going to get sidetracked by red herrings."

"They're not red." She threw a furious glance at the handkerchief still clutched in my hand. "They're a lot closer to black."

"All right." I struck the table, but not hard enough to call attention to us. "So she kissed me. So what?"

"And you fought her off desperately to protect your virtue."

"Sometimes we have to make personal sacrifices to achieve our objectives."

"Some sacrifice!" She sniffed a couple of times. "You reek of her perfume."

Mara wasn't going to be thrown off the scent. Literally, in this case.

But I tried anyway. "Her perfume *was* pretty strong," I said. "I think she called it Euphoria."

"On you it smells like euthanasia."

"All *right*," I said again and raised my hands in surrender. "I plead guilty to all counts of moral turpitude. Now. Do we go on with the investigation together or do I go it alone?"

She smoldered a few seconds and muttered, "Together. . . . But don't you get sidetracked again."

By this time I was smoldering, too, but I kept my voice calm. "All I learned was that Brenda is hiding something. What did you find in her office?"

She sighed. "I found a blackjack in her desk drawer."

"One of those things they call a 'sap'?"

"Yes."

"Why would she keep a sap in her office?"

"Why would she take one home with her and kiss him?"

"You're changing the subject," I said.

Her eyes flashed. "You could use a little changing yourself."

I'd been holding my temper in check, but now it blazed. "I thought we were going to go on together, but if you keep—"

Mara started and grabbed at her pocket. Her hand emerged with a visibly vibrating cell phone. She answered, then listened silently. Her face grew grim.

The noise level of Dolt's music seemed to jump about ten decibels, and my internal musicians countered feebly with Brahms' "Lullaby."

Mara folded the phone and returned it to her pocket, her face deadly serious. She spoke in a voice scarcely audible above the surrounding din.

CHAPTER TWENTY-ONE

"That was Dr. Sheldon. He says Laila Sloan was married to Gifford Jessel."

CHAPTER 22

Dr. Sheldon's bombshell left us speechless for a moment. Then Mara explained: "On a hunch, Dr. Sheldon checked the Insburg marriage records for Dee Laila Sloan. We already knew she and Gifford Jessel overlapped one year at the college there. Dr. Sheldon found they'd married in the fall semester and divorced six months later in the spring." She showed a sardonic smile. "Contrary to Tennyson's opinion, in the spring *that* young man's fancy turned *away* from thoughts of love."

I would have scored another point for her erudition except that the quotation was too common. Besides, my temper was surging up like a thermometer in an oven. No one likes to be lied to, and now we'd caught every one of our suspects in either an evasion or a bald-faced lie. Pappas had concealed his time in prison. Bob Harkins lied about his teenage fling with Laila, and heaven only knew what Brenda had hidden beneath the web of fabrication she'd spun for me before she tried to bribe me with a kiss. Now Gifford Jessel had joined the liars' brigade. He'd said "I hardly knew the woman" when, for heaven's sake, he'd been married to her.

To further confuse the issue, three of the four suspects had warned me of danger if I pursued the investigation. How could I tell which ones were afraid I'd learn embarrassing facts about their pasts and which were afraid I'd learn who committed the murder?

"What are you going to do?" Mara asked. From the concern on her face, I realized my anger must have showed.

I checked my watch. "Giff still has office hours today. If I hurry, maybe I can catch him."

"Watch your temper," she said. "I don't think he'll let you off with a kiss."

"He'd better not try," I said. That was a dumb thing to say, but I couldn't think of anything better. And I couldn't blame Mara for being angry with me. She'd risked her job by searching Brenda's office, and she had every reason to think I'd been playing more than drop-the-handkerchief with Brenda.

"Before you go, I want you to know one other thing," Mara said. "Several times lately I've been watched by a man who doesn't look like a student. That began soon after all our suspects saw me coming out of the science center. I've wondered if there's a connection."

"You need to call campus security," I said.

"I'm not ready for that. Men have stared at me before and not meant anything by it." Unexpectedly, she blushed. "When I'm sure I'm being stalked, I'll call security. Not before."

Her mind was made up, so I drove to the campus and parked in front of the science center. I climbed the stairs again to Gifford Jessel's eyrie and found him at his desk. When I entered, he clasped his hands before him and twiddled his thumbs. The high table still occupied the left-hand wall and the one hardwood chair the right-hand.

Without invitation, I sat in the chair and asked, "What would Socrates say about that gesture?"

Giff twiddled some more. "Not being foolish, Press, he wouldn't waste his time on it. What brings you up here again?" He emphasized the word *again*.

"Last time I came, you didn't tell me you were married to Laila Sloan."

The twiddling stopped, but his hands remained clasped on the desk. "*Were* married? That's a sloppy use of tenses, Press. I didn't tell you I *had been married* to Laila because it was none of your business. Speaking of which, I suggest you mind it."

"You made that suggestion last time by way of Plato's *Republic*. I'd be happy to oblige, except that Captain Staggart keeps trying to pin Laila's murder on me. That being the case, I have to keep filing a non-concurrence." For some reason I felt obligated to sound just as stuffy as Giff. But to move things along, I added, "The quickest way to get rid of me is to tell me about you and Laila."

"No, that's not the quickest way."

He showed a smile I didn't like, and I remembered Mara's finding a pistol in his desk.

"But I'll let it serve in this case," he said. "I've already explained this to Staggart, and he was very understanding."

"Now help me understand," I said.

Giff tented his fingers. "I was a very young and naive freshman at Insburg Community College. I felt flattered when a sophomore like Laila—she still called herself Dee then—paid any attention to me. Like a fool, I thought it was me she loved. It turned out someone had convinced her I must be independently wealthy or I couldn't afford to study a noncommercial field like philosophy. It never occurred to her

that I came up dirt-poor and never learned to need money."

He sighed. "After we were married, we had a couple of wild months together before she found out she'd been wrong. She stayed with me for a while—room and board, you know—but she took jobs on the side and kept the money for herself. She said she was working as a waitress." He gave a sad laugh. "In a way, she was. But she worked in one of those . . . *gentlemen's* bars." His tone gave a sarcastic emphasis to the word *gentlemen's*.

He waited and I said, "That wasn't good." I couldn't think of anything else to say.

He continued, his face expressionless. "When I found out, I filed for divorce. She moved out, and I never saw or heard from her until she showed up here. Then we had one brief conversation: she wouldn't tell about our marriage if I wouldn't tell about her former employment. That was it, except for a passing hello or two."

"Do you know any reason someone would want to kill her?"

"Dozens." He gave a bitter laugh. "Considering her character, there were probably hundreds. I considered it myself before I divorced her." He sighed again. "No, I don't know of any reason since she came to Overton."

So I had dead-ended again. I stood and said, "Thanks for talking to me, Giff. You'll let me know if you think of anything helpful?"

His eyes became gray ice. "No, I'll let Staggart know. He's trained to deal with murderers, but professors aren't. Remember what Socrates said about not trying to do someone else's job."

"I remember," I said, and made the long trek back down the stairs. Socrates was right, I thought with chagrin. If Staggart would do his job, Mara and I wouldn't need to do it for him.

Mara and I had both been depressed when we left Dolt's, and my

interview with Giff didn't help. My depression hit bottom as I entered my darkened house with its silent piano. I'd had only coffee at Dolt's, so I made a quick sandwich. Ham with cheese this time, just for variety. I was finishing with a cup of instant coffee when the phone rang.

Cindy's voice came soft and sweet, as it always did. "Are you still all right, Daddy? I've been worried about you with the trouble at the college."

"I'm fine, Cindy," I said. "Kind of tired after a full day, but basically fine."

"I'm glad, 'cause I've been praying for you." Her tone changed. "Is it still okay for me to spend Thanksgiving with Heather?"

"Of course, dear." My parental caution went on orange alert. "Why? Has something changed?"

"Oh, *Daddy*," she said, her tone eloquent with her opinion of overprotective parents. "It's *the same way we talked about*. Just Heather and me. The boys are staying somewhere else."

"All right, sweet one." I tried to sound enthusiastic. "Have a good time and take care of my girl."

"You know I will, Daddy."

For the second time I could almost see her squirm.

She rang off, and I dropped onto the bed as I had the last time she called. Cindy's voice, so much like Faith's, reminded me that Faith had died on that same bed, and I surrendered once again to the memory of her final hours.

We'd brought her home because she wanted to die among the things she treasured. She wanted music, so I put on the CDs of her choice. In her last two days we worked through much of her library, each sonata or symphony more poignant because she would never hear

it again. The sounds of those final minutes burned into my being with unquenchable fire.

Faith knew the time, somehow, and saved her two favorites until last. One was Jascha Heifetz playing the Beethoven Violin Concerto—exquisite melody, controlled power and passion in the first movement, then the lyric slow movement flowing without pause into the joyful abandon of the finale.

The music's emotions became mine as I sat at Faith's bedside and held her hand. She lay with eyes closed, smiling at passages that pleased her especially, occasionally squeezing my hand to lead me into sharing her pleasure.

Last came the Rachmaninoff Piano Concerto no. 2, which she had performed magnificently with the state symphony orchestra. Her eyes remained closed through the solemnity of the opening chords, but her fingers moved on my hand. I knew that in her mind she experienced every note as if she were playing it herself. At times she emphasized accented notes with a faint squeeze. At others, her hand lay limp in mine, the smile eclipsed from her lips.

She stirred again as a flute introduced the slow movement's plaintive melody over quiet broken chords from the piano. I know no movement more filled with passionate longing, and Faith's smile came again as the music's emotion deepened. At long last the violins returned with the fullest, most intense development of the theme. And at that moment of singing violins Faith's spirit slipped away from her body, which yet lay with a smile on its face, its lifeless hand in mine.

I think it was also that moment when the music passed from Faith's soul into mine, where it still resides.

Out of respect for the music she loved, I remained by her side until the concerto's final chords sounded and the home we had made together lapsed into the silence that yet prevails.

Already in despair from the futility of my investigation, I relived those darkest moments of my life in the depths of a grief that never ends.

At some point in my despair, mercifully I fell unknowing into the velvet blanket of redeeming sleep.

CHAPTER 23

I woke Wednesday morning determined to give up the investigation. In pursuing it I'd committed felonies that could send me to prison, and I'd led Mara to do the same. If she was being stalked, I'd also led her into physical danger. All I'd accomplished was to revive forgotten scandals that could destroy the happiness of my friends. And I was no closer to finding the murderer now than I was when I started.

I tried to phone Mara to tell her my decision, but she didn't answer either her land line or her cell phone. I left no message and hoped to catch her later between classes.

Something about making a decision, even a tough one, tends to restore the spirit. So I felt reasonably positive by the time I entered my office.

But not for long. On the center of my desk lay a sheet of paper that shouted a message in bold type:

LAY
OFF

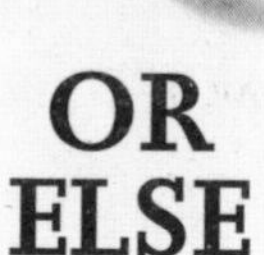

OR ELSE

It was computer-printed, of course, and I later measured the type as 72-point.

My initial shock gave way to a sense of being violated, which then erupted in a blaze of fury. If the violator had been there, I'd have tried my best to smash him. But he wasn't there, so my anger gradually sank into frustration. I could do nothing until I knew who left the warning.

Hurried footsteps sounded in the hall. Then Mara stood in my doorway, anxiety in her face and a sheet of paper in her hand. Without looking, I knew what it contained.

She spoke in an unsteady voice. "I found this in the middle of my desk."

"I have one just like it," I said. "Dean-Dean says two passkeys are missing besides the one I stole. It looks like somebody used one of them."

Mara bit her lip and grimaced. "I came to the campus early to tell you I was quitting our investigation. We weren't accomplishing anything, so I thought it was time to stop."

"And now?"

Her chin raised that expressive fraction of an inch. "We have to continue. We must be getting close."

"Are you still being stalked?"

"I don't know. I didn't see him this morning."

"And you still want to go on?"

She speared me with a glance. "Are you going to back out?"

I found myself adjusting my trifocals. "I tried to call you earlier to

say I was quitting. But not now. You must be right about our getting close." Something popped into place in my mind. "These messages are a challenge as well as a warning. I couldn't quit now if I wanted to."

"Good." She rewarded me with a smile. "What now? Do we take these to the police?"

"How can we?" I'd already puzzled over that. "The first thing they'll ask is, 'Lay off of what?' We say, 'Our investigation.' They ask, 'What have you done?' Then we either have to lie or confess to several felonies."

Her smile faded into tightened lips. "So we've painted ourselves into a corner."

"Only about this warning. Your being stalked is different. A stalking report from any good-looking female is always credible on its own merits."

For a second time, she blushed. But she only said, "I'll have to think on that. If it keeps up, that is." She looked at her watch. "I have to teach my class. Call me later and we'll decide what to do."

When I agreed, she jogged away down the hall—no small feat for someone wearing a pantsuit and pumps. I remembered how genuine her smile had been, and it occurred to me how rarely she smiled.

I barely made it on time to my nine o'clock class, in which today's topic was one of my unfavorites. We studied historians who say the American Revolution was motivated by the founding fathers' promoting their own economic interests. You can find plenty of cases when they did, of course, but you can also find plenty when they acted directly against their own interests. I have trouble covering this topic objectively because I believe in the motivating power of ideas. Materialistic interpretations always fall short.

Nevertheless, I got through it okay. After class, a student met me at

the door and said President Cantwell wanted to see me.

What have I done now? I wondered. But since wondering would do no good, I headed across campus to the executive center. When I reached Mrs. Dunwiddie's office, I found Dean-Dean standing by her desk. He looked up with an irritated expression.

"I can't see you now, Professor Barclay," he said. "I'm busy with a priority project."

"That's all right, sir," I said. "Some other time, then."

He stretched himself up to his full five feet eight and retreated into his office before my internal bassoon could toot more than twice.

Mrs. Dunwiddie looked concerned. "Did you want to see the dean?"

"No," I said, "but I didn't want to disillusion him by saying I didn't."

She suppressed a middle-aged giggle, resumed her officious voice, and said, "President Cantwell is waiting."

The J. Cleveland Cantwell who greeted me was quite different from the one I'd known before. He pointed me to a chair, then came around his desk and sat facing me, a frown creasing his brow.

"Two churches have dropped us from their annual budgets," he said. "Neither would explain why. The cause may have been Laila Sloan's death. It may have been something else."

No wonder he looked worried. He'd always bragged we were on the budgets of more than a hundred churches.

He rubbed his fingers together. "Other things aren't going well, either. Two of our athletes had a fight in the gym last weekend. One required six stitches in his head."

"I hadn't heard about that," I said, still wondering why he'd sent for me. It didn't help that my head echoed with a weird duet between a bass violin and an oboe.

"In any case, Press," he said, "you were right yesterday. I did need to hear that debate."

He'd never used my given name before, and this was the first time I'd heard him speak in a conversational tone instead of his formal pontifical mode.

When I didn't say anything, he continued. "Yesterday, I found some of the speeches profoundly shocking. I hadn't realized people would actually use their classes for . . . well, for *indoctrination* . . . or that they would coerce students into signing ideological statements."

"It's been going on," I said. I didn't ask him where he'd been for the past thirty years.

He wiped his brow. "I hadn't realized how far from its roots this college has traveled."

Again, I said nothing. I particularly didn't remind him that we were a university rather than a college. After all, he was the one who'd renamed it.

He sighed. "I want to stop the drift before it goes too far, but I don't know where to start. I thought maybe you and some of the older faculty would have some ideas." He looked up hopefully.

"I don't know anything about administration," I said. "I just teach history. I guess my main suggestion would be to talk with Dr. Sheldon out at the assisted-living center. He's retired, so he has no turf to protect. He'll talk straight with you."

That last was the understatement of the year. Dr. Sheldon would probably talk straight *through* him. But Cantwell would find that out soon enough.

He again rubbed his fingers together. "Perhaps we've been too lax in hiring faculty. I wonder about that Wiccan woman. . . . There's no telling what she's palming off on her students. . . ."

"I'd keep her," I said, trying to sound thoughtful despite the alarm rising in my throat. I was glad I'd made a few discreet inquiries about her. "Her students say she stays objective and never proselytizes. One asked what she thought about some point in Christian theology, and she said, 'Why do you care what I think? You do your own thinking.' Then she outlined the major interpretations and gave him references for further study. That's the kind of faculty I'd keep."

He nodded. "I see what you mean."

I wasn't going to let that one go. "Her students will tell you the same thing I did."

He nodded again. "I was wondering about some of the . . . the *ideologues* who spoke yesterday. . . ."

Talking about other people's jobs made my flesh crawl. "Traditionally, academic freedom says they can speak openly without fear of penalty," I said, walking on eggshells. "I think I'd look more to the hiring process."

A smile flickered briefly across his face. "I shouldn't have asked you that."

He stood and extended his hand. Like an actor putting on makeup, he turned on his normal rhetorical mode. "Thank You for Coming By, Professor Barclay. Please Be Assured that I will give your comments Full Consideration."

I shook the extended hand. "Thank you for asking me, sir. I do recommend talking to Dr. Sheldon. You might also try prayer."

He made no response and, feeling like the hypocrite I was, I showed myself out. In my spiritual numbness, I hadn't prayed in a long time. Who was I to tell him to pray?

Physician, heal thyself.

Mrs. Dunwiddie questioned me with her eyebrows as I passed

through her office. I answered with a smile and a shrug, which ought to inspire a week's speculation in the campus gossip circles.

The door to Dean-Dean's office stood open, and the executive center's custodial associate stood before him. The custodian was a red-faced man who wore jeans and a blue denim work shirt, with a red bandanna hanging out of his hip pocket. He spoke in outraged innocence.

"*No, sir,* Mr. Billig, I have not *never* put *no* mothballs in *no* part of this building at *no* time."

I admired his Chaucerian grammar, but thought it politic not to linger for more.

The interview with President Cantwell left me feeling like a juggler with too many plates in the air. I already had to worry about my classes, investigating the murder, losing friends because of it, Staggart's trying to pin the murder on me, the murderer's—or someone's—threat to "lay off," and Dean-Dean's accusing me of falsifying my personnel file. Now Cantwell had made me feel partly responsible for the direction of the college. Then I had to top it all by adding the question of prayer. That gave me at least two more plates than I could handle.

So I went to lunch. Another grilled cheese sandwich washed down with coffee.

Listening to the faculty chatter in the grill, I could almost make myself believe the world had returned to normal. Mara sat across the table from me, not saying much but somehow making me feel better. The male and female composition instructors laughed about a student's getting Bayreuth confused with Beirut, and she recycled her standard complaint that her students were recent transfers from Catatonic State. We dutifully laughed with them.

Everything *felt* really normal until Brenda Kirsch showed up. She wore that emerald-green warmup again, and she stopped by our table

long enough to flash me a luminous smile and rub her hand in circles on my shoulder.

"Friends, Press?" she asked.

"Friendship is a wonderful thing," I said.

She laughed and moved away with that long-legged stride, half athlete and half ballerina.

"What did you do, Press?" asked the female composition teacher. "Give one of her athletes an *A*?"

"Maybe she just likes history," I said.

For several seconds I didn't look at Mara. When I did, I wished I hadn't.

She looked right through me and said, "In spring the sap runs free."

"This is November," I said.

"So the sap is out of season." She picked up her books and stalked out.

The female composition teacher looked puzzled. "What did she mean by that?"

I tried to look innocent and said, "She's been reading up on botany."

My afternoon class went well—more on the ideals of knighthood and scholars' speculation on how much they were actually practiced. So by the time I got back to my office, I'd almost forgotten my troubles.

They came back with a rush. I'd carefully placed the "lay off" message in a locked drawer of my desk. The drawer had been jimmied open and the document was gone. That left me with no physical evidence to prove I'd received a threat. And it left no doubt about something even more frightening: I was being targeted by someone who passed through locked doors as easily as a ghost.

CHAPTER TWENTY-THREE

I was still gazing at the desk drawer, half-stunned and trying to make sense of things, when I realized someone was standing in my doorway.

It was Threnody Harkins, and the set of her jaw told me this was no social call.

CHAPTER 24

I'd never thought much about Threnody except that she came from a good Northeastern family and pronounced monosyllabic words like *school* and *pool* with an extra syllable. For a woman named after a funeral dirge, she'd always seemed fairly cheerful. But the look on her face as she stood in my doorway told me I'd have to revise my opinion.

Threnody was an attractive brunette, somewhere in her middle thirties, with an olive complexion and dramatic amber eyes. As always, she was immaculately dressed: a businesslike maroon jacket dress with the skirt covering the knees—stockings, of course, and pumps with medium heels. She carried a coat with an ocelot collar over her left arm and a stylish purse in that hand. Add hat and gloves, and she'd be dressed for a formal tea.

For all of her femininity, though, she was sturdily built and athletic. Everyone knew she lifted weights, and she'd earned a formidable reputation on the racquetball court. The few males foolish enough to play her came away regretting it.

She looked at me now with an expression most people reserve for fire ants.

"Come in, Threnody," I said. "How can I help you?" I was glad to be standing behind my desk.

She marched up to the desk and pointed her right index finger at my face. "Why are you trying to ruin my husband?"

Her gaze of amber fury never left my eyes, and her finger remained pointed at my face.

In such situations, I find a convenient refuge in becoming officious. So I adjusted my trifocals and said, "The intention you attribute to me, Mrs. Harkins, is quite foreign to any I have ever entertained. Why don't you sit down and explain what we're talking about?"

Her finger did not move. "Don't pull that stupid professor act on me, Preston Barclay. Answer my question."

"For heaven's sake, Threnody." I raised my hands, palm upwards, in front of my shoulders in what is commonly called the French salute. "I don't have a clue. Would you mind explaining?"

I knew exactly what she meant, but I wasn't about to admit it.

She simmered for a few moments, then lowered her pointing finger and found her way to a chair. She perched on its edge, hands clutching and unclutching the purse in her lap. Her ocelot-collared coat still hung from her arm but now dragged on the floor. I hoped she didn't send me the cleaning bill. Though she'd calmed down a bit, I kept the desk between us.

She glowered at me and said, "You've been digging up dirt on my husband and I want it stopped. He's under enough strain already with the police searching his office and our house, frightening our daughters to death. Why do you want to drag out that old court record for everyone to see?"

That jolted me like catching hold of an electric eel. I hadn't heard about any court case, old or new. Until then I'd wanted only to appease the woman and get her out of my office. Now I had to find out what she knew that I didn't.

"Old court record?" I said. "Which one?"

She blinked, and her mouth hung open. "Oh, my," she said, "if he's lied to me again . . ."

"What would he have lied about?"

"He only told me about one court case. If there's more than that one—"

"Which one did he tell you about?"

"The one Laila tried to blackmail him with. The larceny."

"That's when she got convicted and put on probation?"

"She and all of her gang. She was eighteen, but the others were still juveniles. Their records were expunged when they met the terms of their probation. That's why I said—"

"Laila tried to blackmail Bob with that?"

She spread her hands in resignation, the coat still on her arm and her purse resting in her lap. "She tried to involve him in something new—said if he didn't, she'd tell the college administration he'd been convicted of larceny. And she'd tell me about their involvement and the other sordid things she'd gotten him into. They committed God-knows-how-many larcenies and burglaries, but they only got convicted of one."

"Did Bob agree?"

"He did not." Her jaw set. "He came to me and confessed. He asked my forgiveness for not having told me about the relationship and their string of crimes. And I forgave him—though not before I made him sweat. Then he asked what he should do about Laila. He never was any good at decisions, and he can't stand confrontation."

"What did he do?"

Her eyes took on a faraway look and a smile crept onto her lips.

"*He* did nothing. If he had, he'd only have gotten in deeper." She sat very straight in her chair. "I went to see Laila in her office and told her a good, whopping lie. I said Bob had told me all about their relationship before he married me, and I married him anyway. Then I said if she didn't leave my husband alone, I would personally tell the administration about her criminal background and the scheme she'd tried to blackmail Bob into joining."

"What scheme was that?"

She laughed, a cruel laugh I hope never to hear again. "I don't know. Bob didn't understand it himself. But I never let her guess that. And I did one other thing while I was at it."

"What was that?"

She showed a self-satisfied smile. "I slapped her face. So hard it snapped her head around. And I said if she didn't leave my husband alone, I'd . . . I'd come back and kill her."

For the first time, she sat fully back in her chair, satisfaction still written on her face.

It wasn't written on mine because I was having trouble keeping up. It didn't help that my internal orchestra was playing the can-can theme from Offenbach's *Gaîté Parisienne*.

Threnody's words "leave my husband alone" echoed in my head, along with the fragments "ter leave h" and "y husband" on the paper scraps we'd found in Laila's house.

"Did you ever write Laila about this?" I asked.

"Of course not." Her eyes narrowed. "I'm not that foolish."

"Did Laila ever write you or Bob?"

Now she looked concerned. "No. Why do you ask?"

I made a hasty excuse. "Someone told me the police found torn paper fragments in Laila's house. One had the word 'husband' written on it."

She frowned. "Were any names mentioned?"

"None that I heard. In any case," I lied, "my information is third-hand."

She moved again to the edge of her chair. "Now you have to tell me about the other court case you mentioned."

Another hasty excuse. "It must have been one of those other larcenies. I heard the court threw the case out before trial." It pricked my conscience that lying came more easily with every whopper I told. Practice makes perfect, I guess. But in deference to my conscience, I made a mental note to chastise myself sometime in the future. Far in the future, I hoped.

Threnody sighed. "I'm glad it wasn't something Bob didn't confess. It's a terrible thing to learn your husband has lied to you."

"I can imagine," I said. That seemed a safe comment.

Her eyes narrowed again. "You still haven't told me why you're digging up dirt on my husband. What have you got against him?"

"Nothing." For once I could tell the truth, though not all of it. "Everyone in the science center that afternoon is under suspicion for Laila's murder. I've heard Captain Staggart wants to pin it on me. Since I didn't do it, I'm trying to find out all I can about Laila, hoping I'll find evidence to point in another direction. That's what led me to Bob, among others."

"What others?"

"I'd rather not say. Anyone in the science center that afternoon."

"What will you do with the information about Bob?"

"Nothing if he's not the murderer." I saw no reason to tell her that

Mara and Dr. Sheldon knew all that I did.

"Bob is not the murderer," she said. "He's a big man, strong as an ox. But he's soft inside. He doesn't have the stomach to kill anything."

She was probably right, and I felt sorry for Bob. As a teenager in Laila's hands, he'd shown less backbone than a mud pie. He apparently wasn't showing any more under Threnody's management. I remembered then that he seldom opened his mouth in faculty meetings. I saw him now as a man who could manage nothing more resistant than the chemicals in his lab.

Except in a fit of fury. When I told him about his photo with Laila, he'd have hit me if I'd been standing close enough. No, I couldn't scratch Bob from my list of suspects. Not yet, anyway. Then I remembered something else.

"That faculty trip to Las Vegas—did you notice anything about Laila then?"

Threnody looked thoughtful, then shook her head. "Laila paired off with the other single woman, Brenda Kirsch. We didn't see them again except once or twice in the casino."

"Did any member of the group win or lose an unusual amount?"

She thought again. "No one bragged or complained about it. I won a little, Bob lost a little. That seemed to be the story for everyone." She stood. "I have to drive Amy and Suzie to their piano lessons. Will you promise you won't hurt Bob with any of this information?"

I decided it was safe to come out from behind my desk. "If he's not the murderer, he has nothing to fear."

She walked up to me and offered her hand. "I'll take that as a promise, Press."

I accepted her handshake. She had the firm grip of a man, no doubt from her weight training. That sparked another idea.

"There is one question," I said, prolonging the handshake. "Threnody, where were you at the time of the murder?"

Her grip tightened on my hand till I thought she would wrench it off. The amber eyes again blazed with fury, and she gritted out the words through clenched teeth.

"That's for you to find out."

She did not merely release my hand. She threw it down with a violence usually reserved for snakes. Then she swept out of my office with a most unladylike curse, the ocelot-collared coat still hanging from her arm.

I slumped at my desk with my head in my hands. I'd made another enemy, and the information received brought me no closer to finding the murderer.

The phone rang. It was Mara. An angry Mara.

"Someone stole the warning I showed you this morning," she said. "He broke the lock on my desk drawer, but he must have used a passkey on the office door. How is it with you?"

"The same," I said. "No marks on the office door, but the desk drawer had been jimmied. How about your stalker?"

"Still not definite. I caught him watching me once today, but he didn't follow. Too much is happening too quickly, Press. We need to talk. Seven o'clock at Dr. Sheldon's?"

Her voice trembled with suppressed anger, but for once the anger wasn't directed at me. I hoped she'd forgotten my lunchtime brush with Brenda Kirsch.

"Seven o'clock sounds fine," I said, and we broke off.

Then I remembered it was Wednesday, and my ancient malaise moved in. It smothered me in a blanket of black muslin that chafed my psyche like sandpaper. I sat there brooding over my failures until

evening descended into dark. If I was going to make my seven o'clock appointment with Mara and Dr. Sheldon, I'd better go home and grab a sandwich.

I followed the narrow walkway down the hill, grateful that night hid my despair from the eyes of others. I dreaded returning to my dark house and silent piano, but facing its emptiness was something I couldn't escape.

I opened the storm door with one key, the heavy inner door with another. The hinges squeaked, and I made a mental note to find some graphite. I closed both doors behind me and moved into the hall.

A shadow with upraised arm appeared on my left. The arm descended and something hard struck a stunning blow above my temple. Pain flashed through my head and neck, and some distant part of me knew I was falling. Then my inner darkness engulfed the entire world, and I knew nothing at all.

CHAPTER 25

The drummer was a lunatic on amphetamines, performing madly on an ensemble Gene Krupa would have envied—snare drums, cymbals, bongos and basses, with assorted triangles, tabors, and timpani thrown in. He must have had eight or ten arms like Shiva the Destroyer, for the world had never heard a drum solo so frenetic.

No, I was wrong. There were two eight-armed drummers, wildly out of sync with each other, both utterly mad and both sent by Shiva to destroy my five heads.

No, I was wrong again. It was Shiva who had five heads, so maybe I was Shiva, bent on destroying myself. All of my heads ached and felt frozen, as if I'd somehow landed upside down in an iceberg.

"Press, wake up."

The voice came from beyond the mad drummers' pummeling. I didn't answer. I was too busy being destroyed.

The iceberg changed position on my heads and the voice grew insistent. "Press, wake up. We have to get you to a doctor."

The drums kept pounding.

"No doctor." My words came from deep beneath the ice. "Just need

to get out of this confounded iceberg. You have the key?"

"The key to your survival. Like getting you to a doctor."

The voice had lost patience. I didn't see why. I had no classes until morning.

"Press, you idiot, don't be stubborn. *Wake up*."

The voice was Mara's. I reached up to feel my heads and found only one. That was one too many. A bowling ball kept bouncing around on the inside, and the drummers kept pounding on the outside. With an effort, I opened my eyes.

I lay on my back in the entryway to my house, a pillow from the living room couch under my head. Mara sat cross-legged beside me, leaning forward to replace the iceberg on my head with a colder one.

I heard myself ask, "What are you doing here? You're supposed to be at Dr. Sheldon's."

"So are you," she said. "Be quiet and help me get you out to the car. You need a doctor."

That was the last thing I needed. "No doctor. Need sleep."

"Let's see the doctor. Then you can sleep all you like."

"No." I closed my eyes. "Sleep first, then doctor."

She protested more, but gave in when she saw I was going back to sleep anyway. She helped me up and steadied me as I staggered into the bedroom and flopped on the bed. I didn't like sleeping in my suit, but asking her to help me take it off didn't seem appropriate. The last thing I remember, except for the mad drummers' pounding, was a blanket being laid over me and the iceberg returning to my head.

After several decades of nonexistence I woke in pre-dawn darkness. The clock's luminous dial showed five thirty. My head still ached, throbbing now to the deliberate beat of a bass drum attuned to my pulse. But the demented drummers had gone back to their asylum. An

easy chair across the bedroom held the shadowy form of Mara, curled up in a blanket. When I groaned up into a sitting position, the ice pack fell off my head.

That woke Mara, who stretched and asked, "How do you feel, Press?"

I took inventory. "My head aches, but I've worked through headaches before. What happened?"

"When you didn't show up at Dr. Sheldon's, I came to check on you. The front door was standing open and you were lying facedown on the floor. Someone had slugged you good. The knot on your head looked like an ostrich egg. I turned you over and iced you down. You wouldn't let me call a doctor like a sensible person would, so I decided to wait it out until morning."

"I didn't need a doctor," I said. "I've been slugged before."

"Sure. Another average day in the life of a history professor."

It seemed too ungrateful to say she needn't be sarcastic. Thanks to her keeping the ice on me, the lump on my head was no larger than an agate. So I didn't say anything.

"You'd better call the police," she said. "Your house has been broken into and you've been assaulted. That's two felonies, and no telling what comes next."

"So I should tell the police someone didn't like our investigating Laila's murder? You know where that would lead. We've committed a few felonies, too."

"We haven't bashed anyone's head."

"That won't make any difference. To police, a felony is a felony. Besides, it looks like somebody is getting desperate. As you said, we must be getting close."

She didn't answer, but looked off into space in the dark bedroom. My internal musicians turned off the bass drum and changed to

Chopin's saccharine-sweet "Raindrop" Prelude. The monotonous repeated note throbbed in rhythm with my heartbeat.

After awhile I said, "Thank you for all you've done, Mara. Give me a couple of minutes for a shower, and I'll fix us some breakfast."

She sprang to her feet and her blanket fell to the floor. "No, you won't. And don't you dare turn on a light. I'm already compromised, with my car parked in front of your house all night. I have to get it out of here before your neighbors wake up."

"I'm sorry," I said. "I didn't think of that."

Even in the dark I could see her chin lift. "You're lucky you can think at all. Now don't move until you hear me drive away. After that, you can turn on all the lights you want."

She moved quickly through the dark house, grabbing her coat from another chair and disappearing toward the entryway. I heard the front door open and close. The house seemed suddenly empty again.

With Chopin's repeated note still throbbing in my brain, I groped my way to a front window and watched as she opened her car door. Quietly, so the neighbors wouldn't hear. She left the interior lights on long enough to put her key in the ignition, then eased the door almost shut until the interior lights went out. She was using all the tricks to keep from drawing attention. Everything went well until she turned the ignition.

Bright light flashed under her front wheels and a loud boom rattled my windows. Red smoke billowed from the car's hood. Mara leaped from the car and looked back and forth as if wondering which way to run.

I raced out to the car. Before I got there, she'd gotten control of herself and popped the hood lock. Without thinking, I raised the hood. That was a dumb thing to do because anyone smart enough to bomb a car

would be smart enough to set a booby trap for idiots like me. I stood there coughing as red smoke surged up from the engine compartment.

Lights blinked on in my neighbors' houses, and people peered out windows. Mara could forget about getting away unnoticed, but I couldn't worry about that now. Moving to one side, I looked beneath the still-cascading smoke to see what had happened.

"It's a smoke grenade," I said. "It's fastened beside the engine block, and there are fragments that might have come from a big firecracker. Some of your wiring is hanging loose."

Mara received the news with a stoical expression. She held up her cell phone and quirked an eyebrow at me. I nodded and she dialed 9-1-1. The situation had gotten too far out of hand to keep the police out of it. That blow to my head could have been a bullet to the heart. The smoke grenade in Mara's car could have been a real bomb. We had stirred up something we couldn't control.

The neighbors poured into the street while we waited for the police. I had all I could do to keep them from pawing over the car.

Pretty soon, Brenda Kirsch pushed her way through the crowd. She wore royal-blue warm-ups and moved with her characteristic strength and grace. I wondered what had brought her. She lived four blocks away, but was she moved only by curiosity about the explosion? Or had she known something beforehand?

She stared at the car and asked, "What's all the fuss, Press?" Her eyes surveyed the crowd, then me, then Mara.

"Someone bombed Mara's car," I said.

The last wisps of red smoke threaded up from the engine compartment. The crowd muttered in the background. In the growing predawn light, I could see people still arriving a block away.

Brenda showed a knowing smile. "Strange that Mara could drive

CHAPTER TWENTY-FIVE

from her place all the way here before the bomb went off."

I said nothing. Mara looked the other way.

Brenda laughed. "You said the words, Press. Friendship is a wonderful thing." She pushed her way back through the crowd, still gliding along with that graceful stride.

I didn't look at Mara and she didn't look at me.

Fortunately, the police arrived. Four of them. More fortunately, Sergeant Spencer came with them.

"I thought you were detailed to homicide," I said.

"Still am." His voice was all business. His eyes scanned the scene. "When anything involves one of the suspects, someone from homicide tags along. What happened?"

While several policemen sealed off the scene with yellow tape, I briefed Spencer about Mara's car but said nothing about my being attacked. To his credit, he didn't ask what Mara was doing there. He called for the bomb squad, posted one man to guard the crime scene, detailed three to question the crowd, and led Mara and me into my house.

I learned later that questioning my neighbors proved futile. No one had heard or seen anything.

"All right," Sergeant Spencer said when we were seated in the living room, "tell me the whole story. Not just the summary." He may have been my former student, but his steady gaze showed he was in command.

I looked at Mara and she looked at me. Her barely perceptible nod gave me license.

"When I came home last night—around seven o'clock—someone slugged me." I pointed to the knot above my temple. "The next thing I knew, Professor Thorn was waking me up."

Mara took it from there, telling why she checked on me and explaining that my bullheadedness about seeing a doctor—her exact expression—caused her to stay and monitor my condition all night.

Sergeant Spencer's face gave no clue as to what he thought of our story, but he made the obvious follow-up. "If you surprised a burglar, Professor Barclay, I can understand why he would knock you out before you recognized him. But why would he break into your house? You live in a low-crime neighborhood and, if you'll pardon my saying so, professors are not the most lucrative targets for robbery."

I shrugged. "That puzzles me, too."

He turned to Mara. "Why would anyone want to put that whatever-it-was in your car?"

Mara duplicated my shrug and showed an admirably puzzled expression. It occurred to me that she'd have a promising career as an actress. In the silence, my internal musicians switched to something baroque that I couldn't identify.

Sergeant Spencer clasped his hands in his lap. "This leaves us two possible motives: harassment or warning. You're both connected with the Laila Sloan case, and strange things have been happening during our investigation—"

"What kind of things?" I asked.

He gave me a hard look, then sighed. "Your book that turned up in the victim's office the second time we searched it. I made the first search, and I know it wasn't there then. Not even Captain Staggart believes either of you wrote those e-mails."

"He gave a good imitation of believing I wrote one," I said.

Spencer looked away. "That's just his manner. And someone broke into the victim's house. Afterward, we found a few things that weren't there on the first search."

I'd intended that they find the safe-deposit box key and the two slips of paper, of course, but I didn't dare ask what else.

"Staggart took my toolbox to prove I was the burglar," I said.

"You fit the description a neighbor gave, but the lab says your tools weren't used for the break-in." Spencer laughed. "The technician thought they hadn't been used in years."

"They don't help with teaching history."

"I daresay."

It struck me that he had a remarkable vocabulary for a policeman. Then I remembered how astute he'd been as a student. He sat there looking both curious and confident, and I wondered what he'd come up with next. I think Mara probably wondered, too, though she put on an admirable show of detachment.

Sergeant Spencer took a deep breath. "That brings us back to your problems last night and the motive for them. It had to be either harassment or warning. I vote against harassment."

He leaned forward and delivered his own bomb. "Now: just what have you two been up to that would provoke that kind of warning?"

CHAPTER 26

I considered pretending innocence or giving Sergeant Spencer the French salute, but something in his gaze said if I ducked the question he would cook my goose. In any other situation that might have been an interesting figure of speech, but not here.

"We've poked around some," I said. "Captain Staggart should have known those e-mails were bogus, but he acted like he intended to use them against us. While he wasted time harassing us, he might not catch the real murderer. So we made our own investigation, beginning by learning all we could about Laila Sloan. That's about it. We've been asking questions."

"What did you learn?" Spencer's set expression gave nothing away.

In answering, my historian's skills in sifting reams of data and remembering its sources served me well. I couldn't very well say, "Now that you mention it, Sergeant Spencer, we committed a few burglaries, but we did it for a good cause."

So I told him what we knew about Laila, but omitted what we'd learned from personnel records and from searching her house and office. I finessed the high school annual source by saying that Bob

Harkins had admitted his affair with Laila, and that Threnody had confirmed it and added the fact of his expunged conviction. I mentioned Pappas's jail time, Laila's brief marriage to Gifford Jessel, Brenda Kirsch's evasions, Threnody's confrontation with Laila (minus her threat against Laila's life), and the fact that all of them had warned us against continuing our investigation.

Mara then described the computerized warnings that later disappeared, and added her belief she was being stalked. Sergeant Spencer noted her description of the alleged stalker, and I described the two toughs Dr. Sheldon had pointed out to me.

"The stalking and last night's attacks on you are new to us, of course," Sergeant Spencer said, "and you've added a few details we didn't know before."

I started to ask which details, but he cut me off. "Thanks for sending Penny Nichols to me. Because of her we know why Laila mailed so many packages."

That brought Mara and me to the edges of our chairs.

"Laila was involved in a small-time racket," Spencer said. "It works like this. Someone answers one of those work-in-your-own-home ads and finds all he has to do is receive packages and mail them to new addresses, mostly overseas. It's easy work: he gets maybe three or four packages a month and he gets paid fifty dollars a package, so he doesn't ask questions. That way he doesn't know he's fencing stolen property—like that notebook computer Penny Nichols brought in."

Mara interrupted. "I drove Laila to mail three packages the afternoon she was killed. She said she'd had trouble with a clerk at the western branch post office, but I wondered why she went all the way to the eastern branch when the central was closer."

"Laila wasn't content with small-time," Spencer said. "We've found

three students besides Penny who received mail for Laila, each under a different name in a different post office box. Laila spread out her transshipments among the three local post offices and several in neighboring towns. She played the market for all it was worth."

At that point I almost let the felonious cat out of our bagatelle. "That explains—"

". . . why Laila chose that particular post office." Mara cut me off.

"My exact thought, Mara," I said. I'd almost said that explained how Laila could afford all her expensive electronics, which we couldn't know about without having been in her house.

Sergeant Spencer gave each of us a sardonic look, then spoke deliberately to the wall beyond us. "I'm glad you haven't done anything you shouldn't have. Well-meaning citizens sometimes blunder into breaking the law, and then there isn't much we can do to help them." He looked at each of us in turn. "What will you do now?"

Mara and I exchanged glances but said nothing.

"What would you suggest?" she asked after a pause.

"You're not obligated to do anything," he said. For the first time since his arrival, he grinned. "But something you did provoked a reaction from someone. It could be dangerous, but if you keep doing the things you've been doing—within the law, of course—you might shake something loose."

"It might shake my head loose from my body," I said.

"Just a thought." He rose to leave.

A plainclothes policeman we hadn't seen before entered without knocking and spoke to Sergeant Spencer. "I'm Robinson from the bomb squad. We've taken samples for analysis, but I'm certain there was nothing but a jumbo firecracker and the smoke grenade." He turned to Mara. "You're lucky, ma'am. It could just as well have been a

bomb. The wiring was sophisticated—the work of a professional, not some rube prankster. By the way, your car will need a lot of work before you can drive it."

Sergeant Spencer thanked Robinson and asked Mara if she wanted him to have her car towed.

"Not now," she said. "I'll take care of that later."

I knew she couldn't afford the tow or the repair, but she wasn't going to admit it. She accepted Spencer's offer of a ride back to her apartment and left without so much as a glance in my direction. By this time I knew her well enough to recognize her inner tension. She'd lost her transportation and was strapped for money in a strange city. Beyond that, she had to decide whether going on with the investigation was worth the risk. The same decision had me tense, though I didn't have her financial complications. I hadn't mentioned it, but past experience with the college administration told me we'd soon have other problems. Regardless of how innocent you are, it doesn't pay to have your name connected with scandal.

With a good bit of hustling and in spite of my headache, I got to my nine o'clock class on time, though I forgot to change out of yesterday's rumpled brown suit that I'd slept in. I couldn't tell you what I taught that day. All I know is that somehow I dragged through it. Afterward, in my office, I took more aspirin and tried to forget my headache by grading research papers.

The early crop of papers is usually good, and I love to see young minds grappling with facts. There were a few minor problems. One on eighteenth-century European culture was flawless except for a passing reference to "Mozart's *Eine Kleine Nacktmusic*." I debated with myself if it was a genuine mistake or if the student was trying to slip one by me. In the end, I wrote *sp* over the word *Nacktmusic* and made a marginal

note: *nacht* = *night*; *nackt* = *naked*. It's for distinctions such as this that we spend years in graduate study.

I was still massaging these philosophical lucubrations when Marcus Fischbach knocked at my office door. A senior now, Marcus still presented himself as he had as a freshman: scraggly beard, shoulder-length ponytail, and baggy pants that sagged under the heels of his unlaced Reeboks. In his first year he'd aced my Western Civ course—what students call "getting required courses out of the way." Having removed that barrier to intellectual progress, Fischbach concentrated on business and computer science. So I hadn't seen much of him.

My mind still on research papers, I moved around the desk to sit facing him. I opened with the usual routine questions.

He mumbled the usual vague answers. Then he said, "Professor Barclay, there's something I want you to know."

That and his earnest expression brought me instantly off autopilot. "Why me? Why not someone in your major department?"

He squinted and pulled at his beard. "They might, like, be involved in it themselves. Besides, I know I can trust you."

"Hold on," I said, now on red alert. "You can only trust me to do what I think is right."

"You don't have to do anything," he said. "I just want you to know I think there's something, like, funny about the campus computer network."

"Then you need to tell Mr. Heggan, the network administrator."

Marcus sniffed. "Earl-George? He couldn't find the problem if he'd put it in the pocket of his overalls. No, I won't tell anyone else till I find out what's going on."

This was getting nowhere, so I said, "You'd be smarter to talk to someone in the computer department."

He squinted again and started to say something, but my phone rang. I stood and answered it from in front of the desk.

It was Mrs. Dunwiddie. "Professor Barclay, Dean Billig wants to see you in his office immediately."

"I'll be right there," I said. I hung up and tried to sort things out. Dean-Dean must have heard I'd gotten slugged, and he'd give me what-for for not being the first to tell him. Well, I'd been chewed out before. Afterward, I could get back to grading papers and teaching classes.

"I'm sorry, but I have to go," I said to Marcus. "All I can tell you is not to do anything illegal."

He laughed and stood. "There's nothing illegal about, like, running computer programs. I just wanted somebody to know what I was about."

After locking the office door behind us, I walked to the executive center. I do mean *walked*. My head ached and my internal musicians were grinding out something hideous from what Faith used to call the mid-twentieth-century "ugly-is-beautiful" movement. The last thing I needed was a confrontation with Dean-Dean.

I found Mara waiting in Mrs. Dunwiddie's office.

"What's going on?" I asked.

"Dean Billig will see you now," Mrs. Dunwiddie said in her most officious voice. She opened the door to Dean-Dean's office and ushered us in. I noted with pleasure that the place still smelled of mothballs.

Dean-Dean looked up from his desk and motioned us into two chairs placed facing him. He did not rise. My internal bassoon honked three times and shut down. Mrs. Dunwiddie shut the door from the inside and retreated to a chair behind us. To take shorthand notes, I guessed. This was no routine expression of Dean-Dean's displeasure.

Dean-Dean assumed his most authoritative manner, the effect of

which is always undercut by his squeaky voice. He cleared his throat and said, "It has come to my attention that you two have been involved in unsavory activities. As you both know, unsavory activities by faculty members will not be tolerated."

What was he talking about? Had he found out I'd stolen his passkey?

Mara's blue eyes blazed. "Dean Billig, I don't have the slightest idea what you're talking about."

Dean-Dean blinked before her onslaught. His eyes bounced back and forth without focusing anywhere in particular. Then he drew himself erect and said, "I refer to what you two did last night, of course."

"Like my getting slugged in the head?" I asked. "Or her car getting bombed?"

"It has come to my attention that certain things happened between the two events."

"Like what?" Mara asked.

"Please." Dean-Dean held up one hand. "Professor Thorn, reliable sources say you spent the night in Professor Barclay's house."

Now my temper was up. "Of course she did. She came to check on me when I didn't show up on schedule at Dr. Sheldon's. He couldn't very well drive over in his wheelchair. She found me unconscious on the floor. She did what you'd have done if you'd found her in that condition. She put ice packs on my head until I was able to take care of myself."

"What I might have done is immaterial," he said. "Your neighbors must know she was there all night. Overton University is on the annual budgets of more than one hundred churches. Even if nothing untoward happened, we have to avoid even the *appearance* of unsavory conduct."

"If you want to impress the churches," I said, "you might try putting the crosses back on the entryways."

His jaw tightened, which made it tremble a bit. "That is not an option. There is more to Christianity than mere symbols."

Mara torched him again. "You might start with 'judge not, that ye be not judged.' "

Dean-Dean must have realized he was out of his depth with Mara. He struck the desk with his palm. "Enough! You are both suspended until further notice. You'll appear before the faculty hearing committee next Wednesday afternoon at one thirty."

"Thanksgiving holidays start at noon that day," I said. "Won't committee members be out of town?"

"I have authority to name additional members as necessary," he said.

That meant he could stack the committee with people who'd do what he told them.

"That's hardly due process," I said.

"Enough!" He struck the desk again. "Just be there at one thirty on Wednesday."

Mara wasn't letting go. "What is the charge? Being a Good Samaritan? Being victims of burglary, assault, and car bombing?"

Dean-Dean stood up, signaling dismissal. "Conduct bringing discredit to the college is good enough for now."

Mara did not budge. "I demand to speak with President Cantwell."

"That's not possible." Dean-Dean shifted from one foot to the other. "President Cantwell is away on a fund-raising mission."

"Perch or bass?" I asked.

Dean-Dean glowered at me. "That will be all. You're both suspended pending the faculty hearing committee's action. Your charge, Professor

Barclay, will include giving false information on your application for employment. I have a witness."

I could have said, "I have documents," but I decided to save that for the faculty hearing committee. Dean-Dean had tipped his hand with the business about my application. That revealed the machination of Clyde Staggart behind this episode. As I've said, Dean-Dean always believes the first person he hears. Changing his mind after that is like trying to reinstate Adam in the garden.

So I said nothing and stood up. Mara stood with me and we exited together. Mrs. Dunwiddie showed a worried expression and followed us with her eyes. When I winked at her, she looked away.

Outside, Mara gave me a look like Vesuvius gave Pompeii just before the eruption.

"Not now," I said. "Let's get out of here before Dean-Dean realizes he forgot to place any restrictions on us."

Her gaze held mine as we walked toward the liberal arts center. "What kind of restrictions?"

"He could have barred us from the campus or told us to hold ourselves available. The fact that he didn't gives us more freedom than we had before."

"Freedom to do what?"

"Further our investigation without having to work around our class schedules. Laila's letters of recommendation came from Insburg and Bi-County Consolidated High School. She and Gifford Jessel were married in Insburg. She, Bob Harkins, and Brenda Kirsch all grew up near the western border of the state. Somewhere in that area is a link that should tie this whole thing together. I intend to go out there and look for it."

Mara's blue torch downsized from blast-furnace to charcoal burner.

"I'm in this for the duration, Professor Barclay. You're not going one step without me."

"Okay," I said. My internal musicians broke into a sprightly polka.

I didn't know what we'd find out west, but it ought to be an interesting trip.

CHAPTER 27

We left Dean-Dean's office about eleven thirty, and by two we were on the interstate heading toward Insburg. Leaving town together would have provided more fuel for slander, so Mara took a taxi to the bus station and caught a bus to Sprague's Crossing, the next town west of Overton City.

For my part, I backed my old Honda into a covered position beside the house, hauled my suitcase out my back door, and loaded it into the trunk. Even my nosiest neighbors wouldn't know I was leaving town. I trailed the bus until it let Mara off at a Sprague's Crossing gas station, and I picked her up there. She had changed from the pantsuit she wore on campus into a pair of jeans and the same deep-violet blouse she'd worn on her first visit to my office. She threw her winter coat into the backseat on top of mine. I wore the brown suit I'd slept in, mainly because I'd forgotten to change.

"What is it you know that I don't?" Mara asked when we were westbound on the interstate. She'd been holding the question ever since we left Dean-Dean's office, and she looked ready to burst.

I told her what I thought had happened. "Staggart must have been

the first to tell Dean-Dean about last night. He'd play up all the sordid implications he could and downplay the fact that both of us were attacked. I caught on when Dean-Dean mentioned my job application. Staggart is the one who raised that issue with him."

She turned toward me as far as her seat belt allowed. "What's wrong with your application?"

"Nothing. I listed my Army service as Infantry. It was true: that was my basic branch. The application didn't require anything more. But Staggart convinced Dean-Dean it was false, that I should have listed Special Forces."

Mara said nothing, but turned back to the front. I listened to the engine's low growl and the hum of wheels on pavement as the endless gray highway slid past. My internal musicians cavorted along with a rollicking something in 12/8 time.

Mara turned toward me again. "You promised to tell me why Staggart hates you."

I looked out at the long, empty highway ahead of us. I wouldn't find a better time.

"Staggart and I served with Special Ops in Honduras during the early eighties. We were helping the Nicaraguan Contras against the Communist Sandinista government. In case you don't remember, it looked like the Sandinistas would give the Soviets military bases in Nicaragua. That would have caused all kinds of trouble."

"You don't have to justify the mission," she said. "What happened?"

"I was a lieutenant and Captain Staggart was my commander. I suspected he was taking kickbacks on weapons for the Contras and maybe a few bribes along with them. For a long time I looked the other way because our mission was vital to U.S. interests and its cost seemed less important. Then proof of the kickbacks fell into my lap. That meant I

had to decide what to do about it—whether upholding the law would jeopardize the mission."

I thought I'd squeezed the emotion out of those memories long ago and left only a dry set of historical facts. But now my hands gripped the steering wheel so hard I thought it might break.

Mara's voice came softly. "I can understand the problem."

I grimaced. "I don't know what I would have decided. Before I made up my mind, a team from the inspector general came and put all of us under oath. I told what I knew and nothing more. So did another lieutenant—Richmond Seagrave, the guy who debugged our computers."

"And what happened?"

"Staggart was allowed to resign his commission in lieu of a court-martial. He swore he'd get even with Seagrave and me for ruining his career, though he'd ruined it himself. Seagrave and I brushed it off as an idle threat. And so it was. Until Staggart showed up as captain of homicide in Overton City and I got involved in a murder investigation."

The blue eyes softened. "I'm sorry I got you involved."

"Not your fault," I said. "I'm sorry I got you tangled up in Staggart's revenge."

Her chin lifted. "All right, so we're both sorry. Now who are we going to see in Insburg?"

The question was timely, for we were entering the Insburg city limits. The lump on my head still throbbed, but I refused to give in to it.

"We're looking for one William Murphy, president of Insburg Tool and Trucking, Inc. He wrote a letter of recommendation for Laila."

We pulled off the interstate and stopped at a convenience store with an outside phone booth and, miraculously, a reasonably intact telephone directory. According to the yellow pages, Insburg Tool and

Trucking was located on the access road near the next exit. That was fortunate: afternoon shadows were already lengthening, and I had no wish to stay the night in Insburg.

The company had a large fenced parking lot where eighteen-wheelers and local delivery trucks vied for space around the dispatch point of a single warehouse. The dispatch looked busy as an anthill, so we bypassed it and parked beside the warehouse near a sign that said "Offices."

When we asked inside for William Murphy, reluctant clerks passed us to more offices manned by more reluctant clerks. Eventually we arrived at a bare office that contained a single desk. Behind it sat a woman of perhaps fifty who looked like she could lift an eighteen-wheeler with one hand and repair it with the other. Her name sign read "Blossom Harlow, MRS."

She looked up warily from the papers on her desk and chewed three times on her wad of gum. "What y'all want?"

"We'd like to see Mr. William Murphy," I said.

She took a moment to decide whether I was a housefly or a cockroach. Given my rumpled brown suit, she probably chose the latter. Whatever her decision, she took three more chews on her gum and said, mimicking me, "You'd like to see Mr. William Murphy, would you? So would all them idiots out there loading trucks." She looked back to the papers on her desk.

Mara marched up to the desk and leaned on it with both hands. Startled, Mrs. Harlow stared up at the woman towering over her. I couldn't see Mara's eyes, but I knew from hard experience what it felt like on the receiving end of that gaze.

"We want to talk to Mr. Murphy about a former employee," Mara said. "One who got herself murdered last week."

Mrs. Harlow blinked. "I didn't know you was police," she said.

"We *are* investigating," Mara said. "Now would you take us to Mr. Murphy?"

The woman rose and lumbered heavily to a closed door in the wall behind her. She pounded on it. A voice within yelled "Yeah?" and she yelled back, "Two guys to see you, Bill." Without further ceremony, she opened the door and motioned us in. I didn't realize she'd followed us until she said, "They're cops, though he don't look like it."

William Murphy was a red-faced man of about sixty who wore a white dress shirt with rolled-up sleeves and an orange tie loosened at the neck. His bulging muscles testified to years of manual labor, and his bulging stomach testified to recent years behind a desk. The mass of papers scattered on his desk showed his distaste for office work, and the wadded paper balls on the floor beside his wastebasket showed that his aim left something to be desired.

He gave us a jaundiced look and asked, "What d'ya want?" He did not rise from his chair.

Before I could speak, Mara seized the occasion. "We're investigating the murder of a former employee of yours. We hoped you could tell us something about her."

For a few seconds he chewed on something I hoped was gum, then shifted it into one cheek and said, "It's been ten years or more since I had any female employee except Blossom."

Mara didn't let go. "This would have been about twenty years ago. The woman's name was Laila Sloan, or she might have called herself Dee Sloan."

If he'd shaken his head any harder it would have fallen off. "No such woman ever worked for Insburg Tool and Trucking."

I resisted the temptation to add "Incorporated" and said, "Mr.

Murphy, eight years ago you wrote Laila Sloan a letter of recommendation. I saw it in her personnel file at Overton University."

If Blossom Harlow, MRS., had tried to decide whether I was a housefly or a cockroach, William Murphy looked at me as if he'd decided. "I never wrote her no letter," he said.

"It was on your letterhead stationery," I said, "and it had your signature."

His opinion of my status appeared to descend from cockroach to something considerably lower in the Great Chain of Being. "That letter may have had *a* signature," he said, "but it sure as shenanigans warn't mine." He waited for that to sink in, then added, " 'Cause I don't write letters of recommendation. Someone lists me as a reference, they gives my phone number. People want to check up, they calls and I tells 'em what they wants to know."

By that time I was certain Murphy hadn't written the letter in Laila's file. It was well-written and grammatical, and nothing we'd heard from Murphy showed him capable of writing it. Score another point for Laila's manipulations.

Mara still wasn't satisfied. "Are you absolutely sure a Laila Sloan or Dee Sloan never worked for your company?"

Murphy's face reddened. "You ask 'Am I sure?' " Deliberately, he reached in his hip pocket and pulled out a misshapen wallet, from which he removed a laminated card. "I'm as sure of that as I am that my name is William J. Murphy." He slammed the card down on the desk in front of Mara and leaned back, his face radiating satisfaction.

Without expression, Mara picked up the card and showed it to me. It was a driver's license identifying our host as William J. Murphy, complete with a mug shot taken while he wrestled with a particularly indigestible meal.

Mara spoke as if the others were not present. "This says he's William J. Murphy."

I returned her deadpan gaze. "Then I expect he probably is William J. Murphy."

This was a Mara I hadn't seen before. I didn't know quite what to make of it.

She gave Murphy back his card and said, "Thank you for your time. I'm glad you're William Murphy and not Laila Sloan. If you were Laila, you'd be dead."

Murphy was still trying to figure that one out as we left. Blossom Harlow, MRS., escorted us back into her office and closed Murphy's door. I decided to make a gracious exit.

"Thank you, too, Miz Harlow," I said.

She bristled. "*Mizziz* Harlow." She turned to Mara. "Honey, Bill didn't get things exactly right, or maybe he don't want to remember." She paused.

Mara favored her with a smile. "Yes?"

"'Bout nineteen, maybe twenty years ago there was a girl worked in this office with me for three days. On the first day I caught her looking through desks and warned her. Caught her again on the third day and let her go. But her name wasn't Sloan. It was Jessel. Yep, Dee Jessel it was. But there was more."

"More?" Mara leaned closer.

"Lots more." Blossom Harlow showed a satisfied smile. "On the second day, Bill caught her makin' up to his son—the one what runs our branch up in Omaha nowadays. So we checked up on her. Turned out she was working nights in one of those places they call a 'gentleman's club,' though no gentleman would be found dead within a mile of one. Out there she was known as Dee Luscious. At any rate, Bill said

find a way to get rid of her, so when I caught her lookin' through desks that second time, I sent her packing."

Mara beamed. "So she might have stolen letterhead stationery from one of the desks?"

"She might've," Blossom conceded, "and I wouldn't put it past her to forge Bill's signature. So someone finally gave her what-for, huh?"

"I'm afraid so," Mara said. "Do you know anything else about her, Mizziz Harlow?"

"No, honey. I'm afraid that's all."

Mara showed her another smile. "Thank you very much. You've been really helpful."

With a frown, Blossom scrutinized the knot on my head and asked, "Buster, is your head just naturally shaped like that?"

"Only when I'm growing horns," I said.

We left her puzzling over that and retreated to my car. I admit the treatment I'd received left me somewhat deflated. I thanked Mara for salvaging a situation I'd written off as hopeless.

"You dominated a woman twice your weight, and on her own territory," I said as we reentered the interstate. "Where did you learn that?"

She showed me a smile and laughing eyes. "I was a sergeant in the Army. You should have learned that when you read my personnel file."

Uh-oh. I felt lower than Blossom Harlow's cockroach. "So you knew that, too."

"I'd have done it in your place," she said. "Besides, you stayed in the executive center long enough to read every faculty file backwards if they were written in Chinese."

Her eyes gave me a mild scorching, then turned to the highway ahead. "What's next in our investigation?"

I glanced at my watch. "Towns are scarce west of here. Let's grab an early supper while we're still in civilization. Then it's on to the wide-open spaces of the western border."

We'd found a few surprises in Insburg. I wondered what others we'd find in Laila's home territory. But there was one thing I didn't have to wonder about. We'd better find something fast, or Staggart and Dean-Dean would put us in a worse fix than we were in now.

CHAPTER 28

Supper proved grim but edible. On the outskirts of Insburg we found Brimstead's Family Restaurant, where the fluorescent lights were decorated with flyspecks left over from summer. Or maybe they were antiques. A hefty waitress with a western twang took our orders: ham sandwich for me, BLT for Mara, coffee for both. Mara wanted a Reuben but was afraid to risk it here. For once, she didn't ask for separate checks. Her finances must have been pretty tight.

We ate in silence and I spent the time brooding. I'd come off rather badly at Insburg, and I couldn't blame it all on the brown suit. Truth to tell, I'd hit a stone wall with Blossom Harlow, MRS., and I'd fared no better with William Murphy. Without Mara's newfound skills, we'd have come away empty. On top of that, Mara had zapped me with peeking at her personnel file. On campus, she'd deferred to my knowledge of the territory, but out here we were on an equal footing. Or maybe she was better equipped for it than I was.

I also worried about what Staggart and Dean-Dean might be cooking up. My internals were playing a nice string quartet, but every time I thought of Dean-Dean a bassoon would bleat in on top of the strings.

Nothing like that had ever happened before, so maybe my hallucinations were developing new tricks.

To lift the gloom, I tried a bit of levity. When I paid the check with my credit card, I gave the waitress a serious look and asked, "Do I sign your name or mine?"

"Sign anything you like, Cupcake," she chirped. "It goes on your card anyway."

I signed my name without further comment. Mara made a great study of keeping a straight face. Nor did she comment outside as we fought through a gusty wind back to the car.

Once we had the engine running, though, she mimicked the serious look I'd given the waitress and said, "All right, Cupcake, what do we do now?"

That started us laughing—deep, uncontrollable, satisfying laughter that swept away my saturnine mood. It seemed to affect Mara the same way. I realized we'd never laughed together before, and I rather enjoyed it.

"I had that put-down coming," I said when I could breathe again. "Some Englishman once said, 'When a German tries to be graceful, he falls down the stairs.' The same thing happens when I try to be funny."

"I don't know." She gave me a sardonic blue glance. "I thought you were hilarious. But really, what *do* we do now?"

I pulled back onto the interstate in the deepening twilight. "We drive into Laila's bi-county area and tuck in somewhere for the night. Tomorrow morning we find all the information we can and hope we stumble onto something that brings what we already know into focus."

"We can hope," she said. "We already have masses of information, but none of it points toward solving the murder. Where will we stay tonight?"

I hadn't thought that far ahead. "We ought to find a motel somewhere out there."

"Two motels," she said. "We've started enough rumors already."

"Okay," I said. "Two motels." I should have thought of that first, but I'd been too busy brooding about my poor showing in Insburg.

We drove on into the night, with nothing to see except the highway sliding past in our headlights and nothing to hear except the engine drone and the low whine of tires on pavement. The car seemed an enclosed world, a sealed capsule spinning through space. I felt as if time itself had ceased to exist.

Mara broke the silence. "You told me about your problem with Staggart. I ought to tell you about myself."

I risked a momentary glance at her face and saw intense emotion written there. The last thing I wanted was an emotional entanglement, so I said, "You don't have to tell me anything."

"Don't get noble about it," she said. "I got you into this mess about Laila, and you have every right to know why I'm . . . the way I am."

"I'm not getting noble," I said. "In the Laila business, I'm saving my own skin. And if you'll pardon my repeating myself, you don't have to tell me anything."

Her chin lifted that significant fraction of an inch. "All right, I don't *have* to tell you. You've helped me do things I couldn't do for myself, and you haven't tried to . . . um . . . color outside the lines or anything." Irritation tinged the emotion in her voice. "For sixteen years I haven't told this to anyone, and now for some dumb reason I don't understand I want to tell you. So quit arguing about it and listen."

"Yes, ma'am," I said.

She looked out at the darkness for a few moments, then began. "You've read my file, so you know I was born in rural Kentucky and

named Alice Thornton. My parents raised me in a very small, very strict country church. We didn't travel, we didn't go to movies, and we didn't watch much TV. The church families formed an insulated fundamentalist community. I grew up thinking all men were surly and all women submissive, and that God intended it that way. Every few weeks, the church pounded Ephesians 5:22 into us: 'Wives, submit yourselves unto your own husbands, as unto the Lord.' "

She paused and searched my face, apparently trying to see my reaction. I studied the road and said nothing.

"I never dated," she said. "That set me apart in high school. When I was sixteen, an older man—he was twenty-nine—began taking me home from church. I was flattered. He asked me to marry him, and I accepted because I thought that was God's plan. It thrilled my parents because they believed their daughter was doing what women were supposed to do."

She spoke as if to herself. "I spent the next three years as that man's servant. He took me out of school and put me to keeping his house and vegetable garden. He went to work every day—he was a carpenter—but I stayed home and went nowhere except to church with him."

She paused and I said, "Sounds like the old 'barefoot and pregnant' routine."

She gave a bitter laugh. "He tried that, too, but for some reason it didn't work. Not for lack of effort on his part. He called it my duty. I came to hate being touched."

I could find no way to escape her story. I felt like Coleridge's wedding guest who had to listen to the Ancient Mariner's tale whether he wanted to or not. And the wedding guest didn't have a headache.

"That doesn't sound like much of a life," I said.

"It was no life at all." Mara stared out at the highway. "I had time to read the Bible, though. I learned that the same passage in Ephesians

speaks to husbands as well as wives, and I found Peter's instruction that husbands honor their wives as 'heirs together of the grace of life.'"

She sighed. "I tried to tell my husband that. He told me to shut up and do what I was told. Next day I left him."

"How old were you then?" I hated that man for the damage he'd done to the concept of manhood.

"I was nineteen, with no high school diploma and no saleable skills. I used grocery money to catch a bus into Louisville and got a job as a waitress. I found a woman lawyer who handled my divorce on credit. It took me three years to clear my debt to her. She also helped me change my name to signify a complete break with the past."

"You chose 'Mara' because it means 'bitter'?"

That drew a sad smile. "I followed Naomi's example in the book of Ruth, though our reasons were different. My lawyer also told me about GED tests, so I took one and passed it. That's the first time I realized I had brains enough to make something out of myself. I used the GED to join the Army because it offered educational benefits."

My hands tightened on the wheel. "That wasn't an easy way to go. Some of the drill sergeants—"

"Found out I didn't play their game. That set me apart from the women, too. So I spent my off-duty time earning college credits. I knew my church and parents had lied to me, and somehow I felt a deep drive to find out what was actually true. No matter how ugly the truth turned out to be, I had to know."

"No relativism?" I asked. Now she had me curious. "You couldn't just believe something that made you feel comfortable?"

She looked at me like I'd said the Indians could buy Manhattan back for twenty-four post-Carter pennies. "Relativism is wishing, not thinking. The only reason for believing something is that it's true. How you

feel about it doesn't matter." She caught her breath and continued. "In college after my discharge I studied all the faiths I could find. All except Christianity. My church had cured me of that."

Now it was my turn to sigh. "I understand. Seeing bad conduct by Christians can drive people away from Christianity itself."

She turned to face me. "You're describing an emotional reaction, not a reasoned process. But by the time I figured that out, I'd settled into Wicca as the closest to truth I could find."

"How did a Wiccan get accepted in a seminary?"

"You shouldn't have to ask that." She gave a bitter laugh. "Diversity is the god of the educational world, and several seminaries wanted to prove how inclusive they were. In spite of my having to work my way through undergraduate study, my grades were good enough to get their attention. Three seminaries offered scholarships. I took the best offer."

"That sounds like a tough and lonely way to go." My problems in graduate school looked pretty mild beside her life story.

"I don't allow myself to get lonely. I don't need anything except my job and my discipline. That's why I have to hold on to them. They're why I have to get this Laila mess straightened out."

"We both have to. Unless you'd care to go halves with me on a used-car lot."

"Go halves? I can't even pay to have my clunker fixed." When I looked at her in alarm, she added, "My credit card can cover the motel. It's a stretch, but I can handle it if I keep my job."

Lights appeared in the distance. "That's the town of Bullerton up ahead," I said. "It's a county seat and within fifty miles of every place we need to visit. We're more likely to find motels there than farther on."

"It's your decision," she said. "I haven't even looked at a map."

Bullerton had a population of six thousand, but we found no

motels on the eastern side of town. I was about to decide I'd been too optimistic, but at the western city limits we found two motels side by side. Both appeared undistinguished, but I parked in front of the better one.

"This one's for you," I said. "Use my tag number when you register."

She came back a few minutes later for her suitcase. "They asked no questions," she said. She scowled at the other motel and asked, "Are you going to stay in that flea trap?"

"I'll be fine," I said. "I slept in worse in Honduras."

She looked doubtful but carried her bag into her motel. I watched through the glass doors until she disappeared around a bend in the hall. Though I was certain no one had followed us from Overton City, uneasiness crept into my stomach. Mara and I both had cell phones. But still, she was a woman and she was being left alone in a strange town.

My motel proved to be everything one could wish for in a barracks for migrant workers. Most of the rats had already gone to bed and the cockroaches seemed fairly tame. I found no bedbugs under the mattress when I stashed my brown suit there for overnight pressing. The napkin-thin towel convinced me not to investigate the shower until morning. The bedsprings (yes, *springs*) screeched like a giant cricket fiddling on a blackboard with a hoe file, but I was too tired to worry about it.

For a few minutes I lay still, brooding on the day and the situation. Mara's story had moved me more than I liked to admit. She'd clawed her way up from nothing to earn a Ph.D. Her determination not to be managed and her determination to find truth had cut her off from other people. But now that she had her degree and believed she'd found truth, what was she going to do with them? I wondered if she'd thought of that.

With an effort, I forced my thoughts back to my own situation.

We'd placed a terribly high bet on finding the key to Laila's murder out here in her home territory.

But what if we found nothing?

At long last, haunted by the sound of Clyde McCoy's mocking *wah-wah* mute, I dropped into a restless sleep.

CHAPTER 29

Mara and I survived our night in shabby motels as well as breakfast in a restaurant that made Brimstead's look like Antoine's. A phone call to Bi-County Consolidated High School got me an early afternoon appointment with Morris Wimberly, the principal who'd written Laila a letter of recommendation. I didn't lie too badly—just repeated the story that I was a professor researching a posthumous recognition of Laila for the university yearbook. Who knows? Dean-Dean might even make me write one. If I ever got reinstated, that is.

Nine o'clock that morning found Mara and me approaching Laila's hometown, the tiny farm village of Alfalfa Heights. It lived up to both words of its name. It was built on a mound that towered a full four feet above the surrounding fields. The other land lay flat as a billiard table without pockets, its surface brown rather than green now that the crops had been harvested. A few grain elevators here and there evidenced what the crops had been.

The town consisted of a dozen unpainted buildings straddling a two-lane asphalt county road. Half the buildings stood empty and unrepaired. Two pickup trucks waited by the gas pumps in front of a convenience store. None of the three men inside responded to our inquiry about Laila, but all agreed we ought to talk to Sophie. They seemed to assume I knew who Sophie was.

But I didn't, so I asked, "Who?"

"Sophie Sloan, her mother. You don't know much, do you?"

"No, I don't," I said. "How did you ever guess?"

It didn't take long to find Sophie's house in a town with only six occupied buildings. Hers was an unpainted prefab with plywood walls and floors. A drunken beetle could have crossed the living room in seven seconds flat. Sophie herself must have been close to eighty years old. She was small and canary-thin, but with a deep, throaty voice. Her sharp black eyes offered stark contrast to her gray hair and drab complexion.

She seated us on a faded couch and settled herself into the room's only chair. It stood at a sewing machine buried beneath a pile of men's shirts.

"You've come about Dee Laila," she said. "When I heard she'd been killed, I knew somebody would come."

"Yes, ma'am," Mara said before I could speak. "We hoped you could tell us something about her. The more we know about her, the more likely we are to find out who killed her."

"Who killed her?" Mrs. Sloan said. "That could've been anyone she ever knew. She gave us all reason enough."

Her word *us* gave me a jolt, but I said nothing. Neither did Mara, who merely leaned forward expectantly.

Mrs. Sloan continued, her face sad but without tears. "Dee Laila was the only child Jed and me had, and we loved her too much. Or maybe not enough. We couldn't say no when she wanted something. We lived on our own farm then, and money wasn't too tight. It's no wonder she

grew up thinking nobody else mattered."

Mara and I said nothing. Mrs. Sloan spoke again, now as if to herself.

"Most people get their selfishness knocked out of them at school, but she was born knowing how to make people do what she wanted. She could talk 'em into using their lunch money to buy her candy. Still, things weren't too bad till she turned sixteen and Jed bought her a car. When he did, he bought us two years of nightmare. We never knew where she was or what she was into. She always lied when we asked, so we finally quit asking."

Mara spoke softly. "Did you ever find out?"

"We found out when Sheriff Briarcliff came and arrested her. She'd organized a teenage gang that stole everything in two counties that wasn't tied down. They was only convicted of one burglary, though. They all got probation, and I hear the younger ones got their records cleared. But Dee Laila was eighteen, so her record stood. We was just grateful she didn't go to prison."

"Who were the others?" I asked. This was the first lead to more than we already knew.

Mrs. Sloan frowned. "There was the Wiggins twins, Neila and Sheila. Neila died of pneumonia a few years back, and Sheila moved to St. Louis. Bobby Harkins went off to school somewhere back East and I lost track of him. Lem Peterson was in the group, but he drove his Harley under an eighteen-wheeler a couple of years ago. And there was someone called BJ that I never met. Dee Laila had others in her gang, but I never knew the ones that didn't get convicted. Except, she once mentioned the Wimberly kid, the one that works over at Bi-County High now."

Mara spoke in a murmur. "I know that must have been painful for you. . . ."

The black eyes focused on her but still shed no tears. "That wasn't all. Jed couldn't take it when they found Dee Laila guilty. He just up and left—said he was going into town for supplies, but he left our pickup in front of the feed store and never came back. I couldn't keep the farm up, so I sold it and moved in here."

"And Dee Laila . . . ?" Mara let the question hang.

"I lent her money to go to college over in Insburg. That's the last I heard from her." Mrs. Sloan's gaze shifted to me. "I see you looking around and wondering how I manage to get by. I still have a little something left from the farm. And I can sew."

She pointed to the pile of shirts. "They don't make shirts now with accurate sleeve lengths. Everything's 32/33 or 34/35. So some of these well-off farmers around here pay me to alter their sleeves to the right length. I'm the only one in two counties who'll do it, so they pay pretty well." She laughed. "I thank the Lord for stingy manufacturers. They're what keep me eating."

"Your daughter had quite a bit of expensive equipment," I said. "You should get a fair amount of money from it."

She sniffed. "Any money Dee Laila got is dirty money, and I don't want any of it. Tell them to give it to a church."

"I'll tell them," I said, and stood to leave.

Mara went over and squeezed her hand. "Thank you for sharing. I know it wasn't easy."

Mrs. Sloan's eyes for the first time showed tears. "I wish I'd had a daughter like you."

"And I wish I'd had a mother like you." Mara gave her a quick hug and hurried past me to the door, her eyes averted. By the time I reached the car she had her seat belt on.

"Forgive my question," I said, "but what did happen to your parents?"

"I don't know." She stared out through the windshield. "If they or my husband ever tried to trace me, I never heard of it. I think they wrote me off—put me down the memory hole as completely as I did them."

We drove back toward Bullerton in silence, but her words and those of Mrs. Sloan echoed in my mind. One family was too authoritarian, the other too permissive, and both extremes resulted in total estrangement. Yet the profound mystery of character formation had made the results so different in other ways: Laila so completely pathological, Mara so adamantly ethical.

Our silence continued as we lunched on prefab sandwiches and Cokes at a truck stop and then drove to Bi-County Consolidated High School. It consisted of three connected brick buildings isolated above bare, open fields that seemed as endless as a calm sea.

In spite of the cold wind, we paused outside the car to gaze at the open expanse, and I quoted the line that described my feelings: " 'The lone and level sands stretch far away.' "

For the first time since we'd left Alfalfa Heights, Mara came alive. "That much fits, but not the rest of it. The lines just before that are, 'Round the decay / Of that colossal Wreck, boundless and bare. . . .' There's no decay of any colossal wreck around here. Those buildings look well-maintained. And those fields may be boundless, but they're only bare because the harvest is in and the winter crop hasn't come up yet."

Another score for her erudition. Those lonely years she'd spent by herself—she must have spent them reading.

"All right," I said. "So you've read Shelley. Try this one: 'My glass is full, and now my glass is run, / And now I live, and now my life is done.' "

"Easy." The blue eyes laughed. "That was written by Chidiock Tichborne in 1586 before his execution in the Tower of London. The allusion is to an hourglass."

"I give up," I said. "Look, it's okay that you've read everything, but you didn't have to remember it."

She laughed aloud and changed the subject. "I know you dread this interview, Cupcake, but let's go in and get it over with."

"I can imagine being in my cups," I said, "but not as pastry."

She was gracious enough to let that one pass.

Inside, we checked in with a middle-aged secretary behind a name sign that announced her as Ms. Lydia Tenfife. She reminded me of a medieval dragon guarding a horde of treasure. Remembering the cupcake incident, I resisted the temptation to ask for St. George. Instead, I gave our names and said, "I have an appointment with Mr. Wimberly."

The dragon deigned to announce me over an intercom, and after a while the treasure horde came out to greet me. Morris Wimberly was a sallow-complexioned man of medium build, and he had the manner of one accustomed to telling people what to do. He wore his suit coat unbuttoned in deference to a pudgy abdomen. The suit was dark blue, which meant he out-authoritated my brown one. His face wore an impatient expression.

I introduced myself and Mara and asked if there was somewhere we could talk.

Looking at Mara, he said, "Mr. Barclay, I believe I granted the appointment to you."

Before I could object, Mara looked at me and said, "That's fine, Dr. Barclay. I'll wait out here." She emphasized the title *Dr.*, nicely neutralizing Wimberly's demoting me to Mr.

Wimberly shut his office door behind us and motioned me to a

chair more or less facing his desk. I gathered he liked to keep the desk between him and his visitors but didn't want to seem too obvious about it. He occupied his swivel chair, clasped his hands in the Dean-Dean manner, and eyed me across the desk.

"Well, Mr. Barclay," he said, "you're writing a posthumous appreciation of Miss Sloan. What do you want to know about her?"

I showed him my most innocent smile. "Mainly, I'd like to know why you hired a teacher with a criminal record."

His face reddened. "I . . . uh . . . *we* didn't know about that when we hired her. By the time we found it out, she'd established herself as an excellent teacher and a valuable colleague."

That excuse had more holes than the average golf course, but I let it pass. I needed to shake something loose, and do it quickly before he had time to gather his wits.

"Come off of it, Wimberly." I used the military voice I hadn't used in years. "You were schoolmates with Laila Sloan in this very school. You knew exactly what she was into."

His face turned deeper crimson. "We . . . uh . . . *did* go to school here, but I graduated a year ahead of her. I had no idea what her group was doing until she was indicted."

"Baloney." I stood and leaned over his desk. "You were an active member of her gang. I have witnesses." I actually had only one witness, unless Sophie Sloan developed a dual personality.

Wimberly tried to bluff it through. "What do you think you can gain with that information?"

"I'm also a journalist," I lied. "Laila Sloan's career and the names of the people she manipulated would make a surefire true-crime story. But I'd rather find out who murdered her and limit my story to that. Which would you prefer?"

His hand dropped to his lap. "What do you want to know?"

"Everything you know." I sat back down. "Start with why you hired her."

"You've already guessed," he said. "She blackmailed me."

His face returned to normal color and his tone grew introspective. "For two years before Dee Laila got caught, her group ran wild—burglaries, larceny, vandalism, you name it. I was involved in the first year of those and . . ." He dropped his gaze. ". . . and personally involved with Dee Laila. But I was lucky. I graduated and went off to college before she got caught."

He looked up again, his eyes pleading. "I put all that behind me. Finished college, married and started a family, taught for a while and moved into administration. When this job opened up, I thought it was safe to come back. For several years it was. Then we advertised for a chemistry teacher, and Dee Laila showed up."

"Her specialty was home economics," I said. "She wasn't qualified in chemistry."

Wimberly looked away. "We often hire people outside their academic expertise. The important thing is knowing how to teach and getting along with students."

I'd heard that line before, and it always rankled me. But this was no time to argue educational theory, so I asked, "She made you hire her or she'd tell everything she knew?"

He nodded. "People whose farms and businesses we'd robbed were still around. They might have done more than get me fired." He stirred in his chair. "Strangely, she did all right as a teacher. Not great, but she learned enough chemistry to stay ahead of her students, and they liked her. No trouble there: I'd told her straight out if she got personally involved with one, all bets were off."

"Not great as a teacher? Your letter of recommendation said she was."

He shrugged. "You work in education, so you know the game. If I don't sing her praises, they don't hire her and she hangs on here like an Al Capone around my neck."

"Albatross," I corrected. Considering all we knew about Laila, though, maybe he had the right word. But I needed to know more. "Her file at Overton contains a letter that says she worked in Insburg before she came here, but the man who's supposed to have written it says she never worked there."

Wimberly shook his head. "Trust Dee Laila to pull something like that. She claimed that job on her application here, but I never checked on it. She had me over a barrel."

"If she never worked at Insburg, that leaves five years of her life unaccounted for. Do you have any idea what she did in those years?"

"No. . . ." He looked thoughtful. "Well, once in a group at lunch she said something about 'when I worked in Las Vegas.' I asked her about it later, and she claimed she never said it."

I was getting nowhere again. "Can you give me names from her high school gang?"

Reluctantly, he repeated the names of the Wiggins twins, Bob Harkins, and the deceased Lem Peterson, then added, "There was Brad Bergson, but he moved to Australia ten years ago. Shirley Potter was in it for a while. She's married and lives in Seattle, last I heard. That's all I can remember." He thought awhile longer. "No, there was a little freshman the year after I left. They called her BJ."

"BJ what?"

He squinted into space. "What was her name? Jefferson? Joseph? . . . No, none of those." He snapped his fingers. "Jones. It had to be Jones."

He rose and took two strides to a bookcase built against the wall. His fingers moved along a shelf of yearbooks, finally coming to rest on a single one. He lifted it from the shelf and flipped through it until he found the page he wanted.

"There," he said, holding it up for me to see. His finger moved to one particular photo and stopped. "That's BJ."

The caption under the picture read "BJ Jones." The face above the caption was young and immature, but readily recognizable.

It was the woman we knew as Brenda Kirsch.

CHAPTER 30

One-on-one, Morris Wimberly had the backbone of an amoeba, but as we returned to the outer office he metamorphosed into the stiff-necked administrator we'd met when we came in. It was a remarkable transformation.

We found Mara in deep conversation with the dragon, Ms. Tenfife, who greeted our appearance with an expression like we'd caught her shooting craps. Wimberly made no pretense of a gracious parting, but returned to his office without further comment. After he did, the two women exchanged smiles and handshakes.

"Thank you, Lydia," Mara said. "I enjoyed talking to you."

"And I with you." The dragon kept smiling and holding Mara's hand. "I hope I've been helpful."

"You've been very helpful indeed." Mara gently but definitely disengaged her hand.

Outside, the prairie wind blew cold dust in our faces. The Honda's windless interior brought welcome relief and its heater brought more as we drove back to Bullerton. Mara wiped her hand on her coat, but tried not to be too obvious about it.

"How did you make Ms. Tenfife smile?" I asked. "She looks like she could 'call spirits from the vasty deep.'"

"Unlike your Owen Glendower," Mara said, referring to the Shakespeare character I was quoting, "she calls gossip from the nasty shallow. What did you learn from Wimberly?"

I gave her a summary and asked about the dragon's gossip.

"Ms. Tenfife complained that Laila had more privileges than the football coach. I gather that constituted a serious inversion of the school's value system."

"Positively shocking," I said.

"When Laila began teaching chemistry, according to my source, she thought a valence was something you hung above a window. One Mr. Higgins, a rather fat physics teacher, carried her through that first semester by staying after school and getting her ready for the next day's classes. His wife put a stop to that early in the spring semester, but by then Laila had learned enough to get by on her own. No one ever said she wasn't smart."

"That's our Laila," I said.

"Not much specific after that." Mara made a moue. "Mr. Wimberly always sang Laila's praises, though Ms. Tenfife never saw a reason for it. She sniffed and said Laila always covered all the bases."

I chuckled.

Mara arched her eyebrows.

"Ms. Tenfife doesn't know what Laila did during summer vacations. She would disappear after graduation and not show up again until the first autumn teachers' meeting."

"Disappeared summers," I mused. "The five years before she got this job are unaccounted for, too, though Wimberly heard her say she once worked in Las Vegas. Maybe Sergeant Spencer can follow up on that."

Mara continued as if she hadn't heard. "I turned up one other gem. Ms. Tenfife says Wimberly went to an administrators' convention in Denver last week—the week Laila was killed. Those things usually open on Thursday night and run through the weekend, but Wimberly made a last-minute change and left on Tuesday. Ms. Tenfife says she usually makes his travel arrangements, but this time he made his own."

I gave a low whistle. "So he could have gone to Overton City and committed the murder. We came out here to narrow down our list of suspects, and now we've increased it."

"That's one we can hand off to Sergeant Spencer," she said. "What do we do next?"

"Nothing today." Outside, the shadows lengthened. "Tomorrow we'll drive to Prosperity and see what we can find out about BJ Jones, a.k.a. Brenda Kirsch. With any luck we can be back in Overton City tomorrow night."

She sighed. "Then we'll have to deal with our suspension. I don't look forward to that."

I didn't either, so we finished the drive in silence. The gloom continued at supper in the same shabby café where we'd risked breakfast. My internal musicians were more than welcome while they performed Schubert's Symphony no. 8 ("Unfinished"). We said nothing more than "Good night" as I dropped Mara at her motel. When she disappeared beyond the glass doors, the car seemed suddenly empty.

Back in my migrant-workers' motel, the well-mannered cockroaches deferred to my claim of squatter's rights. The rats apparently had insomnia, but were courteous enough to stay out of sight. For a long time I lay on my bed of screeching springs and brooded on our lack of progress. We'd turned up mountains of dirty laundry on all four of our likely suspects—six suspects, counting Threnody Harkins and

Morris Wimberly—but not one bit of information that made any one of them either more or less likely to be the murderer.

On that happy reflection, and with the bedsprings and my internal piccolo competing in different keys, I fell asleep.

Next morning, overcast skies and a sharp, gusty wind did nothing to dispel my downcast mood. My internal musicians dragged through some kind of funeral march. I hoped that wasn't prophetic.

That day's breakfast proved as perilous as that of the day before, but the sullen waitress had been replaced by a jolly, red-faced woman who liked to question the customers. I ignored her, but Mara answered graciously, eventually confiding that we taught at Overton University.

"How's Johnny doing over there?" the waitress asked.

"Johnny who?" Mara looked taken aback. "We have quite a few students named John."

"Students!" The waitress laughed. "I'm talking about Johnny Cantwell, the man you work for."

Mara blinked, so I interceded. "He's made quite a reputation for himself."

"I don't doubt it." The waitress beamed. "We knew he'd make a success at anything he did when he grew up."

"Were you kin?" Mara asked.

"Next-door neighbors. From the time he was housebroke, that boy had a special knack. He could always find out what people wanted and give it to 'em."

We said nothing, so she continued. "We thought at first he'd make a salesman. When he went to teaching school, we said he'd end up as principal." She laughed again. "We never dreamed he'd be president of a big university."

"He's certainly done that," I said, and reached for the check. "No telling what he'll do next."

The waitress followed me to the cash register and took my credit card. Remembering my fiasco in Insburg, I didn't try to be funny.

"When you see Johnny again," she said, "tell him Bertha Nussbaum said 'Hi.' "

"I'll do that," I said, and Mara nodded agreement.

"I can't believe it," she said as we drove toward Prosperity. "Can you imagine J. Cleveland Cantwell in short pants?"

"No," I said, "but I can imagine his finding out what people want and giving it to them. That's what he's done at Overton, but I don't think he's happy with the result. That last faculty meeting bothered him. I think he's realizing that if he doesn't define what the college stands for, someone else will do it for him."

She frowned. "That meeting bothered me, too, but as a newcomer I didn't think I should comment."

I felt a stab of conscience, though I don't think she intended to criticize my silence. The metropolis of Prosperity consisted of about ten buildings on each side of a two-lane highway. As in Alfalfa Heights, more than half of the buildings stood empty and in disrepair. A single convenience store was the only life showing.

Behind its counter we found an unshaven elderly man in overalls. He said the town used to have a Jones family, but he never knew much about them. He referred us to a man named Sherman at Sherman's Feed Barn. "Turn left at the next corner," he said. "You can't miss it."

He was right about that. The turn placed us facing the front of an unpainted, barnlike structure where the street ended a block away. Above the door hung a paint-flaked sign that announced, "SHERMAN'S FEED BARN, Solomon Sherman, Prop." The barn could have used a prop

because its walls sagged a bit left of plumb. I hoped they wouldn't collapse with us inside.

Most of the barn's dirt floor stood bare, but a wooden platform in a far corner held an assortment of feed sacks. From among them emerged another grizzled, overalled elder who admitted being Solomon Sherman.

I introduced us and said, "We're trying to locate members of a Jones family who used to live here. We heard you might be able to tell us something about them."

His look classified me as an Iranian used-car salesman. "And what kind of bill would ye be tryin' to collect?"

Before I could answer, Mara said, "Press, I think I left my purse unlocked in the car. Would you please check on it for me?"

Her gaze told me to get lost, so I retreated to the car. As expected, I found her purse locked inside. I looked back at the barn. Mara's gestures seemed to plead for Mr. Sherman's favor. He showed a grudging smile that gradually changed to enthusiastic. Before long, he grew as voluble as a carnival barker.

I sat in the car and watched the show. After awhile, Mara returned with a self-satisfied smile while Solomon Sherman, Prop., fondly observed her departure.

"What did you do?" I asked as we drove back to Bullerton. "Bribe him with a month's supply of gasoline?"

"Nothing so crude," she said. "I merely told him BJ and I were roommates in college, and I'd lost track of her. He was happy to help a lady with a problem."

"He thought I was a bill collector. How did you convince him I wasn't?"

"That was easy, too." The blue eyes danced. "I told him you were my boyfriend, and that you never told the truth when a lie would do

just as well. After he got through convincing me I needed a new boyfriend, he told me about the Jones family."

"What about the Jones family?" I didn't ask how she'd answered Sherman about a new boyfriend.

"He said BJ was a loner from the very first—partly because both parents worked and left her to her own designs. There weren't many girls in town, so she played mostly with the boys. She could outrun all of them and outfight most of them. With the ones she couldn't beat, she did enough damage so they didn't seek a repeat engagement."

Remembering Brenda's strength when she kissed me, I shuddered. The knot on my head started aching again.

"She played as many town pranks as the boys," Mara continued, "but she had no real trouble till she was a freshman in high school. Then she got into Laila's gang. Sherman knew about her suspended sentence, but he didn't know it had been expunged. He said she was a good athlete and some out-of-state university gave her a scholarship. Her family moved away before she finished. He heard Brenda married somebody, but he doesn't know who. That's the last he heard of the Joneses."

"Not much there that we didn't know already," I said.

"One thing more." Mara looked particularly proud of herself. "After Brenda and Laila's gang got convicted, one of the town boys made a derogatory remark about Brenda's virtue."

"I'd think that wasn't very wise," I said.

"It wasn't. Brenda brained him with a two-by-four, and he spent three weeks in the hospital. They had to reconstruct part of his skull."

I whistled. We already knew Brenda had strength enough to knock Laila over the head and strangle her. Now we knew she had a history of violence. And we knew she kept a blackjack in her desk drawer.

My head throbbed, suddenly flooding me with suspicion.

Brenda had bashed the head of one person who'd crossed her. Was she the one who did the job on me?

CHAPTER 31

We didn't talk much on the drive back to Overton City, and our mood remained grim. My head continued under siege: the lump on the outside kept throbbing, and one of the mad drummers returned on the inside. I brooded because I'd been slugged, and I worried about my suspension from teaching. All used-car-salesman jokes aside, what would I do with my life if I couldn't teach history?

Mara looked as worried as I felt. Her situation was worse than mine. As a new faculty member, she had no history of positives to mitigate the alleged negatives. There were also questions about her being stalked and what she would do for a car. I knew she couldn't afford to have the old car repaired.

We made two calls on our cell phones. Sergeant Spencer agreed to check on Morris Wimberly's whereabouts at the time of Laila's murder. Mara arranged a meeting with Dr. Sheldon on our way into town and asked him to develop a time line for President Cantwell's earlier years—one we could compare with Laila's. Though the difference in their ages

argued against it, their hometowns were close enough together that they might have met.

We didn't say much for the rest of the trip.

Around four thirty, Dr. Sheldon greeted us like an old lion licking its chops at lunchtime. "Welcome home from the wilds of the west, children. What have you to tell me?"

I held a chair for Mara and asked, "How about President Cantwell?"

Dr. Sheldon waved the question away. He wheeled his chair around to face us and boomed, "All in good time. Now *give*: What did you learn out west?"

Mara summarized our information from Insburg Tool and Trucking, Inc., graciously omitting the fact that we only learned it because of her intervention with Blossom Harlow, MRS. Even more graciously, Mara didn't recount my subsequent encounter with the waitress.

"Hmmmm." Dr. Sheldon kept rubbing his hands like a gloveless explorer in the Arctic. "So if Laila didn't work at the Insburg Whatever-it-is, we have a five-year gap in her time line before she shows up at Bi-County High. Offhand, I don't know how to investigate that gap."

"She once said something about working in Las Vegas," I said, and described my interview with Morris Wimberly.

Sheldon said nothing, so Mara reported her conversations with Sophie Sloan, Lydia Tenfife, and Solomon Sherman. It hurt my ego to recall that I'd initiated the western trip, but Mara had developed most of the information. Not that either of us had learned anything that seemed particularly noteworthy.

To round things out, I somewhat sarcastically reported the waitress's observations about President Cantwell.

Dr. Sheldon's voice softened. "Don't be too hard on him, Press. He's spent his life being a cork. He's always floated at the level of his sur-

roundings and never developed a level of his own. But that last faculty meeting got to him. Now, at age forty-six, he's realized he needs to be a breakwater instead of a cork, and he doesn't know how to make the change. He's never heard of the National Association of Scholars or the Council for Christian Colleges and Universities."

"Overton would have to make radical changes to qualify for the council," I said.

"Cantwell will find that out," Dr. Sheldon continued, "and he has his work cut out for him. Historically, secularization is a one-way street. No college that started down it has ever been able to come back. Cantwell can use your prayers."

That one struck home. I hadn't prayed in a long time. Not that I was bitter about Faith's death, but I was still numb. Three years was a lot of numbness, now that I thought about it. Dr. Sheldon's comment reminded me I needed to push my own pain aside and help other people with theirs. Deep inside, I already knew that. But I'd been too self-absorbed to act on it.

"All right," I said.

"One bit of bad news." The great voice grew low and somber. "Mrs. Jessel died Wednesday night while you were sleeping off that knock on the head. They buried her this afternoon."

"I'm sorry," I said. "We never know what kind of a life people with dementia have. But her passing will take some financial strain off of Giff." My conscience hurt because I'd skipped visiting her these last couple of weeks. I wondered if she'd known the difference.

Mara's eyes teared up. "She was such a sweet lady. She didn't know who was visiting her, but she always received us graciously."

I didn't know Mara had visited her at all. I found out later that in spite of everything else she had going, she'd visited every couple of days.

"I have good news, too." Dr. Sheldon's voice boomed again. "President Cantwell wants me to offer online courses in history."

"That's wonderful," Mara said. "How will it work?"

Dr. Sheldon pointed toward the notebook computer on the table beside his bed. "I log that gadget on to the university network and work through it. Earl-George came out the other day to set up my password and show me how to connect via the Internet. He isn't half as dumb as I thought he was. Did you know he's added an on-campus wireless connection?"

"He's a good computer mechanic," I said. I wasn't prepared to comment further on the ability of Earl-George's synapses to communicate with each other. My private opinion was that you could fly a B-52 between any two of them.

"Well, children," Dr. Sheldon said, "what will you do about your suspensions?"

Mara and I exchanged glances. It seemed incredible to me that we'd traveled together two days without raising that question.

"Nothing we can do," I said, "until President Cantwell comes back from his . . . uh . . . fund-raising tour." I found it politic not to suggest he'd been fishing. "Dean-Dean has made up his mind, and nothing short of a presidential order will change it."

Mara nodded agreement. "I'll try to talk to President Cantwell, too. And maybe Sergeant Spencer can help. He's an alumnus, so the president ought to listen to him."

"If all else fails," Dr. Sheldon said, "I know several good lawyers."

"Thanks," I said. "I hope we won't need them." I stood to leave, and Mara stood with me.

Outside, the last orange streak was fading from the evening sky. The night wind brought a growing chill, and I felt the beginnings of

deep fatigue. As we drove across town, making a ham sandwich at home seemed an onerous task.

"How about supper at Dolt's?" I asked.

"I've got to quit sponging on you," Mara said.

I thought of a snappy comeback, but it involved coloring outside the lines. So I said, "Okay, you can quit as soon as we finish supper."

She sighed and nodded. She must have been tired, too.

At Dolt's we endured the usual aural mayhem and saw the usual crowd of students who, as always, sat here in groups and yelled into cell phones at people who were elsewhere.

Mara ordered the Reuben she hadn't risked out west, and I settled for another ham and cheese. After the waiter brought our sandwiches and gave the customary command to enjoy them, we ate in silence. Truth to tell, we were both too tired to talk.

Over coffee, though, I raised the sticky subject. "I know you don't want to get obligated, Mara, but you can't get along in this town without transportation. Let me have your car towed, and let's get an estimate on repair. I can lend you any reasonable repair cost, and you can pay me back when it's convenient."

She looked pained. "That's sweet of you, Press, but I'm a bad credit risk. I'm still up to my ears in student loans. I live close to the campus. I can walk to work."

"The money is sitting in a bank doing nothing," I said. I didn't tell her it was insurance money from Faith's death, dedicated to Cindy's education. But I knew Faith would approve of my offering it.

Mara's chin lifted. "Press, don't you see that anything we do together will lend credence to Dean Billig's accusations? We can't afford that."

"The offer remains open," I said, "but we need to get your car

towed before my neighbors have the city do it at your expense. At least let me do that."

She gave a deep sigh. "All right." She couldn't have sounded more depressed if she'd signed up for five years in the Foreign Legion.

When I paid the check I scanned the restaurant to see if anyone was watching us. No one was.

"Before we have it towed," Mara said as we drove to her car, "I need to get the papers out of the glove compartment."

I pulled into my driveway and parked. Everything seemed quiet. The neighborhood looked the same as always, and none of the neighbors seemed to be watching. Nevertheless, it somehow felt like that final moment of stillness before the fury of a storm.

I walked with Mara to her car. She fumbled in the glove compartment and emerged with a handful of papers.

She moved around toward the rear of the car and said, "I'd better make sure I haven't left anything in the trunk."

I went with her.

She sniffed and said, "What's that awful smell? I didn't leave anything in there that would spoil." She started her key toward the lock.

"Don't open the trunk," I said.

"Why not?" Her hand stopped in midair.

"Look at the lock," I said. Even in the dark, I could see scars made by ungentle use of tools.

"Oh." Her hand dropped to her side, still holding the keys. Her face showed bewilderment. "Why would anyone do that? I don't have anything worth stealing."

"They didn't do it to take something out," I said. "The question is what they put in. That's a job for the police."

I led her back to my car, took out my antique cell phone, and dialed 9-1-1.

Long ago, in another country, I'd smelled that smell before. I knew exactly what the police would find in Mara's trunk.

The only question was who it would be.

CHAPTER 32

Mara turned up her coat collar against the wind's cold caress as we waited for the police. We did not talk. I think she must have guessed what we'd find in her trunk.

The first police vehicle arrived without siren or flashing lights and parked a discreet distance behind her car. The lone policeman gave her car a cursory glance, then joined us in my driveway.

I told him who we were and said, "That's the car that got bombed Wednesday night. We haven't been near it again until just now. We don't like the smell, and it looks like someone broke into the trunk. We're afraid to open it."

He called in more police, including a few grumpy specimens from the bomb squad. These looked the car over and crawled underneath the trunk area with flashlights. By this time a crowd had gathered. Other policemen moved people back and blocked off a wide area with yellow tape. A television van arrived and its crew shoved cameras in people's faces. Being featured on TV was a disaster Mara and I couldn't afford, so we lost ourselves in the crowd farthest from the TV van.

We need not have bothered. When the first policeman didn't find

us by my car, he summoned us by name on a bullhorn. Now half of Overton City knew the ruckus centered on us. The other half would know it before midnight, what with the TV cameras recording our conference with the police. I wondered how we'd explain this to the faculty hearing committee, much less to Dean-Dean.

By now we had enough policemen on site to put down a fair-sized insurrection. Blessedly, they kept the crowd off of my property. My neighbors didn't fare so well, but that was their problem, not mine.

A bomb squad man took Mara's keys, backed everyone else away, and opened the trunk. When it sprang open he grimaced and recoiled, fanning his face with one hand. Mara stood straight as a statue and just as silent, staring ahead while tears drew glistening snail-tracks down her cheeks.

She didn't need to see what was in the trunk. No policemen stopped me as I walked forward, squinting against the lights held for the TV cameramen. By tomorrow my face would be notorious on the airwaves. I hadn't felt so conspicuous since I testified against Clyde Staggart. This was another thankless and hideous task, but it had to be done.

"Don't touch anything," the bomb squad man said. "Stand out here and look. Do you know him?"

"I know him," I said, my voice quavering. "He's a student at the college." I half-expected someone to correct me and say *university*, but no one did. "His name is Marcus Fischbach."

I didn't say more. I was too distracted by the bizarre spectacle of the body. One of Marcus's hands clutched what looked like a fragment of polished quartz. His ears dangled earrings etched with the outlines of a five-pointed star interwoven in the ancient pentagram design. A pentagram medallion had been thrust into his mouth.

Most striking of all was the ornate handle of a dagger that had been thrust into the body just below the breastbone. I didn't know much about Wicca, but I thought most of those items were used in Wiccan rituals.

Their presence bred sudden suspicions about Mara. Not that she could have killed Marcus Fischbach. We'd left town too soon after I'd seen him alive. Some of her Wiccan contacts might have done it, though. I couldn't imagine why, but maybe Mara wasn't as "solitary" as she'd claimed. Again, she had no alibi for the time of Laila's murder, and she was strong enough to have done it. For that matter, she was strong enough to have slugged me and smart enough to have spent the night nursing me to throw off suspicion. I didn't want to believe any of these things, yet my historian's mind kept forcing me to face their possibility.

My head whirled with doubt, and whatever my internal musicians were playing dissolved again into dissonance. I felt like Milton's Satan must have felt floundering through Chaos, its elements too inchoate for him to either stand or fly.

Still confused and still dogged by TV cameras, I walked back to give the details to Mara. She received them stoically. Her jaw remained set, though tears no longer flowed.

"I don't own any of that stuff," she said. "I don't know where it came from." She stared ahead for a moment and said, "I don't know Marcus Fischbach. I don't even know who he is."

My former suspicions based on theoretical possibilities dissolved before her obvious sincerity. I felt ashamed that I'd ever doubted her. I realized I'd proved again that a historian's hypotheses can lead into error as well as truth. I still didn't understand the Wiccan implements, but instinct told me Mara had nothing to do with them.

CHAPTER THIRTY-TWO

Fortunately, the police kept the TV microphones away from us. Our images would be splashed all over the video, but for the present, at least, our words would remain our own.

Another police car arrived, and the bull-necked Clyde Staggart emerged. He spent a few minutes directing his team, then charged up the driveway to Mara and me.

Leering, he glanced from one of us to the other and eventually settled on me. "Press, you just can't stay out of trouble, can you?"

"I'm not in trouble," I said. "Marcus Fischbach is in trouble, and so are you."

He smirked. "How do you get that?"

I grinned at him with one side of my mouth. "Marcus is dead and now you have two unsolved murders on your hands. I'd call that trouble. Wouldn't you?"

His face reddened. "You'll soon have more trouble than you can handle." He turned to Mara. "I'll talk to you first. Come in the house."

"What house?" she asked. Her stunned expression changed to anger.

Staggart jerked a thumb at me. "His house. Let's go."

He made a bad mistake then. He reached for her arm to lead her away. Almost as a reflex, it seemed, she flinched that arm out of reach and, with the other hand, delivered a resounding slap to the back of his hand.

"Don't you touch me," she hissed.

Anger blazed in Staggart's eyes. "We're going in there, and I'm going to talk to you."

A few moments before, I'd suspected Mara of all sorts of things, but now I found myself defending her. "You're not going in there without a key," I said, "and I'm not giving you the key until she has a witness to make sure you behave."

Staggart flexed his wounded hand a few times. Mara had given it quite a wallop, and I gathered he wanted to make sure it still worked. His glance at me radiated fury, but he waved one of the uniformed policemen over to accompany them.

I handed him the key. "You have my permission to interview her in my living room. You do not have permission to search anything."

He threw another angry look at me, then barked a command for Mara to follow him. This time he kept his hands to himself.

Mara gave me a grateful glance and followed him.

"Take the Fifth," I called after her.

Now I stood alone in my driveway, though a couple of policemen watched me from a distance. Maybe they thought I'd make a break for it or something. The night grew colder and the crowd waxed louder. The TV newspeople scurried around soliciting opinions from people who had no idea what was going on, which apparently is what TV newspeople do best. But at last things were calm enough for me to think.

And think I did. I tried to remember what I knew about the pentagram. I knew it was ancient and ambiguous in meaning. In traditional Christianity it had symbolized the five wounds of Christ. I vaguely remembered it as the emblem on Sir Gawain's shield, elaborated as five groups of five sacred or virtuous meanings. But I also knew some Christians viewed it as the devil's footprint. Heaven only knew how many pagan significances it had. To nature worshipers, the five points represented spirit, air, fire, water, and earth. Anything beyond that escaped my memory.

I knew, though, that the pentagram was an altar symbol to Wiccans, and I'd bet my next paycheck (if I ever had one) that the quartz and dagger had Wiccan significance. But Wicca was supposed to be a religion of peaceful harmony, not violent crime. So was Christianity, but

supposedly-Christian nuts bombed abortion clinics. Maybe the Wiccans had a few nuts, too.

But I was more certain than ever that Mara wasn't one of them. And if, theoretically, she ever did commit a murder, she had brains enough not to incriminate herself with Wiccan paraphernalia. If anything, someone was trying to frame her by committing murder in the manner of a satanic cult. But Wiccans didn't believe in Satan. So whoever killed Marcus Fischbach knew even less about Wicca than I did.

What, then, was I going to do about it? That's where my brain dissolved into quicksand and my internal musicians mocked me with something hideous by Prokofiev.

So I dialed Dr. Sheldon's number on my cell phone and told him what was going on.

"What are they doing with Mara?" he asked.

"Homicide is questioning her," I said.

He harrumphed into the phone a few times before adding, "She may need more help than you or I can give. I know a good lawyer who represented me a few years ago in a rather unfortunate matter. I'll call him if you think it warranted."

"I'll keep an eye on things," I said.

He harrumphed again. "Do that, my boy. Right now I am deeply engaged in that research we discussed earlier this evening." He rang off before I could answer.

I stood awhile longer in the cold, trying unsuccessfully to get my brain back in gear. Mara, Staggart, and the uniformed policeman emerged from the house. Instead of returning to me, they cut across the lawn to a police car. Mara and the policeman got into it. The car pulled away and headed toward downtown. Staggart collected his dogfaced sidekick and strode back toward me. I didn't like the look on his face.

I took my cell phone and hit Redial.

"What is it this time?" Dr. Sheldon didn't like his research interrupted.

"They've taken Mara downtown," I said. "You'd better call that lawyer."

CHAPTER 33

Come inside," Staggart said. "You have questions to answer."

Dogface stood behind him and said nothing. I reconfirmed the fact that he looked like a basset hound and was considerably less attractive than the average mutt. It occurred to me that I'd never heard him speak. I wondered if he could.

"I'll answer the questions here," I said to Staggart, "and you can return my keys now."

Staggart dangled the keys in front of me but kept them out of my reach. "You can come inside or come down to the station," he said. "Your choice."

He had me there. I was too tired to go downtown. "You can use the living room only," I said. "Nothing else."

Dogface and I settled into chairs in the living room. Staggart paced the floor. He was too smart to read me my Miranda rights. He knew if he did I'd take the Fifth and tell him nothing. As long as my words couldn't be used to incriminate me, I'd play along.

He stopped pacing and pointed his finger at me. "What have you been doing since Wednesday afternoon?"

"On Wednesday evening I was getting slugged by an intruder in my house." I pointed to the still-present knot on my head. "Since then I've been trying to stay alive."

"*Where* were you trying to stay alive?" He resumed his pacing.

"It seemed prudent to get out of town—"

"With a good-looking blonde." He stopped pacing and pointed the finger again.

"I'd been assaulted and she was being stalked," I said, and summarized our itinerary. "If you're even half a policeman, you already know we stayed in different motels. So clean up your suspicions."

He stood with hands on hips. "Why did you go to those particular places?"

"Historical research," I said.

His voice rang with sarcasm. "And it just *happened* that everyone you talked to had known Laila Sloan. Why were you interfering with my investigation of a murder?"

"We weren't. We're writing a posthumous appreciation of Professor Sloan." I'd promoted her again, but Staggart didn't seem to notice. He was too busy looking skeptical, so for good measure I added, "I don't know anything about your investigation except that you've lied about me to Dean Billig. A competent investigator should have produced some results by now."

"How well did you know Marcus Fischbach?" Staggart was smart enough to change the subject.

"He took one course from me three years ago and made an *A*. Practically no contact since then. I've seen him once or twice on campus." This was literally true, but I was on thin ice. I might eventually tell Sergeant Spencer what Marcus said to me, but Staggart would only twist that information to convict me if he could.

CHAPTER THIRTY-THREE

"Why would anyone want to kill him?"

I turned my palms up in the French salute. "I don't know. But putting him in Professor Thorn's car looks like further harassment of her and me. You know what I mean: those fake e-mails, my getting slugged, her being stalked."

Staggart waved a hand. "You could have staged all of those."

I rubbed the knot on my head. "If I ever do stage anything, I'll make sure it hurts less."

He must have seen he wasn't getting anywhere. He tossed my keys into my lap a bit harder than necessary and headed for the door. "Keep your nose clean, Press," he called back over his shoulder.

"Take your dog with you," I called after him.

Dogface gave me a dirty look, but he made no comment as he followed his master out.

Through the windows I could see that Mara's car had been towed. The street would never be normal again, but at least it had begun to look normal. The TV people had decamped, and the crowd had gone wherever crowds go when the entertainment ends.

I sat still for a while and wondered about Staggart: Except for taking kickbacks, he'd been a competent Special Ops officer. He'd even pulled off some enviably good operations. Yet his homicide investigation, what little I knew of it, seemed hopelessly incompetent. Was it really that bad, or was something significant going on beyond my field of vision?

I was still mulling that question when the phone rang.

"Press, my boy," Dr. Sheldon boomed. "My diligent researches have been rewarded."

"Congratulations," I said. "Did you know it was almost midnight?"

"Spare me your sarcasm, child," he said. "You'll be happy to know

President Cantwell graduated from Bi-County Consolidated the year before Laila Sloan entered as a freshman. Since they came from different towns, he probably did not know her."

"Wouldn't his family have told him the scandal when she and her gang got caught?"

"By that time Cantwell was a senior in an out-of-state college, and his family had moved away. There's a good chance he never heard about Laila."

Dr. Sheldon rang off, and I stood there wondering what to do next. My body ached with fatigue, but Staggart had stirred my adrenaline too much for me to sleep. My car still held Mara's luggage, so I decided to drive downtown and hope the police didn't keep her overnight.

I'd just parked near the police station when its door opened and Mara emerged with an impressive man who stood about four inches above six feet. He was blessed with the facial features of a male movie star. He also had broad shoulders, wore a dark gray fedora above a navy blue overcoat, and carried a polished leather briefcase. I didn't have to guess his profession.

"Press," Mara said. "I'd like you to meet Brice Funderburk. Dr. Sheldon sent him to act as my counsel, and he got me out by threatening to file a petition for habeas corpus."

The way Funderburk looked at her left no doubt he wanted to win more than just the case.

"Oh." She looked like someone ambushed by an idea. "Brice, this is Press Barclay."

His professional smile looked sincere. "I'm very pleased to meet you, Mr. Barclay."

"Likewise," I said, and made the mistake of extending my hand.

Funderburk had huge hands and used them like the Jaws of Life. I

was lucky to escape without an emergency room visit.

"I'm glad you're here, Press," Mara said. "Now Brice won't have to drive me by your place to get my luggage."

"My taxi is at your service," I said.

Funderburk looked put out, but touched his fedora and took his leave with practiced professional dignity.

"What happened with the cops?" I asked as Mara and I drove toward her apartment.

She turned up her nose. "They told me about the Wiccan artifacts in my trunk. They didn't believe me when I said I didn't keep any. Somehow, they got a search warrant and brought back a load of them from my apartment. They said I'd get off lighter if I'd confess murdering that student. Things looked pretty bad for a while."

Her chin lifted. "Then a policeman who'd searched my place last week told them none of the Wiccan things had been there then. About that time Mr. Funderburk came in and told me to take the Fifth. They let him talk to me alone. After that, he made the habeas corpus threat, and before you could say 'scat,' they let me go."

"He must be pretty good," I said as we pulled up in front of her apartment. I'd never had any luck telling police to scat. Maybe I'd do better if I carried a briefcase.

"I'll take it from here, Press," Mara said as I lifted her bag out of the trunk.

I said nothing.

She started up the walk toward the apartments, then turned and flashed me a smile. "I did enjoy the trip, Press. Thank you again."

She walked away, carrying her suitcase as lightly as if it were filled with helium. I watched until she disappeared around a corner. As it had in Bullerton, her departure made the car seem empty.

It must have been one thirty by the time I climbed into bed. Fatigue ached in every cell of my body, the lump on my head throbbed, and my internal orchestra featured fluttering strings as background to a squealing oboe.

For a while I lay there wondering if Mara would have enjoyed her western trip more with Brice Funderburk. I banished that thought by reviewing everything that had gone wrong since Mara and I found Laila's body. There'd been so many mishaps, it seemed mathematically impossible that anything else *could* go wrong.

Based on past experience, I knew better than that.

CHAPTER 34

Sunday morning brought gray skies and a wet wind that promised rain or snow. I dragged out of bed around eight, labored through another ham-sandwich breakfast, and phoned President Cantwell before he left for Sunday school. I was lucky he wasn't out fishing.

I apologized for the early call and said, "I need to talk to you today, sir. It's important to the college."

"*University*," he corrected. "But I must tell you now, Professor Barclay: I will not Exert Presidential Authority or Usurp Dean Billig's Prerogatives in the Matter concerning you and Professor Thorn."

Dr. Sheldon would have responded by saying "horsefeathers," but with commendable effort I refrained. Indeed, I took great care to remain both civil and subordinate.

"It's not about that, sir," I said. "It's about Marcus Fischbach getting murdered. I'll be talking to the police about it, but since it involves the college I'd rather talk to you first."

That shocked him so much he didn't correct me for calling the university a college.

After a pause, he asked, "What do you want to tell me?"

"Nothing over the phone. But privately, in person, I'll tell you what Marcus said he was going to do about the college."

Another pause. "See me at one thirty in the executive center. I trust you have Something Substantive to report."

"Very substantive," I said, and rang off.

So what would I do with the long, empty morning ahead of me? I could grade research papers, but in my suspended status I probably didn't have authority to do that. I could try to make sense out of Mara's and my investigation, but I'd already hit the wall on that. I'd long since learned that successful research depends on asking the right question. So it finally occurred to me to ask, "Why is the morning empty?"

The answer was simple. The emptiness was not in the morning, but in me. Nor was it a new phenomenon. It was the spiritual numbness I'd lived with ever since Faith's death. So I chose a radical solution. I went back to church.

To avoid well-meaning friends, I sneaked in late and eased into one of the back rows. I'd no sooner settled in than a familiar sense of pain and loss descended on me like a poisonous fog. These morning services had been special times that Faith and I enjoyed together—no, more than enjoyed, for that special sense of being close together and close to God had become part of our very being. To be here without her seemed more than I could bear. I'd been right to stay away, and I shouldn't have come today.

I decided to leave. But my entry had drawn inquiring stares from neighboring pews. A premature exit would draw even more. I would have to remain and endure.

Then the solemnity of organ music flowed in to fill my emptiness and soothe the pain. My internal musicians held silent, and with a con-

scious decision I surrendered to the blessed sounds of the organ. That instrument's meditation was joined by congregational singing, and the deep harmonies of the hymn reinforced my sense that here in this place, in this experience, was the true reality, and the conflicts that had troubled me outside were trivial by comparison. Even without Faith, this was the closeness I'd known before.

But then doubts and questions intruded. If this was something Faith and I had enjoyed together, what right did I have to come seeking it without her? My action seemed somehow unfaithful to her memory. For a few moments I accepted the guilt—indeed, almost welcomed it—as a just punishment for my unfaithfulness. I could only purge that guilt by returning to the empty numbness that had been my life for the past three years.

My emotions commanded that penance, but then my rational faculty demanded to be heard. The closeness Faith and I had known here together was the best of earthly reality. But now she lived, unchangingly, in perfect closeness to the divine Presence—in the heavenly reality of which this earthly reality was only a pale imitation. Surely she should not feel guilty for experiencing a perfection beyond anything I could experience here on earth. Nor should I feel guilty for seeking the best that mortal experience could provide as preparation for the perfect reality of heaven.

In this realization, my guilt and doubt flowed out from me like an ebbing tide. With their departure I again let the prayers and the deep harmonies of hymns prepare me to receive Pastor Tammons's sermon.

His message from Revelation 3:2 was profound: *Wake up, and strengthen the things that remain, which were about to die; for I have not found your deeds completed in the sight of My God*. The pastor had told me before that God wasn't through with me yet, but now he applied that principle to

everyone: We all must continue our development and our service until the Lord calls us home. Whatever struggles we were going through now were part of that development process.

As he spoke, I felt a quickening through all my being, and a complete inner peace I hadn't felt since losing Faith. In the last analysis, spiritual truth has a divine simplicity. Its peace had been here waiting for me all the time; all I had to do was come and embrace it.

Nevertheless, I left quickly afterward. I still wasn't ready for people with good intentions to welcome me as the returning prodigal. But the inner peace stayed with me, a solid foundation of certainty beneath my churning anxieties. My investigation might fail and my career might be wrecked, but the fundamental truth of the Eternal would still stand. Somehow, that made all the difference in how I felt.

That underlying calm stayed with me at one thirty, when an impatient President Cantwell met me at the executive center. He sat behind his desk and seated me in front of it. That meant this meeting was very, very formal, but he nevertheless did not speak in his usual rhetorical mode.

"Well, Professor Barclay," he said, "what do you have to tell me?"

"Marcus Fischbach came to my office on Thursday. He said he thought there was 'something funny'—his words—with the campus computer network. He said he intended to find out what. I cautioned him not to do anything illegal, and he said he wouldn't. The next I heard about him, he was dead."

President Cantwell greeted that information with a hostile stare. "What did he say was 'funny' about the computer network?"

I met his gaze. "He didn't say. We didn't finish the conversation because Dean Billig sent for me and I had to leave."

Cantwell pursed his lips and drummed his fingers on the desk.

"And you assume Marcus's interest in the computer network led to his death."

"No, sir, I don't *assume* it. But I do *infer* it as a possibility the police will have to investigate. In any case, I thought you'd want to ensure the integrity of your computer network, and I thought you'd want to do it quietly."

He drummed his fingers again. "Why haven't you told this to the police?"

"They haven't given me a chance," I said. "They're hung up on the fact that the body was found in Professor Thorn's car along with some Wiccan symbols."

"Her car was in front of your house," he said.

"Yes, sir. It had been there since Wednesday night, the night an intruder knocked me in the head. When I didn't show for a meeting with her and Dr. Sheldon, she came and checked on me. She ended up nursing me through the night till I could navigate again. Meanwhile, someone booby-trapped her car."

He waved a hand. "We will not go into that. We were talking about the computer network. You think I should have some of the computer faculty check it out?"

"No, sir. If someone is doing something untoward with the network, they're the logical suspects because they have both access and the necessary technical knowledge. We need an expert from outside the college, someone who'll keep his findings confidential."

"Do you know someone?"

"Richmond Seagrave works for a computer security firm in St. Louis. I knew him years ago in Special Forces. He's tight-lipped and dependable. I think I can have him in your office tomorrow morning, and the two of you can take it from there."

Cantwell paused again and drummed his fingers. He looked like a man about to jump off a cliff into a promised safety net he couldn't see.

Finally he sighed. "Have your man phone me today, and we'll work something out."

Outside, it occurred to me that I might have set myself up to get fired. I had no evidence beyond the coexistence of Marcus Fischbach's suspicions and the fact of his murder. My inference of possible causation could be totally wrong, and Richmond Seagrave might find nothing out of sorts with the computer network. If he didn't, I'd be seen as an alarmist at best. At worst, Dean-Dean and President Cantwell would see me as a liar trying to divert attention from my suspension. If Clyde Staggart heard about it, he'd imagine a worse motive and look for evidence to prove it.

Strangely, though, beneath those anxieties, my newfound peace held firm.

From home, I phoned Richmond Seagrave.

He greeted my explanation with a laugh. "Press, trouble finds you like male mosquitoes find a blonde in a bikini. You couldn't stay out of trouble if they locked you in a soundproof box."

"Your principle is sound," I said, "but not your analogy. My entomologist colleagues would say you are projecting your own libidinous impulses onto innocent mosquitoes, whose genetic code inclines them to entirely different stimuli." For the sake of simplicity, I did not refute his assumption that my being locked in a box would not in itself constitute trouble.

Seagrave laughed again. "For stuffiness, Press, no one can match a Special Ops type turned academic. Yes, I can shake loose for a couple of days. I'm still curious about that wiped sector on your hard drive. How do I contact this Cantwell character?"

CHAPTER THIRTY-FOUR

I gave him the numbers and hung up, but the phone rang before my hand left the receiver. Cindy's voice came through with its special sweetness, though it sounded like she'd been crying.

"Daddy, is it all right if I come home for Thanksgiving instead of staying with Heather?"

My caution raised its readiness state to orange. "Of course it's all right, dear. I'll be delighted. Is there a problem with Heather?"

"No, not with Heather." She sniffed a couple of times and added, "The problem is Eduardo. He turned out to be a real jerk."

My caution went on red alert. "What has he done?" She'd been so confident about him before, but now I could almost hear her deciding how much she wanted to tell.

"He was so polite when we met this fall in our dorm's residence life program," she said. "I thought I'd found someone I could depend on."

She paused and I asked, "Did he prove otherwise?"

"In spades," she said, her voice low but throbbing with anger. "They'd been teaching us how we ought to be nonjudgmental and inclusive, and it sounded like a really good idea. But last night Eduardo tried to get *too* inclusive. . . ."

She paused again and I said, "He tried to include something that wasn't his to include?"

She sighed. "You could call it that. But the residence life group says I'm being judgmental."

"For rejecting unwanted advances?" This was uncharted territory for me. "I thought the feminist thing was adamant on that score."

She gave a sad laugh. "That's kind of . . . in a different mental compartment. The residential life program's emphasis this month is 'dismantling systems of oppression.'"

"And sexual continence is a system of repression?"

"That's what they're teaching, Daddy. But I told them I wasn't buying it. I said this was my business and I wasn't changing."

Now it was my turn to sigh. With relief. "Good for you, honey. Will you be okay until Wednesday, or do you need to come home early?"

"They're not going to chase me out of here early, Daddy." Her voice rang like iron. "I'll get in their faces every time they mention it."

My heart swelled with pride. "That's the spirit, Cindy. If you stand your ground they'll either come around or prove they're not the kind of people you want as friends." I sounded exactly like what I was, a father preaching to his daughter.

For once, though, Cindy didn't resent it. "That's what I think, too, Daddy. I'll be home around six Wednesday evening."

"I'll be waiting," I said, and we hung up.

Afterward, I sat down and worried the way all parents do when their children leave home and have to cope with the multifaceted threats of a fallen world. In the end, I said a prayer and resigned myself that at present I could do nothing more. Except chide myself for being behind the times. I'd known about indoctrination in the classroom, but now they'd moved it into the dormitories with peer pressure as enforcer.

Cindy would arrive Wednesday evening. But what would she come home to? If Mara and I hadn't found the murderer, or murderers, by the beginning of Thanksgiving break at Wednesday noon, our suspects would scatter to the four winds. And the faculty hearing committee would meet Wednesday afternoon. By the time Cindy got here, I might not have a job.

What good would my newly regained sense of the Eternal do if I lost the one thing that gave my life meaning? The emptiness of the house closed in, made more oppressive by a lyric melody from my

internal strings. The sight of the silent piano brought back grief as sharp and painful as I'd known in the first months after Faith's death. I knew I had to do something decisive or else sink into despair. But what could I do? Grade more research papers in spite of my dubious faculty status? Call Dr. Sheldon? Call Mara?

Before I could decide, someone pounded on my door. I looked out the window and saw two police cars. The pounding came again. Wearily, I shuffled over to the front door and opened it.

Beyond the clear plastic storm door stood two uniformed policemen and Dogface himself.

"Did you lose something last night?" I asked. "Did you come back for your bone?"

He said nothing, but one of the uniformed types held up a paper for me to see.

"We have a warrant for your arrest," the policeman said. "The charge is suspicion of murder."

CHAPTER 35

You might know Staggart would have them handcuff me and march me out to the police car in front of the whole neighborhood. The planned public disgrace didn't work, though, because as far as I could see none of my neighbors were watching. They'd get wind of it soon enough, but at least they wouldn't have visuals to start with.

We rode to the police station in silence, though Dogface gave me a dirty look every thirty seconds or so. At the station he disappeared, and the others booked me and read me my Miranda rights. At that point I took the Fifth and asked for the phone call I was authorized. They responded by isolating me in a tiny room with one shabby desk, two straight chairs, and no phone. I suppose the idea was to build anxiety and maybe keep me under covert observation.

Whatever their intention, I wasn't playing. I sat down at the desk, put my arms on it and my head on my arms, and pretended to sleep.

I almost did sleep. Then the door opened and I looked up to see two uniformed policemen thrust a small, raggedly dressed man into the room. He wasn't an inch taller than five feet, his face hadn't seen a razor

in a week or two, and, judging from his fragrance, he must have been overdue for his annual bath. When he talked, the smell of cheap whiskey flooded the room.

"I didn't do nothin'," he whined. "I was sittin' on a park bench mindin' my own business and they run me in for nothin'."

"If you're smart," I said, "you won't say anything to anyone, including me."

His voice grew confidential. "What are you in for? I bet you didn't do nothin', either."

I'd never seen a more obvious plant. Staggart must have thought I'd forgotten the interrogation techniques we used in Special Ops. What came next? Would this character start a fight so they'd have something to charge me with? Just in case, I rose from the chair and faced him. I certainly wasn't thinking like a professor now.

"I took the Fifth," I said. "If you're smart, you'll do the same."

"I could use a fifth right now," he said. "No kiddin', though. What do they got against you?"

"They don't like my decision to remain silent," I said, "and that includes you. From now on, you're talking to the wall."

He looked hurt. "That's no way to act. We're in this thing together."

I said nothing and watched his eyes.

"You ain't even bein' civil," he said. "You act more like a cop than them guys in uniform."

I said nothing and continued to watch. The little man dropped his gaze. Neither of us spoke. I suppose the two policemen were listening, for a few minutes later they burst into the room and dragged the little man out, protesting all the way. The door closed. Foot-scuffling, bumping, and more protests of innocence came from the hall and then the adjoining room. Sounds of fists striking something soft came through

the wall, accompanied by the supposed victim's pleas for them to stop beating him.

I have to give them credit. They put on a good show. I sat at the desk again, rested my head on my arms, and feigned sleep. The rumble next door climaxed with one tremendous bump, followed by silence. I didn't move.

Perhaps fifteen minutes later, footsteps advanced in the hall, paused at the closed door, and moved on. This happened several more times—part of the war of nerves, I guess. But I never raised my head or gave any sign I'd heard.

Finally, the door opened and I heard two sets of footsteps. I still didn't move.

Someone shook my shoulder, and a deep voice growled, "Wake up."

I raised my head and saw two burly plainclothesmen who were new to me.

The taller one smirked. "It's your turn now. You heard what your buddy got next door." He stood several inches over six feet and had the build of a professional wrestler.

"Did you bring my phone?" I asked. I made a point of not getting up.

He asked, "Where did you get the blackjack?"

"I've already taken the Fifth," I said. "I'm waiting for the phone call so I can get a lawyer."

"We found the blackjack in your office desk," the shorter one said. He had the build of a middleweight boxer. "What would a history professor be doing with a blackjack?"

"Fifth Amendment," I said again. "How about that phone call?"

They exchanged contemptuous glances.

"He's one of those," the larger one said.

"Oh, yes indeed," the smaller one echoed. "He does appear to be one of those."

"Fifth Amendment and phone call," I said, "and tell Staggart his amateur dramatic production didn't work." I lowered my head on my arms again.

The larger detective shook my shoulder. It felt like he was trying to yank it off.

"Look at me when I talk to you," he said.

I looked at him and said nothing. I still made a point of not getting up.

"Whose blood was on the blackjack?" he asked.

I said nothing.

"The marks on your tools match the marks on the car trunk," the other one said. "Why did you do it?"

I said nothing, making my silence as eloquent as I could. But my heart jackhammered in my chest.

The badgering continued for about fifteen minutes, and I met every question with silence.

Finally, the larger one said to the smaller, "Let's let him think about it awhile."

The smaller nodded and moved toward the door.

"Fifth Amendment and phone call," I said.

They gave me a hard look and left, shutting the door behind them. I put my head back on my arms and tried to sleep, but they'd given me something to worry about. Had they really found a blackjack in my office desk, and had my tools really been used to jimmy the trunk of Mara's car? Who was trying to frame me? Staggart or the murderer?

My thoughts whirled like I'd put my brain in a blender, and I

slipped closer to despair. This seemed to go on for hours, though I later learned it was about thirty minutes. Then a single uniformed policeman came in.

"That way," he ordered, pointing.

I moved in that direction and he followed. He didn't seem too worried about me, and I took this as a good sign. He stopped me with a touch on the shoulder and pointed me into another office. This one had a phone.

"One call," he said, and lounged against the doorframe.

Dr. Sheldon was a long time answering, so I gathered he'd been asleep. He should have been, for it was after midnight.

"I need a lawyer," I said. "They've arrested me on suspicion of murder."

"Horsefeathers," he said. "First it's Mara and now it's you. Next thing you know, they'll arrest the pope."

"He's out of Staggart's jurisdiction," I said. "I'm the one who needs the lawyer, and I need him before they figure out a way to hang me."

"They don't hang people now," he said. "They use lethal injection. Besides, you'll probably die of old age before the courts process all of your appeals."

"That's very comforting," I said. "I'm glad to know they put the court before the hearse. But we may need neither one if I get a lawyer tonight."

"That's a terrible pun," he said, "but I'll see what I can do. Confound it, why can't you young people stay out of trouble?" He hung up.

"Thanks," I said to the supervising cop. "He says I didn't win the lottery."

"Very funny," the cop said in a tone that said it wasn't. "Now follow me to the place we reserve for court jesters."

He ushered me into a cell with old-fashioned iron bars. I'd hoped for solitary, but I had five fellow boarders with ages from about twenty up past where you stop counting.

The eldest inspected me from head to toe and said, "I'm in for not payin' at the gas pump." He pointed to each of the others in turn. "Joe here stole a car, those two robbed a convenience store, and him . . ." He pointed to a well-kempt youngster with watery red eyes. "They picked him up for DUI, and then found he had a computer that didn't belong to him. What've they got on you?"

They all stared at me, waiting.

"They caught me with the chief's wife," I said.

The oldster snorted. "He ain't got no wife. She left him last year."

I shrugged. "I imagine that's why he was so upset about it." I was acting less and less like a history professor.

All except the youngest laughed.

"They won't keep you long," the spokesman said. "They'll just harass you awhile and let you go."

"I hope so," I said. I took a seat beside the youngster on the cell's one bench, leaned my head against the bars, and pretended sleep. That seemed the best way to avoid conversation. But my ears stayed wide awake. Going to sleep in this group of petty poachers wasn't a good idea.

After a long time I heard a loud voice calling, "Preston Barclay, you have a visitor." The voice belonged to the policeman who'd guided me to the cell. He escorted me to a small office where Brice Funderburk sat waiting. Funderburk still had a running back's build and a movie star's features, and to these he now added an impatient expression.

"It's two thirty in the morning," Funderburk said. "Don't you professors ever get arrested at a decent hour?"

"I'll try to arrange it next time," I said.

He glared at me. "If there's a next time, you can call someone else. What are you in for?"

"The charge is suspicion of murder. They've hassled me around some, but I don't know the evidence, if there is any."

"If I'm going to represent you, you have to tell me the complete truth," he said. "You can begin by telling me why you kept a bloody blackjack in your desk drawer."

CHAPTER 36

I'm afraid I showed Funderburk an unfriendly face. "If you knew about the blackjack, you already knew I was arrested for suspicion of murder. Why did you ask?"

Funderburk's jaw rearranged itself into a superior smile. "I like to be thorough. Now tell me about the blackjack."

"I have never had a blackjack in my desk, bloody or otherwise. I have never possessed a blackjack nor held one in my hand. I don't think I've ever seen one. If there was one in my desk, someone planted it there."

Funderburk raised his eyebrows. "Why would anyone do that?"

Now it was my turn to glare at him. "For the same reason someone stole a book from my office and planted it in Laila Sloan's office. For the same reason someone sent Laila a bogus love note from my e-mail account. For the same reason someone left a lay-off-or-else note in my office and took it back again while I was in class."

His eyebrows climbed another notch. It was an irritating habit of his. "And what reason might that be?"

"Didn't Professor Thorn tell you? We were trying to find Laila

Sloan's murderer before Captain Staggart could pin it on us. We must have gotten close, because someone planted false evidence on both of us, and we both received threatening notes. I got knocked in the head in my own house, and whoever killed Marcus Fischbach put his body in Professor Thorn's car and left Wiccan symbols there to implicate her."

His eyebrows descended into a frown. "What Mara told me is privileged information between counsel and client. Please confine your comments to your own case."

His first-naming Mara rankled me, but I had no logical basis for complaining about it. "All right," I said. "The police mentioned something about my tools being used to force the trunk on Mara's . . . uh . . . Professor Thorn's car. The cops checked my tools once before to see if I burglarized Laila Sloan's house. They decided I didn't, so they gave me back the tools. I put them away and haven't seen them since."

"So you're saying someone took your tools, too." Funderburk's eyebrows ascended again. I wondered how many calories it took for that exercise. It looked easier than jogging.

"If they were used on Professor Thorn's car," I said, "I'm not the one who used them. Are you representing me or the prosecuting attorney?"

He smiled the bland smile of a man who has nothing to lose. "We are exploring the possibility of my representing you. There are a number of possible defenses against a charge of murder—"

"Only one of them interests me: I didn't do it." I made my voice sarcastic. "Now, my sagacious *counselor*, which of the two murders do they suspect I committed?"

Funderburk contemplated his fingertips. "I don't think they've decided. I should think it depends upon whose blood was on the blackjack. Would you have any ideas about that?"

"If I've never seen the blackjack, how do I know whose blood is on it?"

He stood and raised his eyebrows again. "That would seem a reasonable proposition in logic. If the premise were to prove true, your inference from it would also be true." He cleared his throat. "I will see what I can do for you. In the meantime, you won't want to be going anywhere." He moved toward the door.

"On the contrary," I said, "I very much *want* to go anywhere but here. I presume a good lawyer can arrange that."

He sniffed and said nothing.

"One other thing," I said before he could escape. "Last Tuesday, Professor Brenda Kirsch had a blackjack in her desk. I don't know if it had blood on it."

"How do you know that?" he asked. "You said you'd never seen a blackjack."

"I said I didn't *think* I'd ever seen one, and that I *hadn't* seen the one they claim was in my desk. As to the one in Professor Kirsch's desk, someone else saw it there and told me."

His jaw tightened. "Who was this person?"

I met his gaze. "I'm not at liberty to say. Not until he or she gives me permission."

He said nothing, but stalked out and closed the door behind him. I sat there alone and wondered what the penalty was for murdering one's lawyer. Maybe I could get off for justifiable homicide. In his case, maybe we could call it justifiable insecticide.

I didn't sit there long. The policeman who'd brought me escorted me back to the holding cell. The youngest was asleep on the bench. The other four sat sprawled against a wall, staring into space. I assumed the same position against the opposite wall.

The elder spokesman's eyes probed mine. "I've been thinkin' you didn't talk straight on that story about the chief's wife. Is she blonde or brunette?"

"That depends on how she feels when she gets up in the morning," I said and dropped my head to my chest, pretending sleep. It was an old joke, but it ended the conversation.

I must have slept then, for the next thing I heard was a bored voice calling my cell mates by name. It was daylight. Pairs of policemen escorted each man to "see the judge," as they put it. None of them returned, and I was left alone. The police had taken my watch along with my other possessions, so I had no idea what time it was. After a while, a policeman brought me a cold breakfast whose only virtue was that I didn't have to pay for it.

I spent the morning reviewing all the information we'd turned up on Laila's murder. It still added up to the same thing: nothing. When I got tired of sitting, I got up and exercised—running in place, sit-ups and push-ups, other exercises I hadn't thought of in years. I'd be sore the next day, but right then all I wanted was to get through the morning. My internal musicians alternated between soothing me with lullabies and bugging me with atonal nonsense.

Finally, two cops I hadn't seen before told me to come with them. They led me to the room where I'd met with Funderburk, and I found him sitting there again. This time he looked smug instead of impatient.

He said nothing until the cops left. Then he made me wait a few minutes more while he cleaned his glasses. He put them on, slowly and deliberately, and gave me a condescending glance. "You're free to go, Professor Barclay. I have convinced them of your innocence. At least for now."

"That's good news," I said, "but not good enough. How did you convince them?"

He showed a self-satisfied smile. "The blood on your blackjack was type A. Laila and Marcus Fischbach both had type O."

"You ran the lab tests yourself, I take it?"

My comment did not appear to ruffle him. "If I had, they would have thought the test was biased. But their lab provided objective results. Beyond that, I convinced them I had witnesses who would place you in the western part of the state when Fischbach was killed."

"Staggart already knew that, so why did they arrest me?"

He gave his eyebrows another workout. "An attempt at misdirection, I'd guess. They probably hoped to confuse you with the Fischbach murder and then sweat something incriminating out of you about Laila Sloan. They've done a lot of that kind of thing lately. But if that's what they intended, they came up empty."

"So what do I do now?"

"You are completely free, though it wouldn't be wise to leave Overton City."

"How much do I owe you?"

"You will be billed. But I'll be happy to drive you home at no extra charge."

"Thanks," I said. I didn't relish his company, but it was the quickest way to get away from the police station.

He drove a Mercedes CL600 coupe with Capri Blue exterior and Exclusive Stone Leather interior. I wouldn't have known all that, but he volunteered the information. He also made a point of demonstrating the hands-off phone system on some inconsequential call that made no sense to me.

He navigated the city traffic with casual competence and parked in front of my house. He cut the ignition, removed his glasses, and made a study of cleaning them with his handkerchief. Still focused on them,

he cleared his throat and asked, "Tell me, Professor Barclay, what is your relationship with Mara Thorn?"

I turned and tried to look him in the eye, but he stayed focused on his glasses, which by now must have been the cleanest spectacles in the state. "We are professors on the same college faculty," I said. "At least, we were until we got suspended."

"Come, now." He threw a quick glance at me, put on his glasses, and stared ahead down the street. "Everyone knows you've collaborated on various activities. Do you know why she kept a package of ammunition in her apartment when she had no weapon that would require it?"

"I don't know. You'll have to ask her."

"I did, and she said, 'When the time comes for me to bite the bullet, it will be easier if I have one to bite.'"

"So ask her again. And say, 'Pretty please.'"

He grimaced, still looking straight ahead. "This is getting us nowhere, Professor Barclay. What is your relationship with Mara?"

"We are suspects in two murder cases," I said to his right ear, which was all I had to talk to while he avoided eye contact. "And we've worked together to try to find who the real murderer or murderers might be."

His eyes returned suddenly to mine with an accusatory gaze. "But you were suspended because she spent the night in your house."

"Yes." If he wanted to know more, he'd have to ask.

"And precisely what were you two doing there all night?"

I grinned at him. "You have a terribly suspicious mind. Why don't you ask her?"

His eyes narrowed. "I'm asking you. Do you have a romantic relationship with her?"

CHAPTER THIRTY-SIX

The grin left my face. "My only romantic relationship died three years ago. What happened to yours?"

That last was a shot in the dark, but it apparently hit home. I learned later that he'd been divorced three times.

"That's none of your business," he snapped. "And I *will* ask Mara. She's having dinner with me tonight." He sucked in an angry breath and turned on the ignition. "Get out."

I complied. Funderburk gunned the Mercedes through a screeching U-turn that shed enough rubber to retread a full set of tires. For all his middle-aged air of superiority, Funderburk was acting like a jealous teenager about Mara. A grown man wouldn't ask questions. He'd make his play with the woman he wanted, and if she turned him down he'd look for another.

Mara was far too good for that kind of man. But why did it matter to me? Was I jealous? I dismissed the thought. I'd come to think of Mara as a good friend. I wanted the best for her, but that was the end of it. If she wanted an officious snob like Funderburk, she was welcome to him.

Inside my house, I checked to see if anything besides the toolbox was missing. It wasn't. The black warm-ups that might incriminate me for violating the crime scene at Laila's house still lay in the washing machine where I'd left them more than a week before. I considered getting rid of them, but decided against it. If the police hadn't found them yet, they probably wouldn't.

My internal musicians suddenly went on strike, and the loneliness of the house seeped into my being like a case of the flu. To keep from sinking into the Slough of Despond, I called Dr. Sheldon.

"So you're out of the hoosegow," he said. "Did you break out or did my private shyster spring you?"

"Your vocabulary tells me you've been reading mid-twentieth-century crime stories," I said. "Your shyster did spring me, as you put it, but he'd rather send me to the electric chair."

He snorted. "As I told you before, they use lethal injection now. It's supposed to be painless."

"That's why Funderburk would prefer sending me to the chair," I said. "Where did you find him?"

Dr. Sheldon chuckled. "Let's just say I found him. He has the utility value of a good plumbing fixture. You don't have to enjoy its company, but you keep it around as long as it flushes when you pull the chain."

He'd apparently made an earlier acquaintance with plumbing fixtures than I, for the ones I learned on had handles instead of chains.

But he gave me no time for reflection. "Your friend Seagrave called me. When he couldn't find you, Mara gave him my number. We've set up a meeting with him at my place tonight at seven. He says he's found something interesting."

CHAPTER 37

We'd be meeting with Seagrave at seven, but what would I do with the rest of the afternoon? I called Mara and got no answer. I didn't call Seagrave because he'd have work to do before our meeting. I could stay home and mope, but that would bring back the despondency I needed so desperately to escape. More than ever, I felt unseen forces closing in on me. And I felt time stalking me like a tiger. If our investigation didn't hit pay dirt before Wednesday noon brought Thanksgiving break, we might as well forget it.

So I headed for the campus. I might yet be able to jar something loose. The skeptic in me said the effort was futile. The gambler in me said go for it. I chose to gamble.

I followed the walkway up to the campus, bypassed the liberal arts center, and climbed to the second floor of the science center. I found Bob Harkins in his lab, wearing a black lab apron and shooing a student toward a distant table. None of the students looked up as I entered.

Harkins greeted me with a scowl. "You're not welcome here, Press. You're suspended. You don't have faculty status."

I grinned at him. "You talk like a man with a bad conscience."

His jaw flexed. "You've already tried to ruin my marriage. What dirty tricks are you up to now?"

"If trying to find out who killed Laila Sloan is a dirty trick, I plead guilty. Besides, you messed up your own marriage when you chose not to tell your wife what you did in high school. Speaking of which, I talked to Morris Wimberly a couple of days ago. I gather he shared Laila's affections."

"The past is buried, Press. Why dig it up again?"

"Because in the present we have an unsolved murder. The last time we talked, you got so angry you'd have hit me if you'd been close enough. Maybe Laila made you that angry when you *were* close enough."

Bob's eyes narrowed. "If you keep making wild accusations, Press, you'll make someone angry enough to shut your mouth. Permanently."

"Is that someone you, Bob?" I asked.

He stalked away and left me staring at his back. I felt pretty foolish. I'd further alienated a former friend and hadn't turned up a single bit of new information.

I found Gifford Jessel behind the desk in his eagle's nest. He was leaning back in the swivel chair, hands clasped behind his head as he gazed at the ceiling. I envied the philosopher's prerogative of lounging and gazing.

But not for long. When he saw me, he sat bolt upright and stopped me in the doorway with a restraining hand, palm outward. For a moment I visualized him as Marshal Pétain issuing that famous order at the Battle of Verdun: "They shall not pass." My internal orchestra dramatized the vision by playing "La Marseillaise." Then Giff was again the balding philosophy professor, officious in performing some duty I hadn't heard about.

He let me know in a hurry.

"Don't come in, Press. The dean has appointed me chairman of your faculty hearing committee on Wednesday. We can't talk privately, or it will prejudice the hearing."

"I thought Dean-Dean had prejudiced it already," I said, careful not to enter the office. "The committee members know which side their bread is buttered on."

Jessel frowned. "That's a cynical thing to say."

"I didn't come to talk about that," I said. "I came to say I'm sorry about your mother and sorry I missed the funeral. I was out of town. She was a sweet lady, and I always enjoyed visiting her in the nursing home."

He showed a guarded smile. "Visiting her was like breaking open a piñata. You never knew what would fall out."

I moved to exploit the opening he'd given me. "Sometimes she made perfect sense. Sometimes she said more than she would have in days when she was more discreet."

His eyes narrowed. "Like what?"

I showed him the same grin I'd showed Bob Harkins. "As I said, she was a sweet lady. By the way, I'm still working on Laila's murder. Would you like to tell me any more about that?"

He stood and leaned with both palms on the desk. "I told you before, Press. There's a real murderer around here somewhere. If you keep provoking him, you're likely to get hurt. You and that Wiccan . . . *companion* of yours." He gave the word an unsavory meaning.

I raised an eyebrow. "Now who's prejudicing the hearing?"

His hands slapped the desk. "Get out, Press. I'll see you at the hearing Wednesday afternoon."

So much for philosophical detachment.

My watch said three o'clock—still time enough to chase down one

or two more suspects. I found Pappas, the janitor, in the basement. He greeted me with a hostile gaze and leaned on the handle of a wax mop, his biceps rippling under a shirt two sizes too small.

His guttural voice almost swallowed his words. "What you want?"

In our previous conversation he'd volunteered information he didn't have to. Now he'd turned belligerent. I wondered what had caused the difference.

I grinned at him as I had at Bob Harkins. "I thought maybe you'd changed your mind about saying you saw me someplace you didn't."

He shrugged one shoulder. "Why should I change?"

I dropped the grin. "Because Staggart isn't the only one who knows you served prison time for assault."

He shrugged the other shoulder. "He don't need my word now. Say he got enough on you without it."

That stopped me for a moment. I didn't know what to ask next, but I didn't have to because Pappas had something else on his chest.

"Mr. Staggart say you make out that I kill Miz Sloan."

"I *am* trying to find the murderer," I said. That sounded too defensive, so I added, "If that's not you, who is it?"

He sucked in his breath. "Someone already knock you in the head. You keep on, maybe you got no head for them to knock."

He turned his back and mopped the floor, great muscles bulging with each stroke. That effectively closed the discussion, so I climbed back to the ground floor, taking each step slowly and wondering what to do next.

I didn't wonder long, for I met Threnody Harkins at the main entrance. She gave me a look that made Pappas's glower look like a smile.

"Hello, Threnody," I said. "Been disposing of any more rivals lately?"

She broke eye contact. For a moment I thought she'd walk past

without conceding my existence. But at the last moment she spoke in her best up-East accent. "You will be very fortunate, *ex*-Professor Barclay, if someone doesn't dispose of *you*."

So now I'd talked to four of my five suspects, and all I'd jarred loose were more hard feelings. One part of my mind said quit before I dug myself a deeper hole. The other part said keep digging with the faint hope I might find gold before the hole fell in on me.

I decided to keep digging, and pointed my metaphoric shovel toward the gymnasium and Brenda Kirsch. Her office door stood open and I found her seated behind her desk. Her emerald-green warm-ups emphasized her roseate complexion, and her black eyes glittered as they had at our surreal tea party.

"Hello, Press," she said. "What brings you to the low-rent side of the campus?"

That was a smart opener. The new gymnasium complex had cost more than the sum of half the other buildings on campus. Brenda was serving catnip for my envy, but I hadn't come to argue about the administration's spending priorities.

I tried my own opener. "Tell me what happened to the blackjack you keep in your desk."

Surprise flickered across her face, quickly replaced by studied impassiveness. "What blackjack?"

"The one you keep in your desk drawer," I said.

She showed a coy smile. "How would you know what I keep in my desk?"

"Look," I said, "two people on this campus have been murdered, and I've been attacked in my own home. I know you kept a blackjack in your desk. What happened to it?"

She smiled again. "Now I know who stole the dean's passkeys."

"What happened to the blackjack?"

She looked down and opened the middle desk drawer. "It's gone," she said. She didn't look surprised.

"Suppose you tell me where you got it and why you kept it."

For once she seemed sincere. "You heard that two football players had a fight a couple of weeks ago? I broke it up right after one used a blackjack to split the other's scalp. Having any kind of weapon on campus would get him expelled, and the team needed him. So I kept the blackjack and only reported the fight. President Cantwell put both boys on probation and that was the end of it."

"What happened to the blackjack?" I was getting tired of asking.

Brenda again looked coy. "I don't know. I looked for it after you got slugged—that is, after you *said* you did—and it wasn't there. Some other thief with a passkey must have stolen it."

"Did the sap have blood on it?"

"I didn't examine it." The black eyes flashed. "Now tell me, Press. Who poked around in my office? Was it you or that blonde Wiccan who stays nights at your house?"

"She doesn't stay nights at my house. We were supposed to meet with Dr. Sheldon at his nursing home. When I didn't show and didn't answer my phone, she came to check on me. She found me unconscious and looked after me till I could care for myself."

"Which conveniently took all night."

"I got struck pretty hard." For emphasis, I touched the still-swollen knot on my head. When I did, I wished I hadn't.

"Struck by what?" Brenda laughed. "She *is* very attractive."

"There is nothing between us," I said.

She cocked an eyebrow in disbelief. "It's too bad, Press. I can understand why you prefer a blonde, but you and I could have had a beauti-

ful friendship." She gestured expansively to match her flight of rhetoric. "Why, with your historical imagination and my . . . *attractive qualities*, we could have matched the greatest friendships of history, like . . ."

"Hansel and Grendel," I said.

"Yes. . . . No, that doesn't sound quite right. But you know what I mean."

"I know exactly what you mean," I said. "Were you the one who slugged me?"

The black eyes flashed again. When angry, she looked as fierce as Threnody Harkins. "Professor Barclay, I'd never in my life do anything like that."

"Never in your life? Was it in some other incarnation you brained that boy in Prosperity with a two-by-four?"

Her face reddened. "I'd heard you took your little Wiccan for another overnight out west. You've both been snooping where you have no business. That can be dangerous."

I didn't let the reference to Mara sidetrack me. "What did that boy in Prosperity say that you wanted to put him in the hospital for three weeks?"

"That wasn't my intention," she said, and I had a momentary vision of her black-widow image among the china cups. "I didn't want to put him in the hospital. I wanted to kill him."

"Like you killed Laila Sloan?"

She laughed again. A derisive, humorless laugh. "So we're back to that. No, I didn't kill Laila, though in the old days I sometimes wanted to. And I didn't even know Marcus Fischbach."

"Are you the one who slugged me?"

"If I had hit you, Press, you wouldn't be here to ask. The boy in

Prosperity wouldn't have lived, either, if someone hadn't grabbed my arm when I swung."

She showed a bitter smile. "You're in over your head, Professor Barclay." She turned the formal title into an insult. "If you and your blonde companion keep poking into other people's business, someone's going to send you to join Laila and Marcus Fischbach."

"And who might that someone be?"

"I wouldn't know, Professor."

So now I didn't even have a name.

"You're the one playing detective," she said. "But if you and your pagan professor friend keep doing what you're doing, you're going to find out who it is. The hard way."

That ended the interview. As I wandered back home, I evaluated my afternoon's work. I'd talked with each of our five main suspects and hadn't turned up a single bit of usable information. All I'd accomplished was to make them angry. Angry enough for each to issue a warning that could be interpreted as a threat.

I wondered which one really meant it.

CHAPTER 38

When I arrived at Dr. Sheldon's room that night, the others had already gathered. Our host's wheelchair occupied the usual spot, and Richmond Seagrave sat facing him. His copper goatee glistened and, as always, I wondered if he waxed it. Mara's chair formed a triangle with the other two, though she'd backed off more than the usual distance. I placed my own chair opposite hers, expanding their triangle into a diamond.

"Let's get started, children," Dr. Sheldon said. "I believe Mara has new information."

Her chin raised the familiar fraction that meant she had her wind up. I wondered what had set her off.

"Sergeant Spencer called," she said. "Morris Wimberly's alibi checks out. He really was in Denver when Laila was killed. That takes us back to our original five suspects."

"Except for Marcus Fischbach's murder," Dr. Sheldon said. "The field remains wide open on that one."

"Not quite," I said. "Someone tried to make it look like Mara killed Fischbach, and someone had already tried to throw suspicion on her

for Laila's murder. That suggests a link between the two."

"*Suggests*," Dr. Sheldon repeated. "Not proves. Where is your historian's sense of fact?"

"Historians entertain working hypotheses," I said. "That one is logical enough until a better one comes along."

Dr. Sheldon knew when to change the subject. "Well, Preston, before we approach our chief subject of the evening, suppose you educate us on your accomplishments since my distinguished barrister sprang you from the hoosegow."

"I've managed to make a lot of people mad," I said. "Mad enough to threaten me. But I haven't learned one bit of new information. I might as well have stayed in jail."

Dr. Sheldon raised his eyebrows. "I daresay Captain Staggart can arrange that." With Dr. Sheldon, the eyebrow habit wasn't irritating, as it had been with Brice Funderburk.

He opened his mouth for further comment, but Seagrave interrupted. "You amateur Sherlocks can chase murderers on your own time. My interest is computer capers."

"Enlighten us, then, dear boy." Dr. Sheldon wasn't going to be one-upped by people he defined as children.

"I've never seen anything like this," Seagrave said. "If you'd told me beforehand, I wouldn't have believed it." He gave me a pitying look. "Your colleague Earl-George doesn't have sense enough to come in out of the rain."

"He's not my colleague," I said. "He's staff, not faculty." Standing on protocol is always a good move when you don't know what's coming next.

"You do Earl-George an injustice." Dr. Sheldon assumed his platform-lecture voice. "He does indeed know enough to come in out of the

rain. It is true, however, that he needs a qualified meteorologist to tell him when it's raining."

"Be that as it may," Seagrave said, "he let a stranger sell him the Brooklyn Bridge."

Dr. Sheldon would not be denied. "I take it he should have preferred the Golden Gate?"

Mara's foot beat a light tattoo on the floor. "If you learned gentlemen have finished insulting poor Earl-George, I'd like to hear what's wrong with the computer network."

"Glad to oblige." Seagrave stroked his goatee and looked at Mara, who responded by studying the wall above my head. "When I debugged your computers last week, I suspected something wasn't right with the network. Part of Press's hard drive had been scrubbed, yet he said he hadn't done it. He also said the computer was new when he got it, and he was the only person who used it. That didn't prove anything, of course, but it suggested someone was entering his computer from the network or perhaps somewhere outside of it. That's why I dropped everything and came when President Cantwell requested my services."

His tone grew ironic. "Press, you'll be happy to know your boss didn't hire me on your word alone. He asked for references and checked with them before he committed."

"President Cantwell has complete confidence in me," I said. "That's why I'm on suspension."

Dr. Sheldon harrumphed. "Less byplay, children, and more substance."

"It seems that your network added another server about three years ago," Seagrave said. His voice carried to all of us, but his eyes focused on Mara.

Seagrave continued. "You know Earl-George's reputation for scrounging equipment. So when a well-dressed stranger walked in, claiming to

be an alumnus, and offered him a late-model server with free software and other goodies, Earl-George didn't ask foolish questions. He did think to ask his benefactor's name. The stranger said his name was Joe, and Earl-George was too polite to ask, 'Joe Who?' "

"What did this 'Joe' do?" Dr. Sheldon leaned forward in his wheelchair.

"He installed the server and software and the other stuff," Seagrave said, still speaking to Mara, who continued her study of the wall. "And he worked too fast for Earl-George to keep up. Earl-George didn't worry about that, though. He was getting free equipment from an alum, so how could he lose? Sure enough, the network immediately speeded up."

"Wait a minute," I said. "The alumni donors I know want their gifts documented as deductions for income tax. Most of them want photos of themselves shaking the president's hand while a covey of good-looking college girls throws admiring glances at them."

"Not this fellow," Seagrave said, stroking his beard and looking at Mara. "Joe said he liked to remain anonymous while he performed his 'random acts of kindness.' All he wanted was a signed receipt, which Earl-George was happy to give him. Earl-George had his equipment and the network ran better than ever, so why should he tell anyone where the stuff came from? He kept his mouth shut, accepted compliments for the improved network, and never saw Joe again."

Mara lowered her gaze from the wall and turned her acetylene torch on Seagrave. "Earl-George should have known to 'fear the geeks, even when they bring gifts.' "

It was a bad pun on a good translation of *The Aeneid*. Virgil would have approved of it, but it went right over Seagrave's head. I wondered what he'd done to raise Mara's ire.

Dr. Sheldon wasn't going to be upstaged. "Seagrave," he said, "I have revised my estimate of Earl-George. It is quite possible he wouldn't know what to do when the meteorologist told him it was raining." He paused for effect, then asked, "So what did this anonymous Joseph do to the network?"

"Something I've never seen before," Seagrave said, "and several things I still haven't figured out. But here's the general outline. There's supposed to be a record of everything that goes out of a network or comes into it. This network does produce a record, but the record doesn't stand up under examination. As near as I can figure, that new server leaves the network around eleven every night and does its own thing until about six the next morning. But there's no record to show what it does."

"Wouldn't the lack of a record be pretty obvious?" Mara asked.

Seagrave beamed like a professor rewarding a bright student. "It certainly would. So Joe set up a program to create a false record. I almost didn't find it. At first glance, the rogue server's record seemed good enough. But I noticed that a couple of its entries looked like some I'd seen for the network's other servers."

"That's a fantastic memory job," I said.

Seagrave stroked his goatee and showed a self-satisfied smile to Mara. "I get paid for noticing things," he said. "But my memory wasn't conclusive—only good enough to create suspicion. For proof, I ran a matching program."

He glanced at each of us in turn. I confess I was hanging on every word.

"My program," Seagrave continued, "showed that, in the last month, every log entry for that server between 11 p.m. and 6 a.m. duplicated a log entry from another server."

I whistled. "Setting that up must have taken some fancy programming."

"Joe knew his computers," Seagrave said. "I haven't yet found the program he used. As a matter of fact, there are several areas of the network I haven't been able to access at all. Tomorrow I'll test my hacking skills on them."

Dr. Sheldon cleared his throat. "What do these irregularities add up to?"

Seagrave frowned. "I'm not sure. I do know that some of the campus computers have been zombied—controlled from a remote location and used for heaven knows what. It's what I suspected, Press, when I found part of your hard drive scrubbed. That opens up all sorts of possibilities for computer crime: information or identity theft, changing or deleting important documents, denial-of-service attacks on commercial Web sites, and the like."

"Information theft?" I mused. "Bob Harkins wondered how another researcher duplicated his research and beat him to the patent office."

I was ready to scratch Bob off our list of suspects until Mara spoke up. "When Professor Harkins became a victim, he may have decided to victimize someone else."

Seagrave continued his recitation as if we hadn't spoken. "Computer crimes don't have to be new. Old crimes like fraud, forgery, extortion, and blackmail can be adapted to computers. Let's say you're a moderate-sized firm doing a lot of business through a Web site. One day so many computers access that Web site at once that it goes down—a classic denial-of-service attack by an army of zombied computers. That happens a couple of times, and the company loses several days' revenue. Then someone contacts the company and offers to keep it

from happening—for a price. That's the old extortion racket adapted to the computer age."

Dr. Sheldon's jaw flexed. "Are you implying that some criminal organization—?"

Seagrave shrugged. "I don't know what's going on, except that it's not legitimate. Tomorrow I'll try to find out."

"One thing I don't understand," Mara said. "If someone on the network is misusing it, couldn't you tell which computer it was coming from?"

"You should be able to." Seagrave repeated his praise-for-a-bright-student smile. "But Joe was a very clever fellow. He also gave Earl-George a wireless connection."

"Wait a minute." Dr. Sheldon looked like a thundercloud. "When Earl-George and President Cantwell talked with me about classes on the Internet, they both said wireless access had been added within the last month."

"Cantwell thought he was telling the truth," Seagrave said, "but Earl-George knew better. Part of his bargain with Joe was to keep quiet about the wireless access, and Joe promised to secure the wireless connection with a complex password."

I felt like I'd been hit with Brenda Kirsch's two-by-four. "So anyone with the password, a car, and a wireless-capable laptop could drive within range and connect." I could see my list of suspects fading into irrelevance—assuming, of course, that both murders were somehow related to the network irregularities.

"Exactly." Seagrave looked at me but withheld the bright-student smile. He didn't stroke his goatee, either. "The intruding computer would almost certainly be a laptop. I scanned the hardware and software configurations of all the campus computers. None of them have

been upgraded for wireless capability."

We all exchanged glum looks, and no one said anything.

"Well, children," Dr. Sheldon said presently, "we seem to have reached an impasse. Let us adjourn for now and reconvene when one of us has learned something new."

He wheeled his chair toward the door. I don't think anyone ever accused him of being subtle. The rest of us stood and drifted in that direction.

"Mara," Seagrave said, "I saw that someone drove you out here. Do you need a ride home?"

Her smile stopped short of her eyes. "That's very kind of you, Mr. Seagrave, but I've already accepted Press's offer."

I tried not to look surprised. To change the subject, I said to him, "Sorry I was out of pocket when you arrived in town. I'd planned for you to stay at my place."

He showed a wry grin. "From what I hear, your place is too hazardous for a peace-loving guy like me. Some people get assaulted there, some get their cars bombed, and others get killed. I'll stick with the motel, where it's safe."

"The motel may be safe now," I said, "but remember what happened to Marcus Fischbach when he started poking around the computer network."

Seagrave's grin disappeared. "I'm always prepared." He patted the left breast of his coat where in the old days he'd carried an Army Colt .45 in a shoulder holster. With a final frown at Mara, he departed.

When the sound of his footsteps faded, she and I took our leave of Dr. Sheldon. She said nothing as we walked down the hall, and she avoided eye contact until we drove away from the nursing home.

"What's with you and Seagrave?" I asked.

I expected her to burn me with a glance, but she showed no emotion at all. "He colors outside the lines."

That should have told me to leave well enough alone, but I asked, "How was your dinner with Brice Funderburk?"

She smiled. "I had a great time, but I don't think he liked the decor at Dolt's."

"Dolt's? I'd have thought he'd take you to a four-star restaurant."

Her smile widened. "He asked where I wanted to go, and Dolt's was the only place where we could finish in time for the meeting with Dr. Sheldon. I don't think the good counselor approved of my choice." She closed that subject by raising another. "What do Mr. Seagrave's findings do to our investigation?"

In frustration, I pounded the steering wheel. "I wish I knew. They may mean our little circle of suspects is too small. That business about the wireless connection means we should suspect anyone with a car and a laptop. And maybe the car isn't required."

She drummed fingers on her left knee. "So far as we know, none of our suspects owns a laptop, unless Threnody Harkins does. I heard that all the others have denied owning one. Given the kind of salaries we draw here, they're probably telling the truth. Most of our colleagues have older desktop computers at home but can't afford anything beyond the most basic setup. If any of the suspects did own a laptop, the police would have found it when they searched homes and offices."

"So where does that leave us?" I already knew, but I hoped she'd have a different idea.

She sighed. "It leaves us out in the cold. I don't see any way to proceed."

"Neither do I," I said as I parked in front of her apartment. "Let's sleep on it and see if we think of anything. And we probably need to

talk about our Wednesday afternoon meeting with the faculty hearing committee. Can we compare notes over lunch tomorrow?"

She gave me a straight look. My thought was that we weren't welcome on campus, and we certainly didn't need to be seen together at either her place or mine. I could see her assessing the situation mentally.

"Late lunch," she said, finally. "I have a lot of things to do. Call me about one thirty?"

"Okay," I said.

She thanked me for the ride, rewarded me with a smile, and was gone. I watched until she disappeared around a corner, feeling an irrational disappointment when she did not look back or wave. Once again I became conscious of the car's emptiness. Could this be some new law of nature, that her absence always left emptiness behind?

Fatigue set in as I drove home. Perhaps because of that, my situation again seemed hopeless. I'd been suspended from my job, Clyde Staggart had poisoned Dean-Dean's mind against me, I was the prime suspect for at least one murder, and the house of hope I'd built toward finding the real murderer had just collapsed like a cardboard box in a rainstorm. As if those troubles weren't enough, I was becoming jealous —yes, I had to admit it—of Seagrave's and Funderburk's attentions to Mara, a woman on whom I had no claim at all.

My only consolation was that things couldn't get worse.

I was wrong again.

CHAPTER 39

Tuesday morning brought plummeting temperatures, scudding low clouds, and a wind so wet you could wring it out like a dishrag. We'd have snow soon. It was a perfect day to relax with a fire in the hearth and a cup of hot chocolate in the hand. But I didn't feel relaxed, my house had central heating, and everything in the cup tasted like hemlock.

I saw with stark clarity that our investigation had hit a stone wall. Mara and I were the only suspects with evidence against us. The fact that the evidence was faked posed little problem to Clyde Staggart. It stung my conscience that his hatred for me prejudiced him against Mara. Brice Funderburk had gotten us out of jail, but keeping us out was another story. And if keeping one of us free required letting the other hang, I knew which one he would choose.

I had no idea how to defend myself before the faculty hearing committee on Wednesday afternoon. I didn't know which way Gifford Jessel would jump but, historically, the committee voted the way the administration wanted. That probably meant I'd never teach history again.

Beyond all that, my sense of unseen forces closing in had grown stronger. And my internal orchestra didn't help. Today it played nothing but dirges.

So the morning passed in gloom, and Mara didn't answer when I called at one thirty. When I called again at two, she said she needed more time and would call back. By the time she did, just after three, my bleak mood had sunk into depression. Her mood seemed no better when I picked her up and headed for Dolt's.

"I'm sorry to be so late," she said. "I'd let a lot of things slip and had to catch up."

She didn't look me in the eye when she said it. That set off my suspicions. For all I knew she'd already had lunch with Brice Funderburk.

Dolt's had the usual crowd of students yelling into cell phones and the usual music blasting out of overloaded amplifiers. My internal music played in different keys, creating a painful dissonance for me to think against.

At the same table we'd used before, Mara and I hung our coats on the backs of our chairs. I stuffed my gloves into the coat pockets, while she laid hers on the table on top of her purse. She was wearing jeans—not much protection against the dropping temperatures.

I ordered a cheeseburger and coffee. She chose a Reuben with Coke and asked for separate checks. Her independent streak again. We ate our sandwiches in silence. Afterward, I had a second cup of coffee while she sipped on her Coke.

After a while she focused her blue gaze on me and said, "All right, Chief Inspector Barclay, what do we do now?"

Several smart replies flitted through my head, but I actually said, "I can't think of a single lead we can follow. Like I said last night, I struck out with all of our suspects."

"I had no luck this morning." She blinked back what might have been a tear. "Based on last night's conversation, I thought we could rule out any of our suspects who were incompetent with computers. But Earl-George says they're all fairly sharp, including Pappas. It seems our custodial associate has been taking night courses. I asked which of the group were extra-sharp, and Earl-George said none. So my bright idea ended up on the ash heap."

"You were ahead of me," I said. "I hadn't thought to ask him."

She gave a bitter laugh. "I hoped I might learn something if I talked to the suspects, but I couldn't find the men and wish I hadn't found the women. Threnody Harkins called me something unmentionable and said I ought to be shot. And Brenda Kirsch . . ." Mara shook her head. "That woman lies like a Persian rug."

"I never met a rug that slippery," I said. My black-widow vision of Brenda metamorphosed into an eel, green like the color of her warm-ups.

Mara made a face. "I tried to find out something about that black-jack, but Brenda would only talk about you and me. She said she hoped we'd be happy shacked up in the poorhouse together—if someone didn't send us to join Laila first. She made me so angry I almost hit her."

"Why didn't you? You know karate." Call it a historian's impolitic curiosity.

Mara's hands formed fists on the table. "I'm in enough trouble already. So I went home and packed everything I own. That's what took me so long."

"We still might luck out at our hearing tomorrow." I knew better, but I also realized I didn't want Mara to leave town. "They have no real evidence against us."

She singed me with her blue gaze. "Our only evidence is our own word, and rules for the hearing don't allow representation by counsel.

We stand less chance than goldfish in a tank of sharks."

I tried another tack. "On this packing business: will the police let you leave town?"

She bit her lip. "I'd finished packing before I remembered. On top of that, the person who's been trying to incriminate us may not be through. We don't know what he—or she—will do next."

My foreboding returned, but I tried to argue it away. "That may be a good thing, in a crazy kind of way. The bogus evidence someone planted on us is the only thing that ties the two murders together."

She burned me with another glance. "Every one of our suspects has threatened us, and all we can do is wait for the murderer to move against us and hope it isn't fatal."

"That's about it," I said.

She picked up her gloves and purse. "Then please drive me home, Press. I can worry more efficiently without this background noise."

We paid our checks and walked out to my car. A light snow was falling, but my gloved hands easily cleared it from the windows. I was glad the Honda had a stick shift instead of an automatic transmission. For driving on snow, I like to decide when to shift gears. Still, I drove slowly and hoped other drivers would do the same.

We eased out of the parking lot and made a gentle turn west toward her apartment. I apparently wouldn't have to worry about other drivers. The street stood empty except for a dark-colored SUV parked at one side with the motor running. The snow came down in big wet flakes, but the windshield wipers swept it aside to leave an arc of visibility. I flicked on the rear-window defroster and lines of clear glass appeared where the snow melted.

Through those clear lines I saw that the dark SUV had pulled into the street and was overtaking us. My caution racheted up a notch, but

I drove on at the same slow pace. The SUV slowed and settled in behind.

Mara glanced at the outside mirror on her side. "Is that car following us?"

She spoke without turning her head, and I answered without turning mine.

"We're going to find out."

I flicked on my turn signal and eased through a right turn at the next corner. The snow squished beneath the tires, but the traction held firm. Still, I hoped I wouldn't have to make a sudden maneuver.

The SUV did not signal, but followed me through the turn. I turned left at the next corner and the SUV followed.

Mara pointed to a house ahead and to our left. "Pretend that we came this way so I could show you that house. Don't let them know we think they're following."

"Great idea." I rubbernecked at the house as we passed it, then turned to Mara. We exchanged nods and smiles for the benefit of those behind us.

Her eyes narrowed. "Can you see how many are in the SUV?"

I glanced at the mirror. "Two in the front seats. Big guys. If there are more in the back, I can't see them." I turned left to return to our original street, still driving cautiously in the snow. The SUV followed and duplicated my right turn back onto the main street, heading west through a quiet residential area. Except for the two vehicles, the street was deserted.

"They're definitely tailing us," Mara said. "I'm going to dial 9-1-1." She took my antiquated phone from the glove compartment.

"Your phone is better," I said.

"It's recharging, back at my apartment." She punched a few buttons on my phone and grimaced. "Yours is dead. Do you have a charger?"

"At home," I said. "Our Plan B is to drive to the police station and see if they follow us there."

Even as I spoke, the dark SUV accelerated. It quickly closed the gap between us and moved into the left lane, fishtailing briefly in the deepening snow. My first thought was that they weren't tailing us—that they'd simply become impatient and decided to pass. My second was that I'd better assume the worst.

As the dark vehicle pulled slowly abreast, I released the accelerator. With my deceleration, the SUV appeared to leap ahead. I risked a quick glance at it, and I saw surprise on the passenger's tough-looking face and an indecisive gesture with the pistol in his left hand.

Now half a length ahead, the other vehicle swerved toward us in a classic sideswiping maneuver. I stood on the brake and spun the steering wheel to the right. Not soon enough. My left front fender ground into the SUV's body with a crunch of metal. For a moment, the heavier vehicle carried us toward the curb. Then my brakes took hold and the two cars separated. Both jolted onto the curb and skidded to a stop about three feet apart.

The collision had jammed the SUV's passenger door, but from the opposite side, its driver and another man leaped out.

Both of them brandished pistols.

CHAPTER 40

I did not wait to ask our assailants' intentions. Somehow, my foot had disengaged the clutch and left the engine running. I slammed the gearshift into reverse, released the clutch, and stepped hard on the accelerator. The front wheels spun in the wet snow and for a terrifying moment I thought we were stuck. Then the tires found traction and the car shot backward into the street. I spun the wheel to turn us back the way we'd come, then shifted into low and stomped the gas pedal.

The wheels again spun, then caught and sent the car caroming forward. It wanted to pull left, and I had all I could do to hold it straight. A steady groan from the left front fender told that it was rubbing against the tire. With that friction, we'd have a blowout soon.

In the rearview mirror I saw the two gunmen floundering to find footing in the snow. One steadied and raised his pistol, but apparently thought better of it. They could drive away from a fender bender in this residential neighborhood, but gunfire would certainly bring the police. They might have chanced escaping from a quick kill, but this one was taking longer than they'd planned.

As we gained speed I risked a glance at Mara. She sat upright in her seat, mouth set firm and eyes focused straight ahead. Her gaze did not waver as she spoke.

"Good work, Press. You don't drive like a professor."

I marveled at her control. And she was right. Some instinct from my days in Special Ops had taken over, and I didn't feel at all like a professor. Actually, I felt more like the fox who finds himself the main attraction at a foxhunt.

But I had no time for reflection. Our tormentors had remounted and renewed their pursuit. Their unwieldy SUV fishtailed in the slippery conditions, but it was closing on us again. Then another SUV pulled out from the curb in the block ahead and drove toward us faster than prudence allowed. As it cleared the intersection to enter our block, the driver threw his vehicle into a skid that brought him broadside in the street, barring our passage.

I slammed on the brakes and hoped I could stop before the collision.

"Go left!" Mara's voice rang with an authority I hadn't heard from her before. "Across that lawn."

Still in the skid, I twisted the wheel to the left, downshifted, and hit the accelerator. For a perilous moment we slid sideways toward the blockading vehicle. Then the old Honda responded as its tires found traction. The sideward skid stopped within inches of a collision, and we launched forward toward an elm tree on the left-hand curb. I twisted the wheel to the right. At the last second the car responded. The jolt as we jumped the curb threw us against our seat belts, and bare limbs of the elm scraped my side of the car. Suddenly we were in someone's snow-covered lawn, tires screaming as they searched for traction and the left front tire moaning against the fender. Two more elms loomed ahead and I managed to thread the car between them. Then we were in

the side street, heading away from the ambush.

That raised a new problem. We couldn't outrun the SUVs on a straightaway, for they had far more power than my old Honda. My only advantage was better maneuverability due to the Honda's low center of gravity. That meant twisting in and out of blocks, and this residential district was unfamiliar territory. If I took a wrong turn, we could end up in a cul-de-sac.

"I don't know this area," I said. "I don't know how to get back to the police station."

"Forget the police station." Mara twisted around and looked to the rear. "Turn right at the next corner. They're getting close. Don't be slow with that turn."

I waited till the last second, then braked, shifted, and accelerated through the turn. In the mirror I saw the lead SUV skid past the intersection. The second slowed enough to make the turn, but we had widened our lead.

"Go straight through the next intersection," Mara said. "Then turn left at the second."

"Yes, ma'am," I said, and finally found enough breath to add, "I hope you know where we're going."

"Just drive," she said.

I did. The second SUV was catching up by the time I made the turn. Its driver was better prepared this time, but we again increased our lead because his high center of gravity forced him to be cautious. The other vehicle had recovered and was trailing farther back.

By now I was completely lost. I'd lived in Overton City for decades, but I'd never driven in this section. Vaguely, I knew the interstate lay to the north and there was new development to the west. But I knew no details. I simply followed Mara's directions, controlled the car, and

worried about the blue smoke now pouring from under the left front fender. That tire couldn't last much longer.

I don't know how long we fled. The snow-covered streets flowed by the windows in a blur. Our tires alternately slipped and caught, and foul-smelling smoke streamed from the left front wheel. We dared not go straight for more than a block or two, for the SUVs kept gaining on us. Then Mara would direct a turn and we would increase our lead. We seemed to be working mostly west, but also somewhat to the north. If we got forced onto the interstate's frontage road, our pursuers' more powerful vehicles would quickly overtake us. The snow now pelted down in a veritable torrent of white flakes, and sensible drivers had long since abandoned the slippery streets. Wherever our adversaries cornered us, they would have no witnesses.

"Turn right," Mara ordered.

I did, and suddenly knew where I was. This street would take us north to the interstate, now only three blocks away. Lights of late-closing business showed up ahead.

"Not to the interstate," I said. "We won't have a chance."

"We're not going there," she said. "Get ready to turn left when I tell you."

We sped through the next block with the two SUVs getting closer and closer.

"Turn now," Mara said.

As the black shapes of a few darkened buildings whipped by, a well-lighted parking lot suddenly appeared. I braked and turned into it. At its far end loomed the long, flat building of Amazing Discount Bargains, the huge new twenty-four-hour supercenter widely touted by TV and newspapers. The parking lot lay deserted in the deepening snow, though rotating yellow beacons on two golf carts signaled the presence

of security guards. Witnesses at last! The guards would be unarmed, but the thugs behind us would hardly attack us in front of them.

"Brilliant, Mara," I said.

She pointed to the left-hand entrance. "Park there. We'll call the police from inside."

The left front tire blew out with a sound like a cannon shot, but I wrestled the protesting car onward to a spot near the door. It wasn't an approved parking space, but the guards weren't close enough to stop us. We leaped out and ran for the entrance as the two SUVs pulled into the parking lot.

Inside, Mara cornered the first clerk she saw and asked, "Where's your phone?"

The clerk, a frowsy woman of middle age, showed a bored stare and drawled, "Customers has to use the pay phones. They's outside in the parking lot."

Mara burned her with a glance. "Call your manager."

The woman scratched her head. "He ain't here right now. Him and Mabel went out for a soda."

I expected an explosion from Mara, but none came. Instead, she smiled and said, "I'll catch him when I finish shopping."

She headed for the back of the store and I followed. As we navigated among the racks I glanced back toward the entrance. A big, tough-looking fellow rushed in and stood with hands in topcoat pockets, head turning from side to side as he surveyed the store. He was the mop-haired fellow who'd been watching me in Dolt's. Before he found us, Mara moved us behind the fitting rooms and hurried on toward the rear.

We swept through a lingerie department featuring garments too small for a modest midget, then through a men's section of T-shirts with slogans that would make a sailor blush. Heck, some might even

make a sitcom writer blush. We barged through hardware, camping equipment, and a vast array of fishing poles that would have kept President Cantwell busy for a week. We rounded a rack of waders and faced up against a metal door with a sign that read, "Emergency Exit: Alarm Will Sound."

Mara never hesitated. She slammed both hands into the door's opening bar. The door flew open, and the alarm's raucous *beep-beep-beep* echoed through the store. We stepped outside into snow that now lay ankle-deep. It slopped into my shoes, and I wished I'd had foresight enough to wear boots. Mara fared even worse in her pumps, but she didn't complain. The snowfall suddenly erupted into a blizzard. It looked like someone had carried truckloads of Arctic snow overhead and dropped it all at once. That made the footing difficult, but at least it would cover our tracks.

Mara seized my gloved hand and turned north along the rear of the store. "We have to disappear before they come looking."

When we reached the store's corner, she continued north into the pitch-black of an unlighted field. I had misgivings because we were within a block of the interstate's frontage road, but she seemed to know where she was going. I glanced backward and saw no pursuit. I shouldn't have. When I did, I learned the lesson of Lot's wife, except that I didn't turn into a pillar of salt; I only fell facedown in the snow.

I sprang up quickly and found Mara had waited for me. She did not offer her hand again, but forged ahead toward the lights of a three-story building on the frontage road. Breathing hard, we rounded its corner and stepped into a lighted parking lot with an electric sign that read "Dreamland Motel."

Mara stopped under a light and said, "Let's get you dusted off and presentable before we go in." Her gloved hands brushed at my over-

coat. After a search, I found my handkerchief to wipe my face and clean my trifocals.

"Go in?" I said. "But that's a motel."

"Of course it's a motel. It's where I stayed when I first hit town." Her eyes scorched me, but a smile played on her lips. "Motels have telephones, Cupcake. That means we can call the police. Now come along."

"Yes, ma'am," I said. This was a Mara I hadn't seen before, and I didn't know quite what to make of it. So I followed her into the motel like the obedient cupcake I was supposed to be.

We found the lobby deserted except for a young male who slouched at the registration desk reading the *National Enquirer* and scratching his scraggly attempt at a beard.

He looked up and asked, "Can I help you guys?" His intonation suggested he'd rather not.

"Our car stalled," Mara said. "We'd like two rooms for the night. Nonsmoking. On separate floors."

The clerk turned a blank stare on each of us in turn, then on the floor beside us, so obviously empty of luggage.

Mara showed him her acetylene torch. "You do have rooms, don't you?"

He winced, grunted, and produced registration cards. We filled them out with my car and tag number but our individual credit cards. The clerk gave Mara her key card in an envelope numbered 206. Mine was 312. He mumbled something about continental breakfast from six to nine and dismissed us by returning to his *National Enquirer*.

In the elevator I punched buttons for two and three. "Why the rooms?" I asked. "Why not just use the phone?"

"Those men in the SUVs may come looking for us," she said. "Come

on," she added as the door opened onto her floor. "We'll make that phone call."

Her room contained a king-sized bed, a desk, chair, and the inevitable TV set. A bedside table held a lamp and phone. We threw our wet coats on the desk, and Mara sat on the bed by the phone. With mounting misgivings, I took the chair at the desk.

She must have had second thoughts, too, for she asked, "Do you think the police will believe us?"

"Not if Staggart gets involved," I said. "We're both fresh out of jail. That means we're on their list of undesirables. And we don't know if those mugs are still chasing us. For all we know, they may have left town when they didn't catch us."

"Let's think about it," she said. "Meanwhile, I'll tell Dr. Sheldon what's going on." She punched in the numbers.

While she summarized our problems for Dr. Sheldon, I thought back over the day's events. The attempted attack on us had taken my mind off our failed investigation. We'd evidently gotten close to someone, for we'd made the hit list of professional criminals. One of the five suspects that had threatened us had made good on the threat.

But which one?

I'd hardly posed the question when Mara stopped talking and began listening.

"Thank you," she said presently. She hung up the phone and turned to look at me, her face filled with sadness.

"Sergeant Spencer asked Dr. Sheldon if he had seen us," she said. "Captain Staggart has issued a new order for our arrest."

CHAPTER 41

For several minutes we simply stared at each other. Despair was written on Mara's face, and mine must have showed no better. Somewhere outside, gunmen were waiting to kill us. We'd hoped for protection from the police, but now the police had become our enemies. Even if we escaped the thugs and the police until Wednesday afternoon, the faculty hearing committee would end our professional lives. We were alone and cut off from help of any kind. Even the safety of this drab motel room was illusory. If our armed assailants found us, it would become a killing ground.

Sometimes the future becomes so threatening that we dismiss it and focus wholly on moment-by-moment survival.

Thus it was with Mara. Her chin lifted that eloquent fraction and the despair on her face changed to determination.

"Let's go check out your room," she said.

Why not? We had nothing better to do. We picked up our coats and headed for the door. I opened it a crack and surveyed the hall. It was empty. Quietly, we followed it to the stairwell and climbed to the third floor. No use signaling our movements by using the elevator. Mara

made no comment until I reached for the light switch in my room.

"Wait." She closed the door behind us and felt her way through the dark room to the window. She parted the thick curtains about a finger's width and looked outside.

"They're in the parking lot," she said. "Both SUVs and six men. It looks like they're arguing."

I joined her at the window. Suddenly conscious of her feminine closeness in the dark room, I took special care to avoid touching her. As I knelt and looked through the parted curtains, she stood behind and leaned over me to look. But she seemed as careful as I not to make physical contact.

The two SUVs were the ones that had chased us. The damaged passenger door identified one, and the other was either its mate or a dead ringer. Mara was right about the argument. One man gestured toward the motel and the one facing him pointed east along the access road. The other four stood and watched. The first man gestured again and marched toward the motel.

Would the desk clerk betray us? For a moment we held our positions as if frozen. I heard Mara breathing above me, and my heartbeat resonated like a bass drum. Then, without words, we moved in concert as we both realized we must barricade the door.

By now our eyes had become accustomed to the dim light. The room's darkness was not complete, for a sliver of light crept in under the hall door and allowed us to make out the shapes of furniture. The room was a duplicate of Mara's except that it had two queen beds instead of one king.

Hurriedly, we disconnected the TV and moved it from the chest of drawers onto a bed. Grunting and gasping for breath, we pushed the heavy chest across the room until it rested lengthwise against the door.

We lifted the desk on top of it and crowned that with the TV set. It would fall with a crash if anyone succeeded in breaking in. We saved the desk chair to club the first intruder who made it through the obstacles. As Mara had said, we weren't thinking like professors.

We stood there for several minutes, panting like hounds on a hot day. Mara seemed to know, as I did, that we'd done everything possible and could only wait.

Footsteps in the hall approached our door. Passed it. Receded. The elevator door groaned, followed by the fading hum of the elevator descending. A false alarm. But it made us acutely conscious of our vulnerability.

We waited. In the silence, the room's artificial freshener smelled sickly sweet. The elevator hummed again, crescendoing as it ascended. Its door grated open. Footsteps again approached our door. Passed it. Again receded. Some unseen neighbor had returned from an errand downstairs.

We resumed our places at the window, opening the curtains the barest crack. We needed the light from outside now that our barricade blocked light from under the door.

The five men in the parking lot stamped their feet in the deepening snow and snugged their topcoat collars against the cold. After a long time, the man who'd entered the motel returned and gave something like a shrug. Another argument followed. Finally, three men got into the undamaged SUV and drove east up the access road.

I guessed they'd argued about whether we were in the motel or had escaped in another direction. Apparently they were pursuing both possibilities.

The three remaining men climbed awkwardly into the damaged SUV through the driver's door. They circled farther out in the parking

lot and stopped where they could observe the full face of the motel while their interior was too shadowed for anyone to see what they were doing. It looked like they'd settled in for the night.

"We mustn't show a light," Mara said. "They may be trying to decide which rooms are occupied. They may make a raid later. . . ."

I knew what she must be thinking. Regardless of propriety, this room was our prison for the night. If the faculty hearing committee got wind of it, that would put the coup de grâce to our already jeopardized careers.

But Mara didn't linger on the thought. "Give me your wet shoes and socks," she said. "There has to be a hair dryer around here somewhere."

I gratefully complied, for my feet felt packed in ice. A few minutes later I heard the hair dryer going in the bathroom. I didn't ask how she'd found things in the dim light, but busied myself with peeping out the window. The SUV had not moved, but the absence of condensation from the exhaust meant they'd turned off the engine. Standard cold-weather procedure: Run the engine awhile to heat the interior, shut it down to save fuel. That meant they planned a long vigil.

Mara returned with my shoes and socks. Their heat made an instant start on thawing out my feet.

"Thanks," I said. "I hope you did your own."

I thought I saw a smile in the dim light. "I did them first. That's the only way I could stand up long enough to do yours."

"Our friends have set up shop outside," I said. "It looks like they plan to stay awhile."

She came and stood next to me to gaze out through the curtain. She wore no perfume, but the clean smell of soap made me acutely aware of her femininity. And of how near me she was standing. She left the

curtain open a crack. Through it, light from the parking lot revealed her face as she weighed the situation.

"They don't know for certain we're in here," she said, "or if they do, they don't know which room. If we don't show a light, they won't know this room is occupied."

"We're okay while they're out there," I said, "and at least for right now they've decided not to come in. Maybe holding a gun on the desk clerk is too much risk if they aren't certain we're here."

"If they do come in, our barricade will give us a minute or two of warning." Light through the curtain-crack glimmered blue in her eyes. "We might as well get some sleep now and worry about tomorrow when it gets here."

Before I could answer, she said "Good night," crawled onto the nearest bed, and, without bothering to turn down the spread, buried her face in the pillow. The austerity of her Army training, I guess.

"Good night," I said belatedly, and crawled onto the other bed. That happened to be the one nearer the door. So if the thugs did come in, it would be my job to grab the desk chair and give my imitation of Brenda Kirsch and her two-by-four.

In the silence of the room, fatigue dissolved my bones like salt on a snail. Silence of the room? Yes, silence. I suddenly realized my internal musicians had been on strike ever since Mara and I left Dolt's. In the movies, the soundtrack would dramatize a chase like we'd been through with something like "The Ride of the Valkyries." But in our case I'd not heard so much as a solitary toot.

Just as suddenly, my orchestra returned with a reprise of Barber's *Adagio for Strings*. Gradually, my emotions merged into its solemn sadness. It brought back the deep, familiar ache of my grief for Faith, now made more acute by the presence of another woman here in the room.

Somewhere amid the melody and manic longing, I slipped into the sable nothingness of sleep.

Someone was crying. Cindy? I roused, still only half-awake. Gradually, reality seeped in. A dark room. Dim light around a heavy curtain. Not home. Fully dressed on a strange bed. Not Cindy, but . . .

The crying came from the adjacent bed, quiet gasps stifled in the pillow. Now louder, less controlled.

Mara.

Something badly wrong. She'd never shown much emotion, always tightly disciplined.

The sound grew to deep, uncontrolled sobbing like a soul in torment. Desperate gasps for breath between sobs.

I saw her then in the dim light. She lay on her stomach, hands clutching the pillow tight against her face, body racked with the sobbing.

Without thought, I found myself kneeling on the floor beside her bed, reluctant to speak, fearful of touching her lest I provoke a memory of even greater pain.

But I had to do something. Carefully, gently, I put the palm of my left hand on her back between the shoulder blades. My position was awkward. To steady myself, I rested my right hand on the bed above her head.

"It's all right, Mara," I whispered. "It's all right."

I knew very well it wasn't all right. Our jobs and our lives were in danger. We were alone against gunmen and police and a hostile administration. Things were far from all right, but I had to tell her something.

Her weeping grew more violent, her body now convulsing with

every sob. She did not look up, but she reached out to grasp my hand that rested on the bed. She gripped it the way a drowning person grips even the smallest twig.

I couldn't blame her. For two weeks she'd been remarkably controlled under stresses that grew increasingly threatening, climaxing in that deadly chase by armed gunmen. Even then she'd showed courage and composure. But even the most steadfast courage must falter sometime, so I did not wonder that hers did now.

I have no idea how long she wept. My thighs and shoulders ached from my constrained position, yet I dared not move for fear of sending an unintended signal. For by now, with my hand resting on her silk-smooth back in the darkened motel room, I grew guiltily aware of her soft femininity. Guilty because I'd fallen asleep grieving my loss of Faith, yet now desire, long dormant, crept through my body at the mere touch of a woman I hardly knew.

It took all of my willpower to prevent my hand from moving into a caress. To make matters worse, my internal musicians kept playing someone's orchestral transcription of Wagner's "Liebestod," the "Love-Death" from *Tristan und Isolde*. The passionate music permeated my being until it became my passion, as if the music rather than my will were in control. The title was sometimes mistranslated "The Death of Love," and I wondered whose love for whom.

My struggle between emotion and will seemed endless. Again and again I told myself, fiercely, that my mission was to comfort a distraught friend, nothing more. Through dogged repetition of that fact, and by forcing the seductive music back into a remote corner of my brain, I somehow managed to restrain my rebellious hand.

Mara's grip remained tight on my other hand, but her sobs grew less violent and further apart. Gradually, they subsided into deep, steady

breathing. Eventually her fingers relaxed and she dropped off into sleep. When I was certain she slept, I eased my hand away from hers and tentatively raised the other hand from her back. She did not stir.

By now the aching muscles had spread from my thighs up my back, and I had to drop down on all fours before I could move away. At that moment, during the agony of returning circulation, I sank into the deepest caverns of despair. We would never escape the gunmen outside or the police now waiting to arrest us, and the faculty hearing committee would take away our jobs. We had no hope.

It occurred to me then that I should pray. I'd neglected prayer ever since Faith's death, and it seemed cowardly to beg divine help now that I'd gotten myself into a fix I couldn't get out of. Yet I had no alternative. There on all fours on the motel-room floor I bowed my head and tried to pray.

I found I could not. No matter how hard I concentrated, all that came out were incoherent blubberings for help. Even those seemed to bounce back from the ceiling more meaningless than when they'd gone forth.

In the end I gave it up and simply remained on all fours until the ache left my muscles and control returned.

When I could stand, I moved to the window and looked out. The door-damaged SUV stood in the same place, exhaust from its engine condensing as a billowing cloud behind it.

The thugs had not given up.

CHAPTER 42

Conflicting music. Something lyrical in my head, something hideous outside: body-jarring bass and a voice wailing above it, indeterminate male or female. Radio.

Eyes still closed, I reached over and silenced the thump and yowl. Only the lyrical remained. Back to sleep.

"Press, wake up."

Whose voice? Eyes open. Daylight. Not home. Motel. Clean smell of soap. Mara.

I sat up and rubbed my eyes. The internal lyric continued.

"I hated to wake you, Press, but it's morning. We have to decide what to do."

She sat on the other bed, fresh as the morning itself. She didn't look like someone who'd run through snow and fought through a midnight emotional crisis. Instead, she radiated an inner calm I'd not seen in her before.

"Who turned on the blasted radio?" I sounded peevish, but that was how I felt.

She spoke as if to a child. "I was afraid to shake you because I didn't know how you'd react. I remembered you'd been in Special Ops."

I squinted against light from the uncurtained window. We apparently had a clear, cold day after the snowfall. "Okay," I said. "I'm awake. What now?"

She sat with hands clasped in her lap, tranquil in a mysterious way I'd not seen in her before. "The SUV is gone from the parking lot. I don't know if the men went with it or came inside. We need to unbarricade the door and decide what to do next."

I took time to splash some water on my face and run my pocket comb through my hair. My brown suit didn't look any more rumpled than usual, so I declared myself ready for whatever the day might bring. It would probably bring bad news. The clock said ten past eight, and we had no idea what we'd tell the faculty hearing committee at one thirty.

If we lasted that long.

We spent a few minutes putting the furniture and TV back in place. It seemed more difficult than it had last night. Less adrenaline, I guess.

Mara gave me a doubtful glance. "I suppose we should check out that continental breakfast."

"I'll go get it," I said. "The goons may have come inside, so there's no use risking both our necks. Lock the door behind me. If I'm not back in ten minutes, sneak out any way you can."

She frowned. "Surely they wouldn't try anything in front of witnesses."

"That's what I'm counting on." I showed her a grin more confident than I felt. I left unsaid the fact that I didn't want her involved if the gunmen were there.

As a precaution, I used the stairs instead of the elevator and moved cautiously into the lobby. Nothing suspicious there: only a bleary-eyed

woman at the desk and the sound of a TV and mumbled conversation from the tiny breakfast room. I peeked around the corner, advancing slowly enough to survey each occupant in turn. The dining area was full, no vacant chairs. But it was full with the usual tourist-looking crowd, and none seemed out of place.

No one gave me a second glance as I moved to the food line, though my flesh crawled as I turned my back on the crowd. The food was undistinguished in variety, and the thermal cups for coffee weren't much larger than Brenda Kirsch's teacups. I poured us three cups apiece and took three donuts apiece—glazed for me, chocolate for Mara. Fortunately, there were trays for carrying. Since no one paid any attention to me, I took the elevator back to the room.

Mara sat on her bed and I on mine, with the tray on the bedside table between us. The aroma of fresh donuts and coffee overpowered her characteristic aura of cleanliness and soap. I realized I missed it.

"You remembered my weakness for chocolate donuts," she said.

I tried to look nonchalant. "How could I forget? You presented a memorable appearance with chocolate on your face." That seemed a suitably professorial remark.

Blue fire flickered in her eyes. Then they softened. They seemed different this morning, mysteriously different. But I couldn't define how.

When we finished, she sat solemnly with her hands again clasped in her lap, apparently unaware of the chocolate smudges around her mouth. "Press, I apologize for last night. I shouldn't have gone to pieces like that."

I tried to shrug it off. "With all the stress we've been through, no one could blame you for having a good cry. It cleans out your system so you can deal with what lies ahead."

She looked away, thoughtful. I waited, trying hard not to show my

impatience. I needed her full attention. We still faced every problem that we'd faced last night. Maybe the thugs had backed off, but I could feel the clock ticking—ticking toward noon, when all of our murder suspects would scatter for Thanksgiving—ticking toward one thirty and the faculty hearing committee. We had to wrap things up this morning, and I had no plan at all.

Mara brought her mind back from wherever it had been, and her eyes searched mine. "I wasn't crying because of stress or danger, Press. It was something much worse. And much better. I finally faced up to something I'd been sweeping under the rug for years."

Her eyes grew softer than I'd ever seen them. "You know I was raised in a small country church. Not just fundamentalists, but the most extreme kind. They talked Christianity, but what they really believed in was male supremacy."

"You told me that. I can see why you rebelled against it." The digital clock on the table between us ticked off another minute.

"I wanted to get as far away from it as I could. I tried atheism, but I couldn't muster the blind faith to maintain it." She showed a rueful smile. "We humans have a built-in need to believe in something beyond the physical world. That's how I wound up in Wiccan goddess worship. It filled the need for a godlike power to govern natural forces, and it was the opposite of paternalistic Christianity."

"Hold on," I said. "I thought the Wiccan thing had a male god as well as a goddess."

She sniffed. "It does. Theoretically. But Wicca is cafeteria-style religion: take what you like and leave the rest. I chose to ignore the male god, if there was one, and worship the goddess Diana."

"So what happened then?" Time was flying, but this conversation was important to her. And I admit I was curious.

"I hit some rough spots," she said, "but I managed to work around them. The first problem was finding a coven. I tried several, but other people's cafeterias didn't match up with mine. That's how I wound up as a solitary."

"That worked out okay?"

She sighed. "At first. Initially, I felt a satisfying presence when I prayed to the goddess. Then I began to suspect the presence wasn't as beneficial as I'd thought. That's when I got rid of my Wiccan paraphernalia and held the belief in theory rather than practice. And all the time I knew I was pushing back a question I'd have to answer sooner or later. That's how things stood when I took this job at Overton."

"What happened then?" I'd never heard anything like this.

"Do you remember our first burglary?" She fixed her gaze on me, but this time it didn't burn. "We had breakfast in your car up above the river. You said you wanted a cross on the new fine arts building to dominate the view from the valley."

"I remember." It was a pleasant memory. For a moment I forgot about time.

She continued. "I explained the Wiccan Rede—'An it harm none, do as ye will'—and the Threefold Law, that whatever you do in the world comes back to you three times. Do something bad, and three bad things come back to you."

"I remember all that." I didn't see where this was leading. Vaguely, somewhere in the back of my consciousness, my musicians played something folksy on a zither.

"You asked, 'Where do the *harm* and the *bad* come from? What is the source of badness?' "

"I remember that, too."

"And I ducked the question. You'd brought back the old problems

I'd refused to think about. What is the nature of evil? Where does evil come from?" She sighed again, deeply. "I locked them in the cupboard again that day. Then last night those men tried to kill us, and I came face-to-face with an evil I couldn't duck or deny."

"That's something of an understatement," I said, my professorial pedantry asserting itself.

She ignored it. "So I had to confront the reality of evil. And the only adequate explanation came from Christianity. No other theology I've studied could even come close. That meant I'd spent fifteen years devoting myself to a wrong cause."

"That's why you cried? Not because you were afraid?"

"That's why I cried. I finally conceded that fifteen years of my life were a colossal waste." Though she spoke of last night's emotional explosion, her face radiated calm.

"So what did you do?"

"At first I gave in to despair. I've never cried like that before." The blue of her eyes grew softer. "You helped me when I needed it."

"I was afraid to touch you," I said. "I knew your aversion to it, and with the circumstances and all . . ." I meant the motel room, but I didn't want to say it.

That drew a smile. "You didn't let me misunderstand, and you made me know I wasn't alone."

"I'm glad it helped." I didn't tell her of my battle with desire or that my fingers still hurt from her karate grip.

"And something else happened then." Now she spoke more to herself than to me. "I prayed—to the Lord. I confessed with the sinner's prayer and asked Him to take me back. I wasn't sure it would work after all that I've done and said, but it was all I could think to do. And peace like I've never felt before came over me. It's still here."

"Welcome back," I said. But her words struck at my heart. I suddenly knew I needed to say the same prayer. My three-year retreat into spiritual numbness meant that I needed that prayer as much as she did. I said it quickly, silently, and turned back to her, for helping her seemed the most important thing now.

"I feel welcome," she said. "For the first time in years I feel welcome in this world. In retrospect, I feel awfully stupid that I let the warped actions of a few Christians convince me the whole thing was a lie."

"It's an uncomfortable truth," I said ruefully. "The most obvious argument against Christianity is the conduct of Christians."

"This wonderful Truth, this way of life . . ." She showed a beatific smile. "I'm still in awe of it. But I can't stand still. How do I go on from here?"

Her eyes again searched mine. At that moment I wanted more than anything to help. But I wasn't the best advisor. Nor would the religion faculty be. She needed practical guidance, not more of the academic theory she already knew by heart.

"You remember Urim Tammons? The minister we met in Dolt's? He's the best person I know for what you need. The only thing I'd tell you now is that you can't re-create the emotional experience you've been through. Tammons can guide you beyond that to something more solid."

"Thank you, Press," she said. "I knew you'd understand." The faraway look left her eyes, and they focused sharp and clear on the present. "But right now we have problems to solve." She glanced at the clock, which showed two minutes past nine. "We don't have much time to solve them. What do we do next?"

Aye, that was the question.

I could only wish I had an answer.

CHAPTER 43

For a second time we looked at each other in silent despair. My internal musicians slogged through something mournful that I didn't recognize.

"I don't know what we should do," I said after awhile, "but we're not accomplishing anything here. My car is shot, but I know a rental-car outfit that will deliver."

"Where will we go?" she asked.

"The police will look for us at my house or your apartment." I scratched my head. "Our best bet is the campus. Lots of movement to hide in, and no one will recognize the rental car. If we can do anything toward solving the murders, it will be there."

I called the rental agency. While we waited for delivery, Mara busied herself making the room look like it had had single occupancy. She returned one bed to its pristine state, then turned back the covers and rumpled the sheets on the other. She gave its pillow a final swat to make an indention where the sleeper's head would have lain.

Her eyes twinkled as she advanced on me. "Be a good cupcake, Press, and let me have a hair to decorate that pillow."

I adjusted my trifocals. "Cupcakes don't have hair," I said.

"Then you're unique." She seized a few hairs on the back of my head and yanked, then held them up for my inspection.

"Too many," she said. "We mustn't overdo it." She sifted the hairs back and forth between her fingers until only two remained. "There. Those will be just right." She arranged them carefully on different parts of the pillow.

This was a Mara I hadn't seen before. "You're acting like a character in a John le Carré spy novel," I said. "What, exactly, did you do in the Army?"

She answered only with a secret smile.

"What about your room?" I asked.

Her smile broadened. "I took care of that while you got breakfast."

The clock said nine thirty. I turned back to the window, despondent again. I had no plan at all, not the least glimmer of one. Mara was still buoyant from her glorious reconversion last night, but I hadn't even been able to pray coherently, much less make contact. The judgment hour was closing in, and I had never felt more helpless.

Bitterly, I chided the irrelevance of my musical hallucination, which now rollicked through Haydn's "Gypsy Rondo." But even as I rebuked it, the music slowed and changed key. Without warning, it swept into that wonderful Victor Young cinema score, Faith's favorite, the one that had distracted me weeks before during the faculty meeting. The Susan Hayward theme of doomed romance swelled up to its climax of passionate longing, receded into hope for assurance, then swept upward again to end in yearning for a fulfillment unattainable on this earth.

Under its spell, I stood again in that faculty meeting, disoriented, half of me entranced by a world of musical illusion, the other half

grounded in banal reality. And in that world I again heard Gifford Jessel's voice saying, ". . . bet my laptop no student will sign it."

Laptop!

The word exploded in my mind. Cymbals clashed and the cannons of Tchaikovsky's *1812 Overture* bellowed.

Richmond Seagrave believed someone with a laptop had exploited the campus computer network for corrupt purposes, and all of our suspects had denied owning anything other than desktop computers. Yet, now that music had triggered my memory, I realized that Gifford Jessel had said he owned a laptop.

Was that only a figure of speech? Or did he actually own one? If so, where did he keep it? Mara hadn't found it when she searched his office. And it hadn't turned up in police searches of his office and his home. So where—?

"Our car is here."

Mara's words jolted me out of speculation. I glanced out into the parking lot and saw two late-model Corollas idling while the driver of one walked into the motel with papers in his hand. Two cars? Good. He had his own return ride, so we wouldn't have to waste time with that.

We took the elevator down and met the driver in the lobby. A few minutes later I drove our rental car out of the parking lot, thankful for the car itself, but even more thankful for a heater that worked. The day stood clear and very cold, with a gusty wind that sliced at our ears and swept the fallen snow around in random patterns.

"You've thought of something," Mara said. "Don't keep it a secret."

I explained about Gifford Jessel and the laptop. "It's a very long shot," I said. "He may not have one. And if he does, that still doesn't prove anything. We're still just guessing that Marcus Fischbach got killed because he snooped into the computer network. The only solid fact

connecting the two murders is the attempt to implicate us—especially you."

She shook her head. "That's a lot of assumption. And we still don't know why Staggart ordered our arrest again."

I eased the car around a corner. "If we find the laptop, we'll tell Seagrave and let him bring the police in on it. They won't listen to us."

Mara gave a bitter laugh. "Won't listen to us? Press, you win the brass donut for understatement of the year. But all right. It's not much of a hope, but let's get on with it."

We arrived on campus at nine fifty, when the circle should have been swarming with students changing classes. I'd hoped we could hide by mingling with the crowd. Instead, the circle stood deserted except for a crowd of several hundred students milling in front of the executive center. At the top of the steps above the crowd stood President Cantwell and Dean-Dean. The president gestured as he addressed the massed students, who responded with hoots and chants.

"Oh, my, what's happened now?" Mara asked.

"We don't have time to find out," I said. "Someone will spot us for sure on this bare campus. We'll hide in the liberal arts center until ten o'clock."

She looked at me in alarm. "What happens at ten o'clock?"

"That's when Gifford Jessel has a class, remember? While he's teaching, I'll search his office for that laptop."

"What if he's taken it home?"

"Then I won't find it, we won't pass 'Go,' and we won't get out of jail free."

She sniffed. "If I know Brice Funderburk, we didn't get out of jail free the first time."

We made it into my office without meeting anyone, but I felt

better when we closed the door behind us. The smell of waxed floors and old woodwork made it feel like coming home after a long absence, but that didn't lessen the tension. I felt tighter than a violin E string tuned up to F-sharp. The set of Mara's jaw showed her equally tense. We both knew our future depended on finding that laptop and somehow tying it to the two murders. And we both knew how slim our chances were.

We said nothing as we waited for ten o'clock. Desperation must have showed in my eyes as surely as it did in hers. Once in a while, crowd noise from across the campus penetrated to our ears—vague, rhythmic chants whose words we couldn't discern.

Mara showed a nervous smile. "What could be important enough for all those students to stand out there in the cold? I hope they don't catch pneumonia."

It was so like her to be thinking of someone else, and so like me to focus totally on my own concerns.

"We'll wait till five after ten," I said. "By then, Giff should be well into his class. Same procedure as last time: you sit in the car out front and beep if you see Giff coming."

"You'll need this," she said, and handed me the passkey I'd given her a week ago.

I'd forgotten about that. Apparently I wasn't as focused as I'd thought.

I checked my watch again and said, "It's time."

Tears formed in her eyes but did not fall. "So it all comes down to this," she mused. "We've worked every angle we could think of for two weeks, we've broken more than one law, and we've still come up empty. Now we either score or we lose everything."

"That's the size of it," I said.

"Oh, Press . . ."

A single tear moistened her cheek. My first impulse was to place a reassuring pat on her shoulder, but I hesitated. While I stood there wondering, she stepped close, put her arms around my neck, and kissed me.

It was not a china-cup kiss.

For a few moments I stood stunned. Then I got my wits about me and returned the kiss with enthusiasm. I was not in the china-cup business either.

After awhile she put her hands on my chest and pushed away. "Be careful, Cupcake," she said, silver tear-tracks now adorning both cheeks. "We're dealing with a brutal murderer, and don't you forget it."

I confess that I didn't feel much like a cupcake. Truth to tell, I didn't feel much like anything except maybe that brass donut she'd mentioned earlier.

"Let's get going," I said.

She drove the short distance back to the science center and parked in front. The crowd, mob, or whatever it was, still milled around at the executive center, and President Cantwell seemed to make no headway with it. Every time Dean-Dean stepped up to say something, they booed him into silence. I wondered what the occasion was, but we had no time to find out.

I wouldn't need my gloves and topcoat for the short distance from car to building, so I dropped them on the passenger seat. "Remember the signal if Giff comes back," I said. "Two beeps followed by three more."

"I remember," she said. By now, she'd banished the tears, but apprehension showed in every line of her face. Her eyes were the softest blue I could remember. Her lips trembled as she said, "Be careful, Press."

I nodded and headed into the building.

Our futures, personal and professional, depended on what I'd find in the next five minutes.

CHAPTER 44

Although Thanksgiving break would not begin until noon, the science center was deserted. The empty halls let me climb to Gifford Jessel's office without being seen. Students weren't allowed to leave campus early, but apparently everyone wanted to see what was happening at the executive center. Whatever it was certainly made enough racket. But the noise faded to an unintelligible murmur when I shut Giff's office door behind me.

I searched the desk first because Mara said he kept a pistol there. No use allowing a weapon that could be used against me. I yanked each drawer open and sifted through any papers that might conceal a pistol. My fingerprints would be everywhere, but one more charge against me wouldn't make much difference.

There was no pistol in the drawers.

Giff's desk was one of the old kind with a door for a typewriter compartment on the right. The door was locked. I could look around for something to jimmy it with or I could open it the quick way. Time was ticking by. That crowd-murmur from across campus wouldn't last forever, and Giff might let his class out early. So I took the quick way. I

kicked the compartment door as hard as I could. Nothing happened except that my foot hurt. I kicked again. This time wood splintered and the door flew open.

The compartment was empty.

So I hadn't found the pistol. But I'd come here to look for a laptop computer. A quick glance confirmed my memory that no other place in the office could hide anything larger than a Palm Pilot. That left the false ceiling installed years ago in the older, high-ceilinged buildings when central heating and air-conditioning were added. When Richmond Seagrave debugged my office, he'd removed ceiling tiles from the false ceiling and checked the space above them.

I would do the same thing here. I counted thirty-six tiles supported on a metal framework. But where should I start?

On my first visit to Jessel's office, I'd noticed an unusually high table standing against the left-hand wall. Standing on top of it, a reasonably tall man could reach the panels, so that looked like the logical place to start. I vaulted myself up and sat on the edge of the table, then swung my feet onto it and scrambled erect. My five-foot-ten height put my head just below the false ceiling, but Jessel's six foot three would have placed his eyes above it.

Nevertheless, I could lift the ceiling panels off of their supporting framework. I shifted the panel directly over my head and felt around as far as I could reach.

Nothing.

This wasn't going to work. I couldn't reach far enough from the opening to be sure I didn't miss anything. Frantically, I glanced around the office for a solution. There! On a little corner table stood an unabridged dictionary. I scrambled down, seized the dictionary, and threw it onto the table.

Crowd noise from the executive center grew louder, accompanied by honking horns from a number of cars. The shouting and honking kept growing, now moving in this direction as if in a parade. How could I hear Mara's signal in the midst of that yammer?

But there was no turning back. Another scramble brought me onto the table again, and standing on the four-inch-thick dictionary put my eyes barely above the false ceiling. The light was dim, but I could make out vague shapes ahead of me.

None of them looked like a computer.

Moving gingerly on the uncertain footing of the dictionary, I turned ninety degrees and looked to my left.

Still nothing.

The shouting and horn-honking kept growing louder. It sounded like the mob was marching around the campus circle. I'd better hurry and get finished before it dispersed.

I turned another ninety degrees carefully, but my foot slipped off the edge of the dictionary. I gripped the ceiling's metal framework to keep from falling. My gaze instinctively dropped below the ceiling to verify my balance. Steadied again, I raised my eyes above ceiling level.

There it was.

Unmistakably, a laptop computer.

Exhilaration flashed through me like electric shock. With unsteady hands, I grasped the computer and lowered it into the full light of the office. It was the largest laptop I'd ever seen. It had to be one of those all-capable models designed to replace someone's desktop. It must be capable of performing all the network operations Richmond Seagrave had imputed to it.

Now all I had to do was put it back and notify Seagrave. He and the police could do the rest. Giff would have some explaining to do.

And I had to get out of there before he came back and caught me snooping. A new thought hit me. I'd known all along we were dealing with a murderer, and that it was probably one of our suspects. But that knowledge had stayed in a separate compartment from the knowledge that thugs were trying to kill Mara and me. My knowledge had in fact remained academic—impersonal and nonthreatening, like wondering which of several historical characters had slipped Napoleon the arsenic.

Now for the first time I thought of Gifford Jessel as someone really dangerous. And I knew I had better be somewhere else when he came back.

Outside, the shouting and honking had grown fainter. Above the fading din I could now make out a single horn. Two beeps, then three. Two beeps, then three.

Mara!

I had to put the computer back and get out of here.

But before I could move, the office door opened and Gifford Jessel stood in the doorway. His disapproving gaze moved from me to the computer in my hands and back to me.

There was a reason I hadn't found the pistol in his desk.

It was in his hand, pointed at me.

CHAPTER 45

For days I'd felt time racing by at twice its normal pace. Now it seemed frozen, and Gifford Jessel and I seemed as far beyond its reach as the figures on Keats's Grecian urn.

But we weren't beyond time. The lover on Keats's urn could never receive the imminent kiss, but one flick of Giff's finger would complete his pistol's deadly work on me.

I'd known fear during last night's flight from armed gunmen. But now, certain I faced the murderer we'd sought and looking down the barrel of his pistol, I was paralyzed with terror. I couldn't have moved if I'd tried.

I don't know how long we stood motionless, but I do know the pistol never wavered in Giff's hand.

"You have a bad habit, Press," he said presently, "a habit of being in the wrong place at the wrong time."

He stepped inside the office to a position where he could face me and watch the door at the same time. With at least ten feet between us, he could shoot me dead long before I could grapple with him for the pistol. If I were fool enough to try.

"You have that same bad habit," I said, struggling to keep my voice from trembling. "You're supposed to be in class."

Outside, the crowd noise and horn-honking kept fading as the march around the circle continued. Inside my head, my cerebral musicians played the feathery violin passages Mendelssohn composed to represent Shakespeare's fairies. They provided no consolation.

"My class didn't show," Giff said. "They all went to the demonstration."

"What demonstration?"

"You haven't heard?" Giff smirked. "When your little blonde friend's students heard she was getting fired, they organized a demonstration to save her job. They have our glorious president and dean shaking in their wingtips." The smirk changed to a snicker. "You'll be happy to know the students supported you as an afterthought."

A demonstration for Mara? I was too stunned to answer.

Giff spoke again. "Press, you also have a bad habit of minding other people's business. And you can't say we didn't warn you."

"Who is *we*?" I asked. Terrified or not, I was still curious.

Giff sneered. "You're always the historian, Press, always after facts. I told them you wouldn't quit."

"Told who?" Even through the fear I felt the emotional surge that comes when the last piece of an intellectual puzzle falls into place. William Harvey must have felt it when the theory of blood circulation formed in his mind, or Newton when the mathematical relationships of gravity coalesced into elegant precision. Even insignificant researchers like me live for those rare flashes of insight.

"Told who?" Giff showed a knowing smile. "My colleagues from Las Vegas. Surely you must have realized this was no local operation."

"So everything goes back to that vacation in Las Vegas?" Curiosity

drove my question, but I also hoped Giff wouldn't pull the trigger while he was talking.

The crowd noise seemed to have leveled at the far side of the circle, but it had not gone away.

"Yes, Las Vegas." Giff grimaced. "I gambled and lost. Lost more than I could ever pay with a professor's salary. And I already had a hard time keeping Mom in the nursing home. That's why I gambled. If I won, I could do better by her."

"But you lost," I said. "Laila had connections in Vegas. Did she set you up?"

"I don't think so. She made the trip with our group, but I didn't see her after we got there. All I know is that when I couldn't pay, they took me into a back room and told me what I had to do. If I didn't, we'd take a ride in the country. I couldn't let that happen. Then there'd be nobody to pay Mom's bills at the nursing home."

"Look," I said. "Do you mind if I sit down? This computer is getting heavy." Maybe if I could get off this silly table . . .

"Stay where you are." Giff's eyes flashed and he waved the pistol. "On second thought, get on your knees and face me. Lay the computer on the table."

I did as I was told. My internal musicians seemed unable to leave Mendelssohn's fairyland. I spoke in desperation, yet some distant part of me dispassionately recorded facts as if in a research library. "What did you do for the mob, Giff? I know you ran some kind of racket from the campus computer network."

He laughed. "The boys from Vegas made a dunce out of Earl-George. They set it up so I could run some of their operations through our campus network with no records kept. Except in that computer beside you." He seemed to enjoy explaining. I remembered that he'd

always liked to brag. "They started me out small, arranging for overseas shipment of stolen goods."

"That's what Laila got involved in?"

"You learned that, did you? Yes, she answered a perfectly legal ad in a newspaper. She'd receive a package and get separate e-mail instructions on where to send it. We didn't realize for a while that she was doing it wholesale under different names. We didn't like it, but it didn't hurt anything as long as she didn't know who gave her the instructions."

"But she found out."

"Yes." Irritation showed on Giff's face, as if someone had slipped him a false minor premise. "I still don't know how."

"And that's why you killed her?"

"She had it coming." Anger flared in his eyes. "She called me into her office and tried to blackmail me. If I didn't cut her in, she'd tell the police." The pistol wavered, then steadied. "I still didn't intend to kill her—just stall for a while and let the mob work out something with her as they had with me. But Laila never knew when to quit. She belittled me for letting her catch on to my racket, so I was already angry. Then she made an insulting personal remark about our marriage. Never mind what. But that pushed me over the top."

Outside, the auto horns and shouting grew louder. It sounded like the students were making another circuit of the campus.

Giff didn't seem to hear. He was breathing fast now, as if reliving the murder. "I'd just come in from shopping and had a heavy plumbing tool in my hand—one of those claw-ended rods you use to turn off your water at the water meter. Before I thought, I swung it and hit Laila on the temple. She went down and I hit her twice more. But my anger kept boiling up and reminding me of all the ways she'd insulted me when we were married. I let it control me. She was wearing a silk scarf,

and I choked her with it till I knew she was dead."

He showed a satisfied smile. "She will never insult me again."

"What did you do with the plumbing tool?" I asked. Maybe I could use his arrogance to keep him talking.

"I got rid of it in the river. No one will ever find it."

The outside noise grew louder as the students approached on the circle.

"Why did you try to throw suspicion on Professor Thorn and me?"

Giff laughed again. "You were a natural, Press. People already knew you were weird, and most of them thought you had it in for Laila. Professor Thorn was a loner, too, and the Wicca business made her even more vulnerable. It was pure luck that you two discovered the body. All I had to do was create evidence that both of you had reasons to kill Laila."

"Using a passkey you stole from Dean-Dean," I said.

Giff snorted. "There must be half a dozen of those loose on campus. Dean-Dean would lose his navel if it weren't bolted on."

Even in my fear I thought that a curious anatomical concept, but I let it pass and went for bigger game. "Your package-shipment racket was small-time, Giff. That elaborate computer setup must have been used for more lucrative tasks."

"It was." Giff's pistol alternated between pointing at my chest and head. "We ran the full range of computer crime. Information theft—we stole Bob Harkins's research records and sold them for forty thousand—and we hacked into hundreds of government records. Changed some of them, too, for substantial fees. The people I work for say I'm as good a manager as they've ever seen."

"Such appropriate work for a philosopher!" I said. "What about Marcus Fischbach?"

Giff paused as if wondering whether he should answer. The noise from outside kept getting louder.

"The Fischbach thing wouldn't have happened," Giff said, "if you and your girlfriend hadn't started snooping. I tried to warn you off with Socrates' definition of justice: everyone in a community minding his own business. But you wouldn't listen."

"You weren't exactly minding your own business with that computer network." I couldn't resist the taunt, but it was a mistake. It hurt his pride and raised his anger with me.

"You've heard of Nietzsche's *Übermensch*, haven't you, Press?"

I nodded. "Some kind of superman, if I remember right."

Giff smirked again. "More or less, translated into layman's terms. What it means is that people above a certain level make their own morality. That's what I've done."

I remembered Mao Zedong's claim that "People like me have only a duty to ourselves." But I said, "What about Marcus Fischbach?"

"When you and your blonde professor started meddling, my colleagues in Vegas sent in reinforcements. They thought you'd get the message if they worried you a little. So they stalked her. They only meant to plant a warning in your house—prove they could take you out whenever they wanted—but you walked in on them and they had to knock you in the head. But the two of you still wouldn't back off. Even after they showed they could bomb your cars, you were too stubborn to quit."

"What does that have to do with Fischbach?"

Giff shrugged, but the pistol held steady. "Nothing, except that Fischbach also snooped into something he shouldn't. The powers that be called him to account for it. Then they got cute and tried to frame Professor Thorn for his murder. I tried to explain the difference

between Wiccan practice and satanic rites, but they wouldn't listen. As it happened, she was out of town when they killed Fischbach. So all they got was a mess."

"Yeah," I said. "It was messy for Fischbach, too."

Giff shrugged again.

The crowd outside was getting close to the science center. We had to raise our voices to be heard above the din.

"How did Brenda Kirsch's blackjack turn up in my office?" I had to keep Giff talking.

Giff clucked. His mouth made the motion, but the sound itself got lost in clamor from outside. "How did you know it was Brenda's blackjack, Press? Did you violate the privacy of her office like you've violated mine? No, Press, Brenda had nothing to do with planting it on you. That was my idea."

"Very considerate of you," I said, ignoring the ethical double standard he implied. "You should have taken time to have the blood on it typed. The lab test cleared me."

"We can't have everything," he said.

"Not even as an *Übermensch*?"

We were shouting now as the noise outside reached its height. No one could hear a pistol shot amid all that hubbub.

"You ask facetious questions, Press." Giff grimaced again. "But I've already wasted too much time on you." He raised his arm and aimed the pistol.

"Wait a minute," I said. "People know I'm up here, and you can't explain shooting me. What will you do with the body?"

Giff laughed. "Don't be naive, Press. You're an oddball, you've been in the Army, and you're already in trouble. All I have to say is that a crazy veteran attacked me and I had to defend myself."

I started to say "They won't believe you," but my mouth never formed the words.

The pistol leaped in Giff's hand. Something hard slammed into my ribs. I doubled over as searing pain raced through my body.

Dimly, as if from a distant planet, I heard the dull flat slap of the pistol shot.

CHAPTER 46

For a moment the pain blinded me. As it faded, my vision slowly returned, but everything moved in slow motion. Giff looking at his pistol in bewilderment. A male voice commanding "Freeze." Sergeant Spencer standing in the door, both hands pointing a Glock 9 mm at Giff, who transferred his bewildered look from his own pistol to Sergeant Spencer's.

Time slid back into focus.

"Put the gun on the floor," Spencer ordered. "Now."

Robotlike, Giff complied. Spencer backed him away from the pistol and scuffed it into a corner with his foot.

My side ached, but I found I could move. Still on my knees, I straightened my body up and took an experimental deep breath. I again became conscious of crowd noise from outside. It was fading as the students moved on around the circle.

I moved my hand that was holding my side. Why did it show no blood? I'd been shot. There had to be blood.

Sergeant Spencer had Giff facedown on the floor, searching him.

Giff's voice rose to a whine. "I had to defend myself. He attacked me."

"Sure he did." Spencer spoke through clenched teeth. "That's why he's on his knees on that table."

Giff craned his neck to look up at me. "I *had* to shoot him. But why isn't he—?"

Spencer laughed. "Didn't you know? He's bulletproof. That was part of his Special Forces training."

Mara stood beside me, her face lined with anxiety. "Press, are you all right?"

As the pain subsided, my anger rose. "Aside from getting shot, I'm in the pink of health."

She laughed, a desperate laugh belied by tears in her eyes. "You aren't badly hurt if you can be sarcastic. I'm sorry we didn't come in soon enough."

"Sorry you didn't . . . You were out there all the time?"

Her tears flowed. "Come down off the table, Press. Your present posture does very little for your professorial dignity."

"Dignity, my foot. I've been shot." Nevertheless, I eased into a sitting position, then slid off the table to stand on the floor. To my surprise, I actually could stand.

Vaguely, I heard Sergeant Spencer calling for backup. He kept Giff lying facedown on the floor while he gave the Miranda warning. When he finished, he threw a quick glance at us.

"Don't touch that bullet," he said. "I need it for evidence."

"What bullet?" I asked.

"The one on the floor by your table." He spoke over his shoulder, his full attention remaining on Giff.

I apparently wasn't dying, so I asked Mara, "What's going on?"

"Sergeant Spencer had a falling-out with Captain Staggart over that last arrest warrant, and Staggart dismissed him from homicide."

"So what's he doing here?"

"He had no immediate assignment. He didn't agree with Staggart's warrant, but he felt obligated as a policeman to enforce it. He came looking for us on campus."

"He found you sitting in that car. That's why your beep came too late."

"It didn't come late. I blew the horn till I thought I'd run the battery down, but maybe you couldn't hear it above the horns in the demonstration."

She was right. I had only heard it once the other horns faded.

"Sergeant Spencer did arrest me," she said, "but he agreed to play along when I explained what we were doing. We saw Professor Jessel enter the building and I beeped like crazy, but everyone else was blowing horns, too. So we came up to get you out of trouble."

"After I got shot, of course."

She waved that objection away. "We heard most of what was said, and Sergeant Spencer didn't want to interrupt as long as you had Professor Jessel confessing."

"But I still got shot."

"I'm really sorry about that. The crowd noise got so loud we couldn't hear the last few sentences. We hoped for more, but when we heard the shot, we knew we'd waited too long."

"A slight error in judgment."

Mara burned me with her gaze. "Don't you understand what this means, Press? That confession clears us of both murders."

Sergeant Spencer spoke again over his shoulder, his attention still focused on the prone Gifford Jessel. "You're both still under arrest, technically. But in the light of this new evidence they can't hold you."

You'd think I'd be glad of the good news, but I still felt in a daze,

still only halfway back from the dead and not sure anything was real.

"What I'd like to know," I said, "is why I'm not dead or at least bleeding. Giff hit me square in the ribs."

Mara suppressed something like a giggle. "That pistol in Jessel's office was a clear violation of college rules. It didn't mean he was any more likely to be the murderer than our other suspects, but it did mean he was up to no good. So several days later I replaced his cartridges with some I'd sabotaged—took the powder out and put the slug back in. All they had to drive them was the primer. They wouldn't kill anything bigger than a mosquito."

I looked at her in wonder. "How'd you know to do that?"

For the first time since I'd known her, she beamed. "You once asked me what I did in the Army. I was an ordnance technician."

That explained her secret smile when I asked her the question. She must have remembered the dirty trick she'd played on Gifford Jessel.

Before I could say anything else, Sergeant Spencer's backup arrived and we all got hustled down to the police station. For the next couple of hours, detectives questioned us and took our statements. After we signed them, they told Mara and me we were free to go as long as we didn't leave town. No word of thanks, no other comment: just free to go.

Through all of this, Clyde Staggart was conspicuous by his absence. For obvious reasons, I suppose. But on our way out, I saw Dogface sitting at a desk with a pile of paperwork before him. He looked up at us with a baleful eye. My resentment of Staggart rose up within me and focused on him. In all the times I'd seen him, he'd never spoken a word. I wondered if he could.

So I walked over in front of his desk and said, "'Heard melodies are sweet, but those unheard / Are sweeter.'"

His baleful glance did not change, but he spoke in a mellifluous voice, "'. . . therefore, ye soft pipes, play on; / Not to the sensual ear, but, more endear'd, / Pipe to the spirit ditties of no tone.'" He grinned. "I'm glad you like Keats, Professor Barclay. Have a nice day."

Mara was kind enough not to laugh until we got outside. But once inside our rental car—one of the policemen had driven it to the police station—we both erupted into laughter as we had out west after the cupcake incident. We must have laughed for five minutes before I was steady enough to drive.

It was almost one thirty when I parked in front of the executive center. Time for us to exchange pleasantries with the faculty hearing committee.

We found its members already assembled in the conference room: two from the nursing faculty who'd been wanting my hide ever since the vote to keep chemistry in the curriculum, two other female faculty who'd snubbed Mara all along, and Dean-Dean rubbing his hands together at what, in a court of law, would have been the prosecutor's table. The defense table stood empty, awaiting our presence.

No one greeted us, so I broke the ice.

"Dean Billig and distinguished members of the faculty hearing committee," I said, "I regret to announce that your chairman, Professor Jessel, is unable to attend. It seems he has a previous engagement with the homicide police."

CHAPTER 47

The faculty hearing committee's response to my announcement was more dramatic than I expected. You could approximate the same result by dropping a cougar into a chicken yard. Dean-Dean tried to make the ship go faster by running along the deck, but this time he only ran in circles while my cerebral musicians accompanied him on the bassoon. And his ship remained firmly tied up at the dock. Eventually, he ordered that the committee adjourn—yes, *sine die* —until one thirty the following Wednesday.

That was two weeks ago, and the committee has yet to reconvene. Much has happened in the interim. Some I learned from Richmond Seagrave, more from Sergeant Spencer.

Gifford Jessel is in jail pending indictment for murder, attempted murder, and a menagerie of other criminal actions still under investigation. It turns out he possessed a sizeable bank account in the Cayman Islands, but that has now been frozen.

Even before I found Giff's laptop, Seagrave had convinced President Cantwell to bring in the FBI. My discovery and the involvement of local police preempted the president's decision because the locals had to ask

for federal help anyway once Jessel mentioned organized crime.

According to Sergeant Spencer, Giff's laptop contained some of the records the FBI had failed to find in several raids. When he last heard, the feds were rolling up the syndicate's organization one cell at a time. Staggart was still captain of homicide, Spencer said, but his failure to solve the two murders got him a counseling session with the police commissioner.

From FBI photos I identified two of the six gunmen who'd targeted Mara and me, including the one who got his haircuts in a mop factory. She identified two more. All were professional hit men. When I last heard, two had been arrested in Vegas. DNA comparisons with evidence from the Marcus Fischbach crime scene are pending.

We still do not know the significance of Laila's safe-deposit box key or the enigmatic fragments of paper we found in her house. Nor will we ever know, for we can't ask anyone about them without admitting that we violated a crime scene.

Seagrave also told President Cantwell the reason for Clyde Staggart's enmity toward me. Cantwell then overruled Dean-Dean's proposed actions against me and, for good measure, those against Mara. Our identifying Laila Sloan's murderer increased our credibility enough for Cantwell to believe our story on why she stayed overnight at my house. We knew better than to mention our equally innocent stay in the motel.

President Cantwell also has taken the coed dorm issue off the table and ordered the return of the crosses to the campus entryways—small steps toward leading the university back to its original values. This will be a difficult process, and the degree of his success remains to be seen.

Changes have occurred among some of my acquaintances, while others remain the same. Luther Pappas continues in custodial services, unharmed by the administration's knowledge of his prison record.

Outwardly, Bob and Threnody Harkins maintain their appearance as an ideal couple, but the climate between them makes Nova Scotia seem a tropical paradise. Earl-George Heggan has resigned his staff position and found full-time employment in computer repair, for which he is eminently well qualified. And yesterday I received a wedding invitation from Penelope Nichols with the handwritten notation, "Thanks for your good advice, Professor Barclay. It worked." Once in a long while, a professor actually wins one.

The campus rumor mill says that Brenda Kirsch and Brice Funderburk have been seen holding earnest conversation at a candlelight dinner for two in Overton City's most prestigious restaurant. I wish them well. May he never dislodge one of her china cups or, if he does, may there be no two-by-fours within reach!

Mara and I were reinstated on faculty, of course. The student demonstration for Mara thoroughly cowed the administration, which lives in constant fear of losing students. And Arthur Medford, who organized it, is the leading candidate for student body president next year.

Cindy arrived home that Wednesday evening, bubbling over with her decision to move out of the university residence hall (with its residence life education program), move into an apartment, and look in a nearby church for friends who share her values. She expressed pride in my role as homicide investigator, though the details remained as distant to her as the Battle of Midway.

She and I shared Thanksgiving dinner with Mara and Dr. Sheldon at a family-oriented restaurant. Dr. Sheldon dominated conversation with his plans for online history courses, though Mara and Cindy apparently shared some girl talk during the sacred rites of nose-powdering. Whatever they said, Cindy seemed to accept Mara as my faculty colleague and nothing more.

Between answering police questions and catching up on our classes, Mara and I have seen little of each other, and neither of us has mentioned the brief interlude when we colored outside the lines. For that matter, we haven't seen much of other faculty members. They don't know what to make of our unacademic escapade, so they find it easier to leave us alone. The religion faculty took a wait-and-see attitude toward Mara's reconversion to Christianity, but she is visiting regularly with Pastor Urim Tammons. I've begun attending church again, surprised that people treat me as myself, not as the Grieving Widower or the Prodigal Son. At morning worship last Sunday I saw Mara across the sanctuary, but we did not connect afterward. She will pursue her spiritual journey in her own way.

I've been reflecting on my own journey, of course, especially my sense of that unseen force closing in on me. I'd thought it malevolent when it drove me into deeper and deeper trouble, even into mortal danger. But in the end it did not just drive me *into* difficulties; it drove me *through* them. Nor did I solve the murders by my own efforts. The solution was given to me through my hallucination of the Victor Young music score. As Pastor Tammons said, God wasn't—isn't—through with me yet.

Looking back, I'm thankful for this purging and awakening. I still grieve the loss of Faith. But my spiritual numbness is gone, replaced by a deep inner assurance that stands unmoved beneath the transient anxieties churning above it.

Campus life has resumed its normal patterns. Today Dean-Dean published a memo, replete with the usual comma splices, forbidding the use of cleaning materials that smell like mothballs. I suppose he was responding to my salting his office with them again last night. (That passkey still comes in handy.) Otherwise, I'm feeling more and more

like a professor. In my Western Civ class today I'll try to describe the miraculous shift in methods of thought that occurred in Europe between AD 1600 and 1660. I hope no one asks me to explain why it happened.

My internal orchestra continues, insistent as ever—no further music scores from movies, but a strange new preference for big-band artists like Artie Shaw and Charlie Spivak. So in all the ways I can tell, my life is settling back into comfortable, familiar patterns.

With one exception.

That was no china-cup kiss, and I haven't decided what to do about Professor Mara Thorn.

They Call Her the P.I. Princess.

ISBN: 978-0-8024-6926-7

It's 1947 and Allie Fortune is the only female (and probably the best) private investigator in New York City.

But she's kept awake at night by a mystery of her own—her fiancé disappeared in the war and Allie is haunted more by the unknown than by finding out the worst.

Her work is a welcome distraction and she's just been hired on by a client who isn't telling the whole truth. Mary Gordon's claims of innocence don't fit with her ransacked apartment, being shot at, and the two Soviet agents hot on her trail.

Meanwhile the FBI is working the case because a legendary and mysterious treasure has gone missing… again. The only catch for Allie is her new "partner" Jack, an attractive, single agent who knows how to make her smile.

As Allie and Jack chase after the gold they must contend with the Soviets who also want the priceless treasure back—after all, they stole it fair and square.

by Sara Mills

Find it now at your favorite local or online bookstore.

Sign up for Moody Publishers' Book Club on our website.

www.MoodyPublishers.com

ISBN: 978-0-8024-6362-3

If there is a way into madness, logic says there is a way out. Logic says. Tallis, a philosopher's servant, is sent to a Greek academy in Palestine only to discover that it has silently, ominously, disappeared. No one will tell him what happened, but he learns what has become of four of its scholars. One was murdered. One committed suicide. One worships in the temple of Dionysus. And one & one is a madman.

From the author of The Brother's Keeper comes a tale of mystery, horror, and hope in the midst of unimaginable darkness, the story behind the Geresene demoniac of the gospels of Mark and Luke.

by Tracy Groot

ISBN: 978-0-8024-8989-0